SAVAGE BLOOMS

By S.T. Gibson

A Dowry of Blood

An Education in Malice

Unearthly Delights

Savage Blooms

S.T. GIBSON

SAVAGE BLOOMS

orbit

orbit-books.co.uk

ORBIT

First published in Great Britain in 2025 by Orbit

1 3 5 7 9 10 8 6 4 2

A CIP catalogue record for this book is available from the British Library.

HB ISBN 978-0-356-52325-5
C format 978-0-356-52324-8

Typeset in Sabon LT Std by Palimpsest Book Production Limited, Falkirk, Stirlingshire
Printed and bound in Great Britain by Clays Ltd, Elcograf, S.p.A.

Papers used by Orbit are from well-managed forests and other responsible sources.

MIX
Paper | Supporting responsible forestry
FSC® C104740

Orbit
An imprint of
Little, Brown Book Group
Carmelite House
50 Victoria Embankment
London EC4Y 0DZ

The authorised representative in the EEA is
Hachette Ireland
8 Castlecourt Centre, Dublin 15, D15 XTP3, Ireland
(email: info@hbgi.ie)

An Hachette UK Company
www.hachette.co.uk

orbit-books.co.uk

To all the serpents courageous enough to
break the cycles they were born into, even if that
meant biting off the tips of their own tails

Content Warning

This is a gothic erotic romance, and therefore, it explores themes that may be distressing to some readers. If you choose to proceed, I hope you read with curiosity about desires that may be different from yours and compassionate engagement with themes that may be challenging for you.

Savage Blooms depicts:

- Toxic relationships
- Alcohol abuse
- Sexual manipulation
- Under-negotiated polyamory
- Consensual non-consent
- Group sex
- Genderplay
- Voyeurism and exhibitionism

- Primal chase play
- Impact play
- General themes of dominance and submission
- Child abuse and neglect
- References to past traumatic childbirth
- Hereditary mental health struggles
- Chronic illness, including migraines, chronic pain, and endometriosis
- Forced marriage
- Near-drowning
- Infertility
- Suicidality

In addition, while no sexual activity between blood family members is depicted, incest is discussed and pseudoincest is explored.

Prologue

The land had been lying in wait for half a century by the time the young man arrived. Half a century of dormancy, of the deep, dark sleep of ancient things.

The moment he stepped out of the rental car in his battered hiking boots, a shudder went through the earth. The hares felt it, rippling through the long grass. The finches felt it, rattling the tips of the narrowest tree branches. Even the tiniest wildflowers felt it, coursing up through their trembling roots.

Beneath the earth, an old magic stirred.

He was tall, fair, and quick to smile. There was a girl with him, stoutly built with a bob of auburn curls. He beamed over his shoulder at her, golden and boyish in his goading.

As the young man – barely more than a boy, really –

tightened the laces of his boots, the land rose up to meet him. Misty breezes caressed his scalp through his close-cropped blond hair, briars tugged insistently on his pant leg, and sedge grasses bowed beneath his feet like soldiers saluting their prince. He breathed in deep, filling his lungs with the scent of salt and primrose.

Earth, sea and sky ached to enfold him.

He turned his face up towards the clouds and closed his pale-lashed eyes against the sun. The light slanted across his curved mouth, his strong aquiline nose.

It had been so long. Years of waiting, of slow rot anxiously gnawing away at tangled roots.

The pair of companions chattered, in high spirits as they shared a swig of water from their communal flask. Though the land didn't speak the garbled child-tongue of English, it knew what these two were after. There could only have been one destination, because the story had always been a circle, always a gyre turning in the sky, forever unfolding, forever beginning anew.

The young man strode out towards the cave, and the story began once again, with his name inked like blood on the first page.

CHAPTER ONE

Adam

Adam Lancaster was euphoric. Granted, they had been walking in circles across the rocky landscape for an hour already, and they had been forced to return to the car parked at the edge of the tiny village of Wyke to get their bearings, but Adam wasn't deterred. His blood was singing in his veins from the sheer thrill of being here, in the right country, on the right patch of land. He had never been this close before, not in all his twenty-two years.

Nicola, however, was less enthused.

"I'm pretty sure we walked past every single house in the village," she said, blowing a wind-tossed curl out of her face with a huff. "And none of them match that address. Are you positive this is the place?"

"Completely," Adam replied, leaning against the compact silver Volvo they had rented at the airport.

He produced the letter from his breast pocket, where it had been pressed against his heart, skin-warmed and secure beneath his fleece vest. The paper was soft to the touch, every sharp corner worn smooth with age and handling.

The return address was well known to Adam: it was the brick split-level in a Michigan suburb where his grandfather had lived right up until his death Adam's junior year of college. That had been the year Adam dropped out, mostly because he had acquired enough graphic design skills to freelance without having to flush more money down the drain on tuition, but also because his grandfather's death had been a blow he hadn't expected. It had shaken apart something inside Adam that hadn't quite come back together again.

The recipient address was the mystery he had come to Scotland to solve. It was made out to Arabella Kirkfoyle, and the post code matched Wyke, a town hugging the rocky coast of the south-west Highlands. But there was no house number on the envelope, and no road listed. There was just one word, written out in Adam's grandfather's heavy but neat script: *Craigmar.*

Adam may never have heard of Arabella, and he may never have heard of Wyke, but he recognized Craigmar from his grandfather's bedtime stories. Adam had hounded his grandfather with his bottomless appetite for tales of far-flung adventures. His recalcitrant grandfather had been perpetually grumpy except around Adam, who he spoiled with stories. When Adam had been an awkward, lanky preteen on the cusp of finally grasping the queerness that was already getting him bullied by the other boys, his grandfather would take him on long hikes around Lake Michigan and tell him stories of enchanted fjords and haunted Bavarian forests and always, Craigmar.

Craigmar wasn't just a house, his grandfather would whisper late at night when Adam should have been asleep but was instead wide awake tending the campfire. It was a living place, an ancient stately home ripe with the promise of magic.

At this point, Adam didn't care if half the bedtime stories were made up, or even if all of them were. He was grown now, less interested in enchantment than he was in geology and civic history. He just wanted to feel close to his grandfather again, to close the circle of love and mutual understanding that had been broken when his grandfather had his stroke.

"We must have missed it," Adam said. "We should try again."

"There's only one road in and out of town. And we just walked the length of it, all two miles. I know this is important to you, and I really want to help you find the right house, but can't we stop at the pub first for a a pint or something? Maybe someone inside can give us directions."

Adam leaned a little further over the car's hood, tapping against the metal as he thought. He brought himself closer to Nicola's height as he did so, giving in to that unconscious slouch he had developed in his teen years when he shot up to six feet tall in one summer. Nicola was roughly the size of a thimble compared to Adam, which was to say, five foot three.

"What if they don't want us poking around?" he asked, feigning concern. Everyone they had met on their travels had been more than willing to help them interpret road signs or find milk for their tea at the hostel. If Adam was being honest, he wasn't worried about encountering an unfriendly face. He was worried about having to share this private obsession with Craigmar with anyone at all except Nicola, his very best friend.

"What are they gonna do, run us off with pitchforks?" Nicola snorted. "Burn us in a straw effigy? I doubt it."

"That's dark, Nikki."

Nicola beamed, one of those sunny smiles that inspired countless men and women to throw themselves at her feet back home in the States. It had also been very popular with the locals since arriving in Edinburgh and spending the night partying in the Old Town before getting up early to travel to Wyke. She had been collecting phone numbers like souvenirs at every stop on the road since.

"Oh, come on, they could do much worse," she said, as though this would make him feel any better. "If this was the Iron Age they would slit our throats and dump us in a peat bog as a human sacrifice. But if we're polite,

I'm sure we'll escape with our lives and maybe even directions too. Lead the way."

Nicola gestured across the road to the pub three doors down, a charming red-shuttered stone building with a painted sign that read 'The Hound and Grouse'. Adam's stomach growled, betraying his lofty commitments to his pilgrimage.

"All right, we'll grab a beer and a snack and some directions," he said, striding across the street. Nicola followed him, just like always. Ever since they had befriended each other their freshman year of college, she had been content to let him take the leaps of faith. Whether it was downing a shot at a Greek life mixer, diving off a tall rock into the cold waters of Lake Michigan, or traipsing across Scotland with nothing to guide him but bedtime stories and a single letter, Adam always went first.

He pretended it was because he was brave, but it was really only because having Nicola at his side made him courageous enough to try anything, at least once.

The pleasantly dim light inside the pub came from low lamps on the tables and the fireplace near the back, which made the long wooden bar gleam. It was barely 3 p.m., and at this time of day there weren't many patrons sitting down for a drink. One elderly couple enjoyed a platter of sausages together in the corner, lost in their reminiscing, and some roughscrabble farmer-types filled out crossword puzzles and chatted about overdue spring rains at one end of the bar. A dark-haired young man nursed a porter by himself at the other end.

The proprietor nodded as they walked up to the bar. He was Adam's platonic ideal of a bartender: in his fifties, heavily tattooed, and with a no-nonsense air that implied he had seen the best and the worst of people and was unaffected by any of it.

Nicola ordered a local red ale, delighted to be able to sample a regional brew, and Adam ordered what he was familiar with, a Stella Artois.

"A bag of cheese and onion crisps as well, please," Nicola said. "Also, we've got a question that maybe you could help us with?"

"Fire away," the bartender said as he filled Nicola's glass.

Adam leaned across the bar and lowered his voice slightly, as if there was anyone here who might care enough to eavesdrop on him.

"I'm trying to get in touch with a family friend. She might not live here anymore, but maybe she's got relatives that do? We went looking for her house but couldn't find it."

The bartender set down a bottled Stella in front of Adam, and Adam's hand brought it to his lips automatically. He was parched, he realized. He had been so excited he hadn't really noticed he was getting dehydrated, or that he hadn't eaten anything all day besides cereal and three dried apricots at the hostel in Edinburgh.

"What's the address?" the bartender asked.

"I don't have a house number or a street."

"Then what's her family name? I've lived here my whole life; if she's a local girl I might know her folks."

"Kirkfoyle," Adam said, breezy as you please, like he hadn't been lying awake at night for the last month turning that name over in his head like a riddle.

The bartender nodded sagely, as though this too was something he had seen countless times. A foreign seeker stumbling into his bar looking for some scrap of forgotten family history buried beneath the village cobblestones.

"Well, that's your problem there. The Kirkfoyles don't live in town. They own the town. You must be looking for Eileen."

Having tossed out this titbit, the bartender turned from Adam, good deed done, and began wiping down the bar. Adam's brain struggled to process this information. The idea that his grandfather could have been in touch with someone who owned a whole town was exciting, but it didn't answer his question of where the Kirkfoyles lived, and he had never heard of any Eileen.

"The woman I'm looking for is named Arabella," Adam said. "Not Eileen."

The bartender stopped mid-wipe, then gave Adam the strangest look, like he had just broken some kind of prehistoric societal taboo. Like Adam had eaten human flesh or taken his sister for a wife or touched a dead body with his bare hands.

"Arabella doesn't live around here anymore," was all the bartender said, and then he disappeared into the back room.

Adam slumped down into his barstool, the first feelings of defeat creeping in. He had known there was a chance that Arabella had moved, or even died. Still, he had held the hope of meeting her close to his chest, like an exotic plant smuggled in through customs beneath his jacket.

"You're looking for Craigmar," a baritone brogue put in from nowhere, making Adam's blood sing in his veins. He had never heard anyone but his grandfather speak that name.

He turned and took a second look at the man at the end of the bar, who had drained his porter and was now looking at Adam intently. He probably wasn't that much older than Adam, but he was clearly closer to thirty than twenty, having already crossed that great quarter-life gulf. He wore a green cable-knit sweater and he had overgrown chestnut curls of hair and a frowning, full mouth.

"The house on the hill," the stranger went on. "It's the Kirkfoyle estate."

"Estate?" Nicola chirped, intrigued as a sparrow who had just spotted a feeder full of seed. "Hi, by the way. I'm Nicola Fairweather."

"Finley Buchanan," the stranger put in, flicking a glance her way. His eyes softened slightly, catching the light of the fire. Adam saw they were not indeed brown but very dark hazel.

"Adam Lancaster," Adam said, sticking out his hand for a shake. Finley stood and reached over the bar, his grip surprisingly strong. He was shorter than Adam – most people were – but he had the callouses and sturdy build of someone who worked with their hands. "Do you know how to get to that estate? Craigmar?'

"I certainly do," Finley said, tossing down enough cash to cover his tab as well as Adam and Nicola's. "It's a few miles down the road. Single-track, but it'll get you there. I'm headed there myself; you two could follow me so you don't get lost."

"You're headed there too?" Nicola said, already scooping up her bag. Adam wasn't exactly sure about this; following a friendly stranger down a single-track road to a mysterious estate seemed like a great way to get serial killed, chopped into little pieces and scattered through the woods.

"Why?" Adam asked, suspicion in his voice.

Finley gave him a once-over, as though Adam was the interloper who had yet to earn his trust. Then he gave a very small smile, just enough to tug at the dimple tucked into his cheek, and swung his car keys once around his finger.

"Because I live there, and because my lunch break's over. You're welcome to come with me, or to stay here. But I suggest you decide fast, before the rain starts coming down any harder."

Adam opened his mouth to point out that it wasn't

raining, then paused to hear the drizzle on the rooftop that was slowly building to a steady patter.

Adam had never been afraid of a little rain, and he certainly wasn't afraid of a little adventure. He could handle himself, just like he always did, and he hadn't come all the way out here to give up mere miles from the prize. Besides, with Nicola at his side, what couldn't he do?

"All right," Adam said, taking one more bracing swig of his beer. "After you."

CHAPTER TWO

Adam

Adam dutifully followed behind Finley's banged-up Volkswagen in the rental car, trundling slower and slower as the road narrowed and the rain came down with more dogged determination. It was astonishing how quickly the sky could open up out here. Finley hadn't been lying about the single-track road, it was hardly wide enough for one car, unpaved and uneven, and Adam saw no other way to accommodate the comings and goings of other motorists than to pull entirely off the road.

"How far do you think it is?" Nicola asked, peering to see through the rain. Adam was following so close behind Finley that he could see the way the other man tapped rhythmically at the steering wheel with his thumb, how he glanced up into the rear-view from time to time to make sure they were still following.

"No telling," Adam said. He had searched for Craigmar endlessly in the last few months, but the house wasn't listed on any public maps, and when it appeared in sparse newspaper articles, no address or photos were included. It was likely the owner didn't want Craigmar to be found, which wasn't totally unheard of as far as misanthropic wealthy families went.

It would be nearly impossible to find, his grandfather had told him once, what felt like eons ago. Adam had been ten years old, begging for one more story and up way past his bedtime. *But if anyone could do it, it would be you.*

"We've been driving for fifteen minutes," Nicola said, peering out the window as gorse bushes and scrubby trees rolled past. "Is that what 'a few miles down the road' means to a Scot?"

She nibbled her lip, a surefire sign she was nervous.

"Are you all right with this?" Adam asked. "If you start to feel weird, we can always leave."

"I'd rather deal with whatever's out in the hills than watch you pout the whole flight back to America because you didn't find what you were looking for," Nicola said, swiping on a bit of chapstick and fluffing her bangs in the passenger mirror. "Besides, the weirdo in the Volkswagen is hot."

"A hot guy can still bury you under his floorboards," Adam said. "And he's not hot enough to be worth dying for."

Nicola snorted. "Sure, like you don't have eyes. Anyway, you're my travel guide, remember? I go wherever you go."

Adam's heart clenched. He had spent as much of his college tenure as possible studying abroad or, at the very least, partying abroad on school holidays. He had somehow been to five countries in two years, funded entirely by scholarships or his total willingness to live on rice and beans so he could afford drop-of-a-hat plane tickets. Nicola was relying on his traveling expertise to steer them in the right direction, and he didn't want to frighten her by worrying.

Suddenly, Finley turned left, disappearing behind an overgrown hedge dotted with bloody berries. Adam swerved to follow, swearing under his breath, and then Nicola let out an awestruck gasp.

A huge structure loomed above them at the end of a gravel drive, three stories of wind-lashed gray stone. Every white-framed window in the mammoth structure was dark, and the multiple chimneys atop the peaked roofline were heavily shadowed by the cloud-shrouded sun. The house was situated at the peak of a rolling hill, and as Adam pulled to a stop outside the large wooden front door, he saw that it overlooked a long, cleared grazing green dotted with sheep. The green stretched all the way to the hazy ocean coast at what, in that moment, truly felt like the edge of the world.

Adam stepped out of the car, struck silent by the grandeur of the landscape. Twisted trees edged up against the grazing lawn, as though the wilderness was straining to spill onto the cleared land and re-wild it by force. Even in the haze of rain, Adam could see that the estate must sprawl for acres and acres.

Somehow, it was bigger and more beautiful than even his feverish child's brain had imagined.

Nicola's boots crunched in the gravel as she pulled her hood up against the rain and peered up to see the tip-top of the house, which seemed to pierce the sky with its Gothic peaks. Some of the masonry had started to crumble, the hedges and flowering plants that lined the drive were scraggly, and the ironwork plate over the door that read *Craigmar* was corroded with age, but it was all still undeniably beautiful.

"Lovely old behemoth, isn't she?" Finley asked, striding over with his hands tucked in his pockets. "Let's get indoors before you catch cold. The lord of the manor will be happy to see you both, I'd wager. We don't get many guests all the way out here."

"Lord of the manor?" Adam echoed, falling into step behind Finley. He was aware that things like lords existed, especially out in the Scottish countryside, but it still felt like something better suited to one of Nicola's storybooks.

"Don't worry," Finley said, tossing Adam a grin over his shoulder as he approached the massive oak door. "She barely bites."

Before Adam had any time to figure out what that meant, a huge, waterlogged deerhound appeared from behind a hedge, trotting towards Nicola with alarming speed. It let out a curious whine, its red tongue lolling out between gleaming teeth, and Nicola stumbled back a few paces.

"Smoo!" Finley said. "Who let you free? You're absolutely soaked."

"She's afraid of dogs," Adam said quickly as he stepped between Nicola and the hound. Its coat was the same gray color as a clotted storm cloud. The dog reared up on its hind legs in excitement and Adam, astonished by its size, stumbled back a few paces too. "Send it away."

"Down," Finley barked, with such authority that Adam almost obeyed himself. "Down, now! You should be ashamed of yourself, jumping on guests. Go on back to the house. And no tearing up the garden in this rain, you hear me?"

The dog shook its head, jangling its heavy leather collar and splattering Adam's jeans with mud, then trotted off with a spring in its step.

"Sorry about him," Finley said, shoving open the front door. "He's just a big dumb baby, but I thought I raised him better than that. Come inside and warm your bones."

Finley strolled through a wood-paneled antechamber that was as big as Adam's apartment back home, his shoes trailing damp prints over flagstones that turned to hardwood as they approached the grand staircase. Adam marveled at the feat of woodworking, like a twisting mahogany dragon that curved in on itself to create a landing before stretching into the darkness above. The space was not opulently decorated, and might even have been considered rustic by McMansion standards, but every detail Adam could see, from the mother-of-pearl inlaid coffee table to the gigantic oil landscape paintings hung on the walls, belied money so old most people probably forgot where it originally came from. There were landscape paintings missing from the walls, however, and open spaces on mantles where intricate clocks or jewelry boxes might have previously been displayed, suggesting that even the wealthiest old families needed to buoy themselves through hard times with selling off treasures.

"The lord's a bit eccentric, fair warning." Finley sloughed off his coat and hung it on an iron hook, then held out his hand for Adam and Nicola's jackets. "No need to stand on ceremony, however. Just mind your manners and your host will be more than happy to tell you about Arabella, I'm sure."

Nicola shot Adam a wary look, but Adam just gave her shoulder a squeeze and kept walking. Being invited right in was strange, sure, but rich people were weird, and Scotland had a different hospitality culture than America did, and most importantly, this may be the only opportunity he ever had to get his answers. Finley seemed relatively harmless, and Adam could probably fight him off if he needed to. Hell, Nicola probably could if she needed to. She was short, but she had a low center of gravity and she fought very, very dirty.

The pair followed Finley down a dim hallway, past a small parlor and into the home's formal library. A merry fire, tantalizing despite the somewhat unsettling circumstances, blazed in a walk-in fireplace flanked by carvings of leaping hares. The room was painted sage green and paneled in dark wood, trimmed with wallpaper bearing tiny white flowers and vines. One wall had been turned into a gallery of framed photographs and little postcards, and there were floor-to-ceiling bookshelves lining the opposite wall. A well-loved cognac leather couch beckoned, along with a bar cart topped with a sweating bucket of ice and a decanter of brown liquor.

A woman stood gazing into the fireplace, sipping from a cut-crystal glass.

"Finley," she said in a throaty alto, not bothering to turn to face any of them, "who have you found?"

"Friends, I hope," Finley said. "This is Adam and Nicola, sir. They were down at the pub asking about Arabella."

At that, the woman turned around, a strange gleam in her dark eyes. She was wearing jodhpurs, and a green tweed vest over a white blouse and riding boots. Her thick hair was crow-black, offsetting her pale skin, and she wore it half-up, half-down in a practical style.

"That's the lord?" Nicola whispered to Adam. "She looks like a grad student."

The lord didn't look like any grad student Adam had ever encountered, but he had majored in graphic design, and Nicola had a degree in literature, which tended to attract a much more theatrical type of person.

"Arabella?" the lord echoed, taking her time while giving Adam a once-over. It didn't feel quite like being sized up or quite like being leered at, both of which would have at least been familiar. It felt more like she was committing every detail of him to memory, which was somehow more discomfiting. "Do you mean Arabella Kirkfoyle?"

"Yes," Adam said, relief rushing through him. He had half convinced himself there was no one left alive who might remember that name. No one to answer his questions, and no one to give him closure. "I know this may sound strange, but I'm here on a sort of . . . pilgrimage? My grandfather was very important to me, and he died last year, but I actually don't know that much about his life. I know he spent his younger years traveling, and he used to tell me stories about this place. Craigmar, I mean. But I never knew where in Scotland it was. Recently, I found this . . ."

Adam reached inside his vest and retrieved the letter. It never left his person during the day, and he slept with it within arm's reach at night.

"It's a letter from my grandfather, addressed to this house, made out to Arabella Kirkfoyle. I thought if she were still living here, she might be able to tell me more about who my grandfather was."

Adam swallowed hard, embarrassment rising in his

cheeks. He felt as though he had shared far too many intimate details, but also that he hadn't shared enough for his story to make sense.

"You came all the way out here for that?" the lord asked. "Quite the quest."

"I guess I, uh, don't have a lot else going on at the moment."

The lord of the manor walked right up to Adam, enveloping him with the scent of peaty whisky and her iris perfume. She wore a somewhat worse for wear clan badge pinned to her chest, displaying her family's emblem and motto. It was a leaping hare encircled with iron into which the words "vivere militare est" were carved.

"May I?" she asked, holding her hand out for the letter. Adam wanted to deny her – this was one of the only clues to his grandfather's life that Adam had left – but she spoke with such effortless command. Like she was asking Adam to hand her one of her own possessions that he had simply been tasked with minding. And she looked right at him with those black eyes, blacker than any eyes Adam had ever seen, never once wavering.

"It's very delicate," he said, trying to find the courage to tell her no.

"Precious things often are," she said, the whisper of a smile touching her lips. Between the day-drinking and the jodhpurs and the antiquated formal title, Adam had assumed she was much older than him. But now, up close, he saw that she was thirty at the oldest, perhaps not even that. She and Finley might have been siblings, if it weren't for their obvious difference in social station and the way the lord's complexion, alarmingly pale and latticed with thin blue veins, clashed with Finley's healthy, olive-toned skin. "I just want to take a look. I'll give it right back, I promise."

Adam took a deep breath, then placed the letter into her waiting palm.

The lord made a humming sound in her throat, like she was *very* pleased with him indeed. Adam's stomach tightened, with arousal or with some other more fearful kind of anticipation. It was hard to say.

"Please have a seat, both of you," she said, sweeping a hand towards the couch. "Would you like a drink? You must be hungry from the road. I can have Finley heat up the venison pie from last night, or tea and scones if you want something lighter?"

"Oh no," Adam said. "We're all right—"

"Tea and scones sound fab," Nicola said, plopping down on the couch. She didn't look exactly at ease, but she was good at making herself at home in strange situations. Finley slipped from the room and Adam sat down next to Nicola, eyeing a collection of very old and very complicated-looking board games stacked tidily in the middle of the coffee table.

"How did you come into possession of this?" the lord asked, unfolding the letter and holding it up to the firelight. Adam's heart leapt into his throat, but she didn't toss the note into the flames, just studied the script with a curious furrow between her brows. "Did someone give it to you?"

"Yeah," Adam said. "Whenever my mom finds something of my grandfather's, she passes it on to me. I figured no one else would be interested in it."

"Oh, I'm very interested," the lord said, flipping the paper over as though confirming its veracity. And then, in a curious lilt that sounded to Adam like stories woven by a fireside, she read the letter aloud.

My Arabella,

It's spring here in Michigan, and I've never seen sunlight so bright. It hits Lake Huron like a mirror, and fills your eyes with stars. The people in this part of the country are very friendly, and respect hard work and honesty. I think I might stay here, at least for a little while.

Last night, I dreamed of Craigmar, at Easter this time. I miss your mother's lamb roast, and the bonfires your father built, but most of all I miss going on morning hikes through the hills with you. I wonder if I'll ever dream of anywhere else.

I hope you're keeping well, and I hope these letters aren't inappropriate. But I suspect that you read them and that they make you smile, even if you don't write back.

Yours always,
Robbie

Adam had read the letter dozens of times, but hearing it in someone else's voice made a lump form in his throat. He would go weeks without crying over his grandfather, and then it would hit him all at once. He stared into the fire, willing the heat to dry his eyes before anyone noticed he was getting misty.

"Thank you for sharing that with me," the lord said, handing the letter back to Adam. She squeezed his shoulder before she moved away, an unexpected jolt of human warmth that startled him out of his grief. "I realized I never introduced myself. I'm Eileen Kirkfoyle. Arabella's granddaughter. This is my land, and the fellow who was good enough to give you directions to the house is my groundskeeper."

Adam's shoulder burned where Eileen had touched him. It hadn't escaped his notice that his grandfather's letter could have been a love letter, and if Arabella had been anything like Eileen, Adam could understand the appeal of Kirkfoyle women.

"Pleasure to meet you," Adam said, and he really meant that.

"I'm afraid I don't know much about my grandmother. She died before I was born. But I've lived here all my life, and my family keeps thorough hereditary records, so I still may be able to help you." Eileen sat in the chair opposite Adam and Nicola, leaning forward with her elbows propped on the knees of her spread legs. There was something masculine in the way she carried herself, like a country gentleman trapped in the body of a lithe girl. "I'm always happy to learn more about my ancestors, or any of their friends. It seems like your grandfather and my grandmother were very good friends indeed."

Finley appeared with a wooden tray laden with a pot of steaming breakfast tea, three china cups so well used the paint had started to wear away, a plate of fluffy halved scones, a jar of raspberry jam and a dish of clotted cream. Adam wondered idly if Eileen had any staff outside of Finley, but then hunger took over and he became distracted by getting as much scone inside his empty stomach as quickly as possible without eating like he had been raised in a barn.

"Adam's playing it cool," Nicola said, her pink tongue darting out to lap a bit of jam from her thumb. "But coming out here is all he's been able to talk about for months. We're very grateful for your hospitality and your willingness to chat with us. It's exciting, to finally be at Craigmar."

"You're a very good girlfriend, traipsing all the way out here with your man," Eileen said, smiling behind a sip of tea. "If I were you I would have made him leave me back at the hotel."

"Oh, I'm not his girlfriend," Nicola said, a blush blooming across her nose. She was always quick to correct anyone who thought they were together, which happened more often than Adam would have liked. It wasn't that he hadn't thought about getting with Nicola – he had thought about it an embarrassing amount, actually, when they were out together, or when they were apart, or when he was alone in bed at night – it was that getting with Nicola was out of the question. She was gorgeous, sure, and they were good friends, but they were a bad personality match in the long term. So Adam had never spoiled anything with a short-sighted hookup. "I'm just a friend along for the ride."

"Suit yourself," Eileen said, as though she didn't believe Nicola at all.

Nicola looked affronted at these fighting words. Adam knew from experience that Nicola would box the ears of a frat guy who got too handsy, or yank the hair of a bitchy girl at a bar, and he hated to see what she would do to landed gentry.

"Nicola's been a godsend," Adam said, stepping in to diffuse the situation. "And she studies Scottish folklore—"

"As a hobby," Nicola put in.

"You finished a whole medieval literature degree," Adam corrected, refusing to let her downplay her intelligence. "Anyway, this kind of thing is very up her alley so I'm glad she came with me."

"What a lovely turn of events," Eileen said. "So, how may I be of assistance?"

"Any information you might have about my grandfather would be great. You never heard anyone in your family talk about a Robert Lancaster, did you?"

"I can't say I did. Was he a guest of the family, perhaps? Or brought on the grounds to do some kind of contract work?"

"I'm not sure," Adam admitted. "He never mentioned

why he was here, or why he left. He just talked about it like it was something out of a book, like Avalon or something. It was special to him, I guess. He wanted to come back, there at the end, but he was too sick to travel. I promised him I would go see it for him instead."

"Finley, you've lived here as long as I have," Eileen said. "Does this ring any bells?"

"No, sir," Finley said, hardly glancing at her. He was chewing on his thumbnail like something was agitating him, like he would rather be anywhere else but here. "I just manage the grounds. The comings and goings of the house have never been my family's business."

"When would your grandfather have been at Craigmar?" Eileen went on.

"I'm not sure about that either," Adam said, face heating as he began to realize just how unprepared he was for this conversation. Had it been stupid, coming all the way out here with nothing but a story, a name, and hope? Was he wasting Eileen's time? "Decades ago."

"There aren't many of us left alive who remember that long ago," Eileen said cryptically. "I'm barely twenty-seven. So's Finley."

Before Adam could press further, a deafening thunderclap boomed above the house, making everyone jump. Finley strode over to the window to glare outside, no doubt gauging how much rainfall they were in for and how that might affect his job, but Eileen just slapped her hand over her heart and laughed.

"It's coming down awfully hard," Finley said, shooting a pointed look to Eileen. There was a half beat of quiet, as though they were silently conferring.

"How hard?" Eileen asked.

"See for yourself."

Eileen went to the window and began to make a tsking sound. Adam, who felt this boded ill, joined Eileen at the floor-to-ceiling window, along with Nicola.

It wasn't raining outside; it was absolutely pouring. Adam had waited for cabs in Berlin rain, and he had hiked through Icelandic blizzards, so he felt quite confident there wasn't much weather could throw at him that he couldn't handle. But this was a gray, cold rain, lashing against the house in sheets.

"Is that your car outside?" Eileen asked.

"Yeah," Nicola said. "It's a rental."

"It's not exactly built for mud," Eileen said. "That road you took to get here gets washed out during heavy rains. I'm not sure it's safe for you to drive."

"How long is the rain supposed to last?" Adam asked.

"Until tomorrow afternoon," Finley replied, with the wisdom of someone who knew his way around a farmer's almanac.

"Tomorrow?" Nicola repeated, voice tight. "It can't be that bad, right?"

"I've flipped one car and bogged another down in mud on that road when it comes down like this," Finley said, glancing over at Nicola. If Adam wasn't mistaken, he was standing a little closer to Nicola than was strictly necessary. "Doesn't matter how steady you are behind the wheel, the spring rains have a mind of their own."

"You picked a hell of a time to come to the Highlands," Eileen said. "We'll have two beds turned down for you, of course. Happy to have you until the rain stops. That will give us more time to get to know each other and chat ancestry anyway, won't it?"

"Oh, no," Adam began, loath to impose, "we can't—"

"You'd let us stay here, in this beautiful house with you?" Nicola said, and *oh no*, her eyes were soft with wonder. Adam could never deny her anything when she looked like that, enraptured by the mere beauty of being alive. "You just met us."

"I'm willing to wager that two American tourists aren't going to throttle me in my sleep, but if you get murder on your mind, remember I keep a rifle in my room."

Finley let out an exasperated sound, and Adam expected Eileen to chastise her employee for that, or at least to give him a look of disapproval. Instead, she barely noticed.

"It's no trouble at all, really," she went on. "This house was built for hosting guests, but it's just me here now, most days. A bit of company might not be so terrible."

She gave Adam a warm smile, perhaps a bit more warm than was strictly necessary, her gaze flicking over his body for one hot instant before she looked back out the window.

She was hard to deny, Adam would give her that.

"Thank you," he said, surrendering to this strange turn of fate. He had been dreaming of Craigmar since he was a boy, and now that he was here, he wasn't keen on leaving. At least not until he had explored every nook, walked through every room, drank down every drop of history in this place. If Eileen was willing to allow that, it was all the permission he needed. It wasn't as if they had anywhere else to be. There was the flight to catch back home eventually, yes, but Adam had left most of their itinerary open for side wanderings and unexpected day trips and hopefully, a deep and meaningful engagement with this place his grandfather had left to Adam like an inheritace.

Adam shot a glance to Nicola, who bounced on the balls of her feet in pleasure. She looked totally enraptured by Eileen and the private world of decaying opulence she commanded.

"Finley will show you to your rooms," Eileen said, already drifting away as though this lavish display of generosity was nothing to her, like it was all in a day's work. "Probably a good idea to get some of your things from the car as well. Take your time settling in. I'm not going anywhere."

"We really appreciate it," Nicola said. "If there's any way we can pay you back, or help out—"

Eileen made a sound as though Nicola was being preposterous. "Absolutely not. This is hospitality, and it's my pleasure. Finley?"

"On it," Finley said, and then, as though he had forgotten himself. "Sir."

Finley gestured towards the door, bidding Adam lead the way. Adam exited the library, followed closely by Nicola pressed up against his back, but he couldn't help take one last look behind him at the grand room. He barely caught sight of the groundskeeper grasping the lord's wrist, rough fingers leaving indentations on the milky flesh.

So quickly, and so faintly that Adam might have been imagining it, he heard Finley say in a low, urgent voice, "*Isla*."

The lord looked to her hired help with fire burning in her eyes. Then, she wrenched her wrist free.

This broke the strange, tense spell. The groundskeeper stalked off after Adam and Nicola, leaving the lord alone in her library.

"This way," Finley said, voice a little rough.

Adam and Nicola dutifully followed him up a flight of mahogany stairs and down a twisting series of corridors that Adam probably couldn't find his way along with a map and the light of day on his side.

"That'll be Nicola's room," Finley said, stopping short in a carpeted hallway and pointing out a bedroom. "Adam, your room will be right at the end of the hall. I figured after roughing it on the road you two might like your own space."

Adam wanted to argue. He and Nicola always slept in

mixed-gender hostel rooms when they traveled, but that wasn't quite the same thing as sharing a private room, and certainly not a private bed. He wasn't sure how to complain about being separated from Nicola directly, so instead he said, "Can we have a few minutes to chat and get our bearings? Happy to be shown to my room after that."

"Sure," Finley said, unbothered. "See you downstairs when you're ready."

With that, he was gone, and Adam followed Nicola into her room.

The guest bedroom was small but cozy, featuring a four-poster bed decorated with carved roses, and a small fireplace in the corner. The wallpaper was covered in delicate green vines and tiny pink flowers, giving the room the air of a country garden.

"Can you believe this?" Nicola asked, in the same tone of voice she used to gossip about who was sleeping with who on the intramural volleyball team. "God, this house! It's got to be what, eighteen fifties? Built on older foundations, I bet. And did you see how many books were in that library?"

"It's gorgeous," Adam conceded. "But I don't love being stuck here."

"You don't love being stuck anywhere," Nicola said, tossing herself down on the bed. "But it's only for the night."

"I just wasn't expecting any of this, and we're pretty

isolated out here. I don't even think I have cell service. I can't help feeling like we're putting Eileen out."

"She's just a lonely eccentric with too much time on her hands, and we're free in-house entertainment. She said it herself: there's no one out here but her and Finley. Now *him* I like."

"I don't trust your judgment when it comes to the people you like, no offense."

"Am I not allowed to like people now?"

"Of course you are," Adam said, covering for himself quickly. He had no right to be jealous over Nicola. At the end of the day, she wasn't his. He had made sure of that, time and time again. It was easier that way. Less painful. "I'm just saying, make sure the guy isn't going to go all Ted Bundy on you before you jump his bones."

"You let me have my harmless groundskeeper fantasy and I'll let you keep looking at the hot aristocrat like you want her to step on you with her riding boots," Nicola shot back with a grin.

"I do *not* want her to step on me," Adam said, bristling. The kick of his pulse at the mention of Eileen told a different story. "And did you hear the way they talked? So weird. Every other sentence is like something out of a storybook, like they actually haven't spoken to modern people in ages. She's worse than he is, but still. Let's just play it safe out here, okay? If you get any weird vibes, come find me."

"Obviously," Nicola said with a sigh. "But this is what you wanted, isn't it? Answers with a side of adventure?"

"I guess so," Adam said, trying not to smile. He knew he should be more wary about this (stranger danger and all) but it was hard not to feel like the universe's favorite son right now. It was so tempting to give in to the sense of fatedness that had wrapped around him the moment he laid eyes on the house.

"This might be it, Adam," Nicola said, sobering slightly. She knew better than anyone what this trip meant to him. After all, she had been the one who picked up the phone early that Sunday morning his grandfather died. "I want this to be it, for you."

"Thanks, Nikki. At any rate, we should get back down there before they start thinking we're up here stealing their silver or whatever." He turned to go, pausing at the doorway. Sincerity was sometimes hard for him, certainly harder than laughter and a good time, but somehow he managed it. "I'm happy it's you with me out here. Seriously."

"It's true, I'm pretty great," Nicola said, smoothing her sweater like a proud peacock as she strode past him into the hallway. "Now come on. I want more tea."

CHAPTER THREE

Nicola

By the time Adam and Nicola had retrieved their bags from the car and changed into clothes that weren't rumply and musty from the road, it was past five, and Nicola's stomach was grumbling. The granola bar she had put away at the hostel that morning was gone, and so were the scones from tea, so Finley heated up that venison pie after all. It tasted rich and dark and perfectly gamey, with a pastry crust so flaky Nicola wanted to paint it and capture its beauty. When Finley passed her a plate in the library where they had all agreed to take dinner informally, his warm thumb brushed the delicate skin of her inner wrist.

Nicola expected Adam and Eileen to lose themselves in theorizing about their intersecting family histories over dinner, but Eileen didn't seem in any rush to get down to business. She made casual conversation instead, absolutely delighted with every new detail about Adam's graphic design business and running club, or about Nicola's work as a florist's assistant who spent her nights writing yet-to-be-published fantasy books for children. Eileen didn't even eat that much, just sipped a fresh glass of whisky while she listened, rapt, to the mundane details of Nicola and Adam's lives.

Finley had taken his dinner with them, but stood by the sideboard while he ate, as though allergic to getting too comfortable. He kept finding excuses to linger, polishing the grandfather clock or clearing dishes, and he didn't say much, but he certainly listened. Nicola caught his eyes on her more than once, and she caught herself admiring the outline of his strong forearms and the painfully romantic curls of his hair more than that.

She wondered if it would be poor form to hit on her host's only staff member. She wondered if Finley might like to be hit on.

It wasn't that she was totally incorrigible when it came to her freewheeling desires, it was just she liked meeting new people a lot, and that flirtation (and sometimes even a friendly hookup) was her favorite way to get to know them.

But now, with the sun setting outside behind storm clouds that refused to dissipate, Eileen turned at last to the matter at hand. Her picked-at venison pie sat forgotten on the coffee table as she nestled her chin in her palm in thought.

"What exactly did your grandfather tell you was out here, anyway?" she asked Adam. "Anything interesting besides old masonry and sheep?"

"It's going to sound stupid," Adam said, studiously putting away the last of his pie. Adam might be skinny, but he sure could eat.

"Try me."

Adam set his plate down and gathered himself.

"The story changed every time. He said it was the final resting place of knights, that there was all sorts of treasure buried beneath the house, that it was a gathering place for witches . . . Just stuff to help a kid fall asleep. But he did seem to think that there was something special about this place, like it had some sort of weird energy."

"I can certainly attest that Craigmar is weird," Eileen said, tucking her feet underneath her in the armchair. She was curled up like a cat, boots forgotten by the fireplace.

"How so?" Nicola asked. She always had an affinity for strange stories, ever since she was a little girl scaring her foster siblings with creepypasta recitations. It didn't matter if it was ghosts or demons, faeries or aliens, angels or headless horsemen, Nicola loved it all. The older the tale, the better.

"I won't bore you with specifics, and I'm afraid most of the stories aren't very happy," Eileen said, treating Nicola to her undivided attention. It was a bit intoxicating, like a full snifter of brandy on an empty stomach. Eileen really was beautiful, in a way that felt brutal and unforgiving and yet effortlessly chic. "I was happy growing up here, but it's true that many Kirkfoyles have faced hardship within these walls, and some have even died at Craigmar. This region used to be lousy with Kirkfoyles, but now I'm the last of my line. My own parents drowned in a boating accident just offshore when I was sixteen."

"Gosh, I'm sorry," Nicola said, heart constricting. She couldn't imagine losing every family member you had since she had never known her mother or father to begin with, but she certainly knew what it felt like to be alone in the world.

"That's life for you," Eileen said, unbothered. "But that reminds me. Adam, I want to show you something."

Eileen rose to pull a large clothbound book from one of the shelves, then slotted it into a stand atop the massive oak desk by the window. Nicola had barely noticed it before, but now she saw clearly that it was the sort of desk that stayed in a family for generations, the place where land treaties and marriage contracts and death certificates had probably all been signed.

Eileen turned the pages of the book with delicate pinches between her nails, which were painted with pearlescent lacquer.

"Come over here," she said in that rich voice that left no room for argument.

Both Adam and Nicola rose immediately, and shot surreptitious looks at each other as they approached the desk. Somehow, without ever raising her voice or making a single demand at all, Eileen had them both on short little leashes already.

Finley watched intently from the fireplace, no longer pretending he hadn't been eavesdropping.

Nicola stepped closer to squint at the pages of the book, close enough that she could feel both Adam and Eileen's body heat as they leaned in with her.

Eileen spread her fingers across a list of names rendered in ancient calligraphy.

"These are my family records. All the offshoots of the Kirkfoyle clan, small but proud though we be. Here's my father, and his father's father. And here I am."

Eileen pointed at her name. Eileen Elizabeth Kirkfoyle, born twenty-seven years ago, not a sibling to speak of. Only five years older than Nicola, and in control of a title and land.

"And this," Eileen said, flipping back a few pages to tap at a name, "is my grandmother."

"Arabella was an only child too?" Nicola asked.

A shadow passed over Eileen's face.

"Yes. We don't birth many children in my family. The women tend to experience . . . complications."

"Born in 1960, married in 1977, died 1981," Adam read aloud. "She was only twenty-one."

"Every family has its tragedies," Eileen said, somewhat ominously. Adam might have been completely convinced of Eileen's affectation, but Nicola had hung out with enough theatre majors to know when someone was putting on an air. Eileen's dreary dramatics were a bit studied, a bit like what she thought might be expected of her. But maybe there was an honesty to that as well. "That's all I know about her. My father never really talked about his mother. I'm sure you can understand why, seeing as she died suddenly when he was two. Arabella's husband, my grandfather, didn't last very long after she was gone. He was an out-of-town sort, not built for Craigmar. Died of a broken heart, they say. Pulmonary hypertension, I say."

"Do you think it was your grandmother that invited my grandfather out here?"

"Probably," Eileen said, flipping the book shut. "But we won't know for certain unless we find evidence of him here. Lucky for you, my family has always had too much time on our hands. We keep meticulous records: genealogy, photographs, letters, guest books, all of it. You're welcome to look through whatever you like tomorrow."

Adam looked slightly winded. Even Nicola had to admit the offer seemed lavish.

"We don't want to make you go through all those boxes," she said. "Maybe you can point us towards a local library or something?"

"Kirkfoyles are private," Eileen said with a sly smile that made Nicola feel melty inside in that scared-confused-sexy way she liked so much. It was like Eileen was the cat watching Nicola the songbird out the window, dreaming of devouring her whole. "You won't find any of my family records in town."

"What will it do for you?" Finley asked. It was one of the first things he had said since dinner, and when Nicola glanced back at him, he was giving Adam a strange, heavy look. "When you find what you're looking for?"

Adam looked right back at him, weighing him up with that masculine appraisal that Nicola had come to learn meant two boys were about to fight, or aggressively shake hands, or, less frequently, disappear together into a dark back room at a party.

"I'll know myself better," Adam said. "And I'll know my grandfather better, and maybe then I'll be able to move on."

It was one of the most honest things feckless, free-wheeling Adam had said this whole trip. Finley stared him down for a moment more, then nodded and dropped his gaze as though in submission.

"This is an opportunity for both of us," Eileen said, grasping Adam's shoulder. "I never knew my grandmother, and you knew your grandfather so well you can't let him go. We could discover so much about them, together. How lucky that you found your way to my doorstep."

"It is," Adam said, gazing at Eileen with a high color in his cheeks and light in his eyes. He looked more alive than Nicola had seen him since his grandfather died, which pricked at her just a bit. She might not be a mysterious rich weirdo who lived in a castle, but Adam was lucky to have found her, too.

"So it's decided!" Eileen said with the brisk, single clap one might use to summon a hunting dog. "You'll stay the night, and get some rest, and have a hot shower. Then tomorrow we'll all get our hands dirty with a little research. Finley, you'll help too."

"There are fences that need mending," Finley said, sullen. Was Nicola imagining it, or did he seem bothered by whatever electricity was crackling between Adam and Eileen too? "Bushes that need pruning. And I've got to feed the dogs."

"Then go home and feed them tonight and come back tomorrow with a shining attitude," Eileen said. "For now, I think we should all get a good night's sleep. You're probably exhausted from all this unexpected excitement."

Nicola wanted to protest that it was still early in the night, that she could stay up for another hour of talking or another cup of tea or even a glass of Scotch, but now that she thought about it, she really was bushed. Adam, similarly, had a road-weary glaze in his eyes.

"You're probably right," he said. "You tired, Nikki?"

"Kind of," she said, stifling a yawn.

"I'll show you both back to your wing," Finley said. "The house is confusing if you aren't used to it. Lots of twists and turns."

Adam and Nicola took their leave of Eileen, thanking her profusely for the umpteenth time, then followed Finley up a flight of stairs that seemed entirely different from the one they had taken earlier that day. It was as though the house had been designed to confuse visitors.

"This is you, Adam," Finley said, stopping at his door. "Have a good night."

"You too," Adam said, then looked at Nicola awkwardly. Why was he suddenly acting like he didn't know how to say goodnight to her, like they hadn't done this every night on the trip so far?

"Sleep tight, don't die," she said, prompting him with their customary send-off.

"Sleep tight, don't die," he responded, then stole one more glance at Finley before shutting himself away in his room.

Finley gave a small smile once the door latched. The expression softened his face considerably, giving him a boyish quality. Tiny, weathered sun lines showed at the corner of his eyes, the only indication of his age.

For a minute, Nicola forgot how to speak.

"My room?" she managed, barely half a sentence.

"Around the corner and three doors down," Finley said. "And a word to the wise: the manor can be disorienting at night. I suggest you stay in your room unless it's an emergency."

"Got it," Nicola said, fully aware that this was the part in the conversation where she should say goodnight. She opened the door to her guest bedroom and Finley lingered a polite few feet away as though making sure she could operate the light switch. He was only three or four inches taller than her, just the way she liked best, and he smelled like pine and woodsmoke.

"Anything else?" she asked.

For a moment it appeared like he wanted to say something more. But then, he just nodded.

"No. Pleasant dreams."

"You too," Nicola said, feeling a bit deflated.

With that, Finley was gone, leaving Nicola alone in the darkened room.

In the resulting quiet, she could hear the manor creaking and settling, like a living, breathing thing.

CHAPTER FOUR

Adam

Adam tossed and turned all night. Sleep came only in fitful snatches, and when it did, he was assailed by strange, dark dreams. When he finally awoke and checked his phone to find it was three in the morning, his recollection of the dreams was hazy. He was sure someone had been saying his name, over and over again, in a voice he couldn't recognize. There had been a sensation of liquid cold, like being dragged under icy water, and a constriction in his lungs, from crying, or drowning, or both.

Adam heaved a breath and tried to banish all memories of the dreams. It was hard to sleep in this creepy old place, beautiful though it was, and harder still without Nicola's soft breathing near by. He had found it comforting to doze off with her right below him in the hostel bunk beds.

Adam tossed back the covers and slipped out of bed, the footfalls of his bare feet muffled by the thick green carpet. His room was more than comfortable, with a cushy if creaky queen bed and a writing desk by the window, but he had no idea what to do with himself this late at night. His laptop was charging in one of the only working outlets in the room, and he hadn't brought a book with him. When Adam traveled, he traveled light, with a purpose, and intent to see as much of the world outside his room as possible.

He resolved to go find Nicola, who he suspected wouldn't be able to sleep either. Maybe she had a melatonin gummy, or even better a weed gummy, or at least the sense to convince him to try to go back to sleep on his own.

Easing open his door, Adam crept into the hallway. He navigated mostly by instinct, trying in vain to retrace his steps. But instead of taking him back to Nicola's room, his feet led him deeper into the manor, down stairs and through corridors hung with oil paintings of dogs chasing after wide-eyed hares. The hares gazed up stricken at the sky, as though pleading to an unfeeling God to spare them.

Eventually, he spied a light up ahead, spilling out of a cracked door. Thinking he had somehow found his way back to Nicola, he quickened his pace. But as he drew closer, he saw that it was far too large to be the door to any bedroom. There were muffled voices inside, rising and falling, and the crisp crack of what must have been a fire popping.

Overcome with curiosity, Adam nudged open the door a few inches.

The library was low lit in firelight, which cast long flickering shadows on the bookshelves. Finley was standing in front of the fire, something gripped tightly in his hand. He was barefoot, wearing jeans and a Henley with the sleeves rolled up. The cording of the muscles in his forearms was evident in the stark shadows, and his jaw was set. With an imperious tilt to his chin, he looked like an entirely different person to the sulking groundskeeper Adam had met mere hours ago.

Finley reared back and brought the item in his hand down towards the floor with that crack that Adam had heard earlier.

The sound went through Adam like an electric shock.

A riding crop, he realized.

Finley was holding a riding crop.

Adam's gaze instinctively followed the arc of the crop down to the ground, and then his heart stopped.

Eileen lay on the Persian rug wearing nothing but cigarette pants and a bra, a high color in her cheeks. Her hands were bound with a length of silk, and there were pulsing red stripes across her back where the riding crop had made contact. She huffed out a breath, giving a little sigh as Finley struck her again, and then again, circling her like a predator scenting prey. Finley's eyes tracked her every movement, jumping from the fluttering hollow of her throat to the heave of her chest to the twitch in her bound fingers. It was the kind of perfectly captured focus Adam only saw when people prayed, or when his more academic friends studied for their finals.

When Finley snapped his fingers, Eileen rolled onto her back, and Adam spied the rose-petal pink of her nipples through her sheer lace bra. There was something luridly appealing about the sight; Eileen in dark trousers and very little else, trussed up like the centerpiece of a feast.

Arousal and horror warred in Adam's stomach.

He should not be here.

He should not be seeing this.

Just as Adam was about to hightail it back to his room, Eileen's head lolled to the side, and she made eye contact with him through the crack in the door.

Her dark gaze scorched across his skin like a hot coal.

Adam knew he should have the decency to avert his gaze, but he couldn't bring himself to look away from her. He was transfixed.

Finley didn't seem to notice their unspoken exchange. He abandoned the crop on a nearby settee and leaned down to thread his fingers through Eileen's hair. Sweat shone on her collarbones, evidence of exertion, or desire, or both, and her lipstick was smeared. Finley tugged Eileen up to meet his mouth, his grip punishingly firm, his kiss all the more indecent for its gentleness.

Eileen kissed him back and all the tension sagged out

of her shoulders, her knotted muscles relaxing until her entire body went limp.

Adam pushed himself back from the door, stumbling into the hallway.

Dreaming. He had to be dreaming. Some strange mixture of jet lag, exhaustion and not having been laid in recent memory was conspiring against him, making him hallucinate dark things about his hosts. He needed to find his way back into his body, still doubtlessly asleep in his bed.

With his skin on fire and a churning in his gut, Adam stumbled back towards his bedroom.

CHAPTER FIVE

Nicola

Nicola woke to the thin gray sunlight of an overcast day shining onto her face. She rolled over underneath the goose-feather comforter and let out a groan of mammalian contentment. For a moment she thought she was back in her nest of pillows and blankets in her studio apartment, but then she remembered the adventure of the night before, and her eyes flickered open.

She was still in Craigmar, still wrapped in a wonderful waking dream. She felt like a medieval princess waking to brush out her hair a hundred times and then be latticed into her gown by her ladies-in-waiting.

Nicola slipped out of bed and shivered the moment her feet touched the rug. She wanted to find Adam, but she wanted a cup of hot coffee more, so she pulled her pink puffer jacket on over her tank top and pajama pants and slipped out into the hallway.

In the light of day, the manor was less intimidating. The dark wood paneling glowed russet in the sunshine, and the rugs underfoot, which had seemed dark as spilled blood at night, turned out to be crimson, accented by geometric designs in blue and gold. Nicola padded down the hall, peering out the windows onto the ocean as she went. You could see the water clearly from the second story, as though Craigmar had been built right on the precipice of a watery kingdom.

Nicola followed the sound of running water and clattering cutlery to an open door, which led into the kitchen. Finley stood at the sink, his back to Nicola, filling a gooseneck kettle with water from the tap. Just as she was about to ease back into the hallway, he glanced round and caught sight of her. In a chunky sweater and with his eyes heavy-lidded with sleep, he looked like an entirely different person than the man she had encountered the day before. He was still handsome in a broody way, but now he also looked approachable, sleep-rumpled and touchably warm.

"Good morning," he said.

"Ah, sorry," she stammered. "I'll just go back to my room and—"

"No, you're up now," Finley said, waving her into the kitchen. "Come in and have a cup of tea."

Nicola stepped barefoot onto the tiled kitchen floor.

The room wasn't as large as she might have imagined, but it was bigger than any student apartment kitchen she had ever been in, adorned with copper pots and pans hanging from a rack above the wooden butcher block island. Finley leaned a hip against the island, watching her with another one of those smiles.

Did he only smile when they were alone together?

"Sleep well?" he asked.

"Very. Is Adam up yet?"

"I don't think so," he said, retrieving a chipped mug from the cupboard and producing a tea bag from a tin on the counter. "Can't say I blame him. It's a lot to take in, and so is Eileen."

"It's Eileen now, huh?" Nicola prodded, drifting a little closer. "I thought she was 'sir' and 'the lord' last night."

Finley held out a strongly brewed cup of breakfast tea to her. Nicola accepted it, if only to warm her fingers on the mug. She was more of a coffee girl, but what couldn't she learn to like, with time? She was used to slotting herself into much more cramped, loud houses than this, and getting along with much more unpleasant temporary family members.

Finley wasn't family, certainly. But she liked the way he looked at her, like he knew the way his gaze warmed her from the inside out. Like he wanted to see what she looked like when she was entirely melted.

"Sorry about that whole routine," he said. "She's very particular about formality, especially when it comes to new people, but her bark is worse than her bite. She's not even a lord, not on paper anyway. I think technically she's some minor baroness. But it's a hard job, being head of the manor, and I do what I can to help. You aren't scared of her, are you?"

"I went to private school on scholarship when I was younger. I know girls like Eileen, and they don't intimidate me."

"Good, that will serve you well. Milk?"

"Yes please," Nicola said.

Finley bent over to reach into the fridge, and while Nicola might have been well behaved enough not to stare, she wasn't so virtuous as to not sneak a peek at his firm ass.

"How long have you worked for Eileen?" she asked, easing down onto a nearby stool. The lord's given name felt good in her mouth.

"Oh, a small eternity. My family, the Buchanans, have worked for her family as groundskeepers for three generations. My dad even went to school and moved to Glasgow before he got called back here to pick up the mantle after *his* dad died. It gets its claws into you, this place."

"Did you grow up here?"

"Sure did. I'm the same age as Eileen. We were brought up alongside each other, her and me. Roughhousing in the heather like she wasn't anyone special, climbing trees and scraping our knees."

"That sounds really nice," Nicola said. "I didn't grow

up in one place like that. I can't imagine being a kid here, free to roam in all that green. I don't think I would have come indoors except to sleep."

Nicola glanced up to find Finley staring at her intently, lips slightly parted, as though she had just begun speaking in tongues. She suddenly felt a stone's throw from naked in her thin pajama bottoms, and she wished she had had the foresight to finger-comb her curly bob.

Finley, as though noticing her discomfort, turned to gaze out the window.

"Rain's stopped earlier than expected," he noted. "If you're lucky the roads will be safe to drive on by late afternoon."

"Oh," Nicola said, and she was surprised to find she was disappointed. Getting stranded here might have been bad luck, but it was hard to feel like it was anything but a boon sitting in the hearth-warm kitchen of a country home, chatting over tea with a gorgeous and interesting stranger.

"Do you want to see them?" Finley asked.

"What?" Nicola replied, eyelashes fluttering.

"The grounds. You aren't dressed for it, but I could wait down here while you change. Eileen lays in late, and I suspect Adam is still asleep. It seems a shame not to show you around before you leave. We could be back before breakfast."

On the one hand, it was probably safest to say goodbye to this unknown man and return to her room to wait for her friend – the person she actually trusted in this situation – to wake up. But she also hated the idea of being cooped up, and this unknown man just so happened to have the sort of rough, soft voice she had always been weak for.

"I'd love that," she said.

The ground was soggy underfoot as Finley and Nicola made their way across the grazing green, and there was a mist hanging in the air, but the worst of the storm had passed. Cozy in her jeans and a sweater and securely laced into her boots, Nicola strode after Finley over the uneven ground. He walked with determined strides, not having to watch his footing.

"How exactly does one keep grounds?" Nicola asked. "Or whatever the technical term for your job is."

Finley let out a bright laugh. He was more relaxed outdoors, away from the house. There was an easy slouch in his shoulders and a springy life in his wind-tossed curls. It was pleasing to look at, the darkest parts of his hair against the splash of green in his hazel eyes, only a few shades deeper than the marshy rolling hills. She lost herself for a moment in mentally picking the right colors to capture the scene, because Finley deserved to be rendered with boldness and depth.

"I do anything that needs doing," he said. "Plant flowers and trim hedges, salt the drive in case of ice, uproot any trees that are dead or dying, tear ivy off the house . . . I've been known to do a bit of masonry, a bit of carpentry, even a bit of cooking when it's called for."

"Jack of all trades, huh?"

"Something like that." Finley pointed ahead to the sliver of rocky coast in the distance, and the deep blue waters beyond. "This strip of grass stretches all the way down to the shore, about a mile away. The woodlands go on for acres and acres, entirely uncultivated. Once upon a time they were used for hunting, or for growing mushrooms and berries for the kitchen, but they've gone wild by now."

Finley kept up the pace, leading Nicola further and further from the house. As Craigmar manor shrank in the distance, they passed a few unbothered sheep nibbling at the wildflowers underfoot. One of them let out an inquisitive bleat, then shuffled aside to reveal the tiny lamb who had been suckling from its mother.

Nicola clasped her hands together, overtaken by the sight, and let out a gasp of delight.

"Oh, a baby!" she exclaimed. "It's so cute. I've never seen a lamb up close."

"You haven't?" Finley asked, and a wicked grin passed over his face. "Stay right there."

Taking big steps in his wellington boots, Finley walked right up to the nearest lamb. The mother let out an indignant *baa*, but Finley shushed her like she was a fussy toddler and scratched her behind the ears. Then he tucked the lamb's legs up underneath its belly and carried it over to Nicola, who was practically vibrating with delight.

"Go ahead and give him a cuddle," Finley said, proffering the lamb. "Just mind his teeth. The little ones bite."

Nicola held out her hands and Finley deposited the bundle of wriggling warmth into her arms. Nicola cradled it with the care she would show to a human newborn, holding it safely close to her chest. It smelled earthy and damp, like fresh cut grass, with the unmistakable musk of farm animal underneath. Nicola could feel the rapid patter of its heart through its wooly chest, a tiny miracle in itself.

"Oh," she said reverentially. "Oh my goodness."

Nicola glanced up at Finley and found he was watching her with a strange expression. It was partly pained and partly reverent, as though he were witnessing something holy. Nicola stood there, scratching the lamb behind the ears, and let him look at her, really look.

Then Finley stepped forward and retrieved the lamb from Nicola, breaking the spell.

"You're good with animals," he said, not quite able to meet her eyes. "Shall we keep walking?"

CHAPTER SIX

Adam

Adam awoke to Nicola's prim triple rap on his bedroom door. Blinking the sleep from his eyes, he hauled himself out of bed and staggered over. His mind was still muddy with images from what he thought he had seen the night before. It hovered just out of reach, hazy with sleep, but as Adam grasped for the sense that *something* real had happened last night, everything rushed back with scintillating clarity. Finley's strong hand gripping the riding crop, Eileen stripped half-naked on the floor, their searing shared kiss.

Adam shoved the memories – or the dreams, whatever they were – away before they could make the half hard-on he had woken with any worse. Stifled by the heavy blankets, he had tossed off his shirt in the night, and his chest was still covered with a thin layer of sweat.

Without thinking twice about dressing, Adam opened the door.

Eileen Kirkfoyle stood before him, his freshly pressed clothes in her arms, her dark hair swirled up on her head and held in place with golden hairpins. She was fully dressed, in wide-legged pants that tied in a bow around her waist, and a dour black blouse buttoned up to her throat, but the sight of her brought images of creamy bare skin painted with a high flush flooding back all the same.

Adam opened his mouth, but no sound came out.

Eileen's eyes flickered unselfconsciously across his bare chest, as though she were examining a horse before a pageant.

"You slept through breakfast," she said. "I came to make sure you hadn't died in your sleep."

"Nope," Adam said, voice too bright. "Here I am. Still alive."

"Happy to hear it. Sleep well, I hope? No trouble with the bed?"

She was speaking at a brisk clip, as though she were impatient with him already. Adam glanced at the clock on his bedside table. It wasn't even eight yet. Had he made some social faux pas by sleeping in, or were aristocratic country families the type to get up at the crack of dawn?

"I slept great," he lied.

"No bad dreams?" she asked, in the light-as-air lilt that left everything open to interpretation.

Adam began to feel, for the first time since arriving, that perhaps Eileen was fucking with him.

"No nightmares," he said, forcing a smile.

"Grand. There are leftovers in the pantry if you're hungry. Join me in the library once you're fed."

"Is Nicola up yet?" Adam asked, feeling a bit disoriented and more than a bit naked, but absolutely powerless to close the door. Eileen's eyes pinned him in place like an insect specimen under glass. "I'd like to say good morning to her first, make sure she had an okay night."

"You can, just as soon as she's back indoors. I saw her and Finley through the window touring the grounds. They'll be out there a while, if he has his way. I'll expect you in the library at the top of the hour."

A lick of anger flared up in Adam's chest. Who did this woman think she was, ordering him around? And who did Finley think he was, absconding with Nicola without so much as telling him? And what was *Nicola* thinking, wandering off with a man she had met hours before? It wasn't that reckless connections were out of character for her; quite the opposite, in fact. Adam's night had been ruined more than once by Nicola running off to the bathroom with some girl she had just met at the bar for seven minutes in sapphic heaven, or by her bringing a new beau who hadn't yet been vetted to a group game night. Nicola was good-hearted and generally a decent judge of people, but she was impulsive, and borderline reckless when sex was involved. Adam had tried to talk to her about it once, but she had snapped back at him that he couldn't get through a single trip abroad without getting into at least one situationship, and that had shut him up.

They were both bad at saying no to the greedy little fires within them that burned every hour of the day, begging to be fed with adventure or kisses or the heady rush of a whirlwind twenty-four-hour romance. They had agreed to stick together on this trip, but it looked like that promise went out the window at the first pair of pretty eyes.

Eileen thrust the bundle of clean clothes into Adam's arms.

"No need to stand on ceremony, but I would recommend putting on some clothes. Do you take tea or coffee in the morning?"

Eileen was still pretty in the morning light, but now Adam could see her human imperfections as well: the flyaway hairs sticking out of her chignon, the way her lipstick feathered at the corners of her mouth, the sickly pallor beneath her makeup. Her under-eyes looked bruised, as though from crying or sleeplessness. As a matter of fact, in the unforgiving sunlight streaming in through Adam's window, Eileen looked like a lovely wraith, a thin-skinned blue-veined ghost doomed to haunt her own home.

"Coffee," Adam said, filing all this away. "Thanks for the laundry."

"Certainly," Eileen said stiffly, giving a jerky nod as though she had forgotten an appropriate response to the niceties of conversation. Adam was once again struck by her antiquated speech, like a child who had only learned how to talk to others by reading Frances Hodgson Burnett novels. It seemed a bit pretentious but mostly earnest, and that was the strangest part.

And with that, she was gone, disappeared down the hallway in a gust of iris perfume. Adam was left reeling, feeling half like taking his chances hiking out to find Nicola and half like pursuing Eileen down the hallway towards whatever designs she had for him.

In the end, he realized that he didn't really have a choice.

Swearing under his breath, he kicked off his pajama pants and changed into clean clothes.

The house was easier to traverse in the daytime, and the pathway to the library had been seared into his memory by last night's excursion. That scene hadn't been a dream, of that he was more and more sure. He had really witnessed something unspeakable transpiring between Eileen and Finley, which meant that Eileen had seen him spying with her own eyes. And now, Eileen was either keeping a stiff upper lip about the whole thing and ignoring it entirely for the sake of courtesy, or she was pretending she didn't know to toy with him, batting him around like a cat with a mouse. Either way, Adam hated it.

At least, hatred was the easiest explanation for the way his heart raced as he turned the corner and stepped into the library.

Eileen had, apparently bright and early that morning, brought a number of cardboard boxes out of storage and piled them on the desk. They were the sturdy kind with lids, the kind Adam recognized from the years his mother worked as a legal assistant. The gallery wall overlooked the strange workstation, faces from antiquity peering out at him from gilt frames.

"This is everything I could find in the attic from the years I figure it was most likely your grandfather was here," she said, putting her hands on her hips as she surveyed the mess with bright eyes. She seemed even more excited than Adam was. "And a few boxes extra."

"That's very thorough," Adam replied, not entirely sure what to say. On the surface, nothing about this situation seemed wrong, exactly. Strange, certainly, but strange in a good way, like an unexpected windfall of fortune. Still, that bell of survival instinct that had saved Adam from being mugged, roofied or swindled on countless trips was ringing in the back of his mind. It was very faint, but he still noticed it.

Something was off.

"Going through all this could take days," Eileen said. "Or hours, if we're lucky. Where would you like to start?"

"With something to eat?" he suggested. He needed breakfast, that was true, but asking for something from the kitchen was also an easy way to send her out of the room for a few minutes. "Sorry, I've never been able to work on an empty stomach."

"Oh yes," she said absentmindedly, as though she had forgotten eating was something human beings needed to do. "The porridge should still be warm. We've got toast and bacon too, if you want it."

"Sounds great."

Eileen nodded and disappeared into the hall, and Adam pressed his hand to his chest, trying to identify the root cause of the sudden urge he had to run. He rubbed a circle over his breastbone, trying to massage away that tight feeling. Was Eileen actually acting strangely or was this just him freaking out the moment someone invited him into intimacy, even if it was only friendship and cooperation? He had been more reactive since his grandfather died, more erratic and irritable. Maybe he was just looking for a way to ruin a good thing.

Adam looked up at the trio of hares captured in the stained-glass panel above the window, arranged in a circle with their ears touching. It took him a moment to realize that there were only three ears shared between the hares, joining them together in an optical illusion.

It was beautiful to look at, but upon closer inspection it gave Adam an unsettled feeling, a feeling that only grew within him the longer he looked at it. He had the sinking sensation that he had seen it somewhere before, or even more unnerving, that he was in the presence of something very ancient that his animal hindbrain recognized even when his conscious mind could not.

"Here we are," Eileen said, appearing from around the corner with a serving tray in her hands. The spread had been arranged nicely, even with a sprig of baby's breath in a slim purple vase, and Adam's stomach grumbled at the sight. "Take a load off, have your fill."

"Happily," Adam said. Eileen had brought him a huge serving of breakfast, far more than even Adam could eat, so he asked: "Want some of this toast?"

"Oh no," she said, waving the offer away. "I already ate."

Adam sat down on the couch and began to slather some jam onto a piece of toast, keeping one eye on Eileen. Something about her, and about this whole situation, was starting to make him feel like a hare himself, crouched in the jaws of a trap and waiting to see if the trigger would go off.

"Can I ask you something?" Adam said, just talking to fill the dead air. When Eileen was chatty, she was charismatic beyond belief. When she was quiet, Adam was learning, she gave off an intensely pensive energy. He had never been good with uncomfortable silences.

"Of course."

"Why do you go by lord, even though you're, well, a lady?"

Eileen gave him a sharp grin.

"Lord suits me better, I think."

"Fair enough," Adam replied. His relationship with gender was neither intricate or fraught, but he knew that wasn't the case for everyone.

"How's that taste?" she asked. "Need more maple syrup for the porridge?"

"It's perfect," he said.

"Better than the cafeteria food at Michigan State, I'd wager," she teased.

Adam was once again thrown off balance. That bell in the back of his head rang a little clearer, a little louder.

"I don't think I told you I went to Michigan State, did I?"

"I took the liberty of doing a quick Instagram search last night," she said, casting her eyes back towards the boxes as she took a seat on the other end of the couch. She seemed once again impatient, like he was the one being cagey. "I had trouble sleeping."

"I think we all did," Adam said, a voyeur's guilt welling up inside him.

"Can I ask *you* a question now, since we're getting to know each other?"

"Of course," Adam said, taking a decisive bite of toast. He didn't believe in doing things in half measures. Whatever Eileen asked, he would answer.

"What you saw last night . . ." Eileen said, gaze never wavering. "Have you ever seen something like that before?"

"The rain?" Adam asked, hoping to God she was just talking about the weather.

"No, that indiscreet moment between Finley and I you stumbled in on."

Adam set down his spoon and pushed his porridge a few inches away, giving her a stricken look. Eileen merely smiled back, utterly serene.

"Not up close," he said. He wasn't sure if it was the answer she had been after, but at least it was honest. "And I didn't mean to see anything. I was looking for Nicola. I'm sorry for the . . . invasion of privacy."

"It was an honest mistake," Eileen said magnanimously, like she was granting Adam a royal pardon. "No harm done and no hard feelings. You must be awfully embarrassed. I just didn't want you to feel bad about it, or to think anything was wrong. Everything you saw was perfectly consensual."

The safest thing to do would be to drop this subject now, when Adam had an out, but the only two things stronger than his own live-to-see-another-day instincts were his curiosity about anything he encountered that he didn't yet understand and his inextinguishable early-twenties sex drive.

Also, Eileen wouldn't have been talking about this if she didn't want him to ask, and there was something curious and sexy about that too.

"Consensual?" he repeated, taking the bait she had so carefully laid out for him.

"I know it might look alarming, but I know what I'm doing and so does Finley. It's like play to us."

"Like a game," Adam said, trying to follow. He wasn't an innocent; he knew what he had stumbled across was some kind of kink dynamic, presumably with Finley calling the shots and Eileen obeying. Adam had encountered kink before, if accidentally, and he hadn't really had a strong opinion on it one way or another. He had met a boy in Brussels who wanted to be slapped during sex, and Adam had obliged, if clumsily. His girlfriend during his study-abroad semester in Thailand had been interested in tying him up and using him like a toy, and Adam had given it the old college try. And he had of course seen glossy BDSM scenes during his bored browsing of adult websites, but nothing had ever really lit his fire. Nothing had flayed him open and seared him alive, making his pulse pound in his throat and sweat break out on his palms. Nothing made him feel the way last night had, in those few moments he had stood frozen at the cracked library door.

He had only come out here to hike around the land and keep his promise to his grandfather, perhaps take some pictures of the house and introduce himself to the owners if they were willing to chat. In his wildest dreams, he had hoped for nothing more than a little closure. But somehow, very quickly, he had been drawn into not only Eileen's home but Eileen's confidence, and now he was just as interested in whatever was going on between her and Finley as he was in his own family history.

He wasn't sure how he had waded so far into the murky

waters of Eileen Kirkfoyle without even realizing he was getting wet. It was like she was a siren, singing him in deeper.

"I like my games," Eileen said. "I like to compete, and I like to win. Sometimes, I even like to lose. It's very simple."

Adam made a noncommittal noise. He wasn't sure what to add, but he didn't want her to stop, exactly. Eileen was talking in riddles, and he still wasn't completely sure why she was telling him this, but he couldn't deny the tightness in his jeans. He shifted in what he hoped was a subtle attempt to hide his hard-on.

"Although," she went on with a sigh, "now I suppose I can't go on pretending that Finley is simply my groundskeeper, can I? That was a fun game while it lasted."

"What is he to you, then?"

"Everything," Eileen said somberly, the word plucked from her like a daffodil yanked up by the roots.

"Ah," Adam said, and looked studiously down at his hands. It was hard to hold her gaze when she was flirting with him – she *was* flirting with him, right? Or trying to intimidate him? Were they the same to her? – and harder still when she was suddenly serious.

"And what is Nicola to you?" she asked, tucking her legs up underneath her on the sofa. Her slippered feet were inches away from Adam's thighs. "Honestly."

"I told you. She's just a friend."

"You flew all the way to Scotland to dig up your ancestral history with someone who's just a friend?"

"I did," Adam shot back, hearing the injured tone of his voice as it gave him away. It was hard to deny Eileen anything when she asked for it outright, even the tenderest of truths. Even more concerningly, it was hard to *want* to deny her anything.

"Love is brutal," Eileen said with a sage nod. "If there's anyone who understands that, it's me. You have my sympathies."

Adam arched a brow, no longer able to dance around whatever subject it was they were actually discussing.

"Sorry, I don't mean to be rude, but I feel like maybe you're asking me for something, or trying to tell me something? If I'm reading that wrong, say so."

"What if I told you your grandfather was right?" she said, lowering her voice to a conspiratorial level. Her clasped hands tightened in her lap with excitement. This was not what he had expected. Hadn't they been talking about sex, or love, or some blurry indistinct mingling of the two? "What if I told you there really is something magical about Craigmar, this house, these lands? What if I told you there was something old out there, so old most people have forgotten the proper name for it?"

"Then I would want to see evidence," Adam said, skeptic's rationality never failing him even as the world turned on its axis, even as Eileen devoured him with burning eyes. "But I'd certainly hear you out."

"And I'm happy to share, in time," she said. She gestured

towards the bar cart, heavy laden with Scotch and gin. "Shall we discuss this like civilized people, over a dram?"

"It's not even noon," Adam said, but a tiny smile betrayed him. He was charmed by her, no matter how upside-down she made him feel. Hell, that upside-down feeling might be what made her charming.

"Americans have cocktails at brunch, don't they?" Eileen said, and rose to cross to the bar cart. She held up a bottle of Outer Hebrides gin, distilled with sugar kelp. "Care for something light?"

She swirled the bottle, making the contents slosh invitingly.

If it was a game Eileen wanted, he would play with her. But Adam had always been competitive, and he played to win.

"Over ice, please. Then we can talk."

CHAPTER SEVEN

Finley

He hadn't meant to steal her away from the house, certainly not for this long, but Finley's best intentions tended to fly out the window when pretty girls were involved.

"Watch your step," he said, instinctively holding a hand out for Nicola as she traversed a treacherous slope. The rolling lawn had turned to birch and oak forest a few minutes ago, and her flat-bottomed boots weren't made for serious hiking.

"Thanks," Nicola said, grasping his hand with her warm, soft fingers. Finley's stomach did a somersault. She smelled like daisies and pressed powder and spring rain, and when she grinned at him in triumph as she made it safely down the embankment, Finley wanted to die a little.

He was just showing a guest around the property, he reminded himself. He was doing Eileen a good turn by helping to entertain Nicola, therefore giving her some time to talk to Adam alone. There was nothing untoward about what was going on here.

He might almost believe it, if he repeated it enough.

They slowed as they came across a small cottage in the woods, hewn from the same gray stone as Craigmar and decorated with the same white trim. Smoo and Smug lazed around in the fenced front garden, flanked by sprays of bright yellow daffodils. Finley stole a glance at Nicola to gauge her reaction. His home was modest, and it wasn't exactly modern, but he kept it tidy, and he was proud to have it as his own.

Nicola stopped ten feet from the house, rooted to the spot with wide eyes. Finley wanted to kick himself. She had liked the lamb, so he thought she would like the hounds. But Adam had told him just yesterday that Nicola was afraid of dogs. Why had he even decided to show her where he lived, like that was something that might interest her? *Stupid, Finley.*

"You really are afraid of them, aren't you?" he asked. "I'm sorry, I wasn't thinking."

Smoo yawned, exposing his teeth, which were probably as long as Nicola's pinky finger.

"I was bit by a neighbor's dog when I was five," she said, tearing her eyes away from the dogs just long enough to glance at Finley. "I never really got over it."

"I was going to bring them out walking with us, but I can leave them here instead," Finley said. One of the dogs let out a whine, as if he was aware he was going to be left behind.

"Hush, Snug," Finley chided. "That's Snug there, with the one blind eye. The other one is Smoo."

"Funny names for such big dogs."

"Big babies, maybe. I raised them both on table scraps. They're my best friends."

"They must be very well trained, if you've had them so long."

"They're well-behaved when they want to be," Finley said.

"Is this where you live?" Nicola asked, taking in the house now that she had moved past the shock of the dogs.

Finley just nodded, unsure of what else to say. Would it be too much to invite her inside? He wasn't sure he wanted her seeing all his paperbacks and history books overflowing from the bookshelf and stacked on the floor, or the secondhand armchair he had dragged here from the charity shop, or the stereo he had inherited from his father set up in place of a television. It might expose too much of him, tender parts he didn't want anyone else to see.

"I like it," she said, taking a few more wary steps forward. "It looks like it's been well taken care of."

Complimenting the care he had taken with power washing the stone and repainting the trim and weeding the front garden was probably the sweetest thing she could have said to him, but Nicola didn't know that. Finley did his best to tamp down the way his heart swelled. She was just making pleasant conversation with a stranger, Finley reminded himself.

This is about Eileen. You're only doing this as a favor to her.

"You know," Nicola said, voice high and thin, "my therapist says I should take more risks. Maybe I could say hello to uh, Snug. And Smoo."

Finley shot her a grin, incorrigible as a schoolboy.

"Yeah?"

"Yeah," Nicola said, taking two more tiny steps forward. She was almost at the gate now, which was still securely closed against the dogs inside the garden. The wooden posts were high enough to prevent all but the most determined dog from hopping over the fence, as Finley had learned through trial and error. Unless Smoo went chasing after a squirrel the dogs stayed behind the fence.

Finley let himself inside the garden and shut the gate securely behind him. Then he took a dog collar in each hand and held the beasts close at his side, talking in a low, firm voice.

"Hush now. Behave yourself in front of the lady, boys. You know how to say hello, don't you?"

Nicola approached the fence very, very slowly, as though something might explode if she moved too quickly. Then she curled her fingers around the gate and peered at Snug, who tilted his head at her and grinned. His tail thumped against Finley's leg in a friendly wag.

"How did he lose his eye?" she asked.

"Oh, he was born blind. We've all got our quirks, don't we?"

With a slight tremor in her fingers, Nicola reached her hand over the fence and let it hover a few inches away from Snug's snout. He snuffled at her palm curiously, but then he lapped at her fingers, as tender as could be.

Nicola let out a relieved, if nervous, laugh.

"Good boy, Snug," Finley cooed. "Very nice and proper."

Nicola was brave enough to let Snug lick her fingertips for a few more seconds before she withdrew her hand behind the safety of the fence.

"Very good," Finley said, and this time it was directed at Nicola.

It was a trained instinct, to follow up adrenaline with praise, and it slipped out before he could catch himself. Finley heard the command in it, the tone like he owned her, like she was his to teach and reward, and that made him want to shut himself inside the house in embarrassment until she left. He absolutely should not be bossing around a guest, especially not when it made her blush as red as a strawberry.

"Want me to leave them here while we explore?" he said, bright and quick like a normal, sane, human person.

"Yes please," Nicola said. "But thank you for introducing me to them. And for showing me your home."

Finley patted Snug's head, gave Smoo a scratch behind the ears, then slipped out through the gate and back onto Nicola's side of the fence.

"It's a house, for sure," he said. "But Craigmar is my home. The woods, the beach, all of it."

"You must know every inch of it, then."

"I do. Better than the back of my hand." He noted the position of the sun in the sky. They had been out here a while, and there was still the walk back to the house to contend with. They should really get going soon, before Eileen or Adam started asking any questions. But time moved so fluidly out here, in the birch forest with Nicola smiling up at him, and Finley wanted to steal just a few moments more with her, if only for his own selfish pleasure. "Can I show you one more thing?"

"I'd love that," she said, beaming bright.

It would be all too easy to lose his footing and fall right into the warmth of that smile, losing himself in her brightness.

Finley could already feel himself slipping.

Finley led Nicola up a rocky incline at the very furthest end of the lawn, climbing up and up until they reached his favorite outcropping, the one that jutted straight out over the sea. Below, ocean waves crashed against shining black stones, an endless churn of foam and water. Salt mist sprayed onto their faces. Nicola's cheeks were bright pink with exertion and joy by the time they reached the top, and her hair was somehow even curlier than before from the damp air.

Outsiders never lasted long at Craigmar. The atmosphere was hostile to them, and they withered like foreign plants thrust deep into rocky Highland soil. But somehow, the further Nicola walked out into the wild with him, the more she bloomed.

"God," she breathed, eyes eating up the horizon, "you can see for ever."

"It's where I like to come to think," he said. "There's no one out here to bother you. It's just you and the sky and the ocean, alone together."

"And what do you think about out here?" Nicola asked, half-teasing.

Finley's heart snapped shut like a clamshell. He had said too much already. He needed to be more careful.

"Bit of everything," he replied, carefully nonchalant as he refused to meet her eyes. There was too much at stake for him to run his mouth and ruin everything. He had his orders, and he knew his role. It was safest to stick to the script.

But then again, this hadn't been exactly what he and Eileen had discussed, and Finley certainly hadn't been counting on Nicola, on a total innocent with stars in her eyes.

Well, Finley thought as he caught Nicola giving him a hungry sidelong glance, *maybe not a total innocent.*

But she didn't sign up to be an actor in Eileen's passion play.

"I appreciate you bringing me out here and showing me all these beautiful things," she said, edging closer to him so their shoulders were nearly touching. Finley hunched forward, his hands thrust deep in his pockets, and tried not to notice how near she was. "Especially since Adam and I just invited ourselves over. That's not exactly polite."

A slender needle of guilt slipped between the armor-plating around Finley's heart. It pierced the flesh beneath, drawing blood.

"Don't apologize," he said. "Sometimes the best things in life are unexpected."

He expected it to come out breezy, friendly, proverbial, but his damned earnest nature betrayed him. He heard the way he said it: too honest, too rough.

Finley turned to look at Nicola, and they were suddenly close, so very close.

"That's sweet," she said softly, eyes falling to his mouth. Finley's heart constricted in his chest as heat curled low in his belly. She *had* been flirting with him, then, and she wanted him to kiss her just as badly as he wanted to kiss her. The air was charged and dangerous, fraught with delicious potential. It would feel so good to steal one kiss from this beautiful bright girl, one thing for himself, right here on this cliffside that he loved more than anywhere else in the world.

But he had been alive long enough to know that gambling security for the sake of pleasure always ended in disaster, and he would not be the reason everything fell apart now.

"We should probably get back to the house," he said.

Disappointment glimmered in her eyes, and Finley dropped his gaze as he stepped away so he wouldn't have to see how hopeful she had been. But as he turned, Nicola pushed up on her tiptoes and pressed her lips to Finley's cheek, brazen even in how chaste it was. Her lips were petal-soft and warm, scented with vanilla balm.

Finley stared at her and Nicola stared right back, a slightly exhilarated, slightly spooked look in her eye. Something about that look broke down whatever civilized dam was holding back the all-consuming floodwaters of Finley's desire.

He dropped his head and kissed Nicola.

It was brief, barely more than a peck, but Nicola responded as though he had touched her underneath her jeans. She let out a little sound of pleasure and arched her back up towards him, pressing her full breasts against Finley's chest.

"You don't want me," Finley said, more a statement of fact than an opinion or apology. Finley was a dead-end road for any woman or man foolish enough to walk down it, and he knew that.

"How do you know what I want?" Nicola asked. "Maybe all I want right now is for you to kiss me again."

It was impossible to say who closed the gap first. One moment they were separated, and the next moment Finley was kissing Nicola with ravenous hunger, and Nicola was digging her nails into his shoulders beneath the fabric of his jumper. She made the sweetest sounds, openly wanton, and it only made Finley want to kiss her harder, touch her more. He threaded his fingers through her short hair, grasping lightly.

He usually restrained himself during his dalliances with village girls, reminding himself to be gentle, to go slow. Only Eileen knew and welcomed that dark part of him that craved the intensity of exchanging pain along with pleasure, but something about Nicola made it hard to pretend.

He tightened his grip just enough to hold her in place for his kiss, right on the precipice of pain, hoping she wouldn't notice.

Nicola's breath caught in her throat, and she let out a shuddering gasp as she broke away.

Finley released her as though she was a hot stove.

"I'm sorry," he said, pulse pounding. God, he couldn't even kiss someone without ruining everything. "I didn't mean to—"

Nicola wasn't even looking at him, and she hadn't let him go. She was clutching his arms, staring wide-eyed at something over his shoulder.

Finley swiveled to follow her gaze. He almost missed it, but a life lived tending Craigmar land made him well acquainted with anything out of the ordinary. A pale figure watched them from the edge of the woods, impossibly tall and angular. It stepped behind a tree before Finley could make out any distinguishable features, but he knew well enough what it was.

If he wasn't sure before, the way it never emerged from the other side of the tree, merely winked out of existence, was all the confirmation he needed.

"Did you see that?" Nicola said, voice tight. "There was a . . . a person, or something. In the woods. Right there. I saw it, and then it was just gone. I saw it, Finley."

There was no way for Finley to deny what she had seen with her own two eyes, not when she was gripping him like he was the driftwood that was saving her from drowning. But he had no answers to give her, at least no answers that wouldn't bring everything he and Eileen had worked to protect crashing down.

Finley should let Nicola go. He should apologize for touching her, for bringing her out here in the first place. But even though his brain knew that's what he *should* do, what he did do was smooth a soothing hand over her head and then wrap his arm around her shoulders, giving her a squeeze.

Nicola's panicked breathing began to slow beneath his steady touch, the muscles in her back softening like she had already been taught to seek solace in him, and that somehow made everything worse.

Standing arrangement with Eileen or no, he absolutely

should not be taking liberties with the guests, and calculated distraction or not, he probably shouldn't have taken Nicola this far from the house. He certainly shouldn't have kissed her.

And Eileen *was* going to know, the moment she saw his face. You didn't grow up with someone, share every fumbling first with them, and have them not be able to read you like a book.

Finley reached down and squeezed Nicola's hand, almost in apology.

"We should get back to the house," he said.

CHAPTER EIGHT

Eileen

Skinny though he was, the American boy managed to put away a bowl of porridge with sultanas and slivered almonds, thick-cut country bacon, local sausages and toast, along with a double pour of gin on ice. Eileen, as usual, had woken up with a headache and no appetite, so she sipped smoky peat whisky and nibbled on a biscuit, watching Adam like a hawk. He had exceptionally fair coloring, with white-blond eyebrows, cornsilk hair and a smattering of freckles across his cheeks. Eileen's tastes tended towards dark and handsome, or brunette and pretty, but Adam was more than comely enough.

"Will you tell me about him?" Eileen asked, running her thumbnail along the rim of her glass.

"Who?" Adam asked.

"Your grandfather. You said it was his stories that brought you out here. What was he like?"

"Grumpy," Adam said, a smile touching his lips. "To everyone except me. If I was well behaved he would take me to the comic book store, and sometimes, when I sat still enough to listen, he would tell me stories."

"You're the only grandchild?" she asked, careful to frame it as a question. It was essential he believed she knew nothing.

"That's right," Adam said. "It's part of the reason we were so close. His health wasn't the best there at the end, and he needed help getting around, so I would drive him to doctors' appointments and stuff."

"That's very kind," Eileen said, only half listening. She was sizing Adam up from all angles, trying to imagine him in every room of Craigmar, standing in front of every portrait, sprawled under sweat-damp sheets in every bed. She was doing her best to paint a meant-to-be picture in her head, to grasp for anything that might tie them together faster, more securely.

He was different than she'd imagined. But people always were.

"I've told you something about me," Adam said, gesturing to himself with his fork. Then, he turned the utensil around and pointed it at Eileen. "Now it's your turn to tell me something about you. That's just fair play, isn't it?"

Eileen could have purred, she was so delighted by this turn. She loved nothing more than someone rising to one of her games, but it wasn't quite time yet to show her whole hand. She had to build the suspense first with a few bluffs.

"You don't want to hear what I have to tell you though! You seem like quite the rationalist to me.There's no room for fairy tales in that very big brain, I'm sure."

She was teasing at the truth with him, sooner than she ought. But it had been so long since she had any visitors besides the doctor and her accountant, and it was so tempting to share more than she should, if only to keep Adam – interesting, impossible Adam – in her house and under her watchful eye a little bit longer.

"Try me," he said, curiosity bright in his unwavering eyes. He was one of those seeker types who gnawed at information like a dog with a bone, determined to devour every morsel of truth. Even if Adam had to crack Eileen open with his teeth and lick out her marrow to get at what she knew, he would do it.

Eileen squeezed her thighs together, shifting to alleviate the pulse pounding between her legs. She liked being looked at like that, like she was a puzzle box to be solved, even if she had to be broken open to get at the secrets inside. The breaking was often her favorite part.

"You came out here looking for something more than a little family history, didn't you?" she asked. Maybe it was too wide a swing too early in this game, but she had to try. Eileen grasped her hands together to keep them from shaking with excitement. She never got to share this with anyone, under any circumstances, for any reason. Finley himself only knew because he was as much a part of this story as she was. But Adam was the reason she had been waiting for. Adam was the key. "All those stories your grandfather told you about Craigmar, they weren't just about the house or the grounds. They were about something ancient under the earth, something alive."

Adam made an expression of disbelief, but his body language betrayed him. He was leaning far forward, elbows propped onto knees, as close to Eileen as he could get without actually touching her.

"I've come a really long way to have someone pull my leg. And, not to insult your hospitality, this is a very strange conversation to strike up with someone you've just met."

"I know we've just met," she said, and her mask fell from her face for a moment, long enough for one sentence to slip out. "But I feel like I've known you a very long time, and I suspect you feel the same."

Adam stared at her, lips parted in invitation, eyes glittering in that almost affronted way men had when you startled them.

"And what if I said you were right?" he asked.

Eileen never got to answer him, because a movement over his shoulder through the cathedral window caught her attention.

"Looks like we have guests," she said.

Adam craned his neck to look. Two figures were striding

across the green towards Craigmar, one in bright green wellington boots, the other in a puffy pink jacket.

"Nikki," Adam muttered, with the affection and irritation of someone inconsolably in love.

It was almost enough to make Eileen feel guilty for what she intended to do to him.

Adam fell into awkward silence as a distant door opened, and as Finley and Nicola found them in the library.

"Our intrepid explorers have decided to join us," Eileen said, arching an eyebrow. She had asked Finley to keep Nicola entertained for an hour or two while Eileen got a better read on Adam, but they had been gone an awfully long time, and Finley looked as guilty as a hunting dog that had killed its master's pet rabbit.

"Finley was giving me a tour of the grounds," Nicola said. She was wind tossed and rumpled, blushing to the tips of her ears. It was apparent she and Finley had been doing a lot more than touring the grounds. You didn't have to have Eileen's keenly trained ability to sniff out desire on anyone to see that something had happened between them.

"Ah," Eileen said, drawing out the syllable until she saw Finley wince. No matter how old they got, and no matter how they promised to be better to each other, there was always a brutal pleasure in twisting the knife. Eileen toasted Finley with her whisky. "Getting to know each other better, were we?"

It wasn't that she held Finley's roaming against him, exactly. From an evolutionary behavioral perspective it was good for him to work off excess energy with other people, and he always came back doubly as desperate for her, practically begging to be allowed to bruise her, to kiss her, to even be granted the honor of unbuckling her shoes. Eileen would wander herself, if there was any point to it, or if her ancestral anxiety would allow her to leave Craigmar for more than a few hours at a time. But as it stood, she was generally impatient with anyone who wasn't as finely tuned to her needs as Finley was, as well-trained in all the ways to torment and tease her.

Still, the door she kept cracked in their relationship for Finley to slip out into the night and return in the early morning smelling like sticky-sweet perfume or other men's cologne was a concession and a compromise. If they lived in gentler times, if they were able to be together fully in the way other people were in the unflinching light of day, maybe she would hoard him all to herself.

Or maybe not.

"I was looking for you," Adam said to Nicola. "You look like you had an adventure."

"Just a little one," Nicola said, shooting a glance to Finley. Finley was staring very studiously at the patterns on the floor, but Adam caught that glance.

Finley, God bless him, tried to salvage it.

"Will that be all, sir?" he asked, probably desperate to storm back to his cottage and chop wood or scowl into a book or jack off or do whatever else it was Finley did to calm himself down.

"Oh, jig's up, Finney," she said, using his childhood nickname just to add a little salt to the salve for his wound. "No need to pretend on my account any more."

"You told him?" Finley demanded, thrusting a hand out to Adam as though Adam was the one who had transgressed boundaries out there on the grounds, not Finley.

"He figured it out himself," Eileen replied. Finley would be humiliated if he knew Adam had seen him whipping Eileen the night before and, more importantly, that was information she might want to leverage strategically at a later date. Besides, if he was worried about people watching he might hold back with her, and that wouldn't do at all. "Very bright, this one."

"Figured what out?" Nicola asked, looking between Finley and Eileen and then, very pointedly, to Adam.

"Listen," Adam began, spreading his hands in a helpless gesture, "none of this is any of my business—"

"Eileen and I are romantically involved with each other," Finley said in an admirable display of nerve. "We have been for years."

"Oh," Nicola said, giving Finley a wounded look, her rosebud lips pursed. To her credit, she didn't look sad, only insulted. Eileen always thought women were at their most beautiful when in the throes of orgasm or righteous indignation, and Nicola wore rage very well. "You didn't mention that."

"Sorry," Finley said, miserable as a raincloud. Eileen wanted to press on that discomfort like a tongue worrying at a sore tooth, just to see if he would squirm, but she resisted. There would be time for that later, when they were alone.

"Nicola, duckie, why don't you come over here and sit next to me?" Eileen asked, patting the sofa cushion next to her. Nicola made no move to sit. "There's no need for silly secrets any more. We're all among friends here."

"That's a bit of a stretch," Adam muttered. Eileen could feel him withdrawing the tentative trust he had extended like a vine recoiling from the scorching sun. She would have to try harder to win him over.

"There's no reason we shouldn't all get along," Eileen insisted, polishing off her whisky. The next drink she poured was water, so Finley wouldn't nag her.

"There's also no reason Nicola and I should believe you," Adam said, standing and dusting the crumbs from his jeans. He looked resolute in his leaving, which made panic spike in Eileen's chest. He couldn't go, not now. If she had to tie him to the stair banister to make him stay, she would do it. "We appreciate your willingness to help. But, at the risk of sounding rude, this whole thing is starting to feel a little strange. It's obvious that you two have something going on that we've intruded on, so I think it's best if me and Nicola head off."

"But if you go now you'll never find out what your

grandfather knew," Eileen said, on her feet before she realized she had stood.

Adam didn't reply. He just crossed to Nicola and talked to her in a quick, low voice, as if making a plan or asking if she was all right. She chattered back at a level Eileen couldn't hear, looking nervously to Finley and then Eileen.

Eileen threw a desperate glance Finley's way, as though to say, *Do something*.

"Nicola saw something," Finley blurted, and though it came out rushed, Eileen could tell it wasn't a lie. "Out in the woods."

"What do you mean?" Adam asked, giving the other man a dismissive once-over. "Nikki, what's he talking about?"

"I don't really know," Nicola said, a startled gleam in her eye. "It was there and then it was gone."

Now, she had Eileen's full attention. Eileen took a step towards Nicola and Adam stepped in front of his "friend", instinctively shielding her with his body.

A questing white knight, indeed.

"Can you try to describe it?" Eileen asked.

"We were out by the ocean," Nicola said. "I saw a person in the trees, or . . . Something shaped like a person. I couldn't quite make out the face. But it was there, and it was watching us. I could *feel* it watching me just as much as I could see it watching me. And then it turned and it just disappeared. And I mean really disappeared; I didn't even blink."

Nicola's voice shook slightly, either with fear or with elation, or some heady mix of both. Eileen reminded herself to breathe, to not pummel the Americans with too much strangeness at once. But this was a boon; she couldn't have devised anything better than Nicola seeing something out there with her own eyes.

"I saw it too," Finley offered. "Just for a moment. But I'm sure."

"Nikki, come on," Adam said. "You aren't serious about this, are you? What did he tell you when you were alone together? Did he convince you that you saw something?"

"Finley didn't do anything," Nicola replied, bristling. "I saw something weird out there. I'm telling the truth."

Eileen watched a flicker of uncertainty cross Adam's face. It was only a moment of weakness, the tiniest chink in his armor, but she rushed in to exploit it.

"I'm not asking you to take me at my word," she said. "I can show you something real. Something that will make you understand that Nicola isn't lying to you, and neither am I. Not about this place, and not about your grandfather's stories."

Adam gave her a wary look, stock-still where he stood. He refused to speak, just weighing her with his gaze.

"Come with me, and I'll tell you everything," Eileen lied.

"And why would you do that?" Adam asked.

"Why do men hunt grouse? My reasons are my own. And maybe I'm only trying to help you, Adam Lancaster."

"You're serious about this?" Adam asked Nicola. This wasn't about Eileen any more, she saw that clearly. Whatever happened next, Adam would only do with Nicola's blessing, and for Nicola's sake.

"As a heart attack," Nicola said. "I've never seen anything like that before. It almost felt like . . ."

"Magic," Finley supplied, with that succinct no-nonsense air that made arguing with him impossible. His timing couldn't have been better. Eileen could have kissed him.

Adam looked at Eileen for another long moment, and Eileen wondered if she had misjudged him. He wasn't receptive and he wasn't ready: this would be the final straw for him and he would undoubtedly be on the next flight home, leaving Eileen to her loneliness and her ruin.

But, miraculously, Adam surprised her.

"If I follow you, where are we going?"

"To the cave," Eileen breathed, for once in her life not lying, not even obfuscating the truth. "That's where it all starts, and that's where it all ends."

Adam glanced at Nicola, who was lit up brighter than a Roman candle at the promise of some sort of supernatural experience, or maybe even just a good story. She had mentioned last night that she enjoyed folklore, and now Eileen saw that it wasn't just a pastime, it was a passion.

In the end, Adam conceded, perhaps more for Nicola than for himself.

"Wherever we're going," he said, "I want to be back here loading up the car in an hour."

"Done," Eileen said, euphoric with triumph.

"Wait here for me, will you?" Adam asked. "I need my coat and shoes."

"I'll come with you," Nicola said, and scurried up the stairs behind him, no doubt ready to spill all her theories about what she had seen out there on the grounds, or perhaps her theories about Eileen and Finley. Eileen didn't really care which. As long as it kept Adam curious enough to stay just a little while longer, she was happy.

In the Americans' absence, Finley stepped right up to Eileen, grasped her chin in his hand, and tilted her face up. He held her tightly, not enough to hurt, but enough to ground her in the seriousness of the moment.

"Are you sure about this, Isla?" Finley asked.

He had asked her this countless times before. Her answer was always the same.

"Absolutely."

"There's still time to call it off and send them home. There's got to be some other way to fix this that doesn't involve taking advantage of innocent people."

Eileen snorted, tossing her head like an unruly mare. Finley held her tighter, forcing her to look at him. Now it did hurt, that clarifying sort of hurt that helped her think clearly. He wouldn't leave a mark; he knew the precise amount of pressure it took to bruise her skin.

"No one is innocent, Finney," she said. "Not even doe-eyed tourists. And don't act like you didn't play your part in this. I've got to give it to you: leading them here from the pub was quite the feat."

"I didn't know them then. I was only doing what you asked."

"And you don't know them now. They're as foreign to us as we are to them, and I'll caution you not to trust anything either of them says. All human beings serve their own ends, when it comes right down to it."

"There's got to be a different way to handle this. We can go back to the drawing board, we can do more research—"

Eileen turned her face abruptly and bit into Finley's palm, just hard enough to startle him. Finley swore and shook out his hand, but he didn't move away.

"There's no other way, and you know it," Eileen said, lowering her voice as the sound of footsteps echoed above them. "This is the way forward, Finley, for you and for me. And once it's all done with, we'll finally be safe, and so will Craigmar. Please. I want this to be over. Just let me do what I have to do."

Finley gently massaged her jaw, rubbing away the indentations of his fingers. It always took her breath away, how he could be so restrained in his brutality and so lavish in his tenderness.

"I trust you, Isla. Unto death, I do. But we're playing a dangerous game here. Please remember that."

"I will," she said, pressing a kiss over the spot she had

bitten. A wicked smile tugged at her lips. "Are you going to tell me what happened with that little redhead? Did she taste so sweet? I'll bet she let you feel her up, too. Did it get you hard?"

"I'm not doing this with you right now, they're upstairs—"

Eileen unceremoniously cupped him through his jeans.

"Mmm, you're half hard now. Is that me or is that her?"

Finley gave her an unimpressed look.

"It was a heat-of-the-moment kiss, that's all. She doesn't matter, and it didn't mean anything."

"Then why are you suddenly so protective of her?" Eileen said, squeezing a bit harder. "I think we're a little old to be lying to each other."

"Fine," Finley bit out. He was doing a very good job of pretending like she had no effect on him, but his cock told the truth. "I want her. Is that a sin?"

"I've told you before, there are no sins in Craigmar. If you want her, and she'll have you, I won't hold it against either of you. So long as you'll do me the same courtesy."

These were the terms and conditions of their relationship. They always returned to each other, binary stars circling each other with the undeniable pull of gravity, but they could take their pleasure elsewhere, if they chose.

"And you want Adam, then?" Finley went on, shifting ever so slightly against her hand to seek more friction. "Is that the bargain we're making here?"

"I'll do whatever I have to do to keep him at Craigmar.

But don't worry, I'm not opposed to sharing. There's plenty for both of us; he's certainly tall enough."

"You're absolutely insane," Finley said, but it sounded more like, *I love you*.

Eileen snatched her hand back as the footfalls grew closer, and she was left as flushed as Finley was left erect. He made an irritated noise and adjusted his shirt tail to protect his decency.

"All ready," Adam said, appearing in the doorway in a rain jacket and hiking boots. Nicola was close behind, bundled up and bright-eyed. "Now what's this about a cave?"

CHAPTER NINE

Adam

Adam was not convinced he wasn't being led out to the woods to murdered, but he was certain that if he walked away now, without any answers, he would regret it for the rest of his life. Nicola had told him so, upstairs when he was pulling on his shoes, and she had also told him that if he didn't come with her, she was going out there with Finley and Eileen all by herself. Adam thought this was colossally foolish, but whatever Nicola had seen outside had electrified her so much that she wouldn't be dissuaded.

Adam figured they stood a better chance against death as a team, so he had surrendered to the strange pull of Craigmar and traipsed out with the others into the wilderness.

This must be a dream, Adam thought, hugging the

basket of bread closer to his chest as they hiked up a hill. *I'm going to wake up in my bed in Michigan with a splitting hangover any second.*

Eileen was leading the way and Finley was keeping pace just behind, his hands thrust into the pockets of his oilcloth coat as he took big strides up the hill. They had left the green ten minutes ago, following a circuitous path through the woods led only by Eileen's intuitive knowledge of the land and Finley's occasional corrections with a compass.

As they moved further and further away from the house, Adam considered yanking Nicola in tight and making a mad dash for the car, but he didn't like the idea of testing Finley's loyalty to Eileen. The groundskeeper might have a change of heart and let them run, or he might wrestle Adam to the ground and then drag him all the way to the cave, ultimately in thrall to whatever dark sway Eileen held over him.

He didn't know his hosts at all, Adam realized with a sickly churn of dread in his stomach. He might have been dazzled by Eileen's storytelling and the firelight in her dark eyes last night, and he might have been immensely grateful for Finley's help with the directions and the rooms and the bags, but he didn't really *know* them. Not what they wanted, not who they were, and certainly not what they were capable of.

As if sensing his distress, Nicola reached out and gave his hand a squeeze. She had been tasked with carrying a jug of farm-fresh sheep's milk, which she cradled to her chest as though it were a baby.

"Are we close?" she called up to Eileen, who was taking the hill in determined strides.

"Just up ahead!" Eileen called back. She sounded awfully winded, and Adam almost worried about her health before reminding himself that she could be bringing him out here to sacrifice him to the old gods or something. He should look out for his own well-being first, not to mention Nicola's.

It wasn't very long before Adam felt swallowed up by the woods, devoured by oak and ash and the tangle of wildflowers and thorns underfoot.

Eileen hadn't explained the milk and bread, and Adam got the feeling that she wasn't the type of person who did much explaining at all. But she had said, very sternly as they slipped out the kitchen door, "Drop that bread in the dirt and even I won't be able to help you."

Just about the time that Adam was starting to panic about never being able to find his way back to the house or the rental car again, they summited the final hill, and the view at the top punched the air out of him. A crevasse split open the gray stone of an exposed rock face, so old that trees had grown around it, their roots grasping for fertile soil. The opening was three times Adam's height, but narrow and dark, slick with condensation and lichen. He had done plenty of amateur spelunking on outdoorsy pleasure trips, but this cave didn't feel like any of the ones Adam had explored before. It didn't feel like an invitation to adventure.

It felt like a rip in the fabric of reality, a place where the skin of the mundane world had been flayed back to reveal the wild impossibility beneath.

"What is this place?" he asked, unable to tear his eyes away from the cave. Out here, the air smelled like ozone and mineral-rich water and the intangible possibility of what he could only call magic, even though he didn't believe in that sort of thing and hadn't in a long time, certainly not since his grandfather died. He could hear the crash of ocean waves in the distance, but that was the only sound in the air. There was no skittering of woodland animals, no birdsong, not even the rustle of wind in the trees. It was utterly still, as if all of Craigmar was holding its breath, waiting to see what he would do.

"It's the reason my family built their house here," Eileen said, pressing a hand to her chest as she struggled to catch her breath. Finley rubbed a soothing hand between her shoulder blades, concern creasing his brow. "It was here before the estate, or the town. Before my family settled in these hills at all."

"What do we do now?" Nicola asked, her voice barely above a whisper despite the fact that there was no one out there to eavesdrop on them. She must have felt it too, how strange this place felt, how . . . charged.

Adam had never been superstitious, but something about being here made him understand why people threw spilled salt over their shoulder or crossed themselves to ward off evil.

"Now we make our offerings," Eileen said. "Would you splash a little milk near the mouth of the cave, songbird? Not too close now."

"It's a libation, isn't it?" Nicola asked. This sharp observation took Eileen off guard, and the girls shared a fizzling look of recognition. Adam had never been more grateful for all that Joseph Campbell and Richard Hutton she had read, even though he couldn't make heads nor tails of it. "For the spirits of the land? Or the spirit of the cave?"

"Something like that," Eileen said.

Nicola moved to pour some milk at the mouth of the cave, but she paused at the last moment and began to shimmy out of her sweater. Before Adam could ask what the hell she was doing, she had stripped down to her tank top, flipped her sweater inside out, and pulled it back on again.

"You're a clever one, aren't you?" Eileen asked, looking at Nicola with an expression somewhere between pride and hunger, like she was so pleased with her that she wanted to eat her.

"What was that for?" Adam asked.

"For protection," Nicola said, as though it were obvious. Adam racked his brain for what she was referring to, and something about wearing clothes inside out for protection stirred a spotty memory. Wasn't it supposed to keep away evil? No, not quite evil, something more specific.

Nicola smoothly raised the jug up high and poured a

smooth, white stream of milk onto the earth. Despite the spring rains, the ground swallowed the milk up as though thirsty from drought.

Nicola's face was reverent, utterly focused on this single task. She looked mythic, like she could have been a priestess in Greek robes or a Druid wreathed in leaves, not a lit major in a T.J. Maxx sweater.

"Very good," Eileen said, leaning heavily against a nearby boulder. "The bread now, Adam."

"Tell me why we're doing this again?" Adam said. His hands moved of their own accord, unwrapping the fragrant sourdough loaf from the dishtowel it had been wrapped in.

"It's a ritual," Eileen said with a sigh, as though he were being deliberately obtuse. "Kirkfoyles have carried it out for centuries. What you're making is an offering, to the spirits who rule the land."

Adam didn't even believe in Jesus or astrology, so he certainly didn't believe in land spirits, but that didn't mean that something inside him didn't stir at that word: *offering*.

It thrilled a deeply buried part of him, to think that there were invisible powers out there in the world who might be worthy of things like offerings or rituals or sacrifices, all those things he had read about in books.

This was one of his secrets: It wasn't that Adam refused to believe in anything bigger than himself; it was that he had yet to be impressed enough by anything to find it worthy of his deference.

Now, he wasn't so sure.

"What happens then?" Adam pressed.

"You'll see," Eileen said.

Adam looked at Nicola, her frizzed curls lit up like a saint's halo in the sunlight shining through the trees, and he marveled at the open wonder on her face. She was taking all this in her stride, thrilled to be brought into such a charming folk custom, but he noticed that her hands were shaking. She was frightened too.

Adam had to be brave. For Nicola, if not for himself.

He crouched down in the moss and laid out the bread near the mouth of the cave. As he bent, he smelled not only the rotted tang of decaying leaves and the richness of the soil, but sweetness. Not cream or flour, more like crushed red berries that had been left to ferment into something syrupy and boozy. His mouth watered even as his stomach tightened, instinctive as a bird avoiding a brightly colored beetle whose coloring telegraphed the presence of poison.

The world spun slightly, and when Adam stood, he found that he was dizzy.

"What now?" he asked. "Do we just leave it?"

"We have to tell them we're here first," Finley said. He was wringing his hands like he was trying to rid them of some stain.

Eileen reached into her coat pocket and produced a woven thread strung with tiny golden bells. It looked simple, cheap even, like something Adam might buy in a head shop along with TCH gummies and nag champa incense, but Eileen held them with reverence.

Eileen wound the bells through a nearby tree branch and they tinkled merrily, discordant in the grave atmosphere.

"Now we wait," she said.

"Eileen—" Adam began.

"Quietly," she said primly.

Adam fell silent.

They waited. For five minutes or fifteen, in complete and total stillness, until Adam's feet began to hurt and the cold started seeping into his bones. Until Adam's patience was entirely worn through.

"All right, that's it," he said. "I'm going in there."

"You can't," Eileen snapped, with a vehemence that surprised him, like she was a mother preventing her toddler from rushing headlong into a busy street.

"I wouldn't do that if I were you," Finley said, which somehow felt more ominous.

"Why not?" Adam demanded. He had only been here a day, and he was already exhausted by this whole song and dance. It was obvious that Eileen and Finley were lying to him, or playing some kind of mind game with him, or both. The sky above him darkened in warning as the sun disappeared behind fast-moving clouds. "You're both starting to piss me off, and you won't explain anything. Why can't I—"

A sharp, wild wind kicked up out of the cave, gusting

cool mist and that scent of rotting sweetness into all of their faces.

Cherry tarts, Adam recalled. The almond flour kind he used to show up early to the campus coffee shop to buy, the kind evoked by that damn-near edible perfume every girl his freshman year was wearing. It smelled enticing, or more specifically, like enticement itself. But it also smelled a little bit like death, like the formaldehyde sweetness of a body in a morgue.

The bells on the trees chimed, softly at first, and then louder and louder, as though an invisible hand was shaking them violently. They no longer sounded cheery, but like a wailing call of distress. A squall of sea air joined the wind from the cave, kicking up around them as a new storm brewed overhead. Had there been any clouds in the sky moments ago?

"They know we're here now," Eileen said, with a look of terrified awe in her eyes. Either she was a very good actor or she was just as scared as the rest of them. Her dark hair fell out of its chignon and whipped around her face, and she had to almost shout to be heard over the wind. "Do you believe me now, Adam? Can't you feel it?"

What Adam felt was electricity, scintillating and hot, coursing through him like he was standing in the middle of a lightning storm. And he felt a bone-deep pull he couldn't explain, a need to plunder that cave of all its secrets. He wanted to be inside it, so badly it hurt, he wanted to be one with that emptiness and see what mysteries it held. More than he had wanted anything in his entire life, Adam wanted to *know*.

Adam closed the distance to the cave before anyone could stop him, pausing mere inches from the mouth of darkness.

"No!" Eileen cried, lurching forward. She would have tackled Adam to the ground if Finley, in an impressive show of strength, hadn't gripped her by the bicep and hauled her backwards. Nicola stood frozen, the jug of milk dropped to her feet, her hands clapped over her ears, and Adam knew that if he didn't seize the moment now, he would never have another opportunity.

Adam didn't really care what going into that cave would prove or disprove. He just wanted to find it out for himself either way.

He thrust his hand into the cave. That darkness was strangely cool, almost vicious. Like he had dipped his fingers into a cold lake and not into thin air.

He opened his mouth to declare that it was fine, that there was nothing to worry about, that he was going to have a look around and come right back.

Then, a long flat tongue lapped against Adam's palm, just as a hot, humid mouth closed around his wrist and bit down right through the skin.

Adam was so shocked he didn't even scream. It was Nicola who screamed, and Finley who hauled Adam back from the cave with his arms looped around the other man's middle. Adam gasped for air, staring stunned at the blood trickling from puncture wounds on his hand. The blood was what shocked him back into awareness, and adrenaline flooded his veins as he tried to break free from Finley's firefighter hold.

"Leave it," Finley said, as though he were ordering a dog to drop a bone. The sky overhead darkened rapidly as the bells rattled hard enough to crack. "Just leave it."

Eileen yanked the Kirkfoyle clan badge from her chest, tearing her sweater in the process, and held it out in front of her like a crucifix. She stood in the gap between Adam and the cave, teeth bared, voice ferocious.

"Not him!" she snarled. "Not this one, do you hear me? This one is mine! Not yours!"

Finley held a hand out for Nicola and she rushed to him, abandoning the jug where it lay. Then Finley began to haul Adam and Nicola back towards the house, away from the strange wind and the shrieking bells and that sickly-sweet smell that enveloped Adam's senses.

"No," he said, gritting his teeth through the pain in his throbbing hand. His mind must be fracturing, coming to pieces in the presence of something that simply was not possible. He didn't know what was real, he didn't even know up from down. He just knew he couldn't leave now, when something so scintillatingly impossible had just broken into reality with a bite that also felt like a kiss. "I want to see. I want to know what's in there! Don't make me go."

In the end, it wasn't a discussion. Eileen yanked and

Nicola pulled and Finley gave Adam a firm shove on the back, and the next thing Adam knew he was half-stumbling down the hillside. Eileen grabbed Finley's hand like her life depended on it, and Nicola clutched Adam's good wrist as they stumbled over stones and heather, two pairs of frightened mortal creatures fleeing an encounter with the supernatural.

Adam's lungs screamed for air as their jostling turned into a flat-out run once they reached the grazing green. The clouds rolled meanly above them, like they were chasing them down.

No matter how far away from the cave he got, Adam could still feel that ache in his bones, begging him to stay. And through the scent of turned earth and macerated grass, Adam could still smell cherry tarts and longing.

Overhead, the skies cracked open, dousing them with rain.

CHAPTER TEN

Nicola

Nicola was soaked by the time they got back to the house. Her teeth chattered as she ducked through the door, and she shed her sweater immediately. It hit the hardwood floor with a wet slap as Adam ducked in behind her.

Finley and Eileen lagged behind, moving agonizingly slow up the path as Eileen struggled to breathe. The lord was leaning heavily on her groundskeeper, and in the end, Finley had to carry her bridal-style the last fifty feet and over the threshold. Eileen protested loudly, trying her damnedest to twist out of his grasp.

"Put me down. I don't need to be toted around like a toddler."

Nicola locked the door behind them, breathing a little easier with solid wood between her and whatever was out there on the grounds. It wasn't that she had no sense of what she had just encountered. It was that she had a very good idea of what had just happened, and that scared her even more.

Fairy stories were fun when they were pressed between the pages of a book, just cultural memory and dead ink. They weren't supposed to come to life.

"You're embarrassing me," Eileen snapped, swatting at Finley. She looked dangerously pale in the warm lighting of Craigmar's chandeliers, with tendrils of hair sticking to her neck like the tentacles of an octopus. There wasn't a drop of color in her lips.

"You're embarrassing yourself," Finley grunted. "Now stop struggling or I'll sling you over my shoulder like a sack of potatoes."

"To hell with you," Eileen spat.

"You pushed yourself too hard. You need rest."

"I can do as I please in my own house, on my own land. Are you lord now or am I?"

"I'm the only one with common sense; you figure out the rest."

Adam and Nicola stood dripping mud onto the expensive rugs underfoot, sharing an awkward glance. Nicola's heart was still pounding. She would be hearing those tiny golden bells in her dreams for days to come.

Eileen and Finley bickered for a moment more before he put her down with a huff.

Adam shook the water from his hair like a dog and Finley looked every inch a bedraggled cat who had fallen into a tub. Eileen began to fastidiously pin back her hair and wipe the stray droplets from her face. It reminded Nicola of a war-rumpled lioness cleaning blood from her claws.

"Well," Eileen said, stomping down the hallway towards the kitchen, "I hope you're very happy with yourself, Adam. Now they've got a taste for you."

"What's that supposed to mean?" Adam demanded, all but tearing down the hallway after Eileen. Nicola followed close after while Finley trudged behind, sulky.

In the kitchen, Eileen swatted on the tap and filled up the gooseneck kettle. Once that was boiling, she tossed open a cupboard and retrieved a first-aid kit, which she then threw down on the small wooden table in the kitchen. The table was an ancient, banged-up thing, probably used more for preparing food than entertaining.

"Sit," Eileen ordered. "All of you. Adam, let's have a look at that hand."

"I'll do it," Nicola said as she took the seat nearest to Adam. She didn't think Eileen would hurt Adam, but she trusted herself with him more.

"Have it your way," Eileen said. "He doesn't want my help, anyway."

Nicola scrubbed her hands clean with goat milk soap in the large farmhouse sink, then gingerly took Adam's wounded hand. There was a semicircle of puncture wounds on the top of his hand, and a few to match on the palm underneath. They were real and undeniable, inflamed and red, still weeping water and blood.

They didn't look quite like animal bite marks, nor quite like the indentation of human teeth.

It was more like Adam had been bitten by a human mouth full of very sharp animal teeth, but Nicola tried not to dwell on that too much.

"It was the iron that kept them away, wasn't it?" Nicola asked as she ripped open an alcohol cloth and retrieved some bandages. She watched Eileen warily, trying to play this right. Perhaps Nicola had been too naive earlier, too swept up in the beauty and romance of a Scottish whirlwind vacation to notice all the warning signs. Eileen knew more than she was telling, and there was something dark just beneath the surface of this place, like rot beneath floorboards. And while it probably would have sounded crazy to most other people, Nicola was willing to make an educated guess about what kind of sickness might be in the bones of Craigmar. "That brooch you wear. And they didn't bother Finley because of his earrings."

"Clever," Eileen said, giving Nicola one of those hot, sharp glances that felt like a piercer's needle puncturing skin. "You've known from the start what you were dealing with."

"I thought you two believed in it," Nicola said, swabbing Adam's palm with alcohol no matter how he hissed. "But that's not the same as believing in it myself. Although now I'm not so sure."

"What are you all talking about?" Adam demanded.

"Faeries," Eileen said, like it was the simplest thing in the world. Nicola's heart fluttered at the word, the word she had been turning over in her overexcitable brain.

"Be serious, Eileen," Adam groaned.

"I'm being dead serious," Eileen replied. "You wanted to know Craigmar's secrets? We can start with this one: this place is lousy with faeries."

"I've been willing to put up with a lot from you," Adam said, and now he was angry, genuinely angry. He tried to clench his hand in Nicola's grasp but she pried it back open. The wound wept afresh. "This is too much. Don't insult my intelligence, please."

"Any other explanation you have, I'll be happy to hear it."

Adam fell silent at that, glowering down at his bleeding hand. Finley, who had looked like a dam ready to break from the moment he set foot in the house, finally crumbled.

"Tell him, Eileen. The whole of it. Or I will."

Even steadfast Finley, it appeared, had his limits. Eileen glared at him, mean enough to shame the sun for shining, and he stared right back, unbothered.

There was something very sexy about him when he looked at her like that, like she had no power over him whatsoever. It was so compelling that Nicola still noticed how beautiful it made him look, even through the haze of fear and the air of confusion in the room and the fact that she was waterlogged and cold.

"You mean little nude people with butterfly wings?" Adam cut in. "That's what you're asking me to believe grabbed me, a fully grown man, and bit me hard enough to draw blood?"

"That isn't what a faery is," Nicola said, tossing the dirty alcohol wipe aside as she carefully peeled open a band-aid. "That image in your head is a Victorian invention."

Now every eye in the room was on Nicola. Adam was looking at her like she was speaking Greek, Eileen was looking at her like she was Christmas Day come early, and Finley was looking at her with frightened awe. Nicola blushed, turning back to her work patching up Adam.

"Go on, sparrow," Eileen said, "you know the stories. Tell him."

"In the oldest stories the faeries are ancient, powerful beings, the size of humans," Nicola said carefully. She wasn't sure how her mental Rolodex of folklore could help right now, but if there was ever a situation that called for it, it was this one. "They have their own society and culture, and they play by their own rules. Humans are entertainment to them, or a nuisance. They enjoy playing tricks on us. But humans can keep themselves safe from faery interference through certain rituals, like turning clothes inside out or wearing iron jewelry."

"Very good," Eileen said. She took a deep breath, as though bracing herself. "Nicola knows part of this story, so I suppose I ought to tell you the rest, shouldn't I?"

Eileen plucked up the steaming kettle and poured four mugs of chamomile tea to steady their nerves. Then she sat down at the fourth seat at the round kitchen table, creating a perfect unbroken circle, and began her tale.

"Before this land belonged to the Kirkfoyles, before it belonged to any man, it belonged to the fae. Human expansion and industrialization drove them underground, into the secret chambers of the earth, but they didn't die. They're still out there, waiting for their chance to reclaim the land. They emerge occasionally, for reasons only they know. Nicola saw one when she was out hiking with Finley. Adam, you just met another one out at the cave. Sorry for the pageantry. I'll admit I like my dramatics, but I didn't know how else to get you to understand. I'm of the mind that magic is something you can only know in the biblical sense, through experience. No one can make you believe in it with words. You have to feel it pull at your bones."

Adam opened his mouth to protest, but something about that last sentence made words die on his lips. For a moment, at least. Then he blinked and shook his head.

"That's a bedtime story," he pushed back. "It has to be."

"Then what do you think took a bite out of you?" Eileen asked, eyes flashing. "What do you think drowned my parents, all those years ago?"

"Isla," Finley said gently. Eileen took another deep breath, then quieted. She was gripping her mug so tight her knuckles were white.

"The Kirkfoyles have lived on this land since the fifteenth century," she said, staring at the table. It sounded like every word pained her, like she wasn't used to saying any of this out loud. "We outlasted rebellions and invasions and transfers of power, and we managed to keep our holdings in the process mostly through canny marriage, and keeping to ourselves. But there was another foe out there in the hills, besides the English."

"The fae," Nicola supplied, urging Eileen on. Eileen's knee brushed hers under the table as she leaned a little closer, as though borrowing some of Nicola's nerve.

"A long time ago, before the Kirkfoyles were even a formalized clan, they lived in peace with the fae. They bartered with them and carried out the proper rituals to show respect, and intermarried from time to time. But with time something . . . soured. Both parties wanted more power, more land, and war broke out. The only thing that put a stop to the bloodshed was the treaty. The fae went underground, and my family ceded the realm beneath the hills to them. In return, the fae would let my family live aboveground unbothered."

"So what happened?" Adam asked. He was trying to sound cynical, but Nicola knew he was intrigued. She could feel it in the way his pulse pounded in his wrist.

She hadn't let go of him after carefully affixing his bandages. And he hadn't pulled away either.

"The fae would only honor the agreement if there was a living Kirkfoyle ruling from Craigmar. If my line dies out or moves away, the treaty is null and void, and the fae reclaim the land."

"They'll take over the house and the grounds?" Nicola asked, running the calculations in her head. If Eileen wasn't taking them for a ride, and if what she was saying was right, that was an awful lot of land.

"When the treaty was signed, the Kirkfoyles owned quite a bit of the countryside," Eileen said, biting the inside of her mouth. "If the treaty is broken, the fae have every right to overrun at least four neighboring villages and towns, not to mention the Craigmar estate. And the fae keep their bargains, but in letter alone, not in spirit. For generations, my line has been afflicted by unexplained illness, madness and death. Kirkfoyles have gone missing in their own backyards, and they've washed ashore on their own beaches dead. People have tried to leave, but they always end up back here, in the end. Even if it's only to come home to die."

"You're saying they've killed people?" Nicola asked, blood running cold. Eileen was sweating through what was left of her makeup as though unearthing family secrets better left buried.

"Our neighbors underground are capricious and territorial. I'd wager they're worse than your stories, Nicola.

I knew, growing up, that there might be one day where I woke up an orphan. I just thought, somehow, that I had more time."

"You mean to tell me faeries killed your parents?" Adam said, sounding brusque and boyish and so, so rude. Nicola stamped on his foot under the table, and he hissed. "*Ouch*, Nikki."

"My parents were both excellent mariners, and the sky was clear the day they went out sailing. Still the boat capsized," Eileen said, eyes flat. She sounded utterly exhausted. Like she had been trapped in this story for a hundred years. "Water is a portal, Adam, just like a cave. You learned that today, surely. At any rate, I'm the last of my line. The last Kirkfoyle that hasn't flung themselves off a cliff or died in childbirth or wasted away upstairs from old age. So please forgive me if I've been vague, or even misled you deliberately. But you see, no one knows about this place, absolutely no one. Kirkfoyles keep to ourselves, and we guard our secrets jealously. And then you show up one day saying that your grandfather was here, that he knew my grandmother, that he told you for years and years that Craigmar was magic? You see now why I couldn't let you leave. Not until you understood."

"And what am I supposed to understand?" Adam asked.

"That you're meant to be here. That you're meant to help me figure out how to save this place."

Eileen's chin dimpled, like she might cry, but then she sighed and her face smoothed out perfectly. Finley twisted the iron stud in his ear over and over, a nervous tic. And Nicola gripped Adam's hand and waited to see what Adam would do.

"I'm sorry," Adam said after a long while. "I just don't think I can believe that."

Eileen stood with a huff, too quickly for Nicola to stop her, and stormed out of the room. In the resulting awkward silence, Nicola became sure that they would never see their strange host again, certainly not until they took their leave.

But then, Eileen returned with a pewter box in her hands. It was battered, like a little girl's trinket box that had seen considerable wear and tear over the years.

"If you won't believe me, then please just trust me on one thing," she said.

She opened the box and produced a thick men's ring, flecked with the beaten marks of a blacksmith's hammer.

"You're giving me jewelry?" Adam asked as she pressed it into his palm.

"I'm giving you iron. It's the best protection I know. My family wears it to ward off our neighbors. That ring was my father's. It will keep you safe, even if you only wear it long enough to make it safely into your car."

"This is a family heirloom," Adam said. "You can't just give it to me."

"I've got no family left," Eileen said with a shrug. "And I'd rather you live a good long life aboveground then get snatched away to faeryland. I've got something for you too, birdie."

Eileen reached back in the box and produced a long-chain necklace, with a single iron charm dangling from it. The charm, Nicola realized as Eileen dropped it into her hands, was a tarnished Scottish thistle.

"That was mine, when I was a girl," Eileen said. "Wear it faithfully and it will keep you safe. I'll help you pack, if you want to go. I'll even have Finley guide you as far as Wyke. But you asked me to tell you about Craigmar, and that's the truth of it."

Nicola searched Eileen's expression for any indication of a lie, but there was none. Eileen just looked wrung-out and a desperate, staring at Adam with the cracked lips of someone who, long denied water, had happened upon an oasis.

"Well, what do you want me to do?" Adam asked, huffing out a disbelieving laugh. "We can't just stay here with you."

"Why not?" Eileen asked, with such a vulnerable hope that it nearly broke Nicola's heart.

"We have hostel reservations, and a plane home to catch in a week."

"Then forget your reservations and stay the week," Eileen said. "If you decide to stay longer than that, I'll buy you new tickets home whenever you like."

Nicola paled. She knew damn well what those tickets had cost, especially since she had saved up for six months to buy her round-trip flight.

"We couldn't let you do that," Nicola said.

"Nicola, I'm rich. It's nothing. Certainly nothing compared to the help you two might be able to give me. You have an obvious expertise in this area as a student of folklore. Your quick thinking out at the cave is exactly the sort of thing we need. And Adam, I do believe that there's something here about your grandfather we're not seeing. Something that could lift the weight of centuries of family suffering off my shoulders. Quite frankly, you're the first break I've had in this case for years. And this big old house feels so empty this time of year, when everything is coming back to life outside. Even if your grandfather is a dead end, it would be nice to have some company for a little while."

Adam and Nicola shared a long, silent look, weighing their options without having to speak. The choice was obvious: turn back towards safety and the known challenges of the regular world, or walk hand in hand together into something darker and stranger and altogether more exciting.

There was nothing waiting for Nicola back in Michigan except closing shifts at the florist's and a half-finished children's book manuscript on her computer that wouldn't write itself and bumble dates that went nowhere. There was nothing good guaranteed to come of staying at Craigmar, but there was certainly potential, of real magic, of a chance at deeper connection with Adam, of luxuriating in all of Eileen's wonderful strangeness, of uncovering what lay beneath the warmth glimmering in Finley's eyes.

Nicola had spent so long with no proper home, no safe place to rest that she hadn't carved out for herself. And while Criagmar wasn't home, it was a place she felt welcome, wanted even, and that was more intoxicating than any faery story.

Nicola already knew her answer. But more importantly, she knew Adam, and more than anything, she knew that deep down, Adam wanted to be a hero.

"Say yes," she said quietly.

Adam sighed and surrendered.

"I guess I don't really need to be in the States to get my freelance jobs done. I brought my laptop with me, just in case, but Nicola, I know you've got to work and—"

"The shop will manage fine without me," Nicola said. "And this is the perfect place to work on my book. Maybe I'll actually get it finished while you help Eileen go through those family records."

"So you'll stay," Eileen said, letting out a relieved breath.

Finley, who had been observing the conversation very quietly and very intently up until now, said: "If you stay, I'm sure Eileen will give you full run of the house and grounds. But you've got to promise to follow her rules, about the iron, about following our traditions, about keeping the good neighbors happy, all of it."

Nicola felt an unexpected thrill at those words. She didn't consider herself the kind of person who liked following rules as, well, a general rule. But something about doing exactly what Eileen said, beautiful brutal Eileen with her impossibly dark eyes, made the prospect more appealing. Nicola would probably do anything Eileen asked when she looked at Nicola like she was now, like Nicola was a flower whose petals she wanted to pluck one by one.

"I promise," Nicola said, a little breathlessly.

"I promise," Adam said, like a pact.

"Thank Christ," Eileen said, slapping the table. A bit of color was returning to her cheeks. "Finley, could you get the rest of their things from the car? They'll be staying with us a while."

"I'll help," Adam said.

Finley gave a curt nod, his gaze fixed on the table. Why couldn't he look Adam in the eye?

"Ready when you are," Finley said.

Adam and Finley pulled on their coats, talking in a low murmur about weather or cars or whatever else men who didn't know each other well talked about, and then left Eileen and Nicola alone in the kitchen.

Eileen leaned across the table, smiling conspiratorially.

"It will be so nice to have another girl in the house again," she said. "Especially one as clever as you."

Nicola smiled back, feeling a bit like a songbird who had wandered into a snare. To her surprise, Nicola found that a dark and needy part of her liked that feeling, especially if Eileen was the one holding the other end of the rope.

CHAPTER ELEVEN

Adam

Adam's head swam with possibilities as he followed Finley out to the car. Yesterday he had been a college dropout on a quest to find a dead man's bedtime story, and now he was the guest of an aristocrat who treated him like the knight who might be able to free her from her tower. And then there was the matter of Finley, the man who looked at Adam like a trespasser and at Nicola like a revelation. Adam distrusted him instinctively, for reasons that made his stomach knot up when he tried to make sense of them.

The ground squelched under Adam's feet, rocky gravel knocked loose by the coagulating mud beneath.

Finley was silent for most of the short walk, keeping his shoulders hunched forward as though he were trying to physically ward off conversation. Adam took the opportunity to steal a glance him, sizing the other man up. Adam was considerably taller with a runner's physique, but Finley was a bit brawnier, with the build that came from a lifetime of outdoor labor.

When Finley finally spoke, in a soft baritone that almost got snatched away by the wind, it took Adam by surprise.

"Did you know?"

"Know what?" Adam said, slowing his about-his-business stride just a touch.

"About the Kirkfoyles' curse."

"No."

Finley made a *hmph* sound in his throat and stopped at the rental car, which still sat parked at the edge of the drive with its tires sunk into the mud.

"Eileen wasn't joking about that rain," Adam muttered, retrieving the key fob from his pocket.

"She doesn't often joke," Finley replied.

"You seem to know her better than anyone," Adam ventured as he popped the trunk. He had a penchant for wiggling the truth out of people, even when it was uncomfortable for them. It was his nature to seek brutal honesty above all things. "How long have you two been an item?"

"Since we were teenagers."

"And before that?"

"There's never been anyone else. No one important, anyway."

"Interesting," Adam said, hauling his battered Kankan out of the car and handing it to Finley. They had brought their duffels of clothes in last night, but Adam had kept his laptop in the car along with his passport, just in case. Nicola had left her mauve toiletry bag with all her lotions and potions in the car as well, and Adam carried that one himself, because he didn't like the idea of the other man touching her things. "Do you really take this whole faery thing seriously? Does she?"

"Faeries are one thing Eileen is dead serious about," Finley responded, shouldering the stuffed backpack without any effort at all. "And I've lived on Craigmar land long enough to see with my own two eyes things you couldn't even dream of."

Adam slammed the trunk shut with more force than was necessary, then started back to the house. There was something about Finley that got under his skin. Adam wasn't sure if it was his brusque tone or his connection to Eileen or the way he looked at Nicola or even the fact that under different circumstances, Finley would have definitely been Adam's type. There was something disconcerting about all those factors swirling together in one person, so Adam just kept his eyes fixed straight ahead.

Adam thought Finley had gotten the message about them being done talking, but he spoke again just as they approached the looming oak doors.

"Eileen may seem . . ." Finley faltered, as though finding the right words was challenging. "High-spirited. But she's a very sensitive person, at the end of the day. I'll ask you not to abuse her hospitality. Or her trust."

"I wouldn't dream of it," Adam replied. Finley's tone was bringing down his mood, and his hand still throbbed, and that strange sweet scent at the cave had given him a headache. He wanted to lie down. "Nicola and I are very grateful to be put up for the time being. And we're happy to help Eileen in any way that we can."

If it were possible, Finley's expression darkened even more at the mention of Nicola's name. Adam bit the inside of his cheek. He didn't know when he was going to be alone with Finley again, hopefully never, so he should take advantage of the opportunity to level with Finley now.

"Nicola seems to have taken a shine to you," he said in a tone that he hoped was slightly threatening in a still pleasant manner.

"Is this the part where you tell me to stay away from her?"

"This is the part where I tell you to be careful. She got her heart broken last year by some asshole on the lacrosse team. I would give her space, if I were you."

Finley shot him a glass-edged look that had Adam spoiling for a fight, for closeness, for some kind of intimate violence that would burst the tension between them like a soap bubble.

"Why, because she's yours?"

Finley, for some unhinged reason, was trying to get a rise out of Adam, and as much as Adam hated to admit it, it was working. He always got defensive when people mistook him and Nicola for a couple, but he got even more defensive when she started running around with someone else. It was a bad quality, he knew that, but Finley, with his strange ties to Craigmar and entanglement with Eileen, was the last person Adam wanted to see Nicola involved with.

"No, because I don't want to see her getting hurt," Adam said.

"I have no intention of hurting her," Finley said, and there were his cards, out on the table. "If anything, I have every intention of making her feel very good."

Adam considered shoving Finley against the ancient oak of the doors, maybe balling Finley's collar in his fist and holding him there while he did . . . something, but that seemed dangerous in more ways than one. He didn't want to piss off Nicola or Eileen by roughing Finley up, and he didn't quite trust himself to get that close to the other man. Besides, he couldn't stop Nicola from doing exactly what she wanted, especially as far as romance was concerned.

"I'm the closest thing to family she's got left," Adam said, putting his cards down right next to Finley's.

"If you're just family, you won't mind my stepping in, then."

"We'll see what Nikki decides," Adam said, just to remind Finley who had known her the longest.

"That we will. Right of the lady to choose, isn't it? Glad we could sort that out."

Finley took Nicola's toiletry bag from Adam without

another word, bumped open the door to the house with his shoulder, then tossed a final glance back to where Adam stood fuming on the doorstop.

"You shouldn't carry anything with that hand for a while," Finley said, disappearing into the house. "Welcome to Craigmar, Adam."

In the resulting quiet, with nothing but birdsong and the rustling of high grass to break the silence, Adam wanted to scream.

Adam did his best to get more settled in his room, trying to break the living-out-of-a-suitcase habit since he may be here for a few days, maybe even more. He took in the room as he put his army-rolled clothes away in the chest of drawers.

He could get used to sleeping here, he thought. That thought felt a little bit dangerous but it also felt a little bit good, like slipping into a hot Epsom salt bath after a long, hard run.

Adam resolved to learn the layout of the house as quickly as he could, so he wouldn't have to rely on Eileen for directions – or worse, on Finley. He only got turned around once before he found Nicola's room, which she had marked with a silk scrunchie wrapped around the doorknob. She always thought of everything.

"Nikki," Adam said, rapping on the door. "You in there?"

There was a rustling of fabric through the door, then a high, startled: "Uh, yeah! Just a second."

Adam heard what sounded like bedsheets being tossed back and something small, like a tube of lipstick, clattering to the floor. A moment later, Nicola threw open the door. She looked even more windswept than after coming back from her walk with Finley.

Underneath the scent of old furniture and Nicola's Daisy perfume, Adam caught an undeniable whiff of sex.

"Were you jilling off?" Adam said, laughter bubbling up to disguise just how turned on he was by that thought: Nicola touching herself in broad daylight under those expensive sheets, her inner thighs glistening, her toes curling as she reached for that sweet spot inside herself. "Come on, you couldn't even wait for it to get dark?"

"I can do whatever I want in my own room," Nicola said with a scowl. Adam wasn't surprised she had owned up to it. Nicola was frank to the point of oversharing when it came to her sex life, which sometimes complicated being friends with her. "It's all that adrenaline from the cave. I needed to flush it out of my system."

"Looks like you were giving yourself a very thorough flushing," Adam said, nodding to a purple travel-sized vibrator lying on the floor behind her. "Since when do near-death experiences turn you on?"

"Since when do you care what turns me on?" Nicola shot back, tossing the door open wider to welcome him into her room. With her usual complete lack of self-consciousness, Nicola retrieved her vibrator, washed it off along with her hands in the ensuite bathroom, and then tucked it away in a little satin bag in her duffel.

"I don't care," he said, bristling. "But I'm allowed to think it's weird."

"I once saw you get hard because a shot girl in New Orleans asked you to hold her drinks while she took a piss. You don't get an opinion on what's weird."

"Fair," he said, tossing himself down onto her bed. Not too close to the rumpled sheets, but close enough that he felt a small guilty thrill at soaking up the last whisper of her body heat from the mattress. Nicola continued the chores she had apparently left half-finished to attend to her own pressing needs, like lining up her skincare and toothbrush on the sink, and hanging up sweaters in the wardrobe.

She glanced over her shoulder at him, arching that eyebrow that told him he was about to be cross-examined.

"Are you going to tell me why coming out here was so important to you?"

Adam shrugged. "I told you. It's one of the big things me and Grandad shared before he died. I feel like I owe it to him to come, you know?"

"Yes, but there's something else, isn't there?"

Adam let his gaze drift out the window, watching a cluster of sheep meander over the grazing green below. Somehow, it was always easier to unburden his heart to Nicola if he wasn't looking right at her.

"It's going to sound crazy," he muttered.

"I've told you before, Adam, nothing is crazy. Not to me, anyway."

"I felt suffocated in Grand Rapids. Like my life was going to be the same every single day if I didn't change something. It was all work, sleep, the same bar every weekend, repeat. I tried to think of the last time my life really felt, I don't know, full? And I realized it was when I was listening to my grandad tell me those stories. I guess I'm just trying to get that feeling back. Does that sound stupid?"

"No," Nicola said. "But it does sound exactly like something you would say."

"So it does sound stupid," Adam said, a smile pulling at the corner of his mouth.

Nicola picked up a throw pillow and swatted at him, resulting in a burst of laughter from Adam.

But then Nicola gnawed on her lip, a surefire sign that she had something to tell him.

"What is it?" Adam asked, snatching the pillow away and rearing back as though he might hit her with it if she didn't answer. "No lying, Nikki. We've got to put up a unified front out here."

"It's just . . ." Nicola kept gnawing, so long that Adam thought he might go crazy waiting for her to spit it out. "I'm worried you don't really believe me. About what I saw out there in the woods. It was real, Adam. It was like something out of a nightmare, but I know I was awake."

"After that freaky-as-hell weather and getting my hand nearly bitten off by a badger or whatever, I'm not writing anything off," Adam said.

"It wasn't a badger, Adam. You know that."

"A wolf, then. Do they have wolves here?"

"It wasn't that either," Nicola said, slamming the wardrobe shut. She took two sharp breaths through her nose in that exercise her therapist had taught her. Adam didn't understand the finer points of Nicola's emotional regulation troubles, but he knew she was working on managing the outbursts.

He paused to think his next words through more carefully. Nicola was undeniably prone to flights of fancy. She had once put away two wines in quick succession at a holiday party and decided that she could see angels dancing in the light of his tiny Christmas tree. But that didn't mean she was wrong about this, and it didn't mean that everything Eileen had told them was a lie either. Adam didn't quite believe in the faery angle, but he certainly believed in places that had bad energy, or families that couldn't break free from an ouroboros cycle of misery so all-consuming it felt supernatural. There was something going on here, whether it was swamp gas or a trick of the light or roaming wild animals or, maybe, even something supernatural. Something to explain the way he had felt standing at the mouth of the cave, like every single one of his atoms was on fire. Like he was being pulled forward by a force his body responded to even as his mind rebelled.

"I'll keep my eyes peeled for anything creepy. If you see anything else, let me know. Let's just not jump to conclusions until we're sure, okay?"

"Okay," Nicola said, taking one more deep breath. "Thanks for believing me."

"I always believe you," Adam scoffed, like he was irritated by her doubt. Not like it was a testament to his unwavering devotion.

Nicola gave him a golden smile, and for a brief, flickering moment, Adam felt at home.

CHAPTER TWELVE

Eileen

Something about the excitement of the morning triggered one of Eileen's unpredictable migraines, so she retired to her room to sleep it off. As it turned out, she slept for four hours. When she finally emerged in the late afternoon, her eyes puffy from sleep and her hair lazily tied into a ponytail with a ribbon, the sun outside her windows was low in the sky. Eileen felt as though she were a rumpled female Christ, emerging from her tomb after a sleep like death.

She hoped her guests were settling in and learning their way around the manor. Finley would no doubt have helped them, as grumpy as he might be about new blood at Craigmar. Finley was often grumpy, so that didn't bother Eileen much. He always went along with what she wanted, bad attitude or no. And she hadn't missed how he had done his best to protect Nicola from

Eileen's designs, or the way he had thrown his arms around Adam to haul him bodily back from that cave.

Finley had never had anyone else to defend besides Eileen, nor had he ever had a single person in the world who could be relied on to come to his defense as sure as he came to hers. They had only ever had each other.

But now, the world had expanded. The knife's-edge balance of Craigmar, so painstakingly maintained by Eileen and Finley's games up until this point, was tottering under the weight of Adam and Nicola.

Eileen had worked very hard to cultivate ironclad privacy at Craigmar, so she and Finley could be left in peace, but she did, occasionally, find herself lonely. She knew Finley must as well, from his occasional ventures into town to chat up someone at a pub and sometimes even go home with them at the end of the night. New people in the house, much less pretty young people, weren't the worst thing in the world, especially not when it came to what Eileen had in mind.

Dr Dasgupta had asked her during one of his house calls why she never left Craigmar. He had tried to convince her to go somewhere warmer for a season, to breathe gentler air and get the sun on her face. Eileen had brushed him off with a fib about her delicate health.

It wasn't that Eileen didn't want to leave Craigmar, that she didn't dream of sailing away to some new and glorious country. It was simply that she *couldn't* leave, not without bringing ruination upon them all. She was pretty sure she could, technically, walk off the grounds without turning to dust. But she hadn't been beyond the boundaries of the estate since her parents died, because there were no other Kirkfoyles left now to sit grim watch for their neighbors under the ground. She barely even went into Wyke, even though that was technically within the bounds of her family's land and therefore covered by the treaty, because she didn't like risking it, and because she didn't like the people in town much either.

Dr Dasgupta might have been a friend of her father's, and he was a good man, but he wasn't family. He could never understand the truth. So Eileen always lied.

But now, even though Eileen could not leave Craigmar to find diversions, entertainment had come to her. It was like when she was sick in her pre-teen years, laid up for days at a time, and her mother would put on shadow puppet shows for her at the end of her bed.

Adam Lancaster wasn't a puppet, exactly.

But Eileen still very much enjoyed pulling his strings.

Eileen paused in her mirror to wipe the mascara smudges from under her eyes and to straighten the iron badge on her lapel, then she went in search of her impossible American.

She found him on the stairs, staring up at a painting of her father. Eileen had learned how to creep through the house undetected at a very young age, and effortlessly dodged creaking floorboards as she approached. As she peered down at Adam from the upstairs landing, she saw he was unaware of her presence.

Eileen drank in the sight of him, his strong profile and long pale lashes and well-sculpted mouth. He looked so different from her, from Finley, from any of the handful of people she regularly saw. She could get used to looking at a face like that, maybe even for a very long while.

Despite his laid-back mannerisms and Midwestern accent, in that moment, with his shoulders back and his chin tipped up to admire the painting, he looked like a prince. Like one of Arthur's knights who had gone searching for the grail and found a girl instead.

"That's my father," Eileen said, making herself known. "He was very handsome, and very kind."

Adam's blue eyes cut over to her, and Eileen's heart stuttered. He really was lovely, in that arrestingly fair way that read more Scandinavian than Scottish. Eileen mentally chided herself as she made her way down the steps towards him. This was a mutually beneficial arrangement of her design, nothing more. She had to remind herself of that, lest her heart run away with her.

"I'm sorry for your loss," Adam said.

"It was years ago," Eileen replied, coming to a stop on the step above him. "The hurt has scarred over by now. But I appreciate your condolences."

"Finley said you had a headache. Are you feeling better?"

"As better as I'm liable to feel anytime soon."

Eileen gazed up at her father, who shared her porcelain skin and dark hair, but with warm hazel eyes so unlike

Eileen's piercing black gaze. Her eyes, her father had once told her, were a little piece of the moonless sky from the night she was born. They didn't come from her father or her mother, they were entirely hers and hers alone, and she was the first Kirkfoyle in generations with eyes like that. Eileen had wondered, ever since she was a girl, if her eyes marked her as different somehow, doomed by a story that had been set in motion long before she was born. Her eyes had always felt like an omen, fitting for a girl born wearing the legacy of a dying family around her neck like an albatross.

"How are you finding your rooms?" Eileen asked Adam, reminding herself to stay present and not drift off into memories. "Comfortable, I hope."

"Very comfortable. We appreciate it."

"Then why does it sound like you're about to apologize for something?"

Adam stepped up onto Eileen's stair, and suddenly he was taller than her again. He was taller even than Finley, who was only a hair's breadth taller than Eileen, and she felt slightly loomed over as Adam looked down at her.

This was, for Eileen, not an unpleasant sensation at all. Her heartbeat quickened.

"Do you really think I ended up here for a reason?" Adam asked, pitching his voice low as though he were afraid of being overheard. "That we're supposed to help each other?"

"I don't think, I know. Have you ever felt the truth of something like that, deep in your bones?"

"Yes," Adam said quietly, with such a naked vulnerability that Eileen could have kissed him.

Finley stalked past at the bottom of the stairs, then paused as though struck by lightning as he looked up at Eileen and Adam. Eileen casually took another step down the stairs, putting a little more breathing room between her and Adam.

"How are things, Finney?" she asked, as though she hadn't been caught on the edge of a dalliance.

"Well enough," Finley said, giving Eileen a hard look before continuing his determined walk towards the library.

Eileen sighed heavily.

"He's in a mood. I should make sure he's all right."

"Did I do something wrong?" Adam asked, craning his neck to see further down the hallway Finley had disappeared into.

"Besides having the audacity to be good-looking and friendly?" Eileen said, slapping him companionably on the shoulder like they were old school chums. "Not at all. Why don't you do a bit of exploring before dinner? Then you and I can start digging through those records."

With that, she was gone, jogging down the stairs to go find her dearest friend and sometimes tormentor and lover, always lover.

Finley was standing in front of the stack of boxes on her father's desk, gnawing on his thumbnail.

"Are you pondering the mysteries of cardboard?" Eileen asked, swinging the library door gently shut behind her. There was only one surefire way to make up with Finley in an expedient fashion, and it required privacy. "You can get it at Tesco, I'm told."

"They're not going to buy our story," Finley said, barely looking at her. She didn't need to ask what he was referring to. It was damn near the only thing they had been talking about – or fighting about – for months.

"Yes, they are," Eileen said levelly. It was a voice of total authority, the voice she used to talk to her lawyer.

"Adam is going to kill you when he finds out."

"No he won't," Eileen said, walking over to the desk to take one final look at the arrangement of papers. It looked unintentionally messy, perfectly accidental, just as she'd hoped.

Finley came up behind her and wrapped his strong arms around her waist, resting his chin on her shoulder. He smelled like rain and sweet hay and the greenery of outdoors, and maybe the musty edges of those old books he kept stockpiled in his cottage. It was sexy and soothing and so perfectly *Finley.*

Finley let out a big breath, just a little bit shaky. He was wound tight as a pocketwatch.

"You look like a pageboy with your hair tied back like this," Finley said, nuzzling the ribbon at the nape of her neck. "Like one of those girls who sing the boy parts in operas."

Eileen knew very well that he knew the precise word was *contralto*, that he was once again downplaying his own intelligence to make her feel better about having him trapped here doing manual labor for all eternity. It wasn't that she hadn't offered to pay to send him back to university after he had been called home at the end of his first semester to care for his ailing father, or that she didn't keep him in a steady supply of all the books he could want. It was that Finley's devotion to her, miserable though it was some days, prevented him from ever abandoning her to Craigmar. If they were stuck here, he had told her many times before, then they would simply make a heaven of hell together.

The old guilt welled up inside her. Eileen decided to tamp it down with her most tried and true method before it had time to snap her up in its jaws.

"And how would you fuck me?" Eileen asked over her shoulder, a smirk playing at her lips. "If I was your boy?"

It was enticing, imagining Finley's hand wrapping around the bob of an Adam's apple in her throat, before sliding down her flat chest to grasp at the hardening length in her trousers. Eileen could see it so clearly, more clearly than she saw herself in the mirror some days. It was all too easy to envision what she would look like as a proper heir to Craigmar. Her father's wavy hair and her mother's fair coloring and those dark eyes that were nothing but Eileen, transformed by the merest alteration of genetics into a boy worthy of her family name.

Finley said nothing, merely moved his hands on either side of her to brace her against the desk as he kissed behind her ear. She could feel his desire, in the hitch of his breath and in the insistent press of his body against hers, but she didn't know if he was going to take her roleplaying bait or not. Sometimes he was inexhaustibly creative, an actor's actor in the bedroom, and other times he got sullen when she asked him to play a part, insisting that he wanted to have her as himself and no one else.

"Would you be rougher?" Eileen pressed, arching back against him. He needed a distraction from his worry. They both did. "Or sweeter?"

She wasn't sure which one she preferred: the fantasy that Finley might push her harder, driven by the competitive camaraderie of men, or handle her with more care, as intuitively aware of her own limits as he was of his own body. Both possibilities made the pulse pound hard between her legs.

In response, Finley used one hand to tug her trousers and panties down over her ass. She shuddered, her sensitive skin exposed to the draft of the house. When Finley squeezed her upper thigh, still bruised from where he had bitten her in a moment of petulance last week, she let out a moan.

"I'd fuck you like I always have," he said, the warmth in his otherwise stern voice the only indication that he was playing a part. She would hardly know he was smiling if she hadn't been going to bed with him for the better part of a decade. “Hard and rough, on top of all your father’s furniture, praying I can come before he catches us.”

Eileen leaned further forward over the ancient desk as Finley unzipped his jeans. She heard him take himself in hand, giving himself a few stokes as he continued to weave a whole world with nothing more than words.

“If you were a boy,” he said, wetting himself by sliding the head of his cock along her entrance. He would penetrate her only when he was ready, only when she was driven mad with desperation. “It would be easier to sneak around. I could have taken you out drinking without your mother waiting up all night for us, and I could have sucked you off in the pub toilets while people banged on the door. We could have played sports together without worrying about ripping your pretty dresses, and I could have fucked you for my prize if I won.”

This was what Eileen had been after, Finley’s near-diabolical talent for sexual storytelling. She thanked the godless sky that he liked to read, and that he liked to root around in her mind until he found the perfect imagery to make her whimper.

“Finley,” she gasped, but he silenced her by pushing her down against the wood with a firm hand. Eileen barely had time to notice that the desk still smelled like her father’s favorite fountain pen ink before Finley sheathed himself inside her. It was all hot skin-on-skin union.

They hadn’t bothered with a condom in a long time.

Finley started to fuck her with the jackrabbit rhythm she most often witnessed him applying to himself with his own hand. There was a selfishness to his relentless pace, a complete disregard for any notion of chivalry, that made heat curl in the base of Eileen's spine. He knew how she liked it best, senseless and greedy.

"A boy wouldn't beg or cry," Finley rasped, still holding her down. He pressed in tighter, nudging her legs indecently wide so he could find greater purchase inside her. "A boy would hold still, just like that, and be so grateful for this."

Eileen wanted more than anything to reach between her legs and tip herself over the edge into orgasm, but Finley had left no room for her to do so, and moreover, he didn't seem to care about her satisfaction right now. Paradoxically (and probably exactly to Finley's design), this disregard only got her hotter, making her pant while he took her.

"We could have been best friends, and no one would have ever known anything," he said, voice tightening along with the muscles in his thighs as he neared his own climax, faster than Eileen would have expected. Something about this scene was working for him too, or maybe he was just working all the stress from the last few days out of his system, or maybe seeing her with Adam had only made him want her more. "We could have been friends, and no one would have ever tried to keep us apart."

Pain shot through Eileen's chest, chasing the spirals of

lust. Finley was good at what he did, but sometimes he pushed too hard. Sometimes, in trying to create a world of fantasy, he uncovered the thorniest of truths instead.

"Inside me," Eileen ordered. It would have fit the scene better if she had pleaded, but her head was swimming with visions of lives that neither of them would ever live, and disorientation made her grasp for power. For station. For the little authority that was left to her as the ever-ill girlchild heir to a legacy of rot and ruin.

Finley bucked against her once more, twice, then spilled into her with breathless obedience.

Eileen squeezed her eyes shut and tried to catch her breath. The moment Finley pulled out, that old, aching emptiness opened up in her heart again.

She wondered sometimes if there was a sinkhole inside her, always hungry and never satisfied no matter how much cruelty or pleasure she poured into it.

Finley retrieved a tissue from the desk and gently wiped her clean. Eileen yanked her pants back up over her hips, shrinking away from his touch.

"Why bother?" she asked, mood careening towards dour. "Nothing will come of it, anyway."

"Eileen," Finley said with a long-suffering sigh. They had talked about this many, many times. It never got any easier. "It's not your fault."

Eileen knew, intellectually, that he was right. Dr Dasgupta had told her as much. She still felt like she was the root cause of their suffering, however.

"In less polite times they would have called me barren," Eileen said, barking out a laugh as she tightened the ribbon in her hair to prepare for the work she and Adam had ahead of them. "Like I'm some sort of wasteland."

Ten years of sex between them and three years of trying, really trying, and they still hadn't been able to conceive. Finley had done his very best, in the beginning, to pretend like he might be the broken one. He tried to keep her in good spirits, to insist that they just needed to try harder, in new and exciting positions. There was no one else he would rather raise a child with, he told her, no one else he would entrust with such a gift. Moreover, a baby would forestall their doom and keep the Kirkfoyle line strong for at least one generation more. Then Eileen and Finley could enjoy the happiness they were entitled to, the happiness that had been denied to them by the circumstances of their births and the wishes of Eileen's family. They could spend their days chasing a little girl through the heather or lifting up a little boy into the trees so he could pluck the highest apples, not worrying about being overrun with supernatural invaders. Maybe they would even finally get married, when it was all over and done with.

Eileen had never conceived, of course. Endometriosis, Dr Dasgupta had said, and considerable scarring in the womb.

Eileen didn't call her condition anything other than what it was: a curse.

"I really hope this works," she muttered, the satisfied throb between her legs already abating. Nothing kept her happy for long any more. Nothing sated her. "I don't think I can go another year waiting for madness or death to claim me. I'm tired of wondering if I'm going to fall and break my neck every time I leave the house, or get swallowed up by the earth, or succumb to some other Shakespearean tragedy."

"They haven't killed you yet," Finley said, echoing the words Eileen always told him every time he worried.

"I hear them more, these days," she said, gazing out the window. She wasn't sure why she was telling him this; it would only make him more anxious. But Eileen had never been able to keep a single secret from Finley, not one, no matter how ugly. "Bells out my window, or voices singing in the middle of the night. Calling me underground. Sometimes, I want to listen to them."

Finley didn't say anything at all in response. He just walked right up to her, wrapped his arms around her as tight as they would go, and pressed Eileen to his chest. She dug her fingernails into his back and took a deep, shaky breath, blinking away her shameful tears.

"We're going to find a way through this," Finley said into her hair. "One way or another. I swear it."

CHAPTER THIRTEEN

Adam

Adam tried to take Eileen's advice and entertain himself by exploring the house, but he just got turned around again. When he found himself once again on the threshold of the library, he couldn't be sure how he got there, but Eileen was waiting for him.

"Welcome," she said in that antiquated lilt, looking up from a stack of papers on the desk.

"Hey," Adam responded, shrugging off his backpack. "I brought my laptop in case we wanted to look anything up online."

"Good thinking," Eileen said.

Adam drifted past the bookshelves, slower this time, taking in the titles. It was mostly old novels and local history and books of letters from philosophers and politicians Adam had never heard of. He plucked up one of the histories, flipping through the pages until he discovered an illustration protected by tissue paper in the center of the tome. It was a penciled rendition of the rolling hills of the Craigmar estate, the house a tiny smudge in the distance.

"How old is this drawing, do you think?" Adam asked, setting the open book down on the table before Eileen.

"A hundred years old or so, I'd say."

"It doesn't look any different than the view outside the window now."

"Craigmar changes at a glacial pace. She was the same when my father was a boy, and when his father's father was a boy. Industrialization improved the machinery we used and the speed at which we were able to communicate with the outside world, but not much else changed."

"Where does the money come from?" Adam asked, realizing too late that his all-too-American curiosity about local economics might come off as tactless. Eileen didn't seem bothered.

"Investments, real estate and sheep, mostly. I own most of Wyke, the little village you passed through to get here."

"So you're a landlady," he said, a smile pulling at his lips as he flipped through the books, admiring another sketch of the rocky coastline beyond the grazing green.

"More or less," she said.

Adam glanced up to find that Eileen was standing very close to him, her dark eyes fixed on his face. For a moment, he was seized by the thought – the hope? – that she might kiss him.

He cleared his throat and closed the book.

"Sorry, I got distracted. Where do you think we should start?"

"It seems wisest to start with my grandmother," Eileen said, turning from Adam as though sensing his self-consciousness. Eileen hoisted up an iron poker and stabbed at the crackling fire, still warming the room well into spring. It was colder out here on the coast than it had been on the drive over from Edinburgh, and the house was impressively drafty. "From her birth up until her disappearance."

"Disappearance?" Adam said. "I thought you said she died."

"I'm sure she did, eventually."

"Well, how did she disappear? What happened to her?"

"I don't know," Eileen said, shrugging one shoulder. "No one does. Maybe she managed to run away from this place without getting dragged back. That would have been a feat."

Adam's hand hovered over one of the boxes of family records, and Eileen nodded, bidding him on. Adam removed the lid and peered down into piles of handwritten letters, some stored safely away in their envelopes, others unevenly folded or crinkled at the edges.

"Looks like this is one of my mother's boxes," Eileen said, picking up a letter and running her finger over the name it was addressed to. *Jennifer Kirkfoyle.*

"They all smell like flowers," Adam said. "And maybe raspberries?"

"Guerlain Idylle," Eileen responded with a fond smile. She pressed one of the letters to her nose and inhaled deeply, her face softening into a girlish smile. "Her signature perfume. She was a prolific letter-writer. It was her favorite way to keep in touch with her friends back in England. She sprayed every letter with that perfume."

"Is England where she met your dad?" Adam asked. He found that he was truly curious about Eileen's tangled family history, and not just about the way it may intersect with his own. She was a riddle of a girl, and part of him hoped her upbringing might hold some clues to help him solve her.

"At Cambridge," Eileen said, removing letters by the handful and beginning to sort them into piles. Categorized by the person her mother had been in correspondence with, it looked like. "They were university sweethearts. My mum wasn't Scottish, though. She was a blonde English rose, if you can believe it. I look nothing like her."

Adam couldn't parse her tone, nor read the expression in her downcast eyes, so he asked: "Did you two get along?"

"I always took more after my father. We were both quick to anger and quick to affection. It wasn't that my mother and I didn't get along; I know she loved me very much. I just think she wasn't sure what to do with me, most days."

"So it was just the three of you out here, growing up?"

Adam went on, taking up a handful of letters and sorting through for his grandfather's name.

"That's right. My father's father was long dead by the time I was born. It's a miracle he lasted long enough for my father to go away to university. My grandfather always had a weak heart; cardiac arrest did for him at the end. At least that's what the doctor said. Personally, I think some creature from underground frightened him to death. That's one of their favorite ways to pick off the nervous ones in my family."

Adam still wasn't sure how to approach the whole family curse thing, or Eileen's bone-deep conviction that there were magical creatures out in the woods who wanted to kill her, so he tried to keep the conversation focused on more mundane things.

"Didn't you get lonely? It doesn't sound like you ever left Craigmar to go to school."

"Certainly not. I wasn't well enough, and I didn't like other children much. But how could I have been lonely? I had Finley right next door. He's all I ever needed."

Adam stopped what he was doing and stared at her. She spoke so plainly, as though it were the simplest thing in the world. Adam couldn't tell if she was putting on a strong face by being dismissive, or if she really didn't see how that was not at all normal.

"Have you *ever* left Craigmar?"

"Of course. When my parents were still alive, one of them would stay here while the other took me into town, or on drives to see the countryside. I went to Glasgow once, for my tenth birthday. That was exciting. But my father called my mother in a panic, and we had to come home early. He had volunteered to stay behind and watch the estate, but then he started hearing voices in his sleep telling him to jump from the third-story window."

"Did your dad have, like, mental health stuff going on?" Adam asked delicately. It was probably invasive, but he *had* to ask. He had to know that Eileen was at least considering the fact that perhaps faeries had nothing to do with her family's hereditary propensity for emotional anguish and sudden death.

Eileen let out a sharp bark of a laugh, like a Pomeranian. "Don't we all! Let's move on to the next box. I don't think there's anything relevant in this one." She carefully stacked her mother's letters back in the box, then wiped the perfumed dust from her hands. "Let's try photos next. What did your grandfather look like?"

"A lot like me," Adam replied, scrubbing at his eyes. They were already burning from looking through the letters, and they had barely started. There must be eight boxes piled on this desk, and Eileen said there were more in storage. "Blond hair, blue eyes. Not as tall, though."

"I can work with that," Eileen said, placing her mother's box of letters on the ground and hoisting a box labelled *Memories* towards them both. She popped the lid to reveal stacks of loose photographs, along with a few bound albums.

"Do you think there'll be pictures of him in with the family stuff?"

"Probably not, but it's worth trying," Eileen said. "If you'll recall my father's portrait, Kirkfoyle blood runs strong. We tend towards dark coloring, not fair. No matter who we marry, that brunette hair tends to pull through. If your grandfather is here, he'll be easy to spot."

"You're sure you're okay with me going through all this with you?" Adam said, fingers itching to touch the yellowed photographs.

"Why wouldn't I be?"

"I don't know, it just seems . . ."

"Intimate?" Eileen asked with a wolfish smile. "Maybe I like being intimate with you, Adam Lancaster."

Adam ignored the way his cheeks heated at that remark, then nodded and plunged his hands into the photographs.

Eileen helped him sort the photographs into piles, stopping occasionally to introduce him to a family member via their ghostly visage, imprinted forever on Polaroid. Adam saw countless pictures of her parents when they were young and in love, Jennifer gamine-slender and grinning with her long honey-straw hair tousled by the wind, James with his arms slung around his wife, looking slightly bohemian despite the expensive clothes with deliberate five o'clock shadow and his waves of dark hair curling past his ears. He also saw a couple of pictures of a teenage Arabella, one in which she was striking an arabesque pose, in tights and ballet shoes, on the upstairs landing, and another in which she was dressed for some type of formal event in the library, primly done up in a cream brocade dress. She looked very much like Eileen, if Eileen's long oval face was pinched into a heart, and if Eileen gave off ultra feminine energy as opposed to unexpected but alluring androgyny.

"Is everyone in your family ridiculously good-looking?" Adam muttered, pausing for a half second too long on a candid picture of James in evening dress smiling rakishly over a glass of champagne at the camera, no doubt held by Jennifer.

"Are you trying to use my dead family to come onto me?" Eileen asked with a smirk. "How macabre."

She bumped shoulders with him companionably, and it put Adam enough at ease to flirt back, if only a little bit. There was no harm in a bit of good-natured flirting, right? Society was basically built on flirting.

"You seem like the type of person who appreciates a macabre compliment."

"Maybe I am."

Adam was quickly forgetting what the purpose of this exercise was, especially when Eileen's eyes slid languidly to his mouth. But then she looked past him and let out a gasp of triumph.

"Ah! Is this him?"

Adam didn't see the picture at first among the dozens of photographs spread out on the table. But then Eileen plucked up a single Polaroid, and a knot formed in Adam's throat.

Robert Lancaster stood in three-quarters profile, gazing out over the green with his hands tucked into the pockets of an oversized gray wool coat, his scarf catching in the wind. There was no date on the photograph, no hint to who had taken it, and no seasonal indicator in the gray haze of the sky above Craigmar, but it was definitely him. Robert was young in this picture, maybe not yet twenty. His head of stick-straight blond hair hadn't begun to thin, and his cornflower eyes – Adam's eyes – were clear.

"Oh my God," Adam said, pinching the photograph tight between his fingers like a gust of wind might snatch it away.

"It is him, isn't it?" Eileen said.

"It's him," Adam said, eyes suddenly stinging. He blinked away the tears, more a physiological response to unexpectedly seeing his grandfather than an expression of sadness. "That's my grandad."

"He was here," Eileen said, squeezing Adam's bicep tight. That touch anchored Adam to reality, to the solid warmth of Eileen beside him, and he was grateful for it. "He was *here*, Adam. You were right."

"Yeah," Adam said, nodding and trying to keep his head. "But we still don't know *why* he was here, or for how long, or what he knew about Craigmar."

"He knew about the faeries. I feel it in my gut. My grandmother must have told him."

"Maybe," Adam conceded. "But I'd like more details, or at least a little more evidence."

"And there's time for that," Eileen said, dark eyes suddenly softer than Adam had yet seen them, softer than he thought possible. "But we don't have to rush. You can just enjoy this small win for now."

Eileen fell silent as they both gazed at the photograph, taking in every detail.

"He looks happy," Eileen said after a long while, and it was this simple statement that made a stray tear trickle down Adam's cheek. He swiped it away quickly with his fist, and Eileen, thankfully, didn't say anything about it.

"Can I keep this?" Adam asked. "I'll make sure it stays safe."

"Of course," Eileen said. "I'm happy you have this photograph, at least. And, for what it's worth, I'm glad you found your way here."

Adam looked at her, the chestnut highlights in her dark hair shining in the light falling through the windows, and allowed himself, for one moment, to feel that same happiness his grandfather must have felt discovering this place and its strange, lovely people for the first time.

"I am too," he said.

CHAPTER FOURTEEN

Nicola

Adam and Eileen stayed locked in the library for hours, chatting in excited voices about whatever was in those boxes. Nicola gave them their privacy, not wanting to insert herself too much in whatever shared quest they were on, but she poked her head in once to say hello and then again to bring in a tray of tea with honey, for which Eileen and Adam seemed grateful. Eileen called her "chickadee" when she thanked Nicola for her hot cup of Earl Grey, which made Nicola blush. At first, the avian pet names had felt dismissive, like Eileen was making fun of her, but they were quickly starting to feel affectionate.

After tea, Adam invited her to sit with them in front of the fire. Nicola brought her sketchbook with her, and drew the rolling hills outside the window while she warmed her bones. Her newest story was about a goblin, the littlest in his family, who wanted to go to school to learn arithmetic. The pastoral environs of Craigmar made for fitting scenery, and Nicola privately hoped that she could steal a little of Craigmar's enchantment to make her next book proposal irresistible to publishers.

Finley had become scarce, and even though Nicola knew he had chores to do and a life to live beyond that, she couldn't help but feel injured. She reacted poorly to perceived rejection – her therapist thought it had something to do with all that abandonment in childhood – but she still wondered how much of Finley's disappearance had to do with Eileen making a show of tightening his leash. She also wasn't pleased with Finley's failure to inform her that he was dating Eileen, quite seriously it seemed, but then again, she didn't think either of them had expected to share that all-consuming kiss by the ocean.

Finley reappeared late in the day, his curls damp with mist from the walk over from his cottage, to suggest that they all break for dinner. There was still some bread left over from the cave offering, and Nicola sat at the kitchen table eating a thick slice smeared with sweet butter while Finley and Eileen buzzed around preparing soup. It was wrenchingly tender, watching these two people who knew each other better than they knew themselves bicker about how much salt to use and laugh about how bad Eileen was at chopping carrots. It made Nicola a little jealous, having a front-row seat to such deep and abiding love. But there was also something deliciously warming about being brought into this intimate world, like a child safe in the embrace of her parents' love dozing in the backseat as they chatted and drove. Adam's presence made it even sweeter, as he sat with his knee touching hers running through possible timelines of his grandfather's visit to Craigmar in pencil on a napkin.

At one point, probably when he thought no one was looking, Finley leaned over to Eileen and bit her shoulder while she was stirring the soup. It was an affectionate bite, and he smiled when he did it, but it was still hard.

Nicola's stomach curled with lust at the sight, but then Finley was mincing parsley and the moment was over.

They all ate in companionable quiet, as though they had known each other for two years and not two days. Nicola kept having to swallow down emotion along with her soup, stirred up by the simple domesticity of the moment. She was doing it again, imprinting on people who barely knew her.

Nicola had always been desperate to hoard all the love in the world for herself, even to her detriment, or the annoyance of other people. She wanted to entice Adam into cuddling with her on the couch by the fire, even though that would make things weird between them, and she wanted to crawl between Eileen and Finley and sleep there, held in the matrix of their affection for each other, but that was wrong.

She needed to be normal, or at least act normal.

"Those dogs are going to have me up bright and early,"

Finley said after the dishes had been cleared and they had all finished the bread with a bit of jam for dessert. "I should get going."

"You letting Snug and Smoo run you ragged again?" Eileen teased. "I hope they aren't sick."

"No," Finley replied. "Snug's been having nightmares, if you can believe it. He'll cry and nose at the door until I let him sleep on the bed with me."

"Oh, to be loved the way a man loves a dog," Eileen said drolly.

In reply, Finley leaned down to kiss her goodbye, but Nicola caught the way his fingers threaded in her hair and tightened, just enough to sting pleasantly. The same way he had threaded his fingers through Nicola's hair just the day before.

Nicola squeezed her thighs together under the table and forced a smile as he left, giving a little wave for good measure.

"He's sort of gloomy, isn't he?" Adam asked when Finley had gone, not in an unfriendly way. "Just like, in general?"

"I don't mind," Eileen said with a chuckle. "Girls like that sort of thing. Isn't that right, Nicola?"

Nicola felt herself blush ferociously, and Eileen laughed brightly while Adam smirked at her, and for one shimmering moment, she felt loved so she could hardly stand it.

That night, as she lay in bed listening to the house

creak in the wind, she tried to memorize the feeling of soft down pillows beneath her head, her belly full of warm soup, the security of Adam sleeping just around the corner. There would be no telling when she felt this safe again, or this at home. She had learned to enjoy these little stolen moments whenever she could.

The next day, Nicola woke to the sound of a gunshot.

She scrambled out of bed to peer outside the windows, wondering if a hunter had wandered too close to the manor.

Instead she saw Eileen, dressed in riding boots and a linen blouse, pointing a long rifle into the sky.

Nicola tugged on her shoes and zipped her pink puffer over her nightdress, then hurried down the stairs and out the kitchen door, propelled by curiosity and no small amount of concern. As she rounded the house, she saw that Eileen stood next to a rusty mechanical contraption.

Eileen pulled a lever, and the machine hurled a spinning object high into the sky.

"Pull!" she shouted, as though there were anyone out here who might be hit.

The lord followed the arc of the object with the barrel of her rifle, the gun held high against her cheek and braced against her shoulder, and then fired with devastating accuracy.

The object shattered in midair.

Nicola wandered over, zipping her puffer up higher. Eileen caught sight of her and gave a victorious smile.

"Morning dovey!"

"Hi," Nicola said, resisting the urge to clamp her hands over her ears as Eileen swung the gun through the air and successfully broke another clay pigeon. There was something a little scary and a little thrilling about standing this close to the action. It was very similar to how she felt whenever she was in close quarters with Eileen, actually. "You're in high spirits."

"Nothing like bracing spring air to do the body good," Eileen said, lowering her gun and turning to face Nicola. Her eyes were bright, feverishly so, and there was an exerted bloom in her pale cheeks.

"Were you sick?" Nicola asked delicately. She couldn't help being curious.

"I'm always sick. That's the definition of chronic illness."

"Oh, I'm sorry."

"Why? It's just a fact of life, nothing for you or anyone else to be sorry for." Eileen squinted at Nicola, as though she were a target Eileen was sighting, and then she sighed, resigning herself to the truth. "I have chronic fatigue syndrome, endometriosis, asthma, and migraines besides. I am a veritable cocktail of ailments, and have been since adolescence. Some days are good, others aren't."

"Is today a good day?" Nicola asked.

Eileen grinned with all her teeth.

"Yes, thank Christ. I don't think I could take another afternoon caged up in my room. You and Adam caught me at a good time; I was bedridden the week before you arrived." Eileen proffered her gun to Nicola with one hand. "Do you want a turn?"

"I've never even seen a gun up close," Nicola said, shaking her head quickly. "I'm good."

"Oh, it's easy," Eileen said. "I'll show you. Stand here, in front of me. Feet shoulder width apart."

Nicola considered begging off with some excuse about having shaky hands, or being a pacifist, but Eileen's confidence was infectious. Besides, there was something appealing about holding a real gun, about the sensuality of the gunpowder smell in the air.

She stepped forward in the dewy grass and let Eileen place the rifle into her hands. It was surprisingly heavy and warm from Eileen's touch.

"The safety's on, so you don't have to worry about shooting anyone in the foot," Eileen said, adjusting the rifle in Nicola's grip. She was quick and efficient, correcting Nicola's posture as she went. "The trick is to not be afraid of the gun. There will be some kickback when you fire, but not enough to knock you on your arse."

Eileen moved behind her, pressing their bodies together, and Nicola was enveloped in Eileen's scent. She smelled like cracked peppercorn and pressed irises, and her long hair tickled the back of Nicola's neck as the lord helped her hoist the gun into the air.

"Trust the strength of your arms," Eileen murmured, her lips nearly brushing Nicola's overwarm earlobe. "Look down the barrel at that little bead near the mouth of the gun, that's your north star. And no matter what you do, don't take your eye off the target. You want to give the signal?"

"Pull!" Nicola called, feeling silly and exhilarated at the same time.

One of the clay pigeons flew into the sky, and Nicola obeyed Eileen's instructions, keeping her eye trained on the target as it spun through the air. A heartbeat passed, then two, then Eileen's finger slid down to curl around Nicola's and pull the trigger.

There was a loud bang, a kick of recoil that shoved Nicola back into Eileen, then, gloriously, the clay shattered in midair.

Eileen let out a triumphant whoop, then took the rifle back from Nicola and slung her arm around her shoulders in a tight hug. Nicola, whose brain felt a little fuzzy from all the close contact, could do little but hold on.

"Well done, well done!" Eileen said. "You're a natural."

Nicola understood Adam and Finley a little better right now, at least the way they hung on Eileen's every word.

"I didn't realize shooting lessons were included in Craigmar hospitality," someone said, and Nicola turned to find Finley leaning against a nearby tree, watching them both with a strange, hard glitter in his eyes.

"Want a go, Finney?" Eileen asked, thrusting the gun out to him.

"You know I don't like guns. Don't let her bully you

into taking up her hobbies, Nicola. Next thing you know she'll have you out with the hounds hunting hare."

It sounded like he was half joking, but Nicola balked at the idea of killing a real animal, especially the fat hares that she had spied hopping across the green from her bedroom window. Still, she was enjoying getting to know Eileen better without either of the boys around.

"I wanted to learn," Nicola said, the wind sweeping her short curls back from her face. She stuck her chin out imperiously, the way she did when she wanted the last word on something. Finley had barely spoken to her over the last day, despite the surface-level pleasantries at dinner. He didn't get to give her the cold shoulder and then show back up to boss her around.

Finley's frown deepened, but he said nothing more to Nicola. Instead, he turned to Eileen.

"Dr Dasgupta is going to be here in an hour, and he's going to wonder why you aren't in bed."

"And I'll tell him that I no longer need to be confined to my room."

"He ordered bedrest, Eileen."

"What does he know about what my body needs? Fresh air and exercise, that's the cure for what ails me."

"He's been your doctor since you were a child," Finley said flatly. "I think he knows a thing or two about what you need."

"Bah," Eileen muttered, and hoisted her gun back up against her shoulder. "I'd stand back, if I were you."

And with that, their conversation was over. Eileen went back to shooting her clay pigeons, and Nicola was left standing awkwardly with Finley, who was quietly fuming.

Nicola turned to him and opened her mouth to say something, anything, but then he just gave a curt nod and started away from her with his long strides.

Nicola jogged to catch up. If he ran, she would chase, at least until she was sure he didn't want to be caught.

"Did I do something wrong?" Nicola asked as she came up alongside him.

"I don't know what you mean," Finley said, not meeting her eyes. Nicola wanted to scream. First he stared at her like she was a gift from God, now he couldn't even be bothered to acknowledge her existence.

"You've been avoiding me."

"I've been busy."

"Well, you've also been rude," Nicola said, temper stirring inside her chest. "Listen, if I overstepped myself with that kiss, just say so. I don't want you angry with me. We've all got to get along out here."

Finley stopped suddenly and turned around, and she nearly collided with his broad chest. His hands came up to stabilize her shoulders.

"You think I'm angry with you?" he echoed.

"You've certainly been acting like it."

"Nicola." Finley swiped a hand over his face and made an anguished sound in the back of his throat. How was he even more gorgeous when he was miserable? "I'm not angry. You've done nothing wrong. I'm staying away from you because it's what's best for both of us. Nobody in this house needs any more complications."

"But what if I like complications?" Nicola asked, pushing up on her tiptoes just a little bit. It was so hard to rein herself in around Finley, especially when he had that tortured line between his brows.

"You're making this whole situation very hard on me," Finley said weakly, taking another step towards her as though their bodies were tethered together by an invisible thread that was slowly but surely pulling tighter.

"Is this about Eileen? Because if what you two have is exclusive, I'll respect that. I don't want to come between anyone."

"No, the boundaries of our relationship are . . . permeable. There have been others. For me, at least."

"Then maybe . . ." Nicola said, her heart fluttering in her throat. Careful. She needed to be careful. Come on too desperate, and he could cast her aside. "Maybe we can go for another walk sometime, you and me?"

"What about Adam?" Finley asked, and Nicola thrilled at the fact that he hadn't, exactly, said no to her.

"Adam isn't interested in me."

"I wouldn't be so sure about that."

Surprise bloomed in Nicola's chest, nearly knocking her backwards. Questions spilled out of her mouth like water from an underground spring.

"What do you mean? Did you talk to him? What did he say?"

"I've already said too much," Finley grumbled, turning from her and starting his walk back to the cottage.

Nicola jogged to catch up with him one more time, threading her arm through his so they were walking side by side. Finley looked down at the point of contact like it physically pained him, but he didn't pull away.

"Listen, Finley, I'm sorry for kissing you. I can be a little aggressive when I like someone, and I don't always think about the consequences."

"I like that you're aggressive," he said, with a rich darkness in his voice that made Nicola's heart beat even faster. "I like that you know what you want, and I like talking to you, and I like kissing you."

"Then what's the problem?" Nicola said quietly.

"You don't know what it's like dealing with me. The way I treat the people who get close to me . . . It isn't right."

If Finley was trying to turn her off the idea of getting close to him, he was doing a terrible job of it. Curiosity and desire flared in Nicola's chest, and it took all the restraint in her body not to beg him to show her exactly what he meant. She hadn't wanted someone the way she wanted Finley in a long time, and she was determined to have him, one way or another.

"You mean the way you treat Eileen?" Nicola asked, walking at a brisk clip. She realized, hilariously, that Finley wasn't actually going anywhere. They had simply circled the house and ended up right back where they started. "Not that it's any of my business, but Eileen seems to like it a lot, and so do you."

"You're a very determined person," Finley said, huffing out a sigh.

"I think it's one of my best qualities. Tell me to stop, and I'll stop."

"I don't want you to stop."

"Then can we at least try to be friends?" she asked. "I'm not asking for anything more than that right now."

"Friends I can agree to," Finley said, smiling back at her. It was unspeakably satisfying, getting him to crack a smile.

"The doctor will be here soon," Finley said, glancing back at the house. "I should get going. But thank you for coming after me. I'm not used to being the one who gets pursued. It . . . feels good."

"You're fun to pursue," Nicola said with a coquettish smile. "But I'm pretty fun to chase down too."

Finley parted his lips to say something more, but then he just gave another one of those short nods and disappeared into the house. Nicola was left feeling bubbly and victorious, like she was a bottle of New Year's champagne. The wind toyed with the curls at the nape of her neck, and it almost felt like the brush of a lover's fingers.

Then, the strangest sensation that she was being watched crept in. Nicola turned to face the trees that crowded up against the little cottage, but there was nothing there. She shuddered despite the spring sun breaking through the clouds overhead, then started her walk back to the house.

CHAPTER FIFTEEN

Finley

As far as Finley's memory reached back in time, there was Eileen. Eileen peering down at him through the bannisters as their fathers discussed lambing season while Finley, feeling much younger than ten, worried he might be turned out of the house at any moment for tracking mud on the rugs. Eileen on his thirteenth birthday, throwing stones at his bedroom window to tempt him outdoors to play a cutthroat game of cribbage on a blanket spread out on the grass. Eileen at fifteen, panting and ferocious beneath him after he chased her down and knocked her to the marshy ground for intentionally spilling coffee all over his only nice sweater. She had been angry with him for something, Finley didn't remember what. All he remembered was the way her pulse pounded in her wrists as he pinned them over her head.

She had thrown her head back and laughed at the sky, euphoric despite the mud seeping into her dress. She was wind-bitten and wild, more animal than girl, glaring at him with glittering eyes. She had dared him to touch her, dared him to kiss her, and when Finley had sharply bitten her bottom lip instead, she had let out a moan that destroyed any resolve Finley had left.

They had made love quickly, devouring each other even as a light mist began to fall. Finley had been equal parts intoxicated and terrified – of Eileen, of her cruelty, and most of all, of how his own cruelty came awake in response. He had tried to be gentle, to slow down, but every time he drew away, Eileen dug her sharp half-moon nails into his back and begged him not to stop.

Afterwards, Eileen was left with blood on her thighs and tangles in her hair, and Finley was left feeling all at once emptied and full, excruciatingly aware that now they had begun this, there would be no end to it, not ever.

Now there was only Finley and Eileen, a two-headed hare, stretching on into eternity.

They had been born days apart, Finley in the run-down county hospital at a healthy eight pounds, and Eileen in her parents' room in the big house, wailing and pale and prematurely sick even then. It was as though they couldn't bear to be parted for a single moment of their lives, as though even in the womb, they knew they were meant for each other. It was as though every gulp of cold air in a world in which the other had not entered burned like poison, and Eileen, who had never been one for waiting, or for kindness, had nearly killed her mother by coming early to the birthing bed.

Jennifer Kirkfoyle had forgiven her daughter the moment Eileen was put into her arms, but Eileen had never forgiven the world. Not for separating her by the circumstance of her birth from Finley, who she adored to the point of sacrilege, and not, Finley thought some days, for the injustice of being born at all.

"What's the prognosis?" Eileen asked, holding still as a statue for her blood draw. Dr Dasgupta looked a bit put out with her, but he had been put out with her since she was a teenager, and Eileen didn't seem too worried about it. She was draped across a chaise longue in the small, dim parlor, surrounded by her board games and decks of cards. Finley had only turned on one lamp, hoping to spare her from another migraine spike.

"You aren't dying, but you do need to be more careful," the doctor said, in his posh London accent with a hint of Bangladesh. Dr Dasgupta had known her since she was a skinned-kneed child who spent her days chasing Finley around the grounds, and he had never once called her "sir". "You need to give yourself more time to recoup from your bad days. If you keep pushing yourself like this, you're never going to fully recover."

"I'm never going to fully recover anyway," Eileen said, wincing a bit as the doctor removed his needle from her arm. "So why handle myself with kid gloves?"

Dr Dasgupta's frown deepened. He had grown a mustache after his marriage last year, and the facial hair made him look even more serious than usual.

"That's no kind of attitude to take. There are people in your life that care about you and want to see you as well as you can be."

The doctor's eyes cut over to Finley, and Finley dropped his gaze. There was no need to shrink from Dasgupta, and certainly no need to pretend that Finley and Eileen hadn't been carrying on together for ages. Dasgupta had known about their dalliance before anyone in Eileen's own family: he had discreetly prescribed her birth control pills before realizing she had no need of them. Still, Finley had never been entirely comfortable around the other man. And it wasn't because the doctor was unkind, or because he was judgmental.

It was because he saw Finley and Eileen exactly as they were, not two star-crossed lovers from a chivalric tale, but two troubled young people who could neither stop hurting each other nor walk away from each other.

Finley had only been to church a few times as a boy, before his Catholic mother ran off with her traveling guitarist, but looking at Dr Dasgupta made him feel the same way looking at the priest had: like he was too recognized, too known in all his shortcomings.

"Can you give me anything else for the migraines?" Eileen asked.

"Nothing more than what I've already given you," he said, carefully slotting her vials of dark blood into his well-loved leather bag. "Your best medicine is sleep, and limiting your stress, especially during menstruation, and avoiding alcohol."

"Well, none of that is likely," Eileen muttered.

The doctor swept his hand over his hair, always perfectly slicked back with fragrant pomade, and took a careful breath.

"Listen to me, Eileen. I promised your father I would always look after you, as your doctor if not as your friend. I know you think I live to lecture you, but I'm only worried. Your immune system can't withstand these long nights and rainy walks outdoors. You're in delicate health and—"

"We're done here," Eileen said, hauling herself up out of her chaise. Her gaze was shuttered, and Finley knew that look well. There would be no reasoning with her on this, at least for a while. "Run your tests and send me your reports. Meanwhile, I will continue to live my life."

Gregory Dasgupta and the late James Kirkfoyle had been university chums, and the doctor had been one of the only consistently present adults in Eileen's life after her parents' death. After the accident, she had been shuttled between various tutors, therapists and specialists, but she was always delivered back to Dr Dasgupta when all was said and done.

Finley worried that sometimes, it was that very devotion

that made her hostile towards the doctor. Eileen always had trouble trusting people who stuck around her for too long.

Dr Dasgupta shook his head, beginning to pack all his supplies back into his case.

"Either you can choose to rest or your body will make you," he said. "That's all I have to say."

"Noted," Eileen said, retrieving a fat cigar from her front vest pocket and clipping off the end with a tiny golden guillotine. Finley could have killed her. She barely smoked, certainly not cigars, and he was positive she had produced this prop simply to drive her doctor insane. She stuck the cigar in her mouth and dramatically rifled through her pockets. "Got a light?"

The doctor rolled his eyes.

"I'll see you next month," he said, putting on his hat and moving towards the door. "In the meanwhile, try not to get yourself killed."

He nodded at Finley as he passed, and Finley nodded back. They didn't speak much during the doctor's home visits, but Finley had his number. He had texted Dasgupta countless times when Eileen was up in the middle of the night throwing up from period pains, or laid up with a migraine so bad she could only tolerate total darkness. Dasgupta always texted back promptly, and he always asked if Finley needed any help or anyone to listen.

Eileen waited until Dasgupta was back in his car and backing down the drive to abandon her cigar in a nearby box, along with five others that hadn't even been unwrapped.

"Have you ever considered being cooperative with him?" Finley asked, arms crossed as he leaned against the doorframe. "It might help things."

"Irritating dear old Gregory is one of my great pleasures in this life," Eileen said, holding an arm out to Finley and beckoning him over to the settee. "Speaking of pleasures . . ."

"No," Finley said: crisp, succinct, a little mean. He liked to pretend that it was Eileen who got off on trading power and Finley who got off on trading pain, but there was an undeniable joy in telling her no and watching her fume about it. He liked knowing he had that power over her, at least. "I'm not rewarding you for bad behavior."

"When have I ever been bad?"

"Every day of your life."

"Come on, Finney. I'm trying to be sweet."

Finley settled down onto the settee and nodded at the ground. Eileen, who knew protocol well enough even if she didn't always abide by it, dropped to her knees beside him.

"You've been avoiding me all day," she said, unable to keep a little of the petulance out of her voice.

This was not going to be a tender reunion, Finley decided. If Eileen wanted to touch him so badly it would be on his terms and for his pleasure only.

"Show me how much you missed me, then," Finley said, leaning his temple against his fist as he watched her unbutton his fly. Eileen wrapped her fingers around his cock, stirring him to life.

"Mouth," Finley ordered. "Slowly."

Eileen did as she was told and wrapped her lips around the head, making Finley's breath catch in his throat. He suppressed a small gasp, not wanting to give Eileen the satisfaction of getting to him so soon. It was better for both of them if he pretended he didn't have a hair trigger when it came to Eileen.

She worked all the way down to the base, pushing herself until her eyes watered, and applied just the right amount of pressure with her tongue.

"Pace yourself," Finley said, threading his fingers through her hair. "You're liable to be down there a while."

Eileen groaned despite her full mouth. Cockwarming was one of Finley's favorite punishments, as it was something he enjoyed immensely that frustrated Eileen no end. The ache in her jaw by the end and the spoiled satisfaction of keeping every stitch of her clothes on and being forbidden even from touching herself was usually enough to set her straight.

Eileen forced herself to slow down, breathing through her nose as she dragged her tongue up and down, swirling in circles around his cock. Finley spread his legs further, slotting his fingers through Eileen's hair and rubbing an encouraging circle at the nape of her neck with his thumb. He took one shaky breath, then slid right back into the rhythm of silent togetherness that formed the foundation of his relationship with Eileen.

Sex was a threaded needle that stitched them together, bone to bone. The instant it had become available to them, they had used it to make promises to each other, to tease each other, to unify after arguments, and of course, to torture each other in a hundred tiny ways. When Finley was sure of nothing else, he was sure of Eileen. He was sure she wanted him, and he was sure he wanted her.

"You've been spending plenty of your time with the Americans," Finley said, smoothing her hair back from her brow as she bobbed her head up and down, agonizingly slow. Any faster and he would yank, forcing her to soften her mouth, pause, and start from the beginning again. "Maybe I don't like watching you making doe eyes at Adam and falling all over yourself whenever Nicola smiles at you."

"Who can account for the whims of the flesh?" she said, coming up briefly for air.

"Whim of your flesh?" Finley asked, capturing her by the chin and pulling her away from her studious work. "Or whim or your heart?"

"Don't get jealous on me, old man. You know I don't go in for that. I thought you didn't either."

"Maybe I'm jealous," Finley said, wiping away the slick from her plush lower lip with his thumb. "Or maybe I'm the only one exercising caution here. Have you thought of that?"

"I have everything in hand."

"Everything? Even Adam? What makes you think you

can possibly get him to agree to what you have in mind? He's no idiot, Isla. He'll riddle it out in time."

Eileen rolled her eyes and wrapped her fingers around Finley's length. Finley opened his mouth to snap out a warning, but then he let out a distinctly helpless groan as she squeezed.

"Take me to bed," Eileen said, suddenly insistent. "I can't stand it. Look, I'm begging."

"You're awful."

"I'm liable to be worse if you don't fuck me expeditiously."

Finley looked into her eyes for a long moment, a muscle in his jaw tightening and untightening.

"Say please," he said eventually, his voice quiet. Somehow, they always ended up here. Somehow, no matter how much Eileen gave of herself, no matter how much flesh she offered up to be bruised or how many acts of service she carried out, Finley always ended up sounding like the one begging.

For a scrap of humanity from his beloved, for a tiny concession of sweetness.

Finley often wondered who really held the reins in this relationship: Finley with his command words and leather toys and strict expectations, or Eileen, with all the money and status in the world dripping like silk through her fingers. The boy with a sadistic streak, or the girl who refused to be denied anything.

"Please," Eileen bit out. Nasty and short, like a child

shaking hands with the schoolyard foe who had bested them at jacks.

Finley wordlessly wrapped his hand around the nape of her neck and tugged her onto the settee like a kitten by the scruff. Then he covered her with his body and gave into her entirely.

CHAPTER SIXTEEN

Adam

Life at Craigmar was idyllic, a watercolor blur like something out of one of Nicola's paintings. Adam and Nicola took their breakfast with Eileen and Finley every morning, and one breakfast turned to two turned to four, until Adam realized that he had been at Craigmar nearly a week without even noticing.

They all chatted in a friendly manner as they buttered their toast and sweetened their porridge with a drizzle of honey (Nicola) or a tot of whisky (Eileen), going over findings from the night before. Adam spent his days exploring the grounds, answering emails from one of the window nooks in the house, or, most often, poring over records with Eileen in the library. They had gone through all the letters and photographs and had moved on to legal documents, just in case there was a clue. Nicola often sat in the library as they worked, wetting her paintbrush thoughtfully before dabbing watercolors into her sketchbook.

Finley, in a display of chivalry that Adam wished he had thought of first, had picked up Nicola a simple but serviceable set of paints and three brushes from town. Nicola had beamed at him, kissing him on the cheek very close to his mouth, and Adam had seethed from his seat on the couch. But then Eileen had leaned over his shoulder from behind the couch, her cheek very close to his as she asked if he would like to take a closer look at some land grants with her, and Adam had taken petty comfort in that.

Finley was spending more of his time in the house these days, often dropping in once his chores were done to provide aid in sorting papers in the library, or to fix a quick meal in the kitchen to keep them going long into the night. Adam was pleased to see that, when they weren't playacting master and servant, Finley and Eileen split household tasks more or less equally. He might not be entirely sold on Finley, and he might not be a fan of how close Finley seemed to be getting to Nicola, but that didn't mean he wanted to see Eileen mistreat him.

On the sixth night at Craigmar, they were all together in the library at nearly midnight, conversation having long since lulled into a comfortable quiet broken only by the crackle and pop of the fire. Adam was color-grading a website header for a client on his laptop as Nicola dozed next to him on the couch, curled up with her stockinged feet in his lap, a book of pastoral poems forgotten on her knee. Finley busied himself at the bar cart, fixing them all a nightcap before they went their separate ways, while Eileen sat at the desk, chin balanced on her latticed fingers as she squinted down at some of her grandmother's old letters.

It felt normal. Comfortable even.

Adam caught himself in the moment of hopeful longing, smothering it back down under a landslide of rationality. This might feel comfortable, but in a month, it would be nothing more than a story to tell at the bar to get free drinks. Eileen would forget about him, and Finley would forget about him (and Nicola, Adam hoped). Nicola and he would go back to the way things were, back to group hangs over horror movies and pickup volleyball and an ironclad, unspoken agreement to never pursue anything more.

Still, a treacherous part of him wanted to luxuriate in this moment, Nicola half asleep beside him, her cheeks pink and perfect in the warmth of the fire. He considered reaching out to sweep a stray curl out of her face, but just as he was building up the courage, Finley said, "Take a break, Eileen. We'll all have a drink, and then you need to go to bed."

"I'm fine," Eileen said, stifling a yawn. Her eyes were rimmed with red.

"I said, take a break," Finley repeated. His warning tone left no room for argument.

Adam glanced up surreptitiously from his laptop and found that Nicola was sneaking a glance at him too, the same look they had shared countless times that said they would be gossiping later. Eileen and Finley didn't exactly hide their dynamic from Adam and Nicola, and Adam had seen it in action at least once before, but Finley usually resisted the urge to boss his employer around when Adam and Nicola were present.

"Come off it, Finney," Eileen said with a scoff, accepting her drink from his hand and taking a bracing swallow.

"Up," Finley said. "You're hunched over that desk like a prawn. At least sit on the couch while you have your drink."

"I'm fine—"

"Now, Eileen. Make me tell you twice and I'll have you on your knees for an hour."

Eileen scowled at him for a long, agonizingly tense moment. Adam was sure she was going to dress him down, maybe even make him leave the house and go back to the cottage. But then she snatched up her Scotch and soda and seated herself in the armchair across from Adam. She didn't look pleased about it, but she had obeyed. It was as though Finley had tugged on a single thread and shifted the balance of power in the room, without so much as raising his voice.

Finley finished fixing Nicola a brandy neat and Adam a gin and tonic, then nodded at Eileen.

"Will you let me take down your hair?"

It didn't sound quite like a command. It sounded more

like an invitation, but to what, Adam wasn't sure. Still, it was a little harder to breathe while Eileen deliberated, and when Adam stole another glance at Nicola, her cheeks were even pinker.

Was she turned on by whatever was going on between Eileen and Finley? Hell, was Adam? It seemed impossible – there was nothing sexual going on – but his body told a different story.

Eileen nodded, then slipped down from the couch and settled onto the ground, tucking her legs beneath her to maintain ramrod posture. Finley sat on the couch and began to unfasten the gold pins from her hair, taking his time, as though they were the only two people in the world. With more gentleness than his calloused hands would suggest, Finley began to finger-comb out her dark waves and plait them into a sleeping braid, and Eileen, glory of glories, *let him.*

Adam couldn't stop staring at Eileen, sitting perfectly still with her swan-like neck bowed. There was something painfully beautiful about seeing her so . . . pliant. Eileen was a wildfire of a woman, but it appeared Finley's touch could tame her into a docile hearth.

Adam wasn't exactly hurting for sexual experience. He liked getting to know people through sex, and he would try pretty much anything at least once. But nothing had ever made him feel as alive as he felt right now, watching Finley braid Eileen's hair, not even his first time with a girl, or with a boy.

Nothing had made him wonder if perhaps he would like to be the one in the chair, giving out commands, or if he would enjoy being the one sitting on the floor, waiting with bated breath to be led.

"I have a question," he blurted.

"Of course you do," Eileen replied, rolling her eyes without slouching so much as an inch. "You're practically made of questions."

"Be nice," Finley ordered, giving one of her tresses a tug.

Nicola closed her book on the couch next to Adam, a little *thud* that signaled Finley had her total attention.

"How long has this . . ." Adam said, gesturing broadly at whatever was happening between Eileen and Finley. He wished he had better words for it, or at least words that didn't make him feel stupid. ". . . dynamic been going on? If it's not rude to ask."

"From the start in some ways, I suppose," Finley said, hands deftly wrapping strand over strand. "Only for the last couple of years, in others. The structure of it, the rules and boundaries, we talk and agree on together. But the nature of the thing . . . that has a life of its own. That's older."

Eileen closed her eyes, letting the conversation wash over her as Finley expertly braided her hair. Adam had never seen her so soft. It was like she was one of Nicola's brightly colored paints, diffused by Finley's touch as though it was water.

"How did you learn?" Adam went on. He was nothing if not a student of life, after all. This was just a bit of harmless sociological curiosity.

"To take care of her like this? Some of it's through instinct," Finley said, holding out a hand for the hair tie around Eileen's wrist. "Some of it's research. I'll remind you I do have access to the internet, Adam. I might be a hick, but I can read."

Heat coursed through Adam, and not just from arousal this time. Why did the embarrassment just excite him more? If he wasn't careful, he would get hard, which would only embarrass him more, which would only make everything worse.

"I didn't mean—"

"I'm kidding," Finley said with a smile. "Lighten up."

"Okay then, answer my question."

"Pushy," Finley said, like he didn't approve of Adam's behavior, like he might have an idea or two about how to correct it, and now Adam *was* hard, so hard that he shifted the laptop on his thighs to cover the evidence. "Ideally, in situations like this, you'd want to find a mentor to teach you. But Eileen and I didn't have that luxury."

"Could you teach someone else?" Nicola asked.

Every eye in the room fell on Nicola, Finley and Adam staring at her like she was on fire, Eileen acknowledging her with impressed raised eyebrows. Nicola just shrugged, refusing to feel awkward. You couldn't make Nicola feel a damn thing she didn't want to.

"I've never tried," Finley managed eventually. "Are you . . . asking me to show you?"

"Or you could show Adam and I could watch?" Nicola suggested, with that pixie smile that was sweet and sharp at once. "I learn best by watching."

Adam wanted, perhaps more than ever in his life, to play it cool. Instead, he spluttered, "What? Obviously, like— No way! I wouldn't, like, unless—"

"Never mind," Nicola said, picking up her book and opening it up to a random page as though she were actually reading it. "It was just an idea. Adam, if you aren't up for it—"

"I'm up for it," Adam snapped. Was he totally terrified of what a kink lesson from Finley might entail? Sure. Was he going to back down now, when Nicola was clearly trying to get a rise out of him? Absolutely not.

"It isn't up to Adam," Finley said, directed at Nicola. He spoke to her sternly, like she was his to command, and Nicola snapped her mouth shut as though Finley had just gagged her. "It's up to Eileen."

Finley leaned down and began talking to Eileen in a low, quick voice, the words impossible to make out. Eileen nodded and responded back in a whisper, gazing up at him.

Then Finley nodded and said, "Eileen sleeps better after a scene anyway. I can show you a wee something, nothing inappropriate, if she's willing to demonstrate. Does that sound all right?"

"Yeah," Adam said, voice too bright, too eager. He hadn't even known he had wanted this, but now, it was searingly obvious to him that he had been thinking about nothing but this since that first night at Craigmar.

"Stay on the ground," Finley said to Eileen, pressing two fingers into her shoulder in a way that seemed deliberate, like some kind of code. "Adam, will you stand up?"

Adam did as he was told, and Finley held out a hand to him, helping him to his feet. It was only a moment of contact, but it was unexpected, and Finley's fingers were still warm from trailing through Eileen's silky hair. That instant of touch made it harder to breathe.

What the *fuck* was he doing?

Nicola tossed her book aside and leaned forward, studying the scene-in-progress with an academic's eye. Or it would have been academic, were it not for the peaks of her nipples through her thin shirt.

Adam came to a stop six feet in front of Eileen, and Finley pressed a hand between Adam's shoulder blades, straightening his spine. He was slouching, just like always.

"Feet shoulder width apart," Finley said. "You're in charge here, so stand like it."

Adam didn't even have a pithy quip to offer in response. It was so easy to do what he was told, when Finley spoke to him like that.

"Isla," Finley said, using that pet name that Adam had come to suspect carried the same weight as any formal kink diminutive. "Crawl."

Eileen crawled. Hands and knees, nice and slow, before she came to rest sitting back on her heels in front of him. She only crossed a short distance, but those seconds stretched on into eternity. She looked up at Adam, no doubt parsing the wild panic in his eyes, and gave him a mean little smirk, like he wasn't man enough to handle her. Then, as though remembering her manners, she dropped her eyes to the floor.

Finley clapped Adam on the shoulder, then took his seat.

"You're in charge now," Finley said, gesturing broadly at Eileen as if Adam would have any idea what to do with her. "Go ahead."

This had sounded fun ten seconds ago; now, Adam sort of wanted to die. He felt horribly, searingly alive, but he also sort of wanted to die.

"What do I do?" he asked.

"Whatever you want to do," Finley said, like he was telling Adam to hurry up and pick a beer at the pub, not decide how to handle Finley's girlfriend, who also happened to be housing and feeding Adam and Nicola. "Don't get too handsy, obviously, this is just a dry run in case you want to do something like this in the future with someone else. The point is to get comfortable being in control. So. What do you want to do?"

"I want to do . . . what she wants me to do?"

"That's very service top of you," Finley said with a smile that edged right up against patronizing, sparking that instinct in Adam to get physical with Finley in a way that was becoming more and more confusing with each passing day, "but the impetus is wrong. What Eileen wants – I can promise you this – is for you to enact your own will on her. She wants you to make good use of her, in whatever way pleases you best. Isn't that right, Isla?"

Eileen glowed in the light of the fire, especially when she looked back to nod at Finley, eyes shining with perfect trust. This, Adam realized in a lightning bolt of insight from heaven, was not about him. It wasn't even about Nicola, who was watching them with puerile delight. It was about Eileen, surrendering herself to another man at Finley's request, and Finley, holding her in safety and love without even touching her. It was a trust exercise between them, just another game, with Adam functioning as nothing more and nothing less than a piece on the board.

It should have been insulting, to realize they were both manipulating him for their own inscrutable pleasure.

Instead, Adam had never been harder.

"What if she doesn't like what I do?" Adam asked, swallowing through a dry throat.

"Eileen likes having her boundaries pushed," Finley responded. "And if you do something she really doesn't like, she'll use her safeword. What's your word, Isla?"

"Geranium," she said obediently.

Adam flexed and unflexed his hands at his side for a long moment. Then he reached out and very gently tipped Eileen's chin up with his fingers. He expected her to resist, or maybe even burst out laughing, revealing that this was an elaborate prank. But instead, she obeyed, exposing her pale throat and the thrumming pulse in her neck. Adam barely had to apply any pressure.

Finley made an approving sound from the couch but said nothing. That sound, little more than a rumbling hum, dropped right into the pit of Adam's stomach. Moving of their own accord, Adam's fingers trailed slowly up Eileen's chin, coming to brush against her lips.

All he wanted was to touch her right there, very softly, on that mouth the color of a rosebud. He just wanted to brush his index finger over her lower lip and memorize the sensation so he could turn it over again and again in his dirtiest late-night fantasies. But then Eileen did the unthinkable.

She parted her lips, wrapped them around his index finger, and sucked. Adam heard a sharp inhale as she did so, and he was so delirious with lust and that new, strange, tight feeling in his chest that flared up whenever Finley told him what to do, that it took him a second to realize it was Nicola who had gasped.

"Does her mouth feel good?" Finley asked, and there was no *way* he wasn't getting off on this too. There was no way everyone in this room didn't know exactly what they were doing.

In response, Adam slipped his middle finger into Eileen's mouth too, making her moan with delight. The sound vibrated through his palm as he stroked in and out of her mouth, once and then twice. He used his thumb to smear saliva over her lips, leaving them shining and wet. Then he pushed in again, deeper this time, all the way to the back of her throat.

It was a mindless impulse, and it took him a moment to realize exactly what it was he wanted from her, apart from the obvious thrill of the sensation of her tongue.

He wanted her undone, he realized with a kick through his cock. He wanted her gasping and ruined.

"Very nice," Finley said, and Adam wondered if he could come like this, his fingers in Eileen's mouth, Finley's rich, dark voice praising them both.

Adam had no idea what was going to happen next. Even though he was supposedly in control of this scene, as Finley had called it, he felt totally helpless against the riptide that was gathering and pulling them all under.

But then he glanced over Eileen's shoulder and saw something that made him surface from the dark waves with a bruised noise, somewhere between a gasp and a groan.

"What is it?" Nicola asked, already on her feet. The haze of the scene dissolved around them as Nicola came up behind him and put her hand on his shoulder. Eileen rose to her feet, a little unsteady, her pupils blown and her mouth wet, but herself once again. Even Finley was up in an instant, eyebrows drawn together in worry.

Adam stared at the small framed photo on the gallery wall behind Eileen, the one he had looked past a dozen times before. It was a photograph of Eileen's grandmother at

Christmas, school-aged, beaming, with her dark hair in curls and a porcelain doll hugged to her chest. The background was blurry, but there was something there in the corner of the image that knocked the wind from Adam's lungs.

It was a little boy off to the far right, lifting up his hand to grasp at a bulbous ornament on the mammoth Christmas tree. He must have been eight or nine, and he might have been some child of a houseguest, except it was impossible not to notice the exceptionally fair hair, the strong nose, and the cornflower-blue eyes that Adam saw every time he looked in the mirror.

Eileen followed his line of sight, identified the photograph, and then strode over with all the determination fitting her station. She plucked the picture from the wall and, upon realizing it was stapled shut on the back, whacked the photo against the edge of her father's desk to crack the frame. Then, sliding the weathered photo from the mess of shattered wood and broken glass, Eileen held it up to the light.

Adam pressed in beside her, Finley and Nicola close behind. It was the nearest they had all been to each other, huddling around a picture to identify a ghost from the past.

Eileen turned the photo over. On the back, in spindly antiquated script, someone had written: *Arabella and Robbie, Christmas Eve, 1970.*

CHAPTER SEVENTEEN

Robert

Robert pushed up on his toes to reach the Christmas ornament, tantalizingly just out of his reach. It was the sort of blue he only saw on the gleaming heads of the mallard ducks who paddled in the nearby loch. He was so close, close enough that the tips of his fingers gently brushed the rough stripe of silver glitter latticed over the cold glass. He had thought about asking his mother to help him reach it, but he wanted to do it himself. Besides, she was distracted talking to one of her friends with a full glass of eggnog in her hand. He would only bother her.

"Cheeeeese!" Arabella sang, offering a big smile to the photographer. Once the camera clicked and the photographer gave her a thumbs-up, she stumbled backwards in satisfied delight, right into Robert.

Robert jostled into the tree and the ornament crashed

to the ground, where it shattered into a hundred tiny pieces.

"Oh!" Arabella said in distress. "I'm sorry, Robbie, I—"

"*Robert.*"

Robert tensed up as his father strode over, his lips pursed in disapproval beneath his mustache. Robert was usually good at keeping track of wherever his father was in the house, even having memorized the sound of his footfalls, but now, he appeared out of nowhere. Robert loved his father very much and he never wanted to upset him, but he was also a little bit afraid of him, which is how the minister had said children ought to feel about their parents.

"Daddy, he didn't mean to," Arabella said, puffing out her chest like a little gorilla wearing hair ribbons. "I fell into him, and he just—"

"Let him take responsibility for his own actions," their father said. He hadn't raised his voice, but then again, he never had to for Robert to be devastated. "Robbie, did you break that ornament?"

"Yes," Robert said, bringing his thumb to his mouth before remembering that, at eight, he was far too old to be sucking on his thumb.

"You'll clean it up, then. Arabella, go get the broom and the dustpan from the kitchen."

Robert waited for his sister to rush down the hallway before he spoke.

"I'm sorry," he said, lip wobbling.

"Hey now," his father said, a little more gently as he clasped Robert's shoulder in his big hand. "No need to go to pieces over an accident, all right? Men fix what they break, they don't cry about it."

"All right," Robert said, swallowing down the tears. "I only wanted to hold it."

"They're just glass and glitter, Robbie, that's all. Clean this up and I'll get you something better."

"All right," Robert repeated as his sister appeared with the broom.

He dutifully swept up the shattered glass, not missing a single piece, even kneeling down to sweep under the tree skirt for good measure. The party swirled on around him, without anyone taking much notice of a child doing penance over something as silly as an ornament. Still, his face burned with embarrassment. He wanted so badly to be good, but he always ended up doing something wrong anyway.

"There we are," his father said, taking the dustpan and broom from Robert's small hands as soon as the cleaning, which felt like it had gone on for an eternity, was done. "Mind your footing better next time, eh? And Belle, don't jostle your brother like that. He's littler than you. You'll knock him over."

"All right!" Arabella chirped, then ran off to go crawl into their mother's lap and steal a sip of eggnog. Their mother welcomed her without missing a beat, smoothing her hair as she continued to gossip with her friends.

There were fewer people at the party this year, Robert noticed, and there had been fewer people last year than the year before that. Did the grown-ups not want to drive out to the big house from the cities any more? Or were his parents simply not as well liked as they once had been?

"I promised you something better, didn't I?" his father asked. He was a tall, broad man, with wide shoulders and a square jaw and a gut. Robert, who was short for his age and scrawny besides, wondered if he would ever grow up to be so strong.

"You did," Robert said, hope coming to life in his chest.

His father pointed with the broom to one of the countless presents under the tree, a hefty rectangular box wrapped in gold-foiled scarlet paper and decorated with a velvet bow.

"That one's for you."

"But it's not Christmas yet," Robert said, confused and scandalized and thrilled all at the same time.

"Christmas Eve is close enough," his father said, giving him a conspiratorial wink. "Go on. Open it up."

Robert didn't have to be told twice. He set upon the present with frenzied enthusiasm, tearing away the wrapping and tugging off the lid until he discovered, with a squeal of delight, that there was a teddy bear inside. Robbie clutched his newest friend to his chest, relishing in its softness. The fur was caramel-colored and curly, and it looked just like the one in the shop window he had seen when his father took him along on a business trip to Glasgow.

"He's mine?" Robert asked, grinning wide as could be.

"He's yours," his father said, reaching down to ruffle his blond hair. His sister and his parents all had dark hair. Whenever people got confused his father always quickly corrected them, saying that Robert was adopted and just as much a part of their family as Arabella was. "Make sure you give him a proper name. Now go on enjoy the rest of the party."

Robert did enjoy the rest of the party, very much, even when Arabella cheated at jacks and their mother took her side in the dispute. He kept enjoying himself as the adults began to wrap themselves in coats and furs and make lingering goodbyes in the foyer while the cars warmed up outside. He was still enjoying himself as his eyes began to droop, and as he perched himself at the top of the stairs to wait for Arabella to come up to bed. There was no point in trying to sleep when she would be going through her noisy girlish bedtime rituals next door, tossing her hairpins into a ceramic dish and kicking her shoes across the room. Besides, he wanted to hug her goodnight. Robert finger-combed his teddy's curly fur as he waited. He hadn't let go of the bear, whom he had decided to name Tammany – Tam for short – all night long.

His mother drifted by downstairs, removing her earrings with a sigh. His father appeared moments later, and stopped behind her to loop an arm around her waist and kiss her shoulder. Robert was mostly hidden by the banister from this angle, and he didn't think they could see him. His parents talked in low voices, murmuring to each other, until his father pulled away and said, loud enough for Robert to hear. "He'll adjust. He just needs time."

"It's been six years," his mother responded. "I worry he won't adjust, not completely."

"The agency said that happens sometimes. He's his own person, and there's nothing wrong with that. He's bright, and he adores Arabella. Would you rather we be raising a child with nothing between his ears?"

Robert froze with his thumb in his mouth, a jolt of guilt shooting through his stomach. Were they talking about him? Were they mad at him?

"I know you love him as much as I do," his mother said with a sigh. "I just feel guilty some days. It isn't fair of us, to trap another woman's child out here."

"That woman could barely take care of herself, let alone a little boy," Robert's father said, with a sharpness in his voice Robert only heard when he talked about Catholics, or criminals. "We did him a good turn. A sibling was all Belle wanted, and it was the one thing we couldn't give her, for all our trying."

Robert's mother fell silent, wrapping her pashmina tighter around her shoulders. She sniffled, and Robert's father strode forward to enfold her in his arms.

"I've never blamed you for any of it," he said softly,

almost too softly for Robert to hear. "You know that. We're all doing the best we can. Let's go upstairs and put the little ones to bed. It's been a long day."

Robert scrambled up as quietly as he could and tiptoed down the hallway to his room, just managing not to get caught. He yanked off his trousers and pressed shirt and tiny bow tie, then shrugged on an oversized sleep shirt before clambering into bed.

He lay there in the dark, surrounded by wooden trains and countless adventure books, his new teddy bear clutched to his chest, but despite all his toys and the rustling of his parents' feet just beyond his door, he felt like the loneliest boy in the world.

CHAPTER EIGHTEEN

Nicola

Nicola's ears rang as she watched Adam and Eileen and Finley stand shoulder to shoulder at the desk, volleying theories back and forth as they peered down at the photograph. Eileen had her palm pressed between Adam's shoulder blades, leaning in close to speak in a low, urgent voice. Like she had known him all her life, like they were just as close as Adam and Nicola were.

The hothouse haze of Finley's lesson moments before had evaporated, sacrificed to more pressing matters. Nicola couldn't help but feel like she had been forgotten.

"That's got to be your grandfather," Eileen said. "The name's the same, and he's the spitting image of you."

"I always thought he spent time at Craigmar when he was older," Adam said, eyes bright with the thrill of discovery.

"And maybe that's the case," Eileen went on. "But we can't discount the possibility that he might also have grown up here."

"He could have visited Craigmar one Christmas when he was a boy," Nicola said weakly, although she knew in the pit of her stomach that it wasn't true. She knew exactly what was unfolding here, and she knew exactly what it would do to her friendship with Adam. Wrapped up in this ultimate triumph, welcomed home like a prodigal son, he wouldn't need her any more.

"Your grandmother and Adam's grandfather are about the same age in this photograph," Finley noted, tapping his fingers thoughtfully on the desk. "They almost look like siblings."

"My grandfather was an only child," Adam said.

"That's what I always heard about my grandmother too," Eileen put in. "Wouldn't I have heard about a little brother, if she had one?"

"Maybe not," Finley said. "Families keep secrets."

"Yeah, but Robert and Arabella look nothing alike in this picture," Adam went on. "Neither do me and Eileen."

"Lots of people adopt," Finley said, dropping his eyes to the carpet. It was as though Adam had unknowingly brushed a raw nerve, but before Nicola could ask what was wrong, Adam blazed forward with his exploration.

"My grandfather never mentioned growing up here, and he never mentioned a sister. He said he had no family at all."

"Everybody has some kind of family," Eileen said, casting a glance so hopeful towards Adam that it made Nicola sick to her stomach.

Adam, always a little slower on the uptake than Nicola, finally caught Eileen's drift.

"You don't think we're related, do you? Like long-lost cousins or something?"

"Great cousins," Nicola said, chewing on the inside of her mouth. She tried to remind herself that this was not about her, that she should be happy for Adam. But her stomach twisted all the same. "If Adam's grandfather was Eileen's grandmother's brother, that would make you two great cousins."

"We spent all morning looking through family records," Eileen said. "There was no mention of a Robert anywhere."

"Genealogical records can be scrubbed," Finley replied.

"But birth records can't," Eileen said, eyes alight with inspiration. She hauled another cardboard box onto the desk, then hoisted out a dusty black folder. When Eileen opened the folder, the heavy cover slapped down onto the desk. Inside, slipped neatly between sheaves of plastic, were dozens of birth certificates and marriage records.

"Old families have too much pride in their own names to destroy all evidence of any of their own," Eileen muttered, flipping through the pages faster and faster. "Even if the records themselves have been erased, there will be a palimpsest."

Nicola couldn't help but be drawn closer, like a moth

fluttering nearer to a flame that promised the scorching illumination of truth, even if it burned. She sandwiched herself between Finley and Adam, tied to reality by their solid warmth.

Eileen flipped through each page, scanning the name of every child, parent and newlywed. Nothing turned up. Until she got to the back of the book, and Nicola spied a sliver of paper slipped behind Arabella Kirkfoyle's birth record as Eileen turned the final page.

"There's something there," she said breathlessly. "Go back, Eileen."

Eileen carefully slid her nail between the birth record and the document behind it, retrieving a folded sheet of thick paper. When she unfolded it, Nicola's world stopped turning.

It was a certificate of adoption.

"Robert Kirkfoyle," Eileen read aloud, her voice shaking. "Adopted at two years old by my great-grandparents. It's signed and dated by the courts."

Eileen and Adam stared at each other for a long moment, and then Eileen, who Nicola had never even seen hug Finley, stepped forward and embraced Adam.

"Welcome home," she said, voice muffled by his sweater.

Adam's arms came up to wrap tightly around Eileen's shoulders, and Nicola felt like she had just been shut out in the cold.

Nicola slept fitfully that night, when she slept at all. She was acting like a jealous child who didn't want anyone to be closer to Adam than she was, but that didn't mean there wasn't something unsettling going on. Everything over the last few days had happened very fast, and this bombshell revelation was no different. She couldn't imagine her gangly, annoying friend – the same boy who had flunked calculus freshman year because he flat-out refused to respect the attendance policy – as some sort of aristocrat. Adam may be a Kirkfoyle, in name if not in blood, but he was nothing like Eileen.

And then there was the matter of that hug, tight and lingering. Eileen had clutched Adam like she had been waiting for him her whole life, and Adam had held her tight as life itself. Eileen's eyes had been glassy when she pulled away, a euphoric laugh bubbling up, and Adam had clasped her shoulders and grinned at her, as happy as Nicola had ever seen him.

Eileen's reaction Nicola could understand. She had been alone in the world for years, and Nicola, who had never had any family to speak of, could find a bit of pity in her heart for the lord. But Adam was spoiled for family, with not only one living parent but two. He still grasped Eileen like she was his only hope left, like Nicola hadn't been at Adam's side for years as steadfastly as any family.

Nicola lay in bed feeling frustrated with Adam – not to mention worried about what Eileen would do with her now that Adam had been identified as valuable in a way

Nicola was not – until the day dawned pink outside her window.

Then she threw back the sheets, sat down in front of her laptop at the writing desk, and pulled up a new JSTOR window.

Adam might be caught up in the heady euphoria of discovery, but Nicola hadn't forgotten what was at stake. Eileen's hospitality came with a clause: namely that Adam and Nicola would help her uncover a way to dissolve the supernatural contract that bound her family to their neighbors underground.

Nicola fully intended to earn her keep before Eileen got any ideas about discarding her.

Maybe she would find something to make herself feel better about this whole situation in the process.

She didn't look up from her research for three hours, not until her birth control reminder rang and made her jump in her skin. Not until her eyes were stinging from peering at scanned typeset from two-hundred-year-old books, and from flipping rapidly between pages to cross-reference the etymology of repeated names, or the frequency of mirrored symbols.

As she looked to the sun climbing ever higher in the sky, Nicola resigned herself to the fact that, if any of her growing suspicions were correct, she wasn't likely to feel better anytime soon.

Nicola pressed her hands over her face and took three deep breaths. She was spiraling. It had been such a late night, and she had been feeling so many things at once: lust, longing, fear and jealousy. Maybe she was reading too much into things.

Or maybe, she was the only one who was putting the pieces together. And if that was the case, she would never forgive herself for not at least trying to tell Adam.

Nicola yanked on jeans, snapped on a bra, and wiggled into her sweater, then marched down the hallway to rap on the door to Adam's room.

"Who is it?" Adam asked from inside, voice slurred with sleep.

"It's Nikki," she said, trying to sound bright and not at all panicked. "Let me in."

"It's unlocked."

Nicola let herself into Adam's room and found him dozing in a tousle of cream sheets and down pillows, his cheeks flushed as though he had just been woken from a dream. He rolled onto his back, scrubbing at his eyes with a hand, and the morning light streaming in through the window glanced off the curve of his bicep and the plane of his bare chest, shadowed with blond hair.

He really does look like he belongs here, Nicola thought as agony pierced her heart. *Like a prince resting after battle.*

"You need to wake up. We've got to talk."

"I'm awake," Adam said, making no move to either become vertical or get dressed. "And we're talking. What's wrong?"

Nicola paced a tight circle, sinking into the carpet beneath her socks. She didn't know how to get at what she wanted to say without sounding completely off her rocker, or worse, pissing Adam off.

"I've been doing some research," she said, deciding that starting with a neutral fact was probably best. "Into some local folklore and other comparative stories from the region. Cross-referencing them with what Eileen's been telling us about her family, and the faeries."

"That's great," Adam said, still a bit bleary. "But it's so early. It's not even breakfast. There's time for all that later."

He seemed to be under the impression that they had all the time in the world, that the honeyed languor of long days at Craigmar would never end, which sparked her anger. They were only supposed to be here for a week; that was what they had agreed upon together. She understood that perhaps his entire identity had changed overnight, and his priorities along with it, but she was still here with him, and she had every intention of sticking to their plan.

"I'm worried there isn't, actually. Listen to me, Adam." Nicola sat down on the edge of his bed, the way she had done so many times before while pregaming with vodka crans before a night out, or while typing out literary analyses as Adam ate hot honey peanuts and designed websites. Only now there was no party to prep for, no final exam to conquer. It was only her and Adam and this place with its heavy presence bearing down all around them. "I'm worried about you. This doesn't feel right."

"What do you mean?"

"I'm going to say something that might seem out there, but just go with me, okay?"

"Okay," he said, not sounding entirely convinced.

"We can agree that there's something special about this place, can't we? That it plays by a different set of rules. Old rules, governed by what Eileen calls magic."

"Right," Adam said.

"I'm not going to pretend like I understand all those rules, but I know a few of them. The iron jewelry, turning my sweater inside out—"

"And you knew what to do with the milk at the cave, yeah," Adam said, encouraging her on.

"Right," Nicola said. Maybe she could get through to him. Maybe there was still time to pull him back from whatever precipice he was teetering on. "Those rules are preserved in folk traditions, and those traditions are preserved in stories. It's not perfect; lots of things get lost and lots of things get fabricated, but we can still use them as a sort of . . . road map to navigate weird situations."

"You're talking about faery tales?" Adam said, arching a skeptical eyebrow as he took a long swallow from the glass of water by his bed.

"I'm talking about ancestral memory," Nicola said, firmer. She did her best to tamp down her growing frustration, knowing from experience that blowing up at him would only bring conversation to a standstill. "Listen, I'm going to get right to it. Lots of stories are about a hero leaving home to go on a quest, but fewer are about someone returning. In those returning stories, home usually isn't what it seems, and sometimes it's an illusion. A temptation. Do you get it?"

Adam blinked at her, brows furrowed. Nicola wanted to pull her hair out, but somehow she soldiered on, picking up the pace.

"It's a trick, Adam. The castle outfitted with a feast to welcome the hero home is always a trick. It's everywhere, if you just look. Galahad at the castle of maidens, or Gawain at Hautdesert, or Odysseus on the island of—"

"Nikki, you're going too fast," Adam said, reaching out for her. Nicola kept her hands clasped tightly together in her lap. She didn't want him to touch her right now. She wanted him to *listen.* "You're being really academic for first thing in the morning."

"I'm not being academic, I'm being serious," she snapped. "Do I have to spell it out for you?"

"I guess so," Adam said, tossing his hands in the air as though he was completely hopeless, like he was some bumbling husband in a sitcom and she was his longsuffering wife.

Nicola wanted to strangle him with those expensive, cream-colored sheets.

"Don't you think it's a little weird that a week ago Eileen had no idea who you were and now she's rearranged her entire life so that you can be at the center? And don't you think it's weird that your grandfather's picture has been on her wall her whole life and she's never noticed?"

She heard the bitterness in her voice, and she saw the way it stung in the slight narrowing of Adam's eyes, but she didn't care. Sometimes, being right was more important than being nice.

"Eileen has been through a lot, and she's been super generous. She's put us up here for free and cooked for us and she even offered to buy our plane tickets home. I don't think it's fair for you to—"

"What if Eileen isn't the princess locked in the tower waiting for you to save her?" Nicola said, voice nearly breaking. She feared that if Adam wasn't willing to entertain this notion, at least, then he was truly lost to whatever spell Craigmar was weaving. "What if she's the wicked witch?"

"That's a mean thing to say," Adam said flatly.

Nicola deflated like a Valentine's Day balloon forgotten in the back of the florist shop.

They sat in silence for a moment, Nicola scowling down at her hands and blinking back tears, Adam propped up awkwardly in bed as he chewed on his lip. Then, just as Nicola was considering storming out of the room and slamming the door behind her, Adam spoke.

"This isn't a story," Adam said slowly, like she was a fool, like she was a child. "It's real life. It's okay if you feel jealous. I know family stuff is hard for you. I think last night probably just opened up some old wounds."

This was why Nicola had never dated Adam Lancaster. He acted like such a rationalist when it came to other people, but when it came to the whims of his own heart, he always did whatever he felt like.

"That's really patronizing," she said, voice small. The tears stung like hot coals at the corner of her eyes. Another minute of this and she would break, but she refused to let him see her cry.

"I don't even know what you're accusing her of, except giving you bad vibes," Adam said, and now he was the frustrated one. He threw back the sheets and stood, yanking a long-sleeved T-shirt on over his sweatpants. "You're not the only one who has damage about their family. Can you please just let me have this and enjoy it for one day before you start poking holes in a good thing?"

Nicola's blood turned to ice in her veins.

She had a handful of theories about what Eileen might be up to, none of which ended well for Adam, but at that moment, she couldn't care less what happened to him.

"Fine," she said, standing to go. "It was stupid of me to come here, anyway. Enjoy being the chosen one, or whatever the fuck. I'm going for a walk."

"Nikki," Adam said with an exasperated sigh. She thought, in her extravagant rage, that she would like to cut out his tongue the next time he called her that. "Don't. It's freezing out."

"Good," she said. "Maybe I'll die out there and you and Eileen can celebrate by fucking at my funeral."

Nicola slammed the door behind her, hard enough to rattle the doorframes, and strode down the halls. Hot tears streamed down her face as she choked back a sob, her fists bundled up tight at her sides.

Let Adam figure it out himself, she decided.

If he suffered in the process, so be it.

CHAPTER NINETEEN

Adam

Adam didn't follow Nicola as she stormed off down the hall, and he told himself that he didn't care if she caught pneumonia out in the grounds. If she wanted to have a meltdown out on the moors like one of her Gothic romance heroines, so be it. The tightness in his chest was just anger because she was being impossible. And the pain in his jaw from grinding his teeth was just from sleeping so deeply after that late night.

Adam dressed and drifted down the master staircase, moving a little slower than usual. He looked up at the portraits he had admired so many times, wondering what it would look like if his grandfather's face had been captured in oils. Wondering why his grandfather had ever left this place, and why he had never heard about a sister named Arabella, or about any family at all.

Nicola's warning burned in the back of his brain,

reminding him that he didn't have the whole picture. There was probably something here he had missed.

Adam pushed away the thought as he made his way to the ground floor. Sometimes, good things just happened. There didn't have to be an ulterior motive or a cosmic scale being rebalanced. Sometimes, families grew apart from each other then they reunited. It was the oldest story in the world, and it didn't have to have a twist ending.

Adam wandered into the kitchen, expecting Finley and Eileen to have already finished their breakfast, but instead he found Eileen alone, her shirtsleeves rolled up to the elbows, her hands covered in flour. She was trying to pry up the gelatinous dough spread out on the counter with a bench scraper.

"Morning," Adam said with a chuckle. "What are you up to?"

Eileen started, then pressed a flour-dusted hand to her throat while she caught her breath.

"You scared me. I thought you wouldn't be up so early."

"It's nearly ten," Adam said, nodding at the clock. "Pretty late in the day, actually."

"Oh," she said, looking down at the various items spread over the counter. Adam spotted walnuts soaking in a ceramic bowl, butter chopped into irregular cubes softening in a dish, and some sort of poultry defrosting in the sink while still wrapped in butcher's paper and twine. That didn't even cover the utensils, scattered around the kitchen like shrapnel from a cannon blast, and the various plates and cutting boards, of which Eileen had already dirtied a dozen. "I must have lost track of time. I'm not used to cooking big meals like this. Thank God I started early."

"What's the occasion?" Adam asked. "Had a hankering for something more than eggs and toast?"

"You're the occasion," she said, like it was the simplest thing in the world. "I gave up hopes of ever having a family years ago. You're nothing short of a miracle."

Adam felt suddenly dizzy, like Eileen had poured half a bottle of her cooking wine right down his throat. Being looked upon with any sort of approval from Eileen, spoiled and beautiful and hard to please, was heady. But being looked at like *this*, like he was the answer to her every fervent, secret prayer, was intoxicating.

"Um," he said. What else could he possibly say in response to that? "Can I help?"

"Certainly," Eileen said, with a wide, dazzling grin.

"What are we making?"

"Duck with rosemary jus and minced nut stuffing, yeast rolls, and a salad with radishes from the garden? Unless that's not enough?"

"I think it will be plenty," Adam said, sidling up next to her at the kitchen counter. "You didn't have to do something like this just for me."

"It's a celebration for all of us. After all, you're only reunited with a great cousin once, right?"

She sliced the dough into portions, then deposited a

lump of would-be-roll into his hands and began to instruct him in shaping the bread. Adam tried not to lose track of what he was doing, but he kept getting pulled back into her bottomless dark eyes, or gazing at her inviting mouth. She stood with her hip pressed against him, the scent of her skin and her makeup and her iris perfume cutting through the cooking smells, and if he wasn't careful – or rather, if he was very wicked – he could see right down the open collar of her shirt.

Adam couldn't tell if learning that he and Eileen – legally speaking if not genetically so – were related worsened his attraction to her or abated it. It was fucked up for his very not-platonic feelings about Eileen to be so tangled in his overwhelming feelings of relief and joy at being reunited with a lost relative, but they only got more tangled the longer he looked at her. He wanted to hold her hand and listen to her tell him everything about her life up until the point they met, and he wanted to lift her up onto the counter and push her pencil skirt up around her hips and kiss her pussy until she cried and, most strangely and most powerfully of all, he wanted to drop his head to her shoulder and weep.

It wasn't technically incest, he reminded himself. They were barely related at all, and didn't share a single strand of DNA. This was fine. He was going to be fine.

He managed to get the rolls into the oven without burning himself or committing any sort of sex crime, and Eileen seemed so proud of having completed the task that he didn't even point out that the rolls should probably go in last, not first. Nicola came through the kitchen door just in time to see Eileen feed Adam a bite of the minced nut stuffing, which featured too much mace but was otherwise very good.

Nicola shook the drops of rain, which had just begun to patter against the window, from her hair and sloughed off her coat.

"It smells good in here," she said, to Eileen, not to Adam. "But sort of like burning. Is something in the oven?"

Eileen swore loudly and wrenched open the oven door, leaning down to rescue the rolls. Adam tried to catch Nicola's eye to no avail. She didn't look upset any more, but her eyes were rimmed red from crying, and she was making a point not to acknowledge him. He had been on the receiving end of this silent treatment often enough to know it could last minutes or days.

This was exactly why Adam had never dated Nicola. She liked to wring her hands and weep about how people weren't kind enough to her, but if you pissed her off, even accidentally, she was cruel as anyone else.

"No need to worry!" Eileen said brightly, as though everyone was holding their breath to see how her bread would come out. "They're salvageable! Just more browned than I intended. Hello, sparrow. Been out for a bit of fresh air?"

"I walked to the ocean," Nicola said, sitting down at the kitchen table. She still surveyed Eileen with suspicion, but she looked a bit chastened, like she had come to the conclusion that she had been too hasty earlier in labeling Eileen a villain. What sort of villian baked bread for her houseguests, after all? "Just needed to stretch my legs and think."

"That's what walks are good for. Did you see Finley when you were out there?"

"No, I haven't seen Finley all morning."

"Hmm," Eileen said, disapprovingly. "Neither have I."

"Can I help?" Nicola asked. "This looks . . . involved."

"It's fun," Eileen corrected. "And yes, you may. Chop those radishes for me, will you? And wash those spring onions while you're at it. You're on salad duty with Adam. I'm going to see if Finley is in the library."

She stalked out of the room in search of her groundskeeper, leaving Adam to chop vegetables with Nicola in icy silence. This could go on for an eternity if he didn't at least try to get through to her, so he took a risk and made a joke.

"Looks like you didn't freeze to death out there after all."

"I didn't want to give you the satisfaction," Nicola sniffed, but then she glanced at him, treating him to the privilege of her gaze.

She was still angry with him, that much was obvious. But maybe they could salvage the day together.

"Good, because I would have been bored without you. Besides, what's the point of coming into a mysterious family if there's no one to keep you humble about it?"

Nicola snorted. It was almost a laugh.

"What do you need me for when you have Eileen to show you the old money ropes?"

"Nobody's said anything about money yet. And I like Eileen. Maybe I even like her a lot. But she's not you. No one is."

Nicola looked up at him, eyes soft and shining, and now she was the one who had him feeling tangled up inside. She was his best friend, and they absolutely should not under any circumstances do anything as stupid as hooking up, but he had never in his life felt more grateful for her. A vision of slipping his hand down the waistband of her jeans and showing her just how grateful he was came to him just as easily as that vision of lifting Eileen onto the counter had.

"Found him with his nose in a book, as usual," Eileen said, striding back into the kitchen with Finley close behind. Finley was dressed for the house today, not the grounds, in a cable-knit green sweater that made him look debonair. Adam caught himself staring at the way it hugged Finley's pecs, then he dropped his eyes into the salad. He was going insane. He needed to get laid, or go for a long hard run, or discover religion and chastity along with it, anything to help him manage all the unruly, confusing desire inside him. He was so horny he wasn't even sure exactly who or what it was he wanted, he just knew he *wanted*, so badly that it ached.

"In my defense, it was a very interesting book," Finley

replied. He scrubbed his hands clean in the sink, mindful to avoid the duck.

"Maritime history is interesting?" Eileen scoffed.

"Very, when lighthouse keepers go missing and are never found again. Do you know what happened in the Flannan Isles in 1900?"

Finley filled them all in on what he had learned about the strange incident that had happened off the coast of the Outer Hebrides, a chilling tale that made time pass quicker and reminded Adam of one of his mother's true-crime podcasts. Finley had a nice voice for storytelling, low and smooth, and he didn't need to raise it to have everyone in the kitchen hanging on his every word. By the time his story was done, it was time to set the table.

By then, Nicola had begun to laugh along with Adam's jokes and shoot him the occasional smile, and Eileen was soaring high on the triumph of having successfully not burned the house down in pursuit of dinner, and Finley was grinning at the rise his spooky story had gotten out of all of them.

As they laid out forks and knives in the formal dining room (Eileen insisted the occasion called for it), their cooperation felt dangerously stable, like something that might last past the week, or even past the spring. It felt, Adam realized with a pang in his chest, like they were a family.

When Eileen disappeared to change out of her flour-stained clothes for dinner, Nicola took her leave to put on something more festive as well. This left Adam standing awkwardly with Finley in the kitchen, making a show of measuring the internal temperature of the duck for far longer than was necessary, just so he would have something to do with his hands. Finley examined his nails, which were already scrubbed spotless, and just about the moment Adam was working up the courage to be the one to break the awkward silence, Nicola came back into the room.

She looked as pretty as he had ever seen her, maybe even more so, if that were possible. She wore the one dress she had brought with her to Scotland, a confection of floral ruffles with a short hemline that showed off her creamy thighs. No shoes, no stockings, just little white socks.

Adam stared at her, a damning beat too long, but Finley and Nicola were too busy staring at each other to notice.

"Eileen will be right down," Nicola said, cheeks dusted with pink. "I'm gonna go sit; see you both in there."

As she disappeared, Finley and Adam shared a glance. Adam wasn't sure what exactly that glance meant, but it felt warm and heavy, like a commanding hand settling onto the back of his neck. The look was only broken by Finley reaching around Adam to pluck up a bottle of claret from the counter and stride after Nicola.

Adam, who had always been one for adventure even when it wasn't wise, squared his shoulders and followed Finley into the dining room.

CHAPTER TWENTY

Finley

The Americans were more than happy to sample the wine while they waited for Eileen to make her entrance at dinner, so Finley met her in the hallway to steal a private moment.

Old habits died hard, and they had been brought up sharing kisses in secret, careful not to rouse the ire of Eileen's parents. James and Jennifer Kirkfoyle loved Finley desperately, but everyone knew well enough that there was no future for the clan heir and the groundskeeper's son. Eileen was supposed to marry someone better born, definitely a boy and not a girl, and probably a friend of her mother's family to bring in more English money to pad the dwindling Kirkfoyle coffers. Those had always been the parameters. A family-approved match had always been a foregone conclusion, even when Eileen and Finley began spending a concerning amount of time together.

Their puppy-dog romance had been discouraged, and then, when they had gotten older and their love had deepened and grown thorns, Eileen's father had reminded her that it was a selfish dereliction of duty to be running around with the hired help. She needed to marry well, at the very least someone with enough money to shore up Craigmar against bankruptcy and dissolution. Eileen was deep in Finley's heart by that point, like a sticky burr in a wool sweater, and there was no extracting her. So they had learned to lie. Eileen had made up a story about breaking things off, and they had gotten very good at pretending they barely knew each other in mixed company. Even now, with no one alive to judge them, they still lived separate lives, carried on their respective duties. Often, their lovemaking had a rushed, illicit tinge to it, as though they might be caught out at any moment.

Some days, it was thrilling, an elaborate game of fantasy and fulfillment that would never end. Other days, like today, it only made Finley sad.

"You decided to stick around to eat with us," Eileen said, stopping a few inches shy of Finley. She was still wearing that tight pencil skirt and the nylons with the line up the back, but she had changed into a silk shirt and let down her hair.

"I'm not going to skip out on a dinner I helped prepare," Finley said. Eileen was used to getting her way and she was certainly getting that, as far as Adam was concerned. Finley had no illusions that his position with Eileen was becoming more precarious the longer Adam was at

Craigmar, and he knew it may be further jeopardized if Eileen's vision for them all came to fruition. Finley still had his pride, though. He wasn't going to beg, and he wasn't going to simper. He was going to conduct himself with decorum. "I've got to eat some time."

"Ah yes," she said. "Wouldn't want me to get the wrong idea about you wanting to spend time with me."

"I saw you yesterday," Finley said, exasperated.

"So tell me you aren't jealous."

"You know I am."

"Then tell me you forgive me."

Finley cupped the base of her skull in his hand and rubbed his thumb across Eileen's lower lip.

"Your games are going to be the death of us both," he said. "When are you going to tell that American boy what you actually want with him? I'm asking you to get it over with."

"In time, my love. I swear it."

Finley pressed his thumb into Eileen's mouth, hooking it over her straight, white bottom teeth like she was a horse to be bridled. She closed her lips around him and sucked obediently, letting him hold her captive.

"Then I don't forgive you," he said, almost sweetly.

He removed his finger from her mouth, leaving her empty and fuming.

"We should get in there," he said, slipping his hands into his pockets and turning to walk into the dining room. Eileen caught him by the wrist.

"Be mine tonight," she said, voice suddenly urgent, suddenly honest. There was no artifice in her right now and that, on its own, was enough to give Finley pause. "Let them see. I don't care."

Finley furrowed his brows. He had always had the most to lose in this arrangement and he had always been the more careful one, reining in Eileen's devil-may-care streak.

"We're discreet for a reason, Eileen. They've seen more than enough already."

"Hang discretion and fuck reason. I want to be yours, in *our* way. Adam and Nicola have no power over us. Besides, I can act how I please in my own house."

Finley examined her for a moment, searching for the tiniest hint of a lie or the whisper of a scheme. Finding none, he put his mouth close to her ear, lowering his voice.

"You've always been excited by the idea of an audience, anyway."

She laced her fingers through his, and warmth bloomed in Finley's chest. This was a pleasure he was almost always denied, carrying on with Eileen, his Isla, in broad daylight, in full view of God and all the saints.

"I love you," she said, the words slipping from her mouth like smooth river stones. They were words she sometimes had a hard time forming, but they were all the more precious when she managed them.

"And I love you," Finley replied, squeezing her fingers.

Without another word, they strolled into the dining room hand in hand.

Adam did a double take when they walked into the room (a very small one, to his credit), but Nicola outright stared. Like a tiny display of tenderness between groundskeeper and lord was more shocking than the wildest carnal imaginings.

"Hey," Adam said. "We already made a dent in the wine."

"Fine as long as I get a glass," Eileen said.

"I'm cutting you off after two," Finley said, slipping easily into the weathered role of dominant. It thrilled him every time Eileen yielded to him, even if he wished she would do it a little more often without the trappings of kink. "You can have one with dinner and one afterwards."

Finley poured Eileen a generous portion from the bottle, knowing she would get bratty if he skimped. He passed her the glass, leaned over to kiss her cheek, then took his seat at the head of the table.

Eileen, with a practiced grace, sank down to sit at his feet. Finley settled a possessive hand on the back of her neck, and Eileen smiled up at him, perfectly content.

This did feel good, he had to admit. Having her as his own not only in private, but in full view of Adam and Nicola. Adam may have a connection to Eileen Finley couldn't compete with, but Finley had been in her veins since they were children, and entrusted with her care and keeping for nearly a decade. That counted for something too.

Nicola was staring at Finley with a wild shine in her eyes and a strawberry hue in the tips of her ears. Even with Eileen's skin warm beneath his hand, he couldn't help but marvel at Nicola, how openly she wore her heart on her sleeve. It was as though she had never learned to be embarrassed of wanting things, like she had never even heard of shame.

"Have you been able to get much work done, Adam?" Finley asked, scooping a slice of duck from the platter in the center of the table and depositing it onto a bone china plate. There was a puerile delight in making Adam and Nicola squirm, but he didn't want to make them outright uncomfortable. Best to keep conversation light and familiar. "The wifi can be spotty out here."

It was all Adam could do to nod. Finley deftly buttered a small piece of bread and handed it to Eileen, who took a delicate, ladylike bite. Even sitting on the ground, her table manners were impeccable.

Finley speared a bit of duck onto his fork and held it out for Eileen, who ate from his hand as though she were a kitten. Finley wiped a droplet of sauce from her lip with his thumb, then brought his thumb up to his mouth and sucked it off. Maybe it was overkill. Finley didn't much care. It felt good to show the Americans exactly who Eileen belonged to, even if such a display was a little mean-spirited.

The more time Finley spent with Eileen, the meaner she made him, and the more pleasure she took in his cruelty. Finley was sometimes worried about that, but most days it felt too good to question.

Adam shifted in his seat, draping his napkin across his lap.

"Um, we've been having a very nice time," Nicola said, doing her damnedest to bridge over the awkward silence. "I've been able to get some writing done."

"That's lovely," Finley said, as though he were the host instead of Eileen. "Are you still working on your goblin book?"

Nicola began chatting amiably about the illustrations she was working on, which thawed Adam enough for him to eventually share more about the website he was building. Dinner passed more smoothly after that. Finley allowed Eileen to retrieve herself a pillow to sit on after it became apparent they would linger over the meal – her submission tonight was supposed to be pleasurable, cozy even, and he wasn't trying to punish her with an uncomfortable position – and he let her speak of her own accord as well. But she mostly listened, pacing herself with her wine, and Finley was pleased with her on both counts.

Like a rare and precious metal, Eileen was at her brightest when Finley applied heat and force.

"I thought we might play a game, after dinner," Eileen said, taking a prim sip of her wine as she stood to help clear the dishes. Finley had loosened the reins on the scene once the final bite was finished, leaning down to murmur that she could stand whenever she wished, but she still lingered close at his side, glancing over for his approval before picking up the sauce dish.

"A game?" Nicola asked, gathering up the silverware.

"Yes," Eileen said with a smirk. Finley knew that look. She had mischief brewing inside her. "A game called Confession."

"I don't think I've ever played that one," Adam said as he appeared from the kitchen.

"It's one of Eileen's favorites," Finley said, a little apologetically. When he had agreed to power exchange with her tonight with an audience, he hadn't thought she would want to play *that* game. He should probably nip this in the bud, or at least warn Adam that—

"It's very easy to play," Eileen said brightly, swirling her wine in her glass. "And, if played correctly, very illuminating."

"I want to play," Nicola chirped.

"Adam?" Eileen asked, pinning Adam to the spot with her eyes in that way that always made Finley feel breathless and panicked and so, so excited. Did Adam feel the same way, being looked at by her like that?

He should say something. He should tell them. But if he put up any fight at all, he would look prudish and boring and Eileen would win. And if there was one thing that Finley would rather die than allow, it was to let Eileen Kirkfoyle beat him at anything.

"I'm down if everybody else is," Adam said, totally oblivious.

"Great," Finley said, tossing back the rest of his wine. Might as well be hanged for a sheep as a lamb.

CHAPTER TWENTY-ONE

Eileen

Eileen had abandoned her slingbacks somewhere between the dining room and the parlor, and now, as she stepped into her mother's favorite room in the house, her toes sank into the plush carpet. The room reminded her so ferociously of her parents that setting foot inside usually elicited angry tears, but tonight, she wasn't alone, and she was in high spirits. There was a light at the end of her family's centuries-long tunnel, and that was worth celebrating in style, in the bohemian-style parlor with its fringed pink lamps and velvet loveseats.

"Oh my gosh, there's got to be a hundred of them," Nicola said, dazzled by the shelves crowded with chess sets, board games, puzzles and tins of antique playing cards. Jennifer Kirkfoyle was a former socialite with more of a head for matchmaking than competition, but she had always indulged her daughter's voracious appetite for games. She commissioned carved jade dice for birthday presents, wrapped riddle boxes to stow under the Christmas tree, and returned from every excursion away from Craigmar, as few as they were, with a new brain-teaser in her purse for her daughter.

"There are seventy-two," Eileen said with a fond smile. "I've counted. My mother had hoped to use this room to entertain her out-of-town friends, but not many friends came calling, so she turned it into a games library for me. I was always allowed to play in here as a child, even after I got too rowdy during a bout of checkers and broke a Tiffany glass lamp."

"You've played all these games?"

"Yes, and I've beaten every one."

Adam was looking at her with something between pity and marvel, and it made Eileen's skin itch. He was looking at her like he understood something about her she didn't even understand herself, and she wasn't sure if she liked that. So, instead of allowing him to speak, she stepped into her role as master of ceremonies.

"The rules of the Confession game are simple," she said, plopping down on the carpet and beckoning for Finley to follow. They sat like children, knee to knee and with their legs crossed. Nicola and Adam followed suit, if a little hesitantly, until they formed a perfect circle of four. "We go around asking questions of each other, one question a turn. The point of Confession is to tell the truth. If you lie, you lose."

"How can you tell if someone is lying?" Adam asked, arching an eyebrow.

"I can *always* tell. The final rule is that, beyond telling the truth, there are no rules. You can exert any sort of influence you want over someone to get them to tell you the truth, and no one can hold it against you in the light of day."

"She's not kidding about that," Finley said, pushing the cuffs of his sweater up to his elbows before yanking them back down again over his wrists. He was nervous. "She once held my head underwater in the loch until I told her the name of the boy I had a crush on."

Finley's eyes didn't leave Eileen's face, but she caught the glance Adam threw his way in her peripheral vision. Was this the first Adam had heard about Finley's long history of falling all over himself over men? And why should Adam, who practically salivated every time Nicola walked into the room and did exactly what Eileen said with breathless delight, even care? She hadn't taken him for someone with a very developed sexual palette. Yet he surprised her.

This, she decided, was interesting.

Moreover, it was something she could use.

"Who goes first answering a question?" Nicola asked.

"Traditionally, one would draw lots," Eileen said. "But I'm willing to take volunteers. Is anyone feeling brave?"

Finley screwed his mouth shut. Nicola looked a little too nervous to go first, so Adam stepped in.

"Sure. I'll go."

"Fabulous. We'll go counterclockwise after you. Me, Finley, Nicola and then back to you."

"Sounds good to me. Ask away."

"Happy to," Eileen said, fixing him with her steely gaze. "Adam: Do you think magic is real?"

"Eileen, you're cheating," Finley cut in. "You can't just blurt out a question. Everyone has to agree on what we're asking."

"The question stands," she said, ignoring him entirely. "Do you think magic is real?"

"Do you?" Adam shot back, knocking her off balance. He was looking at her hard, gauging her reaction. Had he come to suspect that she was lying about the whole sordid family saga, about any of it at all?

Maybe he was smarter than she thought.

"Adam, wait your turn," Finley said.

"If Eileen isn't playing by the rules then why should I?" Adam said, electrifying Eileen to her core. A twist. She *loved* a twist, and she loved a dark horse even more. "And she may have agreed to follow your orders, but I haven't. With all due respect, take it down a notch with the *Fifty Shades of Grey* thing."

Finley looked like he had just been slapped across the face and then spat on for good measure.

"First of all," Finley said, in that voice he only saved for lecturing or winning arguments, "you're in my house, so I would watch—"

"You're all in *my* house," Eileen said with a frustrated noise. "And you're all boring me to death. Stop measuring cocks and answer the question."

Nicola clapped a hand over her mouth, but not before a giggle bubbled up. She was practically kicking her feet with glee, watching Adam and Finley peacock. Maybe Nicola had a little bit of a capricious streak, just like Eileen, and maybe she liked watching men compete to impress women.

Eileen could use that, too.

"I believe that there may be some things out there in the universe that we can't explain," Adam said with a huff. "Is that a good enough answer?"

"Not on your life," Eileen said, at the same moment Nicola rolled her eyes and Finley made a disappointed tsking sound. "Come on now, details. Are you really such a rationalist or not? Aren't bite marks and freak weather enough to convince you?"

"You only get one question, Eileen; now it's your turn to confess," Nicola said, as quick a study as Eileen could have hoped for.

"I like Adam's question," Eileen said, crossing her arms. "I'll answer it. I do think magic is real, Adam. More than that, I know it. And I know better than most that it's nothing to be trifled with, especially by those with no respect for it."

"What's that supposed to mean?"

"One question per round," she sneered.

"My turn," Finley said. "I can't promise how many rounds I'm going to go, so make it a good one." Then, muttering under his breath only loud enough for Eileen to hear, "I know how this game always ends."

Nicola seized the moment, leaning into the circle and asking, "Have you ever seen a faery?"

"Of course. Dozens of times."

"Come on," Nicola whined. "I need details. Tell a story."

"That's not part of the game."

"Oh yes it is," Eileen said, leaning in close and ghosting her lips over his neck. "Shall I motivate you?"

Finley stiffened beneath her kiss, but he didn't pull away. She moved her mouth languidly over his neck, tasting the salt on his skin and feeling the way his Adam's apple bobbed when he swallowed hard.

"Fine," he blurted, and Eileen pulled away with a triumphant grin. He was a piss poor Confession player, and she liked that about him. "There are the lights, out in the woods. Old folks call them friar's lanterns. My dad didn't believe in television; he said I could either read or climb a tree if I got bored, so I spent a lot of time playing outdoors. If I was out at night I would sometimes see a haze glowing off in the distance, but it would always get further away the closer I got. The first time it happened I was so spooked I ran all the way home and barreled through the cottage door, shouting about aliens in the woods. My father gripped my shoulder and said, so serious, 'That was something dangerous, Finn. If you're lucky, they'll cause mischief, and if you're unlucky, they'll snatch you away underground. You ever see something like that again, you stay far away from it, you understand?'"

"Then what happened?" Nicola asked, rapt. Their little circle was getting tighter, and Nicola had leaned so far forward that she was almost able to reach out and touch Finley. Eileen was closer to Adam, too, close enough to see the golden stubble coming through on his jaw after the long day.

"I'd go years without seeing them," Finley went on. "And then overnight, they would be everywhere I looked. After a while I realized they only showed up at certain times. Hard times."

"What do you mean hard times?" Adam asked, rapt.

Finley opened his mouth to speak, then closed it again.

"That's enough, I think," he said.

"*Finley*," Nicola groaned, sounding practically pained. "Come on."

Eileen rolled her eyes, then leaned back into Finley's space and started trailing kisses across his jaw. He withstood her advances valiantly this time, keeping still as a stone.

"It won't work, Isla," he said.

"Won't it?" she asked, then cupped him unceremoniously through his slacks.

Finley hissed, the sound ripping through the air like a bullet, and then seized Eileen by the wrist, hard enough to bruise. Eileen just laughed.

"Come on," she tittered. "You know the rules of this game as well as I do. Nicola, do you want to have a go at getting the story out of him? Or maybe Adam?"

"I saw them the night your parents died," Finley said, tossing her hand back into her own lap.

Eileen had nothing to say to that.

"Why would they have come out then?" Adam pressed, curious as a cat and just as foolish.

"One question per round," Finley said quietly, looking chastened. Once again, he had ruptured Eileen's fantasy with the double-sided sword of truth. "I'm done for now."

"Your turn, sparrow," Eileen said to Nicola, too sharply, too brightly. She hated being caught in a moment of hurt, and Finley's words had sliced right through her heart. Never mind her feelings; dead was dead and no amount of crying would bring her parents back. She couldn't have done anything about it, no matter what Finley did or didn't see that night. "Be a good sport or else I'll have to seduce the truth out of you."

Nicola gave a nervous laugh that sounded like she wouldn't mind that at all. It was a pretty mental image: Nicola whimpering in tortured delight as Eileen slipped her hand underneath the hem of Nicola's floral dress.

Adam opened his mouth to ask a question, but he never got the chance, because Finley beat him to the punch.

"Do *you* believe in faeries?" he asked.

"I believe in lots of things," Nicola said simply. "God, true love, astrology . . . Faeries don't seem so far-fetched, especially considering how long people have been telling stories about them."

"Good, an honest answer," Eileen said, taking back the reins of the game. They were getting lost in the weeds of the supernatural, which wouldn't do at all. There would be time for that later, after everyone had been properly warmed up to each other. She had only intended to use the magic question to set the scene for more intimate talk. "Back to you, Adam. Have you ever thought about sleeping with Nicola?"

Adam made a choked noise.

"We've never slept together," he said tightly.

"She didn't ask if you had, she asked if you had thought about it," Finley said, a flash of command in his tone.

"This is a stupid game," Adam blustered. "I'm tired. You all have fun, I'm going to bed."

"Game's not over, Adam," Eileen said. She hated it when people cut games short, and she hated it even more when people were sore losers.

And then, in a windfall of good fortune, Nicola took Eileen's side.

"There's no harm in answering one question," she said, batting her pretty eyelashes like she was asking to cheat off his chemistry test, not asking him to crack open his ribs and expose his beating heart. There was a sharp shine in her eye, as though depending on how Adam answered, he might win riches beyond his wildest dreams, or he might get his hand bitten off.

Adam looked miserably to Finley, knowing better than to seek any solace in Eileen. Finley merely looked him up and down, disappointed in his sexual cowardice.

"All right," Adam bit out. "I've thought about it."

"I had to give details so you do too," Finley said, twisting the knife. Adam had insulted him, and in response, Finley would humiliate Adam in front of his fair maiden, just for the pleasure of watching him squirm. Eileen was under no illusions about being wicked, deep down, or about the perverse thrill she took in Finley's flashes of cruelty. Watching him torture Adam was as erotic to her as a striptease. "Come on. Let the lady know how you feel. She's been so patient with you. Years and years of knowing each other, isn't it? Don't you think she deserves a little decency?"

"I've thought about it once or twice," Adam muttered, staring at the ground. "Maybe more than that, if I'm being honest."

"Adam," Nicola sighed, and pushed onto her hands and knees and crawled the few feet between them. She sat back on her heels and searched Adam's face, her expression beatific as a Botticelli angel. Everything unspoken between them pulled taught, moments from either snapping or pulling them closer together. "I want to know."

Adam met her eyes. Somehow hungry and penitent all at once.

"I don't want you to hate me."

"I could never hate you," she said, and kissed him on the mouth.

Eileen silently reached out and gripped Finley's knee. He sat still as a statue, but the muscles beneath Eileen's hands were tight.

Adam surged up against Nicola like the waves against the shore, cradling her face with the most delicate touch even as he devoured her. Nicola braced her hands on his thighs and leaned in close, making a sweet, sighing noise as she parted her lips wider and slid her hot, searching tongue into Adam's mouth. If Eileen had been skeptical about them never having gone to bed together before, she was soundly proven wrong. This was not the kiss of two people who had enjoyed intimate access to each other for years, or even for one wild night before. This was the kiss of two people who had been longing for each other every day of their lives without a single moment of consummation.

Eileen and Finley may as well have not been in the room.

When Nicola finally pulled away, Adam stared at her as though under some spell, his fingertips resting lightly on her cheek.

"Do you remember spring break, when I convinced you to come to Barbados with me?" His voice was barely audible. It was like he was in a trance. In the week she had known Adam, no matter how bated his breath when Eileen walked into the room, she had never seen him look at *her* like that.

"I do," Nicola said. Her mouth was wet from his kiss,

gleaming tantalizingly in the low lighting of the parlor. Eileen wanted to kiss the taste of Adam right off her.

"We went out to the dancehall and you were wearing this tiny dress, with all your hair piled up on top of your head because it was so hot. You were dancing on some guy and I couldn't stop looking at you, or imagining pulling you into the bathroom and pushing up that little dress and . . . I wanted you so badly it hurt. I couldn't sleep, remembering the way you looked."

"That was the first time?" Nicola asked.

"Yeah. But not the last."

"A *very* good answer," Eileen said. "God, I love this game."

Adam's eyes cut over to her. He was not pleased with her question, despite the obvious boon he had won by answering with courage.

"Have you ever slept with anyone else besides Finley?" Adam demanded, before anyone else could say a word.

"And why would that be a concern of yours?" Eileen scoffed. Adam wouldn't try to make her confess. He wasn't bold enough, not yet anyway. She hadn't had her talons in him long enough to shape him to her liking.

Unceremoniously, Finley laced his fingers through Eileen's hair and yanked her head backwards, exposing the white curve of her throat. Eileen gasped but didn't struggle, utterly dazed. She hadn't expected Finley to act as Adam's champion in this battle. She hadn't expected Finley to push back against her at all.

"Answer the question, Isla," Finley said, giving another

tug. His grip was punishingly tight, giving her the real, white-hot pain she so craved in private. He wasn't pulling his punches any more, audience or not.

"Never," she ground out, blinking back the water in her eyes. "There's never been anyone else I wanted."

It was Finley who spoke next, not Adam.

"And what about now?"

"No doubling up on questions," Eileen said with a mocking smile. Despite the pain tingling along her scalp and the way her sex throbbed in response, she would not give him the satisfaction of making her beg for release in front of her guests. "Your turn, dearest. Do you want to fuck pretty Nicola?"

Hatred flashed in Finley's eyes. How quickly the two of them spun from affection to bitterness, like ice dancers caught in a death-defying spiral.

"That's enough, Eileen," he said, letting her go as though he had been burned.

"If Adam had to answer, then so should you," Nicola shot back, strapping her arms over her chest. She had more spirit than Eileen had assumed, and if there was anything Eileen appreciated tremendously, it was a high-spirited woman. "It's only fair."

"All's fair in love and war, right?" Adam asked bitterly, glaring at Finley.

"I'm not answering that question," Finley said.

Nicola jutted out her chin, offended by Finley's recalcitrance.

"We'll see about that," she muttered to herself, then stood and crossed the circle.

"What are you doing?" he asked, looking up at her with wide eyes. He looked truly terrified, like he had just witnessed a Marian apparition. Eileen loved seeing Finley unravel and lose his tight grip on himself, but she wasn't used to seeing anyone else hold that power over him. Yet somehow, sweet smiling Nicola with her birdsong laughter and strawberry hair had wrapped Finley's leash tight around her fist.

Nicola braced her hands on Finley's shoulders and sat down on his lap, straddling his hips so they were face to face. The back of her dress hiked up a few extra inches, revealing the generous curve of her bottom beneath a pair of sheer panties.

Finley made an irritated sound, but his hands came up to rest on Nicola's lower back of their own accord, holding her secure against him. She draped her arms over his shoulder, brushing her nose against his in a torturously tender gesture. Adam and Eileen just stared, gobsmacked by the gambit.

"Is it true?" she asked quietly. "Do you want to fuck me?"

Finley had always been bad at Confession; he was too reactive and most importantly, too likely to get frustrated or even wounded by prodding questions. So Eileen wasn't surprised when he scowled at Nicola like she had ruined his night. But she was surprised at what he did next.

Finley made a noise in his throat very much like a growl and crushed his mouth against Nicola's.

Nicola squeaked in surprise and then melted in Finley's grasp. She pressed her body against his, kissing him deeply as he dug his fingers into the sensitive skin of her lower back. Her dress was thin and insubstantial, better suited for an American summer than a Scottish spring, and Eileen could see every curve of her body through it.

She tore her eyes away from the scene and looked to Adam, who appeared blind with rage and tortured by lust, undeniable as the hard-on pressing against his jeans. He was painfully, shamefully turned on, watching his romantic rival devour the girl he'd had a crush on for half a decade.

Eileen had never been as taken with him as she was in that moment.

Nicola rolled her hips experimentally against Finley's body, then gave a shuddering little sigh that captured Eileen's attention once again. God in Heaven, she was getting off. Did she like being watched? Did she like making Adam jealous? Did she take pleasure in cuckolding Eileen? Every option was tantalizing in a different way.

"Well," Eileen said to Adam, clearing her throat. She was aping disaffection, but she felt a red flush creeping across the plane of her chest. "Those two are entertaining themselves, so I think you and I should continue the game."

"It's Nicola's turn," Adam said weakly, mesmerized by

the way Nicola rotated her hips in little circles, the way Finley's ragged breath caught in his throat.

"Nicola is otherwise engaged," Eileen said, more forcefully. She grasped Adam's knee, demanding his attention. "I'll go in her stead."

"All right then. Tell me what's out in that cave. Real talk this time, with details. No bullshit."

Adam probably thought this would put a stop to everything and bring the whole impossible evening to a screeching halt. It was cute, the way he dramatically tossed down his Get Out of Jail Free card. But instead of cutting the game short, Eileen merely smiled.

"You're going to have to try harder than that to get an answer out of me," she said, blood pounding hot and fast in her veins. Whatever came next, consummation or confrontation, she welcomed it.

She never felt quite so herself as she did when she was tangling other people's heartstrings in her deft fingers, like they were nothing more than a cat's cradle. Maybe that made her evil. It wouldn't be her only trait worthy of damnation. But God, it made her feel *alive*.

Eileen stole another glance at Nicola and Finley. Finley had hiked Nicola's dress up around her waist, treating the entire room to an unobstructed view of her round ass.

Was Nicola using Finley to punish Eileen for capturing Adam in her web? Was Finley disciplining Eileen's wandering eye with this American girl, leagues lovelier and bushels sweeter than Eileen would ever be? Or was it simply the seductive influence of Craigmar, wrapping them all up in a blanket of private enchantment that made every desire of their hearts seem plausible?

Maybe they were all trying to punish each other, in their own ways.

Eileen stretched out languidly, letting her knees fall further apart to reveal the lace-trimmed edge of black silk beneath her skirt. That was the final straw for Adam.

He made a disgusted sound – whether he was disgusted with himself or with her, Eileen didn't know and didn't care – and pushed up on his knees to lean over her. Up until that moment, Eileen had been convinced that he was pliable but unsure he was a good fit for what she wanted. He had seemed too earnest, too decent, too unsure of himself. But now, as he looked down at her like he truly despised her and like he wanted her so much it might obliterate him, Eileen saw that he was *perfect*.

Adam flipped her skirt up around her hips, and, without another word, cupped her pussy in his hand. His touch was warm and heavy, making all rational thought evaporate from Eileen's brain.

"This game is called Confession, right?" Adam said, voice low and warning. "Start confessing."

"No," Eileen purred.

Adam slipped his hand beneath the waistband of her panties and quickly located the small bud of pleasure between her legs. She might talk a good game about anyone but Finley being able to catch her eye, but her body was no liar, and it was wet and ready for him.

He circled her clit with his fingers, slow at first and then with more force. Eileen squirmed under his touch, giggling in a teasing fashion, so Adam used his free hand to hold her down by the waist, making her still. The laughter dried right up as her heart pounded against her ribs.

A firm hand was the secret to getting under her skin, as Adam would quickly learn.

"You play dirty," Eileen whispered, her breath ghosting across his mouth without her lips ever making contact. No matter how lovely he looked right now, she refused to kiss him. That seemed more intimate than his hand between her legs. She had only ever kissed her parents on the cheek, and Finley on the mouth. Kissing was one of her favorite things in the world, especially the unhurried, sweet kind that made her heartbeat slow and made her feel, for one long moment, like a normal human girl capable of normal human emotions.

She wasn't sure she could trust Adam with that just yet.

Her hands found the button on his jeans and quickly unfastened it. Adam yanked his jeans down over his ass, revealing his painfully hard length. Eileen wrapped her soft fingers around him and began to stroke, firm and deliberate. She lived for this filthy, furtive kind of sex, the stolen gasping moments that made her feel like she couldn't come fast enough.

The sound of Nicola's rising and falling voice broke through the haze of Eileen's pleasure, and Adam stole a glance in her direction. Eileen watched him watching Nicola, all the hotter because of the agonized line that appeared between his brows.

Nicola had pushed Finley down onto his back on the carpet, braceleting his wrists with her hands and holding them up above his head. Finley looked punch drunk and dazed as Nicola ground her hips against him. Eileen never held him down like that, never used his body for her own pleasure. She enjoyed the friction of a power struggle, but she enjoyed losing the struggle more.

Was this something Finley liked, being bossed around and handled roughly? The thought sent a spiral of heat curling through Eileen's womb, nearly pushing her over the edge.

Nicola broke first, coming with a high-pitched cry that liquified something inside Eileen's brain. Finley followed her shortly thereafter, making a deliciously dirty mess of his slacks.

Adam made a bruised noise, hips bucking. And then, caught up in the unspeakably erotic atmosphere of all four of them debased together on the floor, he spilled in Eileen's hand with a groan.

"I win," Eileen said triumphantly.

"No, you don't," Adam ground out and pushed two fingers inside her. Eileen gasped, a tremor rolling through her thighs. She had never had anyone else but Finley inside her, and he rarely touched her like *this,* plunging her depths like there were secret treasures hidden away in the heart of her for the taking. Adam rubbed a circle against the sweet spot alongside her inner wall.

"Adam," Eileen gasped.

She only lasted a few more moments, then clenched around him as her orgasm swept through her body. She all but saw stars, her vision whiting out for a few exquisite seconds.

Then her forehead dropped down against his shoulder, her chest heaving with exertion.

"The past," Eileen panted, the morsel of truth slipping from her lips unbidden. She hadn't meant to say that. Maybe Adam had won this round, after all. Maybe he was clever enough to match her. "That's what's out in that cave."

CHAPTER TWENTY-TWO

Nicola

The game dissolved quickly after that. Red-faced with pleasure and shame, everyone exchanged goodnights and disappeared to go shower off the evidence of their little victories. Nicola had never been to Eileen's bedroom, but she suspected Eileen lived on the very top floor, up the narrow set of servants' stairs at the end of the main hallway where Nicola slept. That suspicion was only strengthened when Nicola glimpsed Eileen pulling Finley with her up that little flight of stairs.

Adam walked Nicola to her room, just like all those times he had walked her to her car after a night of bar-hopping, only this time, he couldn't meet her eyes. Nicola's thighs still ached from pinning Finley down beneath her, and her lips still tingled from where Adam had kissed her, pressing his confession into her skin. She felt weighted down with wanting and light as air at the same time, perfectly in command of herself and yet totally out of control.

She didn't know what she had been thinking in the parlor. She had wanted Adam, and she had wanted Finley, in a disparate yet complimentary way, and in the heady haze of the game, the answer had seemed so simple: have them both. But now, with a clearer postcoital head, complications swept in.

None of them had talked about any of this. Finley was Eileen's, and Adam was certainly not Nicola's, that much had always been painfully clear.

But Adam had kissed her *like* she was his, like she was the lady he wanted to honor with roses and courtly devotion by day, then despoil and devour by candlelight at night. And Finley had looked up at her with something close to religious devotion, bucking against her and whimpering like she was the cruelest goddess he could ever want to be sworn to.

Nicola, who wasn't used to being anything to anyone, was terrified and intoxicated by it all.

"Um, goodnight," she said now, twisting her fingers as she stood at her bedroom door. Adam was with her in the hallway, only inches away.

She had spent so long resisting the impulse to kiss him that now, with that sacred veil torn right down the middle, she wanted to do nothing *but* kiss him, over and over again.

"Are you all right?" Adam asked, searching her face with his blue eyes. God, he was so tall.

"Why wouldn't I be all right?" Nicola asked. Adam could think whatever he liked about her, but she refused to let him think she was scared of a little light group sex. She had enjoyed a threesome once in her lab partner's dorm room, losing herself in two other girls for an hour before they ate cold Domino's naked in bed and braided each other's hair. She might be sensitive, but she wasn't delicate.

"That was a lot," Adam said, like it was obvious.

"Maybe I like a lot," Nicola said softly, exposing more of herself than she wanted to, right now, so late at night. "Would that be so bad?"

"No," Adam said, breathy and low.

Nicola opened her mouth to ask him if he wanted to come inside, to practically beg him to, but then, to her surprise, he took the initiative. Closing the gap between them, Adam kissed her again, harder this time. Nicola's head swam and her lips burned as Adam pulled away.

"I don't know what's happening to us out here," he confessed. "And I need a little time to make sense of it. But I'm not mad about it."

"Me either," Nicola said.

"Goodnight, Nikki," Adam said. And then, with a little bit of his old stalwart cheer, "Sleep tight, don't die."

"Sleep tight, don't die," Nicola responded. And then, she was alone in the hallway.

Thank God Adam turned the corner towards his room at the end of the hall instead of climbing the stairs towards Eileen's room. Nicola didn't think she could take that.

She slipped into her room and locked the door behind her, peeling off her clothes the moment the latch clicked tight. She stripped off her dress, unlatching her bra and letting her heavy breasts free. Then, wearing nothing but her black cotton panties, she snagged her vibrator from her travel bag and slipped into bed.

Her head swam with a hundred worries and desires and theories. Her MacBook, left open to a half-read JSTOR article, glowed at her from the desk. Nicola was irritated by the light and the reminder of her quest for the truth, and crawled across the bed to snap the laptop shut before nestling back down against the pillows.

She didn't want to think about how anything could go wrong right now, or about what Eileen might have in store for any of them. She just wanted relief from the ache between her legs.

Nicola didn't think she could fuck herself soundly enough to quiet all the longing inside her, but she could certainly try.

She kicked her vibrator onto the highest setting and teased herself for only a minute before thrusting the toy all the way inside herself. Usually she needed more warm-up, but she was so embarrassingly wet that her body took the vibrator with absolutely no resistance. Her fingers grew slick as she moved the toy in and out of her body, faster and harder with every thrust.

Her mind was a swirl of indistinct lust, alighting for one second on Finley's full mouth, then on Eileen's burning eyes, then on the scent of Adam, all mint toothpaste and amber deodorant. She tried to force herself to conjure any garden-variety fantasy: something tame, something that wouldn't muddy the boundaries between her and her friends any more.

But when she came, hard and sudden and with a cry that could no doubt be heard all through the house, she was imagining all three of them, covering her with hands and mouths in a vicious game of conquest, ruining her for their pleasure like she was the mouthwatering centerpiece of their feast of desire.

Nicola caught her breath in the dark for a good ten minutes afterwards, riding out the aftershocks. She had hoped to work all that longing out of her system, but she had barely recovered before she plunged back into *wanting* again. Her stomach tightened with need the moment she turned her thoughts back to Adam or Eileen or Finley. She let out a sound close to a sob as she slipped her fingers back down between her legs, circling her clit in search of a second orgasm.

Craigmar, it appeared, had made her insatiable.

Nicola couldn't say how long she slept in the next day. She had dropped into unconsciousness the night before, utterly wrung out, and hadn't even thought to set an alarm on her phone. By the time she opened her eyes, on her eighth day at Craigmar, the sun was bright through her gossamer curtains and the birds were singing a full-throated chorus.

The date of her flight home had come and gone, and she had barely noticed. Realizing that the plane had taken off without her felt like crossing a threshold, like throwing her lot in with her new friends in a very real and immediate way.

She hauled herself into consciousness, groggy and irritable. Despite all the orgasms, she hadn't slept well, and had been tormented by nightmares. Visions of humiliation floated through her mind as she dressed: Adam shouting at her for committing some sort of infidelity, Finley running into her at a party and pretending like he didn't know her, Eileen lending Nicola a dress only for Nicola to rip it down the seam and sob while trying to mend it. And there had been another dream as well, something darker and more strange. A cold, long-fingered hand encircling her throat, holding her as gently as a farmer might hold a chicken he didn't want to startle before wringing its neck, and an unfamiliar voice whispering her own name in her ear.

Nicola scrubbed her face clean in the bathroom, patted off the excess water, then fastidiously applied mascara, concealer and shimmery lip balm like a soldier preparing for war.

No matter how any of the others felt about what had happened last night, she would not be made to feel ashamed.

Nicola found her way down the stairs to the kitchen without Adam – Craigmar was becoming more familiar with each passing day – and she was greeted by the sound of men's voices as she approached. Nicola paused a few feet from the doorway, listening intently. Eavesdropping had always been one of her favorite vices.

"Did you sleep well?" Adam was asking.

"Like the dead," Finley said. "Eileen's games always tire me out."

"Is Eileen still out cold?"

"She lies in later than most. But I'm sure she'll be pleased to see you when she wakes up."

"Oh yeah?" Adam replied, a teasing challenge in his voice. "I'm sure Nicola will be happy to see you too."

Nicola's heart skipped a beat at the sound of her name, betraying her with girlish hope, and heat pooled in her stomach at the idea of these two men discussing her when she wasn't around, with an altogether more adult sort of longing.

Why did that faint whisper of objectification turn her on so much? She was losing her mind. She had to be.

"Did you and Eileen kiss and make up?" Adam went on. "You two seemed like you were on the rocks last night."

"We're always on the rocks," Finley scoffed. "But yes, we made up. Multiple times."

"I hope you aren't upset with me for what happened."

"You mean you fingering my girlfriend, who happens to be my employer, three feet away from me? I'm not, actually. So long as you aren't upset with me for taking liberties with Nicola."

"Nicola can do what she likes, and we're all grown," Adam replied, in the voice he used to try to make himself sound worldly and experienced. "I think we know how to share."

"And have you talked to Nicola about that?"

Deciding that was as good as any cue she was going to get, Nicola walked through the kitchen door as though she had just arrived.

Finley was leaning against the island pouring some coffee into a glazed mug, looking rumpled and touchable in a green T-shirt and soft plaid pajama bottoms. Adam was wearing one of his traveling Henleys over gray sweatpants and, judging by the imprint of his half-hard cock against the fabric, no briefs.

Nicola was momentarily dazzled by the sight of them both, feeling very spoiled for choice.

"Hey there," Adam said.

"Good morning," Finley chimed in pleasantly, and thank God, he wasn't making anything weird. Nicola didn't think she could stand it if anyone tried to make last night weird. She was utterly earnest about sex, and had always been terrible at playing the cool girl-who-can-pretend-they-care-less game, even in casual flings. "Want some coffee?"

"Yes please," Nicola said, eyes following the way Finley fixed Adam's coffee just the way he liked it, without having to be asked. Had he been paying that close attention to their tastes?

Finley poured Nicola a hot cup of coffee with plenty of milk and a tiny spoonful of sugar, just enough to take the bitterness away, and leaned down to kiss her on the cheek while he pressed it into her hands. Nicola turned her face at the last moment, offering him her mouth, and Finley gladly kissed her on the lips, as sweetly as though they had known each other their entire lives.

Adam watched with raised eyebrows, a small smile on his face. Nicola couldn't help but kiss him too, pressing her lips right over that smile. Adam blinked at her, looking twitterpated and so, so cute.

"Hi," he said, like he hadn't said hello to her moments before.

"Hi," she said back.

Finley looked through the window above the sink, and said with a sigh, "There she goes."

Sure enough, Eileen was trudging up over a distant hill, shoulders hunched against the gray drizzle, wrapped in a coat that didn't look remotely warm enough.

"Is she all right?" Adam asked, one hand drifting up thoughtlessly to rest on Nicola's waist.

"She does this sometimes," Finley muttered, draining his coffee. "Gets a bee in her bonnet about taking the air, or trying to climb a tree or swim the loch. She doesn't know her own limits. I'll call her back."

"I can catch up with her," Adam said brightly. And then, suddenly self-conscious, "If that's okay with you. It's just that you seem to spend a lot of your time making sure she's all right. I don't mind splitting that load with you, if you trust me to watch out for her."

Finley looked startled, like such a thing had never occurred to him. But he nodded, slowly at first and then more resolutely.

"Yes. That would be very nice, actually. No need to lecture her. Just make sure she's not catching her death out there, and try to convince her to come back inside quickly, will you? She isn't supposed to go out in weather like this."

"On it," Adam said, stealing one more greedy kiss from Nicola before pulling his jacket off the coat hook and trotting out the kitchen door.

As soon as Adam was gone, Finley plucked up Nicola's hand and brought it to his mouth.

"Thank you for last night," he said, pressing his lips to her knuckles.

Nicola smiled at him, feeling warmer than summer.

"It was a lot of fun. We should do it again sometime."

"I agree. But I would like to take you out on a proper date too, if you would let me. Consider it an apology for being an ass and fending you off for so long."

"Are you done fending me off, Mr Buchanan?"

Finley gave her a lopsided smile.

"You're a sweetness I don't want to run from, Miss Fairweather."

Nicola took a deep swig of coffee, grinning at him mischievously, and then sat down at the kitchen table. Finley sat down beside her, easy and comfortable, like they did this all the time, like they were more to each other than strangers bonded by shared emotional entanglements.

"Can I ask you something?" she said, gathering up her courage. "About sex?"

"You're very direct," Finley said.

"We can talk about something else, if you want."

"No, I like it. I'm just not used to it. Eileen is a bit more . . . roundabout when it comes to talking about how she feels. Yes, ask me anything."

"The way you are with Eileen . . . Is that the way you are with everybody?"

"You mean, do I want to hurt all my partners?"

"Yes." She leaned in close to study his face. He was so lovely, in a melancholy way. Like a spurned prince from a Shakespeare play usurping his older brother's throne.

Finley took his time thinking, running his thumb along the handle of his mug. Then, finally, he said: "It's hard to say what's me and what's how I've learned to be when I'm with Eileen. But yes, I think this predilection has been with me since the start, and yes, that wanting – to bruise or to bite or to restrain – is always there. But it's not the only thing I like. And I would never do that to someone who didn't like it too. Does that make sense?"

"Perfect sense," Nicola said with a big smile. "And you seemed to like it when I pinned you down last night."

"I did, very much."

"Has anybody ever done that to you before?"

"Never," Finley said, fixing her with a look of longing that felt like pure power coursing through her veins.

"We should do that again sometime too, then."

"I'd like that."

"You'd better be careful getting close to me," Nicola said, with a brittle laugh. For a few moments things had felt so good, so cozy, but now those old insecurities were creeping in like a thief in the night. "I can be a handful."

"I don't think you're a handful."

Nicola could have brushed him off, or smiled and accepted the shallow compliment. If he was just someone she was trying to get with at a bar, or be pleasant enough to to get invited on a second date with, she might have. But Nicola really liked Finley, maybe even as much as she liked Adam, and that was freaking her out so bad she couldn't breathe. It seemed easier, at this point, to confess rather than to disappoint him later.

"My mother surrendered me to the state when I was ten days old. I bounced between foster care and group homes for most of my childhood. Some of the families were better than others, but none of them ever stuck around for long. I was a really difficult kid. I would get jealous of other children and I had horrible separation anxiety and I would have these . . . meltdowns. I still do, if I'm being honest. You only think I'm easy to get along with because you haven't seen me get upset yet."

She punctuated this admission with a laugh, trying to take some of the sting out of the somber topic. But Finley just looked at her with that level gaze that made her feel like she was the only woman on earth.

"That sounds very lonely, and it sounds like you blame yourself for the actions of the adults who were supposed to keep you safe. That's not how family is supposed to treat each other. You're a bright, sweet-natured person, Nicola. I don't doubt that for a moment."

"Thank you. But you don't actually know me that well yet."

Finley laced his fingers between hers under the table.

"No, not yet. But I'd like to. Is that enough, for a start?"

Nicola blinked the sting of water from her eyes.

"Yes," she said. "Definitely."

Finley leaned forward and kissed her, really kissed her, like he might never see her again. Nicola kissed him back, sweet and deep, until she was breathless.

"I appreciate how gentle you are with me," she said, because it was easier than voicing any of the other sentiments that were bubbling up inside her, the ones dangerously close to fondness, or even love. She was moving too fast, hurtling from person to person at the speed of light. It was her damaged attachment style, she reminded herself, or a disordered love map, or whatever other defect inside her soul that therapists had clinical language for.

A shadow passed across Finley's face, and his grip on her hand slackened.

"I don't think I'm very gentle."

"Why do you say that?"

"You've seen how I am with Eileen. I can be selfish, demanding. Cruel. It's not a very gentle thing, to take pleasure from the pain of others."

"I'm not entirely sure what goes on behind closed doors with you and Eileen, but from what I can see, you love her very much. I've seen you acting tender, so don't pretend like it's all whip and chains."

"I hate working with chains," Finley said with a laugh. "They're more trouble than they're worth. And I'm nowhere near skilled enough to use a bullwhip."

His hand smoothed up her back, and his fingers slotted gently into her hair. He rubbed a little circle into the pressure point at the base of her neck with his thumb, sending warmth spreading down Nicola's spine.

"I'm surprised I haven't frightened you away yet," he murmured.

"You're going to have to try a lot harder than that to scare me," Nicola said, tipping her chin up bravely.

"Oh yeah?"

Finley tightened his grip in her hair for a moment, and

Nicola's eyes went wide with surprise, her heartbeat kicking up. The air was suddenly tense, charged with possibility. Then Finley released her and went back to massaging that pressure point, as though to apologize for his roughness.

"I think we like a lot of the same things," Nicola said, suddenly shy. Since when did she have any reticence when it came to talking about sex? "I'm not a shrinking violet. I'm sure if you had any idea about half the things that excite me, you'd be scared off."

"I doubt it. But by all means, try to scandalize me. What do you like?"

It was always easier to think about these sorts of things in the privacy of her own bed than it was to bring them up in mixed company. But she was trying to trust Finley, even the little bit that she could. If she wanted to build anything real with him at all, she would have to be honest.

"Well," she said, taking a shaky breath, "I've always liked the idea of being chased."

"Chased?" Finley echoed, dark delight in his voice.

"Hunted down and ravished, to be precise."

"I've never done that with anyone. I'd like to do it with you."

"Yeah?" Nicola asked, her voice jumping half an octave.

"Yeah," Finley said, nudging her nose with his own. "As soon as we're able. But right now, I'd like to just talk to you, and keep kissing you. Does that sound all right?"

"That's perfect," Nicola said. "And while we're talking,

can we talk about what's going on with Eileen? What's uh . . . What's her deal?"

"We can talk about that until you're blue in the face and you're not likely to find any satisfying answers, but I'm happy to chat things through. What are you worried about, exactly?"

"I know she means so much to you, and not to put too fine a point on it, but you're all she has in the world. I like you, Finley, I like you a lot, but I couldn't live with myself if I ruined something between the two of you. Is she okay with this?"

As though to make her point, Nicola nodded down to her and Finley's joined hands.

"We talked for quite some time last night. She's as comfortable with me exploring my connection to other people as I am with her exploring her own. We love each other, and we'll love each other until we're both cold in our graves, but that doesn't mean we control each other's every move."

"Do you think that means she'll make a move on Adam?" Nicola asked, chewing her lip. Why did romance have to be so hard? Why couldn't everyone just have everything they wanted, with no hurt feelings or complications?

"I'm fairly confident that's what last night was about," Finley said with a curt laugh. "Eileen would rather die than ask for what she wants outright. Everything has to be a riddle with her. My advice to you is: talk to Adam.

See how he feels, make sure no one is lying to anyone about what they're after. Everyone should have equal say in this. Otherwise, I wouldn't worry."

"Okay," Nicola said. And with the sunlight streaming in through the windows into Finley's curls, his hazel eyes warm with affection, she truly wasn't worried at all.

CHAPTER TWENTY-THREE

Adam

Adam was a half-mile from the house when he caught up with Eileen. She had opted to forgo the mellow path through the grazing green and had taken a path that led straight up into the woods. Adam followed, appreciating the burn in his calves and the stretch in his lungs as he hiked up the rocky terrain. He had been a swimmer all through high school and college, and it was still his preferred form of exercise. He longed for the resistance of the water, the rhythmic crash of waves over his head. But the hike was challenging enough, and it gave him the time and space he needed to think.

Adam's thoughts drifted to the game of Confession. As good and right as kissing Nicola had felt, he still couldn't forget the way Eileen's eyes blazed a challenge as he slipped a hand under her panties, the way she had said his name like an oath as he brought her close to the edge.

Most of all, he couldn't stop thinking about that high color in her cheeks when he gave into his meaner instincts and held her down. He had never enjoyed overpowering someone like that before. But there was an animal satisfaction in overcoming Eileen Kirkfoyle, one that probably should have alarmed him. What else did Eileen enjoy, besides being held down? What else might she let him do, if he asked?

Adam's mind wandered again, settling for a moment on the tousle of Finley's curls against the floor, the way he had looked up at Nicola like she was God incarnate while she straddled his hips. Adam had wanted to chalk his arousal up to the general aura of sex hanging in the air, but when he traipsed downstairs the next morning and found Finley brewing coffee, jaw stubbled from sleep and pillow lines pressed into his cheeks, all that wanting had rushed right back in. It was inappropriate to dwell on, surely, no matter how good Finley looked fresh from bed. But Adam *was* dwelling, and all this reminiscing had him half-hard in his sweats.

And then, of course, there was Nicola. Mercurial and irresistible, all honey and light one moment and bared teeth the next. He couldn't stop looking at her, even when he had two fingers inside Eileen, and something about Nicola watching him watching her while Eileen watched Nicola grind against Finley had tied Adam into such a tight, inextricable knot of emotion that he hardly knew what to do with himself.

Everything had changed between them, and yet nothing had.

Adam summited a small hill to find the lord of the manor crouched down in the mud, examining a ghostly white mushroom with a scholar's interest.

"Eileen!" Adam called, and began to close the distance between them.

She rose to her feet with unhurried languor, regarding him curiously. She was wearing a long russet-colored coat over a plum dress that skimmed her bare knees, and her hair was coming loose from its updo. As Adam approached, he noted the sweat on her brow despite the chill of the morning, the way her cheeks were pinpricked with red. The coat was barely fit for early autumn, let alone a spring still touched by morning frost.

"I've been trying to catch you," Adam said, only slightly out of breath. "Finley wanted me to make sure you were all right."

"I slipped out because I wanted privacy," Eileen responded. She was still staring at the mushrooms, deep in thought. "I don't always tell my old man where I'm going."

My old man. Adam wondered for the hundredth time about the nature of what lay between Finley and Eileen, a devotion so honed it was almost painful to witness, yet one that allowed them to pursue other people. It was like nothing he had ever heard of, much less seen in real life.

"You should be careful in the grounds," she said. "Many parts of Craigmar are still wild and uncultivated. I would hate to see the woods eat you alive."

"You seem fine."

"I grew up here. Craigmar is a part of me. It doesn't know you yet. You're still wearing the ring I gave you, aren't you?"

She was being cryptic again, like she had donned her lord-of-the-manor mask in order to keep him at a distance. Compared to last night's gleeful indiscretions, it was a little jarring. Adam showed her his hand, his ring finger bound in iron. Eileen just nodded, harrumphing in her throat.

"What kind of mushroom is that?" Adam asked. He knew it sounded stupid, but wanted to do anything to keep the conversation going.

"I haven't the foggiest," Eileen replied, pressing her lips together tightly as though the mushroom offended her. "They just sprang up overnight."

Adam took a better look at the mushroom, pale and mottled, and realized it was merely one of dozens, sprouting in a perfect circle on the hillside.

"That's a strange formation," Adam said, taking another step towards the fungal ring.

Eileen's hand shot out to grasp his wrist, almost hard enough to bruise.

"Children know their stories well enough not to play in mushroom rings. Place one foot inside that ring, and you might slip right out of time, disappear away to a world where years pass like hours. You could walk out again a decrepit old man."

"Now you're starting to sound like Nicola," Adam said with a laugh. But Eileen was still holding him tightly, her skin clammy against his own.

"It isn't a joke, Adam. You should listen more when Nicola talks. You aren't in Kansas any more."

"I'm from Michigan," Adam quipped, but he took a step back all the same. He looked down at Eileen's hand, frail in the thin morning light, but she didn't let him go. She just stood there with a miserable expression on her face, holding him stiffly, as though waiting for him to do something.

Adam took a wild guess and latticed their fingers together. Eileen relaxed, but only slightly.

"You don't look very good," he said gently. He didn't want to offend her and rouse her ire, but more importantly, he was concerned about her. "Are you sure you're feeling well?"

"I'm never feeling well," Eileen said, sullen. "Apparently my ultimate destiny is only to feel worse and worse until I die."

"That's not going to be anytime soon," Adam said firmly.

"Perhaps," Eileen said, toneless and unconvinced. "Perhaps not."

"Is there some diagnosis here I don't know about?"

"Not particularly. It's just a family trait. We can sense

our own ends, sometimes far in advance, sometimes only days. Maybe you'll sense yours too, when the time comes."

Adam didn't like the sound of that at all. He had to steer her out of these bleak, chilly waters towards something warmer, something that might get her back in touch with her will to live.

"Did you have a good time last night?" he asked hopefully.

"I did," Eileen said with a lupine smile. That was better. That was more like the Eileen he knew. "With you, and with Finley. He and I talked things through. We see no point in any of us denying ourselves, so long as we can all remain civil."

"Then will you let me kiss you?" Adam asked, glancing down at her mouth, which was reddened from the cold. She had such a lovely, severe mouth. He wondered if she kissed the way she spoke, like she was trying to get one over on him, or if her rough edges would melt away under his lips.

"And what if you regret it?" Eileen said, that taunting smile still fixed firmly in place despite the flash of sadness in her eyes.

"I won't."

"And how do you know that, Adam Kirkfoyle?"

She neither pulled away nor drew closer, just leveled her gaze at him in challenge. Adam didn't want to push her too much, but he knew an invitation when he saw one, and he was emboldened by the sound of his name and hers mingling in her mouth. With his heart hammering in his chest, he dipped his head and kissed her.

It was tentative, little more than the brush of his lips against her own. She tilted her chin up and let him lavish her with soft, exploratory kisses that warmed her cold skin and made Adam's chest tighten. He could kiss her for a year and a day and never get tired of it.

Eileen slid her arm around his waist, deepening the kiss, and Adam ran his tongue along the curve of her lower lip. She tasted like a cold north wind and morning dew.

Then, a biochemical warning siren cut through the rosy haze of the kiss.

A strange sensation prickled down Adam's spine, the sudden intuition of danger, and the hairs on the back of his neck stood up.

Watched. They were being watched.

Adam released Eileen and threw a glance over his shoulder. They were entirely alone out here, a mile from the house. Who could possibly find them this far into the wilderness, let alone spy on them?

"Getting shy on me?" Eileen said with a crooked smile. "It's all right if you aren't up for anything more than kissing. But I had hoped . . ."

Adam's attention snapped from the vaguely menacing aura of the woods just beyond the mushroom ring back to Eileen. She was looking at him hungrily, like she was starving, like she might want to devour him and leave nothing left.

A shudder of arousal went down Adam's spine, tingling in anticipation in the small of his back.

"You hoped for what?" he pressed. She had set him up for that, but he couldn't help but ask. Even when the outline of her snare on the ground was so glaringly obvious, Adam couldn't help but step into it.

"I had hoped you had more on your mind when you found me out here than talk of mycology."

"One minute ago you were acting like you didn't even want me to kiss you," Adam scoffed, but he was taking slow steps towards her, as though drawn forward by her rope around his waist.

"Maybe I like making men work for it," she said, with that heartless haughtiness that made him want to dig his teeth into her skin, just to get a red-blooded rise out of her. "Maybe it excites me. What excites you, Adam Lancaster?"

Adam probably should have played it casual. He should have stuck to something safe, like saying it excited him just to kiss her, which wasn't exactly a lie. Or he could play it a little more louche, pretend like he was down for anything if she was, which wasn't exactly the truth.

Adam wasn't totally sure what he wanted from Eileen, but last night had certainly brought a few things that excited him into sharp relief.

"It excites me to hold you down," he said. "Maybe even to hurt you. But it also excites me when you tell me what to do. Especially when you're mean about it. I guess those two things don't really go together though, do they?"

Eileen studied him with those black eyes, hard and glittering, like he was a stallion she was deciding whether to take for a ride or not.

"You'd be surprised," she said, and something about the weight in her voice took him from half hard to so painfully hard he could barely see straight.

What the hell was happening to him out here, with the memory of society's rules and morality so far away?

"I'm a hard guy to surprise," Adam blustered.

Eileen laughed at him. *Laughed*, like she could see all the way through him and out the other side. A gust of wind rippled through her dark hair, laughing along with her. Genuine frustration grew inside Adam alongside his sexual angst. Is this why Finley always seemed at the end of his rope with Eileen? Always on the verge of some outburst of intimate violence that left Eileen grinning and triumphant and Finley debased, even with his hand around her throat?

"You don't want me to tell you what to do. It would frighten you."

"Why do you think that?" he challenged.

"We aren't cut from the same cloth, you and I," she said, smile falling away. "I'm unkind as winter, when you get right down to it. You're warm. Like summer. You can't help but be kind, even in your cruelest moments. I've seen it."

Eileen was talking in spirals again, in circuitous riddles that seemed to lead towards some greater truth just to arch out into incomprehensibility again. But Adam was determined to get closer to the heart of Eileen this time, even if he never found his way through her labyrinth. Even if all trying to solve that labyrinth did was draw him deeper inside.

"I can be cruel," he said, putting steel behind the words. Surely, this is what she wanted. This must be what got her off. That was fine with Adam, so long as she welcomed his participation.

A cold sensation crawled across his skin, that sensation of being watched. Adam pushed it aside. He was being paranoid. And he wasn't going to choke now, not when Eileen so obviously wanted him to take charge.

Eileen glanced over her shoulder into the woods, took a deep breath, and then came to her own conclusion.

"I'm sure you'll learn how, with time," she said, suddenly sad in a way that nearly took Adam's breath away. He had only ever seen anguish like that in museums, in the eyes of painted martyrs. But then the sadness was gone, replaced with a dark mirth that promised exactly the sort of transgressions Adam had been hoping for since he laid eyes on Eileen. "But if you want to show me how mean you can be, I'll let you try."

That was all the permission Adam needed. He slid his hand into her hair, tightened his fingers in the tousled waves, and pulled her into a merciless kiss.

It was inexpert, and Adam's palms were clammy with nervous sweat, but Eileen didn't seem to mind the way his grip shook before it steadied, the way he knocked his nose against hers as he worked her mouth open with his own. She just made a low, animalic noise of delight, then kissed him back, harder than Adam thought people were capable of kissing.

Eileen slipped her cool hands up the back of his shirt, dug her pearlescent nails in at the top of his shoulder blades, and raked them all the way down to his hips. Adam hissed in pain, instinctively breaking the kiss and grabbing her hands by the wrists. Hard, like he wasn't playing a game with her at all.

"Fuck, Eileen," he said, wounded as a child who had put their hand out for a sweet and been given a tadpole. "That *hurt.*"

"Then hurt me back," she challenged, pressing her warm, lithe body up against his. "Show me how angry you are with me. Or are you too good to get your revenge?"

"I don't want to hurt you," Adam huffed, his head swimming with contradictions. "I mean, I do, but not like that, not for real, I—"

"If you want to fuck me, you'll fuck me in the way I like, exactly as I tell you," Eileen said, every word as clear and cold as ice. "If I don't like the way you fuck me, I'll say geranium, and you will stop immediately. You can also stop at any time of your own free will, but if you choose to keep going, you will do as I say until I am entirely satisfied. Do you understand?"

Adam stared at her for a long while, still grasping her wrists tight enough to bruise. He struggled to catch his breath and order his thoughts, to sort through all these rules of engagement that felt so needlessly complex and yet thrilling at the same time.

"What do I get?" he pressed, gathering his courage with a deep breath in the same way he did before tackling the high dive. "If I satisfy you entirely?"

"Permission to do it again," she replied with a wide grin. "Now are you going to do what you've so obviously wanted to do since you arrived here or are we going to chastely walk arm in arm back to the house?"

Adam knew an out when he heard it, and he knew, deep in the part of his gut that alerted him to danger, that he should take this one. Eileen unsettled him, on the same visceral level the mirrored flash of animal eyes in the woods at night unsettled him, but he was still drawn to her powerfully and undeniably, and he was drunk on the small taste of power she had given him, heightened to delirious effect by the total surrender she demanded of him.

"Tell me you want this," he said, edging right up to the end of the diving board. He took Eileen's face in his hands. "Be honest."

"I want this," she said quietly. "More than that, I need you in a way I don't think I've ever needed anyone. So much it frightens me. Is that honest enough for you?"

"Yes," Adam said, and sank his teeth into her plush lower lip.

They kissed like they were at war, Eileen surprisingly strong in his arms as she bit and scratched and giggled at him, like all of his efforts to overpower her were little more than cute. Adam was soon breathless, heat spreading across the back of his neck, but he was determined to beat her at this game. He would not back down now, not when he had her lithe twisting form in his arms, not when she was grinning at him with all her teeth and smothering her gasps like she didn't even want to give him the satisfaction of hearing her moan.

Eileen pulled him down onto the earth, or maybe it was Adam who wrestled her onto her knees in the grass, it was so hard to tell. The world was a flurry of breath and bared teeth, so enveloping that even as that dreadful certainty that they were being watched grew in his stomach, his arousal eclipsed it.

Somehow, Adam ended up kneeling behind Eileen with an arm bracketed around her waist, his free hand flipping up her skirt so he could grip her ass.

"Is this what you want?" he challenged, somewhere between talking dirty and begging for her approval. "You want it hard, in the dirt?"

Eileen only laughed, like he was finally starting to understand her. Adam yanked her simple black thong and fumbled with the drawstring of his sweats. Eileen arched back into him, making impatient noises until his stiff cock slid between her thighs. Adam held her tight against him, refusing to enter her for a few more agonizing moments as he retrieved a condom from his back pocket. He somehow managed to get it open with his teeth, a feat he had never managed before.

"Are you going to fuck me or are you just going to talk about it?" Eileen needled as he rolled the condom on. "I'm getting bored, Lancaster."

Adam made a desperate noise, nudged her knees wider, and sank into her up to the hilt.

"*Yes*," Eileen ground out, like she had been waiting for this for a week, for a lifetime.

Adam kept one arm around her waist and looped the other around her shoulders and collarbones, pressing her so tight against him she could have never hoped to escape. Adam seriously doubted she wanted to, but something about holding her right where he wanted her, right where it felt best to thrust inside her over and over again, wiped any coherent thought from his brain. Eileen surrendered herself utterly, even holding her skirt up for him to grant him easier access, even though the pebbles beneath them were undoubtedly digging into her bare knees. She presented herself to him like a spoil of war, as though he was the king enjoying his tribute. The rougher and more selfish he was, the louder her noises of pleasure got, until she was rubbing herself between her legs with three fingers.

Adam slid his hand down her belly and covered her hand with his own, applying more pressure than she could possibly give herself. He worried for a moment that he might be hurting her in a way she didn't like, but then she tipped her head back against his shoulder and moaned in earnest. She was close, and Adam was hurdling towards his own climax embarrassingly fast. He wanted to get her there, wanted to satisfy her enough that she welcomed him back into her body again and again.

Adam yanked her collar to the side and sank his teeth into the juncture of her shoulder, hard enough to leave teeth marks.

Eileen let out a cry loud enough to startle a rock dove from a nearby tree, and clenched down around him. Adam's own orgasm rushed up like a wave to drag him down into the depths and he spilled into her with a choked gasp, but Eileen didn't relent. She bucked back against him until she was entirely spent, until Adam was so overstimulated he was on the verge of begging for her mercy.

The muscles in his thighs were little better than jelly by the time it was done, so he was relieved when Eileen pulled him down into the grass with her. He didn't care about the damp, cold ground, or the rocks beneath his body. He was wrapped in the smell of crushed moss and sweet rain and sex, draped in Eileen's arms.

"Thank you," she said, pressing the words into his mouth like she was pressing her signet into an oath. "You did so well. I had to know you could give me what I needed."

"I'll give you whatever you ask," Adam said, the postcoital haze intoxicating enough to make him terrifyingly honest.

"I know you will," Eileen purred, stretching out underneath him like a contented cat. "You're such a good little soldier in bed."

Adam probably wouldn't be recovered enough for another round for at least twenty minutes, but his cock kicked weakly at her praise, eager to be used by her regardless.

"Was that mean enough for you?" he teased, trying to regain some sense of normalcy, of control. But nothing felt normal around Eileen, and he would probably have better luck trying to maintain control of a roiling Highland storm.

"Yes," she said, kissing him very softly, almost shyly, like she was embarrassed to be caught acting tenderly. "But I still think you're kind, deep down."

Then, the cuddling was over. She smoothed her skirt down over her thighs, heedless of the mess it hid, and stuck out a hand to Adam. He let her pull him to his shaky feet, the world spinning around him.

Eileen's face hardened suddenly, snapping over Adam's shoulder as though she was displeased by an intrusion. That certainty that they weren't alone flooded back in a sickly rush. Had Finley been out here the whole time? Had Nicola?

He followed Eileen's gaze into the forest, but there was no one there. There were only shadows, so dark and deep they seemed to move of their own accord. A tree branch shuddered and shook, but no hare ran out from the underbrush, and no family of birds rustled in the leaves.

"We should go," she said. "Walk me back to the house?"

She extended her arm like a regency gentleman, like Adam hadn't just knocked her to the ground and fucked her in the muddy grass. Adam took her arm, grateful for the steadying touch, and let her lead him away from the mushroom ring and back towards the manor.

He couldn't help but look over his shoulder most of the way, however, as that ambient sense of presence followed them like a shadow.

He also couldn't quite smother the instinct in the back of his brain screaming at him to run.

CHAPTER TWENTY-FOUR

Nicola

Nicola was aware something had shifted between Adam and Eileen after they returned to the house arm in arm and damp from the rain and smelling like freshly turned earth, and she strongly suspected that something was sex. Nicola had supposed such a scenario might drive her mad with jealousy, but when Adam sidled up against Nicola in the upstairs hallway, murmuring a hello against her neck with the fading scent of Eileen's crushed Iris perfume clinging to his skin, what Nicola felt was hot all over.

She had always taken a guilty thrill in watching Adam disappear into dark rooms at parties with other girls, or return from "stepping out for a cigarette" with another boy with a hickey bit into his neck, but it was better now, because it was unclouded by the pain of pining. Now she could *touch* Adam, she could kiss him in the hallway until he smelled not only of irises but of daisies, and she could press her body to his up against the wall and tease him mercilessly about hooking up with Eileen until Adam, flushed and hard and grinning, divulged just enough details to stoke the fire in her belly.

"And you like that?" Nicola responded between kisses. "Having sex outdoors where anyone could see you?"

"I don't know," he said breathlessly, digging his fingers into her soft hips. "I like everything these days. I want everything, with everyone."

Nicola let out a moan and only kissed him harder, wantonness responding to wantonness. He was the only person she knew who was as much of an unrepentant slut as she was, and she loved him for it.

Then Finley called from downstairs:

"Soup's getting cold, lovebirds! Eileen found a muscadet in the cellar; get down here before she drinks it all."

"I would *not*!" she called back, faux offended.

Nicola and Adam hustled down the stairs with their fingers loosely linked, doing their best to suppress their laughter. Something about the pervading warmth inside the house, balmy as summer from the heady mix of domesticity and carnality despite the rain outside, made Nicola feel pleasantly feverish from her head to her toes.

She could get used to this.

Nicola hoped she and Adam would have the chance to deepen their connection in a more physical way after lunch, but Adam was swept almost immediately into a studious genealogy research session in the library with Eileen, and they even left the door open so Nicola could see that research was actually what they were doing.

Adam and Eileen had an easier rapport after their tryst under the sky, Eileen running her hand along Adam's waist as she directed him to read a passage of a book more closely, Adam tucking Eileen's hair behind her ear as she leaned over a cardboard box to retrieve documents. Finley, regrettably, had to go fix a retaining wall on the east side of the property, which left Nicola to work on her book quietly in the sunniest alcove she could find. It was a padded bench seat set into the windowsill of the stair's landing, under a window featuring a trio of hares captured in stained glass.

Nicola was grateful for the quiet time to pour all of her new-found inspiration into her work. Although it didn't soothe the pulsing ache between her legs much at all.

The next day, Eileen and Adam disappeared into the attic to retrieve more boxes of family records, leaving Nicola and Finley with the run of the manor. Finley had been loitering around the house all day, draping himself across furniture while reading (or pretending to read) *The Hunchback of Notre Dame*, the sleeves of his green henley pushed up around his elbows as though he were *trying* to tempt Nicola. He was freshly showered and smelled faintly of cologne, of vetiver, spiced woods, and sweet, vulnerable tonka. He couldn't have possibly looked more enticing, lounging on the couch with his curls gleaming and his lower lip tugged between his teeth in thought, if he had been trying. And Nicola was pretty sure he was trying.

She remembered what Finley had said to her on the lawn, about never being the one to be pursued. If he was locked into his role as initiator with Eileen, it might feel nice to have someone else initiate for a change. Maybe this was an invitation, if Nicola was bold enough to take it.

Nicola kicked off her jeans in her bedroom, shimmied into her sheerest black tights, stepped into a short cranberry colored-skirt, and swiped on some lip oil. She could hear Adam and Eileen's footsteps above her, confirming that they were still busy sorting through boxes.

If Finley wanted Nicola to be daring, she could be daring.

Nicola let herself quietly into the library, standing barefoot in front of Finley until he glanced up at her, as though only just noticing she was there.

"Hello, Finley," Nicola said, bouncing on her toes. She was excited, but she was also nervous.

"Hello," Finley said, closing the book and tossing it aside. "Can I help with something?"

"I was wondering if you wanted to play a game with me," Nicola said. The ball was in his court now.

Finley sat up straighter, pushing forward in his seat so his knees were almost touching hers. He was perched on the precipice of the couch, as though waiting for her word to pull her down onto the sofa with him, or slide to his knees to kiss the damp spot in her tights.

"What kind of game? Chess or mahjong or . . .?"

Nicola traced the floral pattern of the rug with her toe. She might know exactly what she wanted, and she might be sure down to her bones that Finley was the person she wanted to ask to do it with, but that didn't mean she didn't feel bashful.

"I'd like to play Ravishment," she said finally.

Dark hunger flickered behind Finley's eyes despite his pleasant smile, and something about that total restraint, the way he never moved a muscle or dropped his friendly affect despite his not-so-friendly interest, was enough to make her stomach tremble.

"I like the sound of that game," he said. "But I don't think I've played it before. Can you tell me the rules?"

"It's easy," she said, breath catching in her throat. "I run, and you chase me."

"What happens if I catch you?"

"If you catch me, you get to keep me and do whatever you want with me."

Finley wordlessly slid his hands up the back of her thighs, then cupped her ass beneath her skirt and pulled her closer, until she was standing right between his parted knees. He ran his thumbs across her skin through the paper-thin fabric of her stockings, a rhythmic gesture as soothing as it was inflaming.

"I'd like to chase you, and I'd really like to catch you," he said, voice soft. "But I might not know what to do with you until I catch you. I might want to do anything.

Is there anything you *don't* want me to do with you when I have you?"

Nicola shook her head, lust making her reckless, and then thought better of it. Even she had limits, at least the first time and without proper preparation.

"You could have my mouth, or my pussy," she said, voice little more than a whisper. It excited her so much to say these words, but she was afraid that if she spoke them any louder, something about this perfect, charged moment would shatter. "But not my ass. And I get frightened when I can't breathe. So no choking."

Finley nodded, keeping his expression neutral even as he made a quiet, anguished sound in the back of his throat. He kept nodding as he kissed her belly through her sweater, deliberating with himself.

"Can I do whatever I want with you even if you tell me to stop?" he said into the wool.

Nicola threaded her fingers through his hair, scratching down his scalp to the base of his neck.

"Yes, please. I want you to keep going. I want it to feel nice for you even if it doesn't feel nice for me, because that will make it feel best of all."

Nicola had never felt so turned on or so powerful, standing over a man who looked like he might cry from gratitude for the privilege of bruising her skin.

Finley pulled away and looked up at her, brown eyes somber.

"Are you on birth control?" he asked.

"IUD. Hasn't failed me yet."

"And how will you show me if you want the game to stop right away?"

"I'll say something silly that I wouldn't usually say. Like the word Eileen uses with you."

"What word will you use?"

"Marzipan," Nicola said, the word coming to her unbidden. It was her favorite candy. She wasn't likely to panic and forget that.

Finley huffed out a laugh and grinned up at her. A wolf delighted by a lamb, or perhaps a loyal dog eager to be run hard by his mistress.

"Does a fifteen-second head start sound fair?"

"Yes, yes," Nicola said, nodding fast. Adrenaline was already coursing through her, spiking her heart rate and urging her to run for her life.

"Do me a favor and try not to break anything in the house, or else Eileen is liable to kill me. Either way, I feel like this is going to be worth it," Finley said, letting her go as he rose to his feet. He pressed his hands against the base of his spine, stretching up to his full height, and then glanced down at his watch and waited for the second hand to tick all the way up to the top. And then, with a finality that Nicola felt drop into her stomach like lead, he said, "Go."

Nicola tore out of the library, kicking up the rug in the process, and scurried down the hall. She didn't have the house mapped correctly yet, and the thought that she might run into a dead end or turn the wrong way just to run headlong into Finley, who had grown up here, only made the game hotter. Her heart pounded, blood singing in her veins with a feral terror and joy she probably couldn't describe even if she dedicated a whole book to it.

Alive was the only thing she felt right now, and that was the refrain chorusing in her head as she ran, *alive, alive, alive.*

Nicola tried to hide herself in a narrow broom closet and found she didn't fit in alongside the linens, and then she threw herself against the door to the wine cellar only to find that Eileen had locked it. Nicola had no idea how many seconds had passed, five or fifteen, when she stumbled into the dining room. She was starting to panic now, the ticking clock making her reckless.

The tablecloth didn't reach the ground, but it was long enough to hide her in shadow if Finley didn't look very hard.

Right now, it was her only option, and so Nicola surrendered herself to it, crawling beneath the table and hiding like a child. She did her best to calm her ragged breathing as she waited for the sound of Finley running after her, or perhaps the sound of him calling her name through the house and making cocky promises about what would happen when he found her.

But that wasn't what she heard. What she heard was a series of quick, light steps as Finley began to traverse the house with perfect calm, examining every room with clinical efficiency. There was something genuinely terrifying about Finley taking his time in rooting her out, and that terror made her more wet than she had been in a very long time.

Nicola pressed her hand over her mouth to keep her breathing from giving her away as Finley got closer, pausing only momentarily in the hall to check the closet before stepping into the dining room. She could see his socked feet and jean-clad ankles circling the table, as leisurely as though he were browsing for new packets of seeds at the store.

Nicola squeezed her eyes shut, not sure if she was praying for him to find her or for him to pass her by.

A strong hand thrust beneath the tablecloth and wrapped around her ankle, yanking her out from under the table. Nicola yelped in protest, but Finley was stronger than he looked when he really wanted to handle her with force, and she was soon lying on her back with Finley standing over her.

Nicola froze, really froze, like a rabbit holding still for the sake of its life. Her knees were frozen askew to reveal the underwear beneath her skirt.

Finley took a long look at her, like she was his to devour in tiny bites. Like he might be memorizing the sight of her blushing and frightened to replay in his mind later.

"Boo," he said, and then fell on her mercilessly.

Finley did his damndest to pin her to the ground, locking

his hands around her wrists as he tried to shove them down above her head. Nicola thrashed and writhed, valiantly attempting to fight him off. Finley was bigger than her, but she was wily, and she wasn't afraid to fight dirty.

"Get off me," she snapped, twisting out from under him before he wrestled back on top of her again. "I'll scream!"

Finley covered her mouth with a broad hand. She bit at him, all delirious instinct, and he swore when her teeth nipped his palm.

"*Christ.*"

Now that sounded *real*, like he was really mad at her, like he might want to take that anger out on her, and Nicola let out a whimper.

Finley went after her with renewed vigor, and it was only then that she realized he had been holding back before. There was no play in this now, no levity in the way his fingers bruised her wrists and the way his knee jutted beneath her thighs to open her up and keep her where he wanted her.

"You can fight me all you want," he panted. "It's only going to get me harder."

Nicola saw through the part he was playing to his tacit assent, his permission to keep going, even though she had scratched so hard down his arms she had left raised red marks behind. And he *was* hard, his length pressing into her thigh.

She could let him take her like this and probably have a very good time, but she was having too much fun to give up the game now. More importantly, she didn't want to go down without a proper fight.

Nicola brought her knee up and jutted it into Finley's stomach. He avoided having the wind knocked out of him only by sacrificing his balance. Nicola was able to scramble away and rush out of the room in a string of breathless giggles. Finley gasped in surprise, then laughed himself as he hauled himself to his feet.

So much for keeping in character.

Finley chased her through the house, nearly catching her once and then twice, but she always wiggled away at the last second. By the third attempt, his palms and her arms were slick with sweat, and she slipped off his hook like a wily little fish. They were both panting now, from fear or exertion or desire or some heady mix of all three.

Nicola nearly lost the game by slipping on the hardwood in her stocking feet, but she recovered quickly and dashed towards the stairs.

If she could make it to the second floor, she might be able to hide in one of the spare bedrooms until Finley found her and made good use of the bed.

They never got that far. Finley caught her on the stairs, looping an arm around her waist and bringing her down onto the carpeted runner. Nicola managed to crawl up the final few steps to the landing, until Finley finally climbed atop her for good, pressing her down on her stomach with a firm hand between her shoulders. Nicola shrieked in genuine frustration, pounding her fists against the floor. She had no purchase in this position, no leverage to use against him. She was utterly at his mercy.

She snarled at him, but that sound soon turned into a moan as Finley thrust his hand under skirt and palmed her ass. He shoved his hand between her thighs, cupping her sex from behind as though it belonged to him.

"I can see everything through your tights," he said, mouth close to her ear as he pressed down harder on top of her. She felt like she was being smothered by him, suffocated by his weight and scent and hot breath. "It's like they're barely there. Like you want everyone to see what you've got under your skirt."

Finley hooked his fingers into the inseam and yanked, and Nicola heard the fabric rend in two. The cool air of Craigmar hit her overheated skin as Finley yanked the hole open wider. He kept tearing until they were totally beyond salvaging, until she was presented to him like a Christmas present torn open.

Nicola tried to wiggle away, but Finley held her fast, digging his knees in on either side of her.

"Soaking wet," Finley murmured, rubbing circles through her lace panties until she was squirming. "I think you like being hunted."

"Finley," she gasped. Then, because they were still playing the game, she added. "Please don't—"

Gloriously, Finley ignored her protests. He yanked her

panties aside and shoved two fingers deep inside her. He probably could have given her three without hurting her at all, that was how ready her body was for him.

She was so exposed on the stair landing, right out in the open in a beam of light streaming in from the window. She must look debased like this, being held down and fingered by the groundskeeper. Adam or Eileen could walk in on them at any moment, they could watch Finley do whatever he wanted with her and tell her how dirty she was for asking for this, but that just made it better.

Maybe I really am depraved, she thought distantly, and then all coherent thought left her head as she heard Finley unzip his jeans. He grunted and maneuvered her a little more, keeping her shoulders pinned down as he guided her ass up higher to meet him. The landing rug was scratchy against her cheek, her curls spilling across her face.

"Needy little thing," Finley went on, rubbing the head of his bare cock against her swollen lips. He sounded half drunk, like he had completely unraveled somewhere between the library and the stairs. This is what Nicola had wanted from him all along. To see a good man lay the cruelest parts of himself down at her feet as an offering. To be the tormenting beauty that made someone so self-controlled go to pieces. "I've got something for you."

"Let me go," Nicola protested, but it came out in a breathy moan.

Without another word, Finley thrust inside her. Nicola

gasped as he filled her up, taking her without restraint or remorse.

Finley hooked an arm around her soft middle and pulled her in tight against him, holding her right there on her knees for a long moment. Like he wanted her to feel every inch of him. Like he wanted to memorize what she felt like wrapped around his cock.

It felt so good she forgot to fight him. It felt so good she wanted to cry, wanted to melt right there in his grasp and drip all over Eileen's antique rug.

"You look like an angel," he said, voice rough with want as he pushed her back down. He ran his hand along her arched back as he stroked in and out of her. She didn't think he was pretending any more, either. She thought he was being honest, the kind of bone-deep honesty that some people could only express during sex, right on the edge of oblivion. "You're so fucking soft and sweet and *tight*. You're going to ruin me; ruin me, Nicola."

Finley fucked her faster, taking what he wanted at the speed he needed, which was all Nicola wanted as well. It felt so good, to be plucked like a piece of ripe fruit and devoured until there was almost nothing left of her conscious mind, of her anxieties and hang-ups and fears about the future. There was only Finley and the pleasure building inside her core. She wasn't even touching herself, and she was close to the edge. She always came quickly when she fantasized about playing this game with someone, but actually being in her body for the real thing was almost too much to bear.

He beat her to the finish line, spilling deep inside her with a groan. Nicola whimpered, riding the high of his ecstasy but not yet satisfied herself. She would finish herself off later, in her room. This was better than anything she could have ever hoped for and she had already asked for so much from him, she didn't want to be greedy and—

"Did you come?" Finley asked, still holding her tight like she was his captive. Maybe he wasn't quite done with her yet.

"Oh, uh," she babbled, embarrassment rushing in. Would he be mad at her for not finishing? Would he be insulted he hadn't gotten her there, or irritated at how much time she took? "Not really but I—"

"Roll over," Finley commanded, a little out of breath. "Show me."

Nicola did as she was told and rolled onto her back. She lifted the hem of her skirt so he could see the mess he had made of her cunt, the shredded remains of her tights and panties.

He looked at her like she was a holy idol dipped in gold, like she existed to be not only revered but worshipped.

"Please let me," he said, voice almost broken by the force of his desire. Nicola recognized herself in him in that moment, in the anguished, bottomless want in his eyes. Finley could probably have her in every way, in every room of this house, over and over again until eternity and never be completely satisfied. He could probably want her to the point of sacrilege and still want Eileen, still want Adam or anyone else, still want the sort of consummation that could only be found in the twilight between pleasure and pain. He was like her: needy, greedy, desperate. Always trying to fill a well of intimacy that could never be filled because it was bottomless, because it had no beginning and no end, because it couldn't be drained even if the fate of the world depended on it.

She felt a terrifyingly deep affection for him then, a tenderness rooted so deeply in her soul she wasn't sure she was ever going to be able to dig it out.

"Yes", she said, and hooked one of her legs over his shoulders as he lowered his mouth between her legs. Finley applied himself to Nicola's pleasure with a servant's attentive focus, making her gasp with a long stroke of his tongue through the come dripping out of her and up to the apex of her sex. When he lapped and sucked at her clit, Nicola fisted her hand into his hair and pulled hard, grinding against his mouth with a selfish abandon she had never completely allowed herself with anyone else. Finley let out a whimper of pleasure as she used him to her satisfaction, and something about that noise, so small and willing, was what sent her over the edge.

It took everything inside Nicola not to scream as she came with devastating and eye-watering finality. She didn't realize she was crying until the waves of sensation had crested and then abated, until Finley was leaning over her and wiping the tears from her face. She was shaking slightly, from the adrenaline drop or from the intensity of her orgasm, or perhaps from the knot of emotion forming in her throat. She had never been so totally seen by anyone, in bed or out of it, and now that Finley had looked right into the dark heart of her, she was terrified he would lose interest in her and leave.

Instead of leaving, Finley kissed her with such tenderness she thought she might start crying all over again. He smoothed her hair away from her face and tugged her skirt back down over her thighs, then pulled her into a crushing embrace. It wasn't the drowsy cuddly post-coital embrace she was used to. It was a tight hug, like they had been separated for a long time and had just been reunited.

"Thank you," she whispered, voice wavering with emotion. God, she needed to stop *crying*. He was going to think there was something wrong with her if she didn't stop.

Finley chuckled, the sound rumbling through her chest like thunder. Something about the sound of human laughter put her body a little more at ease, helped her relax into his embrace.

"Thank *you* for inviting me to play that game with you. I think you're some kind of miracle, Nicola."

Nicola clutched him tighter, letting out a hum of animal contentment. They held each other for a long time, breathing in sync as they came down from the ecstatic frenzy they had worked each other into.

"Can I fix you some tea and biscuits?" Finley asked. "Maybe we can just sit together for a little while and have a snack? Selfishly, I think that would be good for me, if that sounds good for you too?"

"That sounds good for me," she said, beaming.

What she didn't say aloud but whispered in her heart was: *that sounds like it could be good for me for the rest of my life.*

CHAPTER TWENTY-FIVE

Finley

Nothing good, Finley had always privately thought, could ever really last. His sullen nature wasn't something he was particularly proud of, and his mother had always said he was the most pessimistic child she had ever met, a surly old man walking around in the body of a little boy. But Finley had only ever known a world in which the fulfillment of his wildest fantasies – a single-bed dorm room with his name on the door, Eileen in his arms calling him beloved – were followed up with tragedy and misery and death. He had lasted all of four months at university before his father had gotten so ill he couldn't tend the grounds any more, and Finley had dutifully returned home to help him pack for his retirement cottage on the Isle of Skye, finding Craigmar unchanged and Eileen waiting for him in the doorway of the big house with wounded eyes. He had heard her tell him she loved him more times than he could count, but every time they tried for a baby, Eileen's brutal monthlies returned with a vengeance, and every time they let themselves dream for one foolish moment about getting married, those dreams would be dashed as the reality of their situation set in. She needed a suitable partner, one who could pad the threadbare bank accounts or at the very least help her carry on her family's grief-filled legacy.

Finley knew that.

It didn't make it hurt any less.

But even though Finley didn't believe in the permanence of joy, the next few days at Craigmar stretched long and languid, like the first day of summer that, every year, felt like it would never end. Eileen was kind to him, circling his waist with her arms and nuzzling her face into his chest while she asked about his day, or asked him to make them a pot of tea. Nicola was charming, telling him about her works-in-progress as she piled her arms with books from his personal library, swearing that she wouldn't dog-ear a single one, and that she would pay him back in kisses. Even Adam was far more pleasant, helping Finley haul firewood and do dishes and inviting him into a spirited but friendly round of checkers in the parlor.

As excited as Adam seemed about being part of Eileen's family – Finley couldn't understand why, as he had never met a Kirkfoyle who didn't end up cursing their own name – he didn't act high and mighty about it, which Finley appreciated. Finley saw Adam and Nicola walking together often, bundled up against the mist as they chatted animatedly to each other, or stealing kisses in the rain, the library, on the master staircase. Anywhere really. They were like the hares depicted in the paintings and stained glass all around the house: sweet and soft and desperate to fuck.

It was damn near close to a functioning household, with chores split four ways and meals made tastier by good company and the sun finally starting to shine more clearly and more brightly with each passing day. The wildflowers would be in full, riotous bloom soon, and Finley very much hoped Nicola would stay at Craigmar long enough for him to show them to her.

Privately, he hoped she would stay long enough for him to show her the autumn leaves too. It was a foolish hope, and greedy besides, but if Eileen was endlessly selfish in every walk of life, maybe Finley could be selfish with his heart, just this once.

He was in such good spirits, despite his built-in aversion to feeling comfortable in his own happiness, that he decided to plant some bluebells in the cauldron-style planters moldering in the shed, and then line the drive with flowers. Finley usually didn't bother with decorating the big house for any reason; it was in a state of marked disrepair, and with no team of staff to see to its upkeep, there was no point in gilding any lilies. But Eileen loved bluebells, so why not take a chance on making things look extra beautiful, just this once?

The bluebells took less time than he thought, so Finley decided to take the scenic route back to his cottage, cutting through the woods and passing by the loch where he had spent so many summer days as a child. It was a small, dark pool, hardly big enough for a boat, but it had made a fine swimming pool for him and Eileen year upon year growing up.

When he crested the hill and spied the loch in the distance, he was surprised to find there was someone in the water, swimming steady laps and sending ripples shuddering out to the edge of the shore. Finley stopped and peered through the trees, wondering if he was going to have to shoo some townie kid out of Eileen's loch. But then the swimmer looked over their shoulder and Finley realized that it was Adam.

Adam's clothes lay discarded in a heap on the banks of the loch, and the sunlight glanced off the muscles working in his shining shoulders. With his hair slicked back from his face, he had a more severe appearance, almost aristocratic. He looked perfectly at home, for all the world like a young lord making recreational use of his ancestral land.

Finley had never been oblivious to the fact that Adam was good-looking, nor that their ostensive rivalry had an edge of eroticism to it. But every time Finley had noticed himself really *noticing* Adam, he had talked himself out of it. So what if Adam's eyes were a shade of blue Finley had only ever read about in fairy tales? That wasn't any of Finley's business. And perhaps it had been thrilling beyond measure for Adam to entrust himself into Finley's hands as the eager student of kink, but surely any excitement Finley felt about that had more to do with Eileen than with Adam. And perhaps Finley was defensive of Adam's well-being, and increasingly concerned about him getting caught in the crossfire of Eileen's moods or schemes. All that meant was that he was a decent person. Nothing untoward about it.

But as Finley watched Adam's strong breaststroke, the reality settled in. Out there, with no one to witness it, Finley really let himself *look*. And for one shameful, secret moment, he let himself yearn.

Then, Finley tore his eyes away.

The last thing he needed in his life was another Kirkfoyle tangling up the strings of his heart. Adam was a distraction he couldn't afford, not if he wanted to keep his sanity. The longer Adam remained at Craigmar, the harder it would be for Finley to keep him at arm's length, but that was exactly what Finley needed to do, for all their sakes.

He turned to go, navigating down the rocky hill.

Then a wordless shout pierced the air.

Adam.

Finley trekked back up the hill and peered down into the loch. Adam was nowhere to be found. There was just a series of ripples emanating from the center of the loch, where bubbles were disrupting the surface of the water. Had he tried to dive down to the bottom?

Finley waited for three heartbeats, then four and then five as he anticipated Adam coming back up from under the water.

Six heartbeats passed.

Seven.

Where *was* he?

Adam burst from the water with a ragged gasp, his arms flailing. Finley's stomach lurched.

Something was wrong.

Adam struggled to catch his breath, then disappeared beneath the waves again. When he came up for air a second time, he could barely keep his head above water.

He was being dragged under.

Finley was watching a man drown.

"Goddamnit," Finley swore, then wrenched off his shoes and shucked off his jacket. He ran down the side of the hill, heedless of the sharp rocks underfoot, and hurled himself down the dock.

Without thinking twice, he dove into the green waters of the loch.

The water was bracingly cold but not shockingly so, and Finley knew this loch from his youth. It was ancient, but it wasn't that deep, and Finley could swim to the bottom before losing his breath.

Adam was thrashing in the water when Finley found him, fighting off some unseen foe. He had kicked up so much sediment that Finley could barely make out anything at all, but strange shadows loomed up behind Adam.

Finley's eyes must be playing tricks on him, because he could have sworn he saw a webbed hand circle Adam's ankle and tug him further towards a watery grave.

Without sacrificing precious brain space to processing what he was seeing, Finley hooked his hands under Adam's arms and began to kick furiously back up towards the surface. Adam was lead in his grasp, heavier than he ought to be, and for a moment Finley believed they wouldn't make it. They were going to die down here. He thought of Eileen finding them both floating bloated and lifeless in the loch, of Nicola's shrieking cries of grief. He thought of his father on Skye, receiving the news with watery eyes.

Then, just as his morbid visions were pressing down on him with the weight of the suffocating water, Finley broke through to the surface.

He gulped in air, eyes stinging, chest heaving. Adam was still a dead weight, and the comparison suddenly seemed all too apt. Finley laboriously kicked through the water until he could feel the silt and stone of the loch bed underfoot, and then he dragged Adam out of the water.

Somehow, Finley managed to get them both onto dry ground. A merciless wind whipped down off the mountains, making Finley shiver, but Adam didn't stir at all, which was more concerning. He had stripped down to his boxers, and his lips and eyelids were blue.

"Adam," Finley pleaded, kneeling on the water-smooth stones next to the other man. "Adam, wake up."

He jostled Adam's shoulder but nothing happened. He couldn't really tell if Adam's chest was rising or falling; if he was breathing, it was only shallowly.

Panic started to rise up in Finley's throat. He didn't know CPR. If Adam died on his watch the girls would never be able to look at him again, and he would never be able to forgive himself.

"Come on, Lancaster," Finley said through gritted teeth. Utterly out of options, he slapped Adam briskly across the face.

Adam stirred with a groan. Then, he rolled onto his side and spat up a frightening amount of water.

Finley rocked back on his heels and let his eyes slide shut.

"Thank Christ," he breathed.

"Finley," Adam rasped, turning those cornflower-blue eyes on his rescuer. "How did you find me?"

"I heard you call out for help," Finley lied. Adam might be full of generous feeling towards Finley for the small matter of saving his life, but he wouldn't take kindly to Finley spying on him.

"There was something . . ." Adam went on, coughing up more water and a green thread of loch grass. "Something in the water. I swear it."

"Like a fish?" Finley said hopefully, half leaning, half falling down onto his back. His chest was on fire from panic and exertion, and he felt a bit lightheaded.

Adam's eyes darkened.

"No. Something big. Something with hands."

"Weren't you wearing your ring?" Finley asked.

"I took it off," Adam spluttered, gesturing towards where the ring lay nestled in his shirt. "It was a gift, I didn't want it to slip off in the water and—"

"Never take it off," Finley snapped, picking up the ring and thrusting it back onto Adam's finger. It was thoughtless, the way he took control, pressing a thumb sharply into Adam's palm to spread his fingers for the ring. After he was done, he grasped Adam's wrist tight like he was a misbehaving child. "Promise me you won't take it off. Say it."

"Fine, Jesus," Adam said. "I promise. I didn't realize I had to wear it twenty-four/seven. I thought—"

"Water is a portal," Finley said, repeating what Eileen had told him so many times, what her father had told her when he ordered her to stop swimming in the loch. "Come on, let's get you back to the house."

"Eileen!" Finley hollered, shouldering open the door to the main house. "Get down here!"

He pulled Adam inside with an arm around his shoulders. Adam could walk by himself just fine, and it wasn't as though he was going to develop hypothermia. Still, holding on to Adam made Finley feel better, so he hadn't let him go.

"What is it?" Eileen hissed, appearing at the stop of the stairs. She was disheveled from bed, her dark hair knotted and her eyes puffy from sleep. Judging by the way she winced against the light, she had a raging migrane. "Some of us are trying to sleep."

When she finally looked down the stairs at them, all the color drained from her face.

"God in heaven," she said. She hurried down the stairs, gripping the banister tight, and took Adam's face in her hands as though to make sure he was still alive. "What happened?"

"He went swimming," Finley said, shaking the water from his curls. He had mostly dried on the walk back to the house, but he was still cold and damp.

"S-something grabbed me," Adam said, teeth chattering slightly. Maybe shock was getting to him, or maybe he just wasn't built for the cold the way Finley was. "In the water. Finley pulled me to shore."

"He took off his ring," Finley went on.

Eileen's eyes flashed, enraged both that their neighbors underground would try to steal Adam from her and that he had been stupid enough to go swimming without wearing his iron.

"What the hell would you let him do a thing like that for?" Eileen snapped.

"I'm not his keeper," Finley responded, bristling.

"Adam, listen to me," Eileen said. "Water is—"

"A portal," Adam said, rubbing some warmth back into his arms. "I've heard."

Eileen glared at him, but she put an arm around him and pulled him in tight all the same. The other arm went around Finley, and the groundskeeper found himself smushed between Eileen and Adam, wrapped in the scent of iris and lake water and damp skin. His hands drifted up of their own accord, pressing against their backs. Adam was cold to the touch, and Eileen was trembling. With fury or with fear, Finley didn't know.

"Adam?" Nicola asked, appearing around the corner. "Oh my God, look at you!"

"I'm fine," Adam said, but he gladly accepted the way she examined him like a nurse and kissed all over his face. "Finley found me."

Without a thought for what the lake water would do to her sweater, Nicola embraced Finley. Finley's chest constricted.

He was trying to let himself enjoy the good things while they lasted. But it was so hard to believe that it all wouldn't be taken away again the moment the truth came to light, and it was harder to believe that Adam or Nicola would want anything to do with them once they found out who he really was. The things he was capable of, and what he was complicit in.

"You need a hot shower and warm clothes," Eileen said, already pulling Adam towards the stairs. "Join us in the library once you've finished. We'll add a few more logs to the fire and you'll feel right as rain soon."

"You've got to listen to me," Adam said, stumbling forward as though in a daze. "There's something out there, in the water, something mean and *strong*—"

"I'd wager there's more than one something out there; it wouldn't surprise me at all."

"Shouldn't you be more worried about that?"

"What happened to you is the exact same thing that's been happening to Kirkfoyles for centuries. I'm far more concerned about your health than I am about draining my loch to keep faeries at bay."

"What the fuck is going on in this place, Eileen?" Adam said, pulling his arm out of her grasp and stopping at the foot of the stairs. She looked down at him from a few steps above, irritated with the pushback, but Finley saw clearly that Adam had scraped the bottom of the barrel of his patience and come up with nothing. The air between Adam and Eileen was tense, pulled taut as a bowstring as they stared each other down.

At Finley's side, Nicola slipped her hand into his own and gave a nervous squeeze.

"I've told you exactly what the fuck is going on," Eileen said crisply. "You're the one who refuses to believe me."

"I've bent over backwards to believe you. I've certainly taken everything you've said in stride. But it feels like every time I go outside something attacks me and—"

"You're right," Eileen said with a nod. "It's probably safest if you don't leave the house for a while."

"You can't keep me on house arrest because *Tinkerbell* is outside—"

"Watch the way you talk about our neighbors," Eileen

said, hissing through her teeth as though warding off the devil.

"This is exactly what I'm talking about," Adam said, stomping halfway up the stairs before turning to look back down at her. Finley thought about breaking up this brewing domestic, but even he wasn't brave enough to come between Eileen and whoever she was locked in battle with. "I don't know what's real and what's superstition, and I don't know what happened to my grandfather here or why he left. I don't even know how long I'm going to have to stay."

"As long as it takes, I'm sure," Eileen said nastily, probably showing more of her hand than she intended to. Eileen was incredibly calculating, but she got sloppy when she was mad.

"Lay off him, Isla," Finley said, desperate to shut her up before she said too much. "He's just had a scare."

"Taking his side now?" Eileen demanded. "How very like a man."

"I can handle this myself, Finley," Adam said, just as ferociously.

Finley relented. No good deed went unpunished, apparently.

"Can you please at least tell me what happened to your grandmother?" Adam went on. "I know that you know why she disappeared, I can feel that there's something you're not telling me—"

"I don't know what happened to her," Eileen said.

"You're lying!" Adam said, smacking the banister with a force that made Eileen start. The Kirkfoyle temper ran just as deep as the charm, it appeared. "What's the point of me being here if you can't even tell me the truth?"

"You're here on my pleasure, Adam Lancaster," Eileen said, voice cold as ice. "And you would do well to remember that."

Adam looked Eileen up and down, as though finally seeing her for the first time. The expression that crossed his face next was pure disgust, like he had turned over a rock and found Eileen wet and wriggling on the underside.

"I'm going to shower," Adam said, and he looked right through Eileen when he said it.

With that, he turned and disappeared up the stairs. Nicola hurried after him, calling his name sharply one moment and then pleadingly the next. Finley was left staring up at Eileen. She looked every inch the miserable fallen angel wreathed in the red halo glow of the stained glass behind her head. Without another word, she stormed up the stairs to her bedroom.

Two hours later, after she had hopefully had enough time to cool down, Finley climbed the narrow set of stairs to the third floor and knocked lightly on her door.

"Go away," Eileen said from inside.

Finley unlatched the door and pushed inside.

Eileen's childhood bedroom was small, by no stretch of the imagination the grand quarters of the lord of the manor. The dark wood paneling of the baseboards and trim contrasted starkly with the sky-blue wallpaper, dotted with little vines. The walls were crammed with framed paintings, mostly of foreign locales, and one large tapestry of a man hunting a unicorn that hung over a small fireplace. A modest bookshelf tucked in one corner boasted books of poetry, myth, fiction and picture books, many of which were antiques.

Finley had asked Eileen a dozen times if she wanted his help moving into a larger room, or into her parents' old master bedroom. Every time, Eileen said no, making up excuses about hauling furniture down stairs and already having the best fireplace in the house. Finley knew, though he was too kind ever to say it out loud, that Eileen refused to abandon the final vestiges of her girlhood, the last time she was truly happy.

Eileen was sulking, fully dressed, under a sheet, looking considerably worse for wear. She was reading a book of poems (probably an affectation to cover up for the fact that she had obviously been crying moments before he arrived, as Eileen hated poetry) and studiously working through the decanter of Scotch by her bed. She drank it neat from a highball glass: no ice, no soda.

"Would you like to come down for dinner?" Finley asked. "If not, I can bring you something from the kitchen."

"I'm not hungry," she mumbled, staring unseeing into her book.

Finley sat down on the edge of the bed, and put out a

hand to squeeze Eileen's socked foot. Even through the covers, she was cold. She was breathing shallowly, her forehead pale and speckled with sweat. The fight with Adam hadn't helped her health, and neither, Finley suspected, had the whisky.

"I shouldn't have told him anything," Eileen said, flipping a page aggressively, like it had personally wronged her. "Now he knows enough to ask questions, not to mention he hates me. It's never going to work."

"It will work," Finley said. That was what Eileen needed to hear right now, even if he harbored serious doubts. "You just need to give him time."

"Time is exactly what we're running out of," Eileen said and snapped the book shut. "They've tried to take him from me twice – *twice*, Finley. What if they succeed next time? I can barely sleep at all any more, the dreams have got so bad. My health is only getting worse, and the money is running out, for good this time. We need new blood. I'm terrified that if we don't do it soon, it will be too late to do it at all."

Finley didn't ask her not to go through with it. He knew how high the stakes were, and he knew it was her only remaining option. Still, he wished she didn't have to.

Eileen glared into the glass, then drained her drink with alarming fluidity. Judging by the dent she had made in the decanter, that was probably her third glass.

"Can I get you some water?" Finley asked.

"I'm not thirsty."

"You've had one too many drinks," Finley said, threading more authority into his tone while remaining mindful as ever about walking the tightrope of Eileen's mood. Being told what to do usually calmed her down, although sometimes she fought back. "Give me your glass, Isla."

Eileen turned her eyes to him finally, and Finley saw they were shimmering with tears. Silently, she surrendered her glass.

"Yes, sir," she said quietly.

Finley loved being a dominant; it fulfilled him like very little else in the world, but it was also exhausting. Anticipating his partner's whims, shoring up their weaknesses, and being their firm foundation was no easy feat.

On good days, dominance was thrilling. It felt like bridling a wild horse and galloping through the trees with the reins tight in his hands, it felt like tempering iron in a blazing fire that answered only to him, it felt like coming home.

On bad days it felt like nothing but loneliness.

Even though he was the dominant here, he understood Eileen's draw to submission on a bone-deep level. How exquisite must it feel, to have someone take the burden of choice away from you?

"You need rest," Finley said.

"Make me rest, then," she replied hoarsely.

Finley stumbled over the next step in their dance, suddenly sure of nothing. He didn't know if he should touch her or not, if he should speak sweetly or order her to sleep, if he should insist she change into pajamas or let her rest in what she was wearing.

She would probably sleep better if he sent her to bed in subspace. The aching tingle of cords around her wrists or a stinging swat on the back of her thighs would undoubtedly distract her from the argument with Adam, at least. But when Finley reached deep down inside himself to find the desire to hurt her, or even the will to, he came up empty.

"Will you try to sleep for me?" he asked softly. "Please?"

Eileen rolled onto her side and pulled the quilt up over her shoulders. Finley's shoulders dropped in relief. In this, at least, she wasn't going to fight him.

As he switched off the lights and slipped out of the room, decanter and glass in hand, Finley prayed to a God he didn't believe in that tonight, at least, she would sleep a dreamless sleep.

He also hoped that God would forgive him for what he was about to do.

Finley retrieved the master ring of keys from his back pocket, the one that had been passed down to him by his father, and very quietly locked Eileen inside her room. He didn't want her getting into any more of the liquor when she was in this state, and if she was telling the truth about those dreams, he didn't want her to heed the siren call of the fae and stumble out into the woods, never to be seen again. He had heard too many stories about her father going into agitated frenzies after days of not sleeping, threatening to kill himself to make the voices in his dreams finally quiet. Finley had witnessed a few of these rants himself, and they still disturbed him, even years later.

Dr Dasgupta had called it bipolar, and Finley believed him. James had been a charming, high-spirited man with a heart full of love, but he was also deeply troubled, prone to dark moods and animated bursts of self-destruction.

Still, that didn't mean that there also wasn't foul work at play. Faeries like to nibble away at minds already loose from their moorings, especially in times of trouble. They just liked to see what you would do.

Finley knew he was doing the right thing. He just hoped Eileen saw it that way when she woke up.

CHAPTER TWENTY-SIX

Robert

"Arabella, wait!" Robert called. "You're going too fast!"

Robert dashed after Arabella through the overgrown grass, following the sound of her pealing laughter. They had begged off their lessons with an excuse about Arabella having food poisoning, and the moment the tutor had disappeared down the drive, Arabella had sprung the locks on the parlor window and wiggled out into the grounds.

Robert had followed, just like always.

Where wouldn't he follow, if Arabella led?

"Keep up if you can!" Arabella called over her shoulder, her dark curls and red hair ribbon streaming in the wind. Robert did his best, slowing only enough to prevent himself from stumbling and cracking his skull on a rock. At fifteen, Arabella was a long-legged gazelle, but thirteen-year-old Robbie had yet to grow into himself.

"Where are you going?" he demanded breathlessly, pulling up alongside her as she slowed. They had cleared the green and were in the woods now, having crossed that liminal threshold into the uncultivated part of Craigmar.

Arabella grinned at him. A bright, wild smile, more creature than child.

"Where do you think?"

"Arabella, no," Robert said, making his voice as serious as possible. It was a difficult task, as it had begun to crack in recent months. "Father will kill us."

"Father doesn't have to know, unless you tattle," she said, giving her brother a sharp pinch on the fleshy part of his upper arm. "Come on, I want to see what's out there."

Robert didn't need to ask where "there" was. He had only been to the cave twice, both times to place offerings of sweets and cream with the rest of his family. The atmosphere of the place had felt . . . wrong. Robert had gotten the strong inkling that he shouldn't be there. He had been raised like any other Kirkfoyle child, taught to give the cave a wide berth and not to trust his eyes and ears when he traveled out there.

Robert knew their strange neighbors were not to be provoked under any circumstances. He knew they were to blame for the curious lights he sometimes saw out his bedroom window in the wee hours of the morning, and for the way his father sometimes paced the hallways at night, muttering to himself until his wife coaxed him back into bed, but that was all Robert knew. He kept a healthy distance from the cave at all times, and he maintained a healthy fear of the fae, even though he had never seen one of them himself. Arabella had, though, or at least she liked to pretend she had in order to frighten him. She said they came to her in dreams, to whisper secrets in her ear and sing her sweet songs.

Robert opened his mouth to protest further, but Arabella had already taken his hand and started pulling him deeper into the forest. Just about the time he had formulated his argument for why they should turn back, they cleared a hill and found themselves face to face with the cave. It loomed before them, flanked by bare trees with twisted branches covered with moist lichen.

"I don't like this," Robert said weakly. "Come on, let's go back. It's so cold out, and Father will be home from town soon. If he finds out we're gone, I'll be the one in trouble, you know that."

"I won't let anybody get you in trouble," Arabella replied, already taking a few steps towards the cave in her soaked ballet flats. She had been obsessed with *Swan Lake* recently and practiced her pirouettes at all hours of the day, and she hadn't bothered to pull on her boots before scurrying out onto the grounds. "Don't you want to see it for yourself? Nobody has to find out."

Robert had to admit, grudgingly, that part of him was

curious. But a bigger part of him was scared, both of the cave and of his father's discipline. He pulled his hand out of Arabella's grasp, but she didn't turn back with him. Instead, she lifted her chin and took a few determined steps into the cave.

It was alarming, how fast the darkness swallowed her up. In one moment, she was totally visible; in another, she was gone. Robert's heart battered against his ribs. He couldn't lose Arabella. He *couldn't.*

Swallowing the last of his pride and his good sense, Robert squeezed his eyes shut and walked into the cave.

At first he blindly navigated by feeling along the damp rock walls and following the sounds of Arabella's footsteps ahead. The air inside the cave was wet and thick with the scent of rotting leaves and the musk of small animals, but as he pushed further into the mountainside, there was another smell as well, like the fluffy hot cross buns his mother baked every Easter. It might have been appetizing if it wasn't so sickly sweet.

"Arabella," Robert hissed into the dark. He put a hand out to grasp his sister, but all he clutched was empty air. "Arabella, where are you?"

"Come on," Arabella whispered back, her voice seeming to come from every direction. It was impossible to tell how far away she was.

Robert took a gulping breath, and tried not to panic. If he panicked, he might suck down all the oxygen in the small space and suffocate, and then Arabella would have to drag his body out, if she could even find her own way back, and then . . .

His anxious thoughts trailed off as the ground began to slope downwards, moving further underground.

And then, there was a faint glow of light up ahead.

Robert scurried towards the light, hoping that they had somehow turned around and were resurfacing into the sun. But the air was getting colder, not warmer, and that saccharine scent was as strong as ever.

Robert hurried forward, and emerged in an underground chamber. Overhead, the ceiling was low and adorned with stalactites, and the mica in the walls sparkled and winked at him as though it was in on some joke. But how? There shouldn't be any light down here at all.

Robert looked to his left, and his heart nearly gave out at what he saw.

A wooden table sat in the middle of the cavern, heavy-laden with out-of-season fruits and a whole suckling pig with an apple in its mouth and buns that looked like his mother's. No, Robert realized as he took a few stunned step forwards, they *were* his mother's, down to the uneven criss-cross on top.

Robert knew with a crushing dread that they had most certainly made a mistake in coming here. But Arabella seemed delighted. She was standing at the table with her hands clasped together, as though the entire spread had been arranged for her pleasure alone.

"Look, Robbie," she breathed. "Isn't it so pretty? And everything smells delicious."

"Look at the lights," he whispered, too terrified to move a muscle.

There were fat, dripping candlesticks on the table, smelling of beeswax and sweet chamomile, but the flames dancing on the wicks weren't the cheery gold of mortal fire. They were an eerie blue, pale as a robin's egg, and they cast a cool light around the room.

"Let's leave," Robert said, finally finding enough courage to reach out and clutch Arabella's arm. Her skin was cold beneath her thin sweater. "Before anybody realizes we're here."

"Not on your life. This is what our family has been hiding from us this whole time? Kindness and goodwill?" Robert desperately wanted to convince Arabella that this felt more like a trap than anything, but she was a thousand miles away already, swept up in one of her wild fancies. "I feel like a princess at a banquet. Just look at those gooseberries, and plums too, as big as my fist!"

"I'm not hungry," he said miserably.

"You know," Arabella said, trailing curious fingers across the edge of the table, "I heard Mother say once that the fae used to be allies with our family. What if this whole time they've been trying to be friendly, and we're the ones who have been rude?"

Robert felt like tearing his hair out. He had been roped into hare-brained schemes by his sister countless times before, and he had often been the one to take the fall for them, but he had never felt as though they were in real danger before. He had never fretted, deep in his gut, that the consequences of their actions might be anything worse than a few licks of the switch or an evening locked in his room without supper.

He should never have come here. He should never have listened to Arabella.

"Please," he said, on the verge of tears. "I'm cold and I'm frightened and I want to go home."

"Then go!" she said with a blithe little laugh.

"Not without you. I won't leave you, Arabella. Not ever."

His pleas fell on deaf ears. Arabella was entranced by the bounty before her, and her face was lit up with delight in the blue glow of the candles. She stretched out one of her hands, plucked up a plum, and brought it to her lips.

"Don't," Robert hissed, at the very moment Arabella's teeth tore through the flesh of the fruit.

Juice dribbled down her chin as she swallowed, and her eyes flashed with triumph.

When Arabella smiled at him, all plum-stained teeth and mischief, Robert felt like he was looking at a stranger.

He felt something fracture between him and his sister then, something he, in his youth, did not have a name for and wouldn't be able to put into words for a long time.

Arabella held the fruit out to him, ripe and bloody and so perfectly bitten. He was tempted, for a hot, strange moment, to slot his mouth over the place where her lips had been and taste what she had tasted. Something about the thin air going to his head or how pretty Arabella looked with her curls askew garbled his emotions, insisting there would be no harm in one small bite.

But then he remembered how angry he was with Arabella, and he knocked the plum out of her hand and into the dirt.

"Robbie!" Arabella shrieked indignantly, suddenly a child no better than him, no matter how much she liked to pretend that being older made her so much more mature. "You beast!"

Robert never got the chance to defend himself, because all the candles in the room sputtered out. The room was plunged into total darkness. For a long instant, there was no sound except the scrape of Robert's breath against his lungs.

Then, in the distance, there was a faint sound. Rhythmic, like drumming.

"Shh!" Robert whispered. "Do you hear that?"

The pounding of drums grew louder, along with a high whine that sounded like viola strings, and the jangling of bells. A strange music, with instruments Robert couldn't place, sifting through the very rock of the walls and growing ever closer.

"We should go," he said again, edging towards the path back home.

This time, Arabella didn't fight him. The realization

that they weren't alone down there must have spooked her, because she jostled against him and started pushing him towards the exit.

They walked quickly at first, but when the music got louder, joined with the distant hiss and chatter of high-pitched, indistinguishable voices, they clasped their hands together and ran.

Robert had been right in his assumption that he would receive the blame. When he and his sister tumbled back inside the house, dew-wet and wide-eyed and stinking of the cave, they had very little to say for themselves. Their mother shouted at them for a full ten minutes before their father hauled them both upstairs by the wrists, locked Arabella in her room, and paddled Robert's hide with a hairbrush. He was too old to be spanked any more, but that didn't take the sting out of his father's blows, and it didn't stop him from blubbering like a baby, either.

He and Arabella never talked about that day again, and Arabella never confessed to her parents that she had eaten faery fruit. But Robert sometimes caught his sister sitting at her window at night, gazing out in the direction of the cave as though drawn by a compulsion Robert could never understand.

As though it was calling to her.

CHAPTER TWENTY-SEVEN

Nicola

Adam hadn't wanted to say much to Nicola right after his fight with Eileen but now, freshly showered and dressed in clean clothes, sitting by the glow of the library fireplace, he was much more forthcoming.

"I should have listened to you," Adam muttered. "She's impossible. We're the houseguests of a crazy person."

"I'm with you on crazy, but we don't have proof that she's a liar," Nicola said, tossing another log onto the fire so it burned bright and hot. Just because they had added kissing and groping and sharing hot Scots with each other to the list of what was included in their relationship, that didn't mean they had taken off giving each other sound advice. Nicola, personally, would like to add a lot more to the list, like proper dates and declarations of affection and sex in every position imaginable, but it had only been a few days since they broke their no kissing rules. Adam was a bit more flighty than her, and needed longer to warm up. She could be patient.

"Don't we? She's hiding shit."

"Almost definitely. But we don't know what, or why. It's also completely possible she's hiding personal, something that hurts to share, something that has nothing to do with us. You two still might be able to help each other, if you can work together without getting yourselves killed. We're all each other has out here, the four or us. It benefits us to cooperate for as long as we have to, whether we like it or not."

"I'm going to bump her off and run away with the insurance money," Adam said, darkly sarcastic.

"Don't let Finley hear you say that," she said with a chuckle.

"Let Finley hear you say what?" Finley asked, appearing in the doorway of the library.

"Nothing, we're just venting," Adam said, running a hand through his hair to slick it back from his face. "Is Eileen asleep?"

"She's certainly in bed," Finley responded, jangling a ring of keys before stowing it away in his pocket. "Hopefully she naps. I locked her in, so there's not much else for her to do."

Nicola's stomach gave an unsteady twist at the sight of those keys in his hand. She wasn't sure how she felt about *that*. Eileen might be ill, and she might be difficult to deal with, but did Finley really have to lock her up like a secret wife in an attic room? Her impression of Finley was of a pragmatic but ultimately gentle person, and that ring of keys in his hand grated against her image of him.

Despite their closeness, there were many things about Finley she had yet to uncover. He had secrets of his own, and a deep and mysterious allegiance to Eileen that Nicola didn't completely understand. Nicola would do well to remember that.

"What if there's a fire?" Nicola asked.

"As long as Eileen doesn't start one, there won't be," Finley said, coming to stand beside her in front of the fire to warm his hands. "You doing all right, Adam? You're looking warmer, at least."

"I'll live," Adam replied. "What the hell happened out there? In the lake, I mean. I *know* something grabbed me, Finley; I swear on my grandfather's grave."

"And I believe you. My theory is that this place knew exactly who you were from the start, even before Eileen did, Kirkfoyle land will always recognize a Kirkfoyle, and so will our neighbors underground. Their goal has always been the same: to get around the terms of the treaty by picking off Kirkfoyles one by one, through accidents that aren't really accidents or through stealing them away underground to do God knows what. They got a taste of you out there at that cave, and now they want more."

"What's in the cave, Finley?" Nicola said, crossing her arms and looking him square in the face. Some secrets she was willing to accept, for a time or for eternity, but this was not one of them.

"Nicola, don't ask me to—"

"I'm not asking," she said, a flash of power coursing through her like a dagger being unsheathed from a blade. If Finley could boss people around, so could she. "Tell me."

Finley relented immediately, looking almost relieved about it, like having the choice taken out of his hands was all he had been waiting for. Like telling the truth was the ultimate balm on his soul.

"It's a gate," Finley said. "Between one world and the next. Between Craigmar and the faery underworld."

"You're telling us that if we walk into the cave . . ." Nicola prompted. She already knew the answer. She wanted to hear Finley say it.

"You won't walk out again. At least not unchanged. You couldn't pay me to go in that cave. Not for all the money in the world."

"I'm surprised all it took was Nikki asking not-so-nicely to get that out of you," Adam said, making it sound like a joke even though there was hurt in his eyes, like he wanted to be the one to have that power over Finley, or the one on the receiving end of Nicola's command. She tucked this observation away for later, when they weren't in the middle of actually making progress at chipping away at Finley's and Eileen's joint stonewall.

Maybe separating them was the key to getting them to talk.

"No use denying the facts. Besides," Finley added, a little quieter as he gazed into the fire, "maybe I'm getting tired of covering for Eileen."

Nicola stood in somber silence with her hands clasped for a moment, like they were all mourning something. Then Finley glanced over at her, hazel eyes anguished.

"That's all I have to give you, Nicola. That's all I know about the cave. Is that enough?"

"Yes," she said softly. And because he seemed to be seeking her approval – desperate for it even – she added, "Well done."

Finley nodded, shoulders sagging in relief. What was he carrying around with him every day that was so heavy? Nicola wanted to take it from him, to give him a place to unburden his heart, even if he had to do it on his knees.

Finley sat down on the end of the couch opposite Adam and beckoned Nicola over to sit in the middle, with Adam on her left and Finley on her right.

"There are some stories that are Eileen's to tell," Finley said, speaking slowly and quietly, like tragedy might strike if he said the wrong thing or in too loud a voice. "And some stories of Eileen's that not even I am privy to. But I'll always share what I can, with both of you. I feel we owe each other that, at least."

"Thank you," Adam said, and the two men shared a charged look, charged enough that it damn near heated the room. Nicola certainly felt herself warm.

"Adam," Finley went on. "You said the day we all got

back from the cave that you smelled something sweet out there?"

"Like booze and fruit and wet sugar," Adam agreed. "It made me feel hungry, but also a little sick. Nicola, did you notice that?"

"All I smelled out there was forest," Nicola replied. Adam settled his hand on her knee, rubbing his thumb back and forth in that nervous tic that was more about stilling himself than soothing her. Nicola took comfort from it all the same.

"I couldn't smell it either," Finley said, draping an arm over the back of the couch around Nicola's shoulders. He leaned back, losing himself in thought. "But I'm not surprised you could. My working theory is that they were trying to tempt you underground. Kirkfoyles are . . . drawn to that place. All of them, without fail."

"But why?" Nicola said. This was a twist in the tale even she didn't understand, an anomaly in the story that she couldn't account for through either research or observation.

"The Kirkfoyles and the fae used to intermarry," Finley said. "I've heard stories about how, for a long time, there were always Kirkfoyles living above ground, tending the estate, while at least one of them lived below ground, bound in marriage as a sort of . . . peace offering. Sometimes black-haired children would just appear at the front door, like they had been sent above ground to visit their families, and every time, the child was taken in without question.

Every Kirkfoyle has a little wild blood in them, and the cave calls to it."

"But I'm not a Kirkfoyle," Adam insisted, leaning over Nicola to get a better look at Finley. They were all very close together on the couch, wrapped up in the conspiratorial cloud of mutual discovery, by the heat of the blazing fire." Well, I am, but not by blood. Why would they want to kill me?"

"They may not want you dead, is what I'm saying," Finley replied, and the puzzle box Nicola had been turning over and over in her mind for a week finally sprung open.

"It wasn't an assassination attempt," she breathed. "It was an attempted kidnapping."

They might not have been pulling you down to drown you, Adam. They might have been pulling you towards another gate, a back door into their world. They want Eileen alone and desperate, so that her family line will finally be extinguished. In their minds, you already belong to them, so why not bring you home? One above, one below."

Nicola stared at Finley for a long moment, stunned into silence. He held her gaze, as though begging for her forgiveness for something done or left undone. He looked every inch the penitent man, like someone who had confessed every sin to the exacting letter. Still, she couldn't shake the feeling that there was something else he wasn't telling them.

"This is too much," Adam said with that performative scoff that meant he was scared.

"This is Craigmar," Finley said.

Nicola burrowed against Adam, slipping her arm through his own. He shifted closer, angling his body towards her so she could nestle in deeper. Tentatively, Finley petted her hair, like he knew no other way to comfort her. Adam watched Finley stroke her curls and said nothing, as though the seriousness of what they were all facing had burned away his petty jealousy.

"They can't have you," Nicola said, with the desperate conviction of a child declaring that their parent would never die. She held Adam even tighter, as though that would help anything. "I won't let them."

"It's okay, Nikki," Adam said softly. "I'm still here."

"But I almost lost you today. Both of you."

Nicola turned to press a kiss into Finley's shoulder, breathing in his scent. Adam's hand tightened on Nicola's knee, gliding a few inches up her thigh. As close as she was to the two men in that moment, it wasn't enough. She wanted to be enveloped in them, to hold them both so tight death could never touch them.

Nicola lifted her face and kissed Finley on the mouth, sweet and slow. Adam's hand disappeared from her thigh, but she reached out and tangled her fingers in his before he could draw away, putting his hand right back where it had been. Then, she leaned over to Adam for their own kiss, earnest and searching. Finley's arm stayed around her shoulders the whole time, his fingers digging a little tighter into her upper arm. Like he wanted to leave a bruise, but was holding himself back.

Maybe she was asking for too much, ruining a vulnerable moment with her greed. Or maybe this was a necessary comfort they could all take from each other, spoken in the body's native language.

"It's all right," Adam murmured, tracing the line of her lips with his own. "Nobody died."

Nobody died. Maybe that was the best any of them could expect, tangled in this strange web of magic and painful history. Her whole life, Nicola had dreamed of stumbling into a fairy tale, but now that she had, she didn't feel lucky. She was scared, and she was confused, and she *ached*, every hour of every day, for the kind of intimacy she feared no one person could give her. Craigmar was poisoning the well of her heart with its heady, dark magic drip by damning drip.

Perhaps, one person would never be enough, not when her heart was so full of Finley and so full of Adam that she felt as though it may burst before she ever felt satisfied.

Nicola didn't know if she was ever going to feel satisfied again. But she could feel good, she knew that much, and she could make other people feel good too.

Nicola kissed Finley again, hungrier, needier, as Adam's mouth dropped to her throat, seeking her pulse under his lips. Then she was kissing Adam again, and then Finley, over and over again in a glorious unbroken circle. Sweetness turned quickly to fervency, made all the more desperate by the adrenaline spike of a brush with death. Finley's arm slipped down to her waist, clutching her close even as Adam's hand tightened around her hip. Finley bit her lip, making her moan.

When she finally broke away, Nicola was gasping for breath.

"I want to do it again," Nicola blurted.

Finley and Adam exchanged startled looks, as though they had just realized that the other one was in the room with them.

"Do what?" Finley asked.

"The lessons you were giving Adam," she said, speaking before she could allow herself to think. "I want to do it again."

"Now?" Adam asked.

"I want to be close to both of you, and I want to help us all calm down, and I just want to be told what to do," she said, her voice nearly breaking. "Neither of you have to if you don't want to, but don't say no just because you're worried about me. I know what I want. Please?"

Finley's mouth pressed into a thin line. He was weighing something internally. Risk, perhaps.

"Eileen's in bed," he said.

"Let me stand in for her in the scene," Nicola said, all but begging. She wasn't totally sure what she was offering, but she wanted to understand what Finley did with Eileen behind closed doors. She wanted to know if she might like it too. And most of all, she wanted to feel Finley's eyes on her the way they had been on Eileen during the last lesson, and she wanted Adam to look at her with that same rapt awe. "I might not have much experience, but I'm a quick study. I'll learn while Adam does."

"It's up to Adam," Finley said, choosing the diplomatic route no matter how his eyes flashed with interest. "It's for his benefit too, and he must be exhausted after the day—"

"I'm game," Adam said.

Nicola had heard him say it a thousand times. It was one of his favorite expressions, tossed out casually before every midnight joyride and tequila shot and round of one-on-one volleyball. She had never thought anything of it before, but now those two words heated her blood. It sounded like an affirmative. It sounded like a promise. Like consent.

"Should I kneel?" Nicola said. When she had watched Eileen last time, it hadn't been with the clinical intention of memorizing her movements. It had been with wonder and shock and arousal. Nicola hadn't exactly been taking notes.

"No," Finley said with a soft chuckle that made Nicola's heart pound. "That's a more advanced technique, and I can think of better ways to bruise your pretty knees another time. We should start with something simple. Something foundational."

His eyes flickered to Adam. Adam tracked the movement, his own eyes dropping down to watch Finley's mouth shape the next word.

"Denial," Finley said.

"Denial?" Nicola asked, still lightheaded from the scare of nearly losing Adam and the horrible revelation of Finley's story and the breathy realization that this was *actually happening*. "I thought kink was about getting what you wanted."

"Sometimes not getting what you want is more fun. Adam, in this exercise you'll be learning patience and control. Does that sound all right to you?"

"Fine by me," Adam said.

"Good. Nicola's right, this might . . . help calm us all down."

Finley stood, and crossed to an armchair on the other side of the room. She expected some regal stance, like a king ready to command court, but instead he pulled his legs up under him and leaned forward over his crossed knees. A scholar then, tutoring pupils for the final exam.

"You can kiss her, if you like," he said.

Adam, who apparently had been harboring his own hopes about experiencing another one of Finley's lessons, wasted no time in turning Nicola's chin towards him and kissing her deeply. Finley said nothing, but Nicola could feel his eyes on her, practically leaving burn marks on her skin.

Adam's hand found her waist, and then slipped up further to cup one of her full breasts. Nicola let out a shaky breath, bringing her hand up to cover Adam's, to encourage him to apply more pressure.

"Don't," Finley said, crisp and final. "Nicola, you're not to touch yourself, do you understand?"

A hot flush of embarrassment crawled up Nicola's neck, but when she shot a glance to Finley, she saw he wasn't upset with her. If anything, he was watching her with appreciation.

"You're not to come until Adam tells you to," Finley said, giving her a small nod as though weighing her assent. Giving her an out, if she were to want one.

Nicola nodded.

"I'm going . . . to make her come?" Adam repeated.

"Only if you'd like to," Finley said. "But I suspect you'd like to."

Adam dropped his face to the crook of Nicola's neck, nuzzling her skin.

"Will you let me make you come?" he whispered, for Nicola to hear, not Finley. It was such a simple, vulnerable question, but it made a lump form in Nicola's throat. She had dreamed of him asking her that for years, and she had convinced herself time and time again that they would never be brave enough to take a chance on each other.

Now, after so many years of fruitless hoping, Nicola still had a hard time believing that Adam wanted this with her. But even if she was just a passing fancy, even if Adam would tuck tail and run like he always did the moment a good thing got too real, she was going to let herself enjoy the moment.

Nicola nodded, giving Adam her consent. His hand slid up her body again, searching fingers slipping beneath the hem of her corduroy miniskirt. It had been a gift from Eileen to supplement Nicola's minimal traveler's wardrobe, and for a moment a memory of Eileen's self-satisfied smirk when she delivered the parcel flashed through Nicola's mind, but then it was gone again.

"You're my best girl, Nikki," he said against her shoulder. He pushed her skirt up over her thighs, exposing the edge of her simple pink panties. Adam's fingers ghosted along the hem for an agonizingly long moment, tickling and teasing as they went.

Then, moments before he touched her where she needed it the most, Finley said,

"Wait. I just thought of something."

Adam made a frustrated noise but he stopped.

"Yes?"

"You two . . . how to put this. I mean. You two *have* fucked before, right?"

Adam and Nicola shared a quick, guilty look, like children caught with their hands in a cookie jar. They understood each other telepathically: if Finley thought this was their first time, he might chicken out, and that would *suck*, so best to put forward a unified story.

"Totally," Adam blustered.

"Lots," Nicola said with a nod.

"Oh, *liars*," Finley said. "I'm not doing this, then. You two deserve to sort that out yourselves before anyone else gets involved, that's sacred, I'm not going to—"

"It's going to happen whether you're here or not," Adam said, with such conviction that Nicola's heart swelled. He did want her, for real, with a sense of sexual inevitability that bordered on fate. He couldn't have said anything to make her like him more. "But I'm having fun and so is Nikki, so what's the problem?"

"I agree," Nicola said. "I'll have Adam with or without you, but it turns me on to have you talk us through it."

Even for someone as forthcoming at Nicola, that one felt maybe a little too frank. Had she just ruined things? But if the way Adam and Finley looked at her, like she was an apparition of the patron saint of horniness, was any indication, she had perhaps just made things better.

"Touch her," Finley ordered, dark and a little impatient.

Adam finally cupped her sex in his hand and squeezed, sending warmth spiraling through her belly.

Nicola's hips bucked into his touch. She ached to press down on his hand with her own fingers, to show him the best ways to please her, but she somehow resisted.

"Denial is a result of trust between two parties," Finley narrated. "Adam, you have to trust her to wait for you, and, Nicola, you have to trust Adam to know when it's time."

"How do I know when it's time?" Adam asked.

"Feel it," Finley said cryptically, then fell back into silence.

Adam and Nicola kissed languidly, losing themselves in each other as Adam touched her over her underwear. She synched her breathing with Adam's, luxuriating in the time he took with her. But Nicola could never forget that Finley was in the room with them, his quiet presence as steadfast as it was inflaming. She felt over-exposed and yet protected with him right there, guiding the proceedings.

Adam's kisses grew more insistent, and the pressure of his hand between her legs gave way to gentle, agonizing circles right over her clit. Nicola wiggled for better purchase, aching to run her hands over her breasts, but she forced herself to breathe slowly instead. She so desperately wanted to do well. Both to please Adam and Finley, and also because she wanted to find whatever sweetness was on the other side of denial.

Adam tugged her panties to the side and teased at her entrance. When he slid one finger inside her, Nicola let out a whimper.

"Good job, Nicola," Finley said. And why wouldn't he be proud of her? He had a perfect view, seated directly across from Nicola's spread legs. The sound of Finley's voice sent a throb of need through Nicola's pussy, which tightened around Adam's stroking fingers.

"Adam," she breathed.

Adam pushed another finger inside her easily, filling her even more. He thrust his fingers in and out of her slowly but firmly, driving her towards the peak of pleasure. She looked into his eyes, giving him all that unbroken intensity that so many people had shrunk from before, but Adam looked right back, utterly captivated.

"Oh God, Adam, don't stop. I'm going to—"

Adam stopped. He withdrew his fingers and resumed cupping her in his hand, just tight enough to remind her who was playing the role of dominant in this scene. Nicola tumbled off the precipice of her orgasm, every lick of electricity in her belly suddenly snatched away. She was left gasping, her fingernails digging into Adam's back.

"How do you feel, Adam?" Finley asked.

Adam glanced over to Finley, a breathless smile on his face. He looked wild and elated and *perfect.*

"Powerful."

"Good," Finley said, his voice lower this time. Rougher. "Again."

Adam resumed his task of pleasuring Nicola, harder this time, more mercilessly, and just as she was edging up against her climax, he once again withdrew his hand.

"Get on your back," Adam said. "I want to taste you."

Nicola knew, realistically, that she could decline. It might feel like too much too soon. But something about the closeness of her orgasm and the sheer thrill of being watched by Finley during this incredibly intimate moment made her want it more.

Adam hadn't eaten her out yet, despite pushing her skirt up over her hips and getting down on his knees before being very nearly caught by Eileen in the parlor yesterday. They had done so much together: helped each other move apartments, nursed each other back to health after hangovers, listened to each other vent about exes, kissed and touched and begged for more, but never *this*.

Nicola laid on her back, letting her knees fall open for Adam. Adam hooked his fingers beneath her panties and pulled them over her thighs and down past her calves, until the scrap of lace was on the floor and she was entirely bare before him.

Adam laid down on his stomach, hooked his hands around her hips, and pressed a kiss to the pulsing heat between her legs.

Nicola's back arched off the couch. She should probably feel embarrassment, stripped from the waist down on an antique couch that didn't belong to her, being eaten out by her friend while someone very much like a stranger directed them. She should surely feel some kind of shame.

But all Nicola felt as Adam lapped and kissed at her was white-hot blinding pleasure. Adam gave head like it was his highest calling in life, like he had been dreaming about this just as long as Nicola had, like he couldn't get enough of her. Nicola threaded her fingers through his hair and tightened her grip, trying so hard not to ride his face to climax.

When she glanced over, she was treated to the sight of Finley pressing the heel of his hand against the insistent erection in his jeans. He was looking at her like her very existence tormented him, like she was the most beautiful woman in the world.

Nicola's whole life, she had been afraid of losing people. Whether it was the circumstances that had stolen her parents, or the abandonment of foster families who complained about a "poor fit" and her "high needs", or the loneliness that resulted from constantly being moved away from her friends, she had come to accept that she was only ever going to end up alone. But in this manor house with Adam and Finley lavishing her with their attention while the threat of magic circled outside their door, she felt fully seen, fully held. Not too much at all, for either of them.

A desperate wish took root in her, that this would never end. That Finley and Adam would never leave her.

A stray tear trickled down Nicola's cheek. It was impossible to tell if it was from sensation or emotion.

"Adam, please," she begged, squeezing her thighs around his head. "I'm ready. I'm so ready. Will you please let me—"

Adam lifted himself from his task, using one hand to brace himself on the couch as the other fumbled with his fly.

"Almost there, Nikki," he said. "You're doing such a good job. Can you go one more round for me?"

"Yes," she said, her voice nearly broken in half from wanting.

Adam retrieved a condom from his back pocket and tore it open. How long had he been carrying it around? Nicola tried to remember how to breathe as Adam wrapped himself in the condom and tugged her closer, not even bothering to remove his jeans all the way.

She looked to Finley one more time, all but drowning in his storm-dark eyes.

"Tell him when you're ready," Finley said softly, with the reverence such a thing deserved.

"I'm ready," Nicola said, and then Adam was inside her

and the world *was* Adam, made of nothing else but his presence and amber-skin scent and his pressure on top of her.

Neither of them lasted long. Within minutes, Adam's thighs were trembling, and Nicola was begging for release in a nearly incoherent string of babble. Adam leaned over her, driving into her deeper and faster.

"Touch yourself," he panted in her ear. "Get yourself there."

Nicola rubbed her clit fast, trying to catch her orgasm before Adam could snatch it away. Adam's rhythm became desperate and stuttering as he approached his own climax.

"You say when, Adam," Finley reminded him, and *God*, that clinical detachment should not be so hot.

"Come for me, Nikki," Adam said.

Nicola's orgasm hit her like a truck. One moment she was whimpering, doing everything she could to pull herself to the pinnacle, and then she was *there*, a sharp stab of pleasure radiating out from her belly as her toes curled in on themselves.

"Fuck, I can feel . . ." Adam said. Then he let out a grunt and spilled into the condom, all sticky heat and sweet release.

Nicola and Adam lay together for a moment, their bodies pressed together, their skin tacky with drying sweat. Then Adam lifted his head, his eyes as bright as she had ever seen them. He was just Adam, the same goofy, kind, frustratingly headstrong young man she had always called her dearest friend. But he was also something else now, something Nicola didn't quite have the words to define but was incredibly grateful for.

"That was amazing," he breathed. "You're amazing."

"Same to you," she said, blushing through her afterglow. She looked over to Finley, her heart pounding in his chest. Would he be pleased with her? Would he be jealous, or disappointed?

Finley was still curled up in the chair, sitting perfectly still as though moving any muscle might cause the dreamy atmosphere in the room to dissipate. His dark curls shaded his eyes, making parsing his expression difficult.

"How was that?" Adam asked, and if Nicola wasn't mistaken, she detected a note of challenge in his voice.

Finley cleared his throat.

"I think everyone had a very good time," he said tightly.

"I'll take it," Adam murmured with a smile, to Nicola, not Finley. Then he stood and said, a little sheepishly, "I should probably go get cleaned up."

Finley nodded, waving him off. Nicola felt Adam lean down and kiss her forehead, and she heard him wander off to the bathroom, but she didn't see any of it, because she couldn't stop staring at Finley. He was taking quick, shallow breaths, and the outline of his cock was still clearly evident through his jeans. How he had resisted getting himself off surreptitiously in the corner, Nicola couldn't fathom.

Then again, maybe he understood denial better than any of them.

"Nicola," he said, with such raw adoration that it made her heart seize.

Nicola tugged her skirt back down over her thighs, then she carefully slid off the couch and onto the floor. Onto her knees.

Never breaking eye contact, Nicola slowly crawled across the room to Finley. She tried to be present with the act, to focus on the pressure of the hardwood under her knees, the stretch in her back. There was a pleasant ache in her sex, a tingle of aftershock still running up her spine.

She didn't stop until she was right in front of him, and then she sat back on her heels and placed her hands on his thighs.

Finley took an uneven breath and uncrossed his legs. Nicola knelt between his knees, her nimble fingers finding the zipper on his jeans. He was hard as a rock when she took him in hand.

"You don't have to," he said, smoothing her curls away from her face and sliding his fingers through her hair.

"What if I want to thank my teacher for such a good lesson?" she asked, then wrapped her lips around his cock.

Nicola had done this many times before, but it felt different somehow, kneeling at the feet of someone she had entrusted her own pleasure to moments before. She bobbed her head up and down, taking as much of him as she could, and used her free hand to cup his balls.

"I'm going to hurt you," Finley said, and it was impossible to tell if he was warning her about what he was going to do next, or if he was prophesying that things would end badly between them. Either way, Nicola welcomed it. She made a humming sound of assent, then dragged her tongue along his length.

Finley hissed, and the grip in her hair grew more forceful, more directive.

Nicola moaned in satisfaction and let him fuck her mouth, losing herself in the experience.

When he came, it was with a jerk of his hips and a strangled cry, softer than she would have expected. Nicola swallowed every drop of him, savoring the taste. She even licked him clean afterwards.

Finley leaned down and pressed his knuckle beneath Nicola's chin, tipping her face up towards his for a kiss. Nicola kissed him deeply, sharing that taste with him, and then she drew away and beamed up at him.

Finley's eyes fell on something over her shoulder. When she looked behind her, she saw Adam standing in the doorway with a dish towel in his hands, probably to offer to Nicola. He wore the strangest expression. It didn't look like betrayal, or jealousy even.

It was more like longing.

"How long have you been standing there?" she asked. This should be fine, strictly speaking. Adam had told her she could do as she liked with Finley, and Finley had responded in kind. But high-minded notions about civility and sharing often flew out the window when the heart got involved.

To Nicola's great relief, Adam didn't seem angry.

"Long enough for a show," he said, and then walked over and held his hand out for Nicola. He pulled her to her feet as Finley tucked himself away in his jeans. "Does anyone want something warm to drink? I can boil water."

"I think Eileen may still have some drinking chocolate in the cupboard," Finley said, standing up. "I'll help you find it. Unless you two want some time to yourselves?"

"You're welcome to join," Nicola said, sliding her arms around Adam's waist. He was warm and solid, and she felt dopamine-drunk and drowsy. "If that's all right with Adam."

"Fine by me," Adam said, and together all three of them walked towards the kitchen.

CHAPTER TWENTY-EIGHT

Eileen

"What's the damage?" Eileen called, cupping her hands around her mouth to help the sound carry. Finley was balancing at the top of a rusty ladder they had hauled out of the gardening shed, taking stock of the state of the roof. In response, he tossed a few crumbling shingles down onto the ground. They landed at Eileen's feet, ancient and useless.

"I'll take that as an indication we might be looking at repairs," she said.

Finley dusted off his hands, then climbed down the ladder and came to stand at Eileen's side. He had left his coat in the house, and his forearms were slick with the mist hanging in the air. Eileen was bundled up in her biggest tweed coat, a newsboy cap protecting her hair from the damp. She had slept nearly twelve hours last night, and woke to the undeniable sense that something had happened in her house when she was asleep, something that she would have very much liked to be consulted about beforehand. Finley's guilty-dog look when she caught him in the kitchen told her most of the story, and the confession he had made when she pulled him into the pantry for privacy told the rest.

Eileen put on a good show, pretending not to care. Why should she? Finley wasn't her husband, and she wasn't his wife. They had always run around with other people, even if Eileen's options had been limited. And Adam and Nicola were the right people to run around with, if it came right down to it. Anything to bond them all more tightly together, to make Adam feel like he never wanted to leave, and to encourage Nicola to support him in his desire to stay.

And if Eileen felt a little bit left out, and like her health had prevented her from participating in a game she would have liked, that was her wound to nurse. She had laid into Finley about locking her in her room, at any rate, and he had insisted it was for her own protection. It felt good to fight with him about *something*, fighting felt familiar, made her feel like there was life left in her yet. And she had won that fight, by such a landslide that Finley had offered to do that chore he had been putting off and look at the roof to make amends.

"Lots of the shingles are shredded from weather, and others have been ripped off altogether," he pronounced. "Your parents didn't ever have this roof replaced, did they?"

"I doubt it. Even then, there wasn't much spare money for large repairs."

"Well, add the shingle damage to the accumulated wear and tear of the years, and we're seriously overdue for calling in a contractor."

Eileen wrinkled her nose and shook her head.

That simply wouldn't do.

"No outsiders," she said. "We'll fix it ourselves."

"Eileen, I'm not a roofer. If I don't break my neck from climbing up there, I'm liable to do more harm than good to the house. I've done what I can to keep the grounds clean and make essential repairs, but I don't have the expertise for this. I know you're tight on money, but this isn't something you ignore. Call a contractor."

Eileen shook her head again, more forcefully this time. Craigmar had stood for hundreds of years, and it would stand for hundreds more. She *was* Craigmar, it was in her blood. It wouldn't fall while she lived.

"You want me to bring a stranger in and tell them that my house needs to be defended against supernatural creatures, is that it?"

Finley sighed long-sufferingly in a way that made him seem twice his age. Eileen resented him for his old-man habits; they only served to remind her that he was technically a couple days older than her, and that he liked to act like it.

"I'm not saying anything like that. I know you don't like bringing in outsiders—"

"It's not that I don't like it. It's that it's dangerous."

"But exceptions have to be made. You see the doctor, don't you? Well, your house needs a doctor now."

"Don't talk to me like I'm a child," Eileen said, turning and walking towards the house with long, determined strides. God, she was *furious* with him. Any of the goodwill he had earned by promising to fix the roof while trapped in the pantry had completely evaporated.

Finley jogged to catch up with her, then caught her by the wrist.

"I need you to listen to me, Eileen. This is getting serious, and I don't think—"

"It's been serious for me from the start," she bit out, her temper snapping like a dry twig. "It's been serious since my parents were murdered. This place is my albatross, Finley, my home, *mine*. I don't expect you to understand."

A dark warning flashed behind Finley's eyes, an indicator that she was skirting too close to a sore subject, but she pressed on, gathering momentum as her anger mounted.

"You can leave anytime you want. You could move to Edinburgh, or go back to university, or go live with your father on Skye. Nothing is holding you here but some misplaced loyalty to my family, from which I release you. I can't leave, Finley, and I never will. I was born here and I'll die here, so I'll make the decisions about what happens to the house."

"*Release* me?" Finley said, barking out an unkind laugh. "You want me gone now, is that it?"

"I don't care what you do," Eileen said, even though she knew she did care, to a desperate, sickening degree. It was just so hard to control her tongue when she was angry, or frightened. She couldn't stop thinking about how close she had been to losing Adam, to destroying an innocent life and her only hope at survival in the process. There was so little holding the fae back from devouring Craigmar whole, just old promises and tenuous magic she didn't totally understand.

Eileen marched back to the main door, but Finley caught up with her again on the threshold. This time, he grabbed her by both shoulders and forced her to face him.

"Let me go or I'll scratch your eyes out," she ordered.

"I'm not here because of loyalty to your family, Eileen; hang your family. I'm here because of *you*, and you know that. How can you say all that when I—"

"Oh, you know I hate it when men grovel; don't start."

Finley shook her hard enough to rattle her earrings, and now he was *mad*, in that way that made the meanness coiled deep inside him strike like a pit viper. Eileen glowered right at him as he laid into her.

"I'm tired of giving you everything and having you throw it back in my face. You can hardly take care of yourself, and you beg me to boss you around and act like your father just so you don't have to think about anything, then you turn around and treat me like a servant the moment I displease you. You're an ungrateful, spoiled headcase and I'm the only one who fucking sees that, but

I'm still here. You *owe* me, Eileen. The things I have done for you, the lines I have crossed, the—"

He bit off the rest of the sentence, all the blood draining from his face. Eileen looked over to find Adam standing in the doorway, Nicola close behind him. She thought they had been gazing into each other's eyes, or having tender missionary sex, or doing whatever else normal young couples spent their time doing. Eileen wouldn't know. All the gazing and fucking in her life had always been coupled with fighting, with manipulation and pain and power struggle.

"I heard shouting," Adam said unsteadily, his eyes flickering from Eileen's face to Finley's tight grip on her shoulders.

Eileen wanted, in a dark, cruel rush, to hit Finley, really hit him. All her carefully laid plains and meticulously placed breadcrumbs of information, and he was about to blow it all in front of the Americans because he couldn't keep his mouth shut.

Eileen shoved Finley away. Hard. He stumbled back a few steps, then moved to grab at her again, but Adam was quicker. With a speed of a track runner, he was out of the house and between Finley and Eileen, gripping Finley's upper arm.

"Everybody take a lap!" Adam barked, holding Finley back. Eileen nearly stumbled in the gravel from the efficiency with which Adam had broken up the fight. "Eileen, go inside. Finley, you're with me."

"Stay out of this," Eileen snarled. "I don't need a white knight to protect me from this stupid—"

"Eileen!" Nicola called, holding out a hand. "Come on, let it go. I hate fighting."

"That's right," Finley said sullenly. "Take the princess to her tower room and serve her tea and crumpets; why should she ever have anything but the best? Why should she ever consider for one instant the way her actions impact other people—"

"That's enough now," Adam said, in that good-natured but firm way that had probably broken up a few bar fights. "Take a walk with me, will you? Nicola, take Eileen inside."

Eileen had half a mind to throw Adam to the ground so she could get to Finley herself. Who did Adam think he was, stepping into something he couldn't possibly understand? She and Finley fought, and they made up. It was the way of things. They had grown up tangled in each other like ivy, starving each other for light, and they were the only ones who really understood each other. She never asked for help. She didn't *need* help.

A touch on her wrist gave her a jolt, and Eileen turned to find Nicola standing at her side.

"Try to breathe, okay?" Nicola said. This simple act of sweetness was so unexpected, so ridiculous, that it broke the spell anger had been weaving around Eileen. She found herself following Nicola into the house, looking over her shoulder to see Adam sling his arm around

Finley's neck in that effortless way of men, bending in to say something soothing.

Then the door swung shut behind her.

"Tea is what you need," Nicola said. "Calms the nerves."

She led Eileen into the drafty kitchen by the hand and put the gooseneck kettle on. Eileen's skin tingled where Nicola touched her, searing her flesh with the impossibility of tenderness.

Nicola fished two bags of chamomile tea out of the cupboard, doctored up a pair of mugs with honey like she was slathering chocolate sauce on the inside of a Starbucks cup, and poured in the hot water the moment the kettle started to whistle. Then she sat down at the rough-hewn kitchen table and motioned for Eileen to sit with her. Eileen sank down into the nearest chair, memories of chopping carrots and peeling potatoes with her mother crowding in despite the circumstances. The knife grooves on the wood were so deep that the table smelled constantly of crushed thyme, her mother's favorite herb.

"Are you, uh, okay?" Nicola said, pushing Eileen's mug towards her. "It looked like Finley grabbed you pretty tight."

"I'm not afraid of a little manhandling," Eileen said breezily, knowing full well she might have done worse to Finley if Adam hadn't stepped between them.

Nicola's brows creased as she stirred her tea.

"But someone putting their hands on you in play, that's different from someone putting their hands on you in anger."

"I suppose," Eileen said, taking a sip of the scalding

tea. It peeled off a few tastebuds, but all the better. She deserved to hurt.

"And you shoved him too, Eileen. Really hard. I saw it"

"I did," Eileen said coolly, putting her tea back down. It tasted like home and freely given love, two things that currently felt like hydrochloric acid on bare skin. "What about it?"

"Your relationship isn't my business, but . . . Well, it sort of is, since Adam is kind of involved with you and I'm kind of involved with Finley. I know we're making this up as we go along, but I just don't want anyone getting hurt."

"I understand," Eileen said, wishing someone would come put a knife through her heart and end this misery for all of them. Maybe that was the simplest escape route. No lies or scheming needed, no collateral damage, just Eileen and her legacy bleeding out on the kitchen floor. She knew herself too well to think she was magnanimous enough to release either Adam or Nicola from their death spiral of lust and lies: it would take eliminating her from the picture entirely for either of them to be free.

"I'm glad to hear it," Nicola said, polishing off her own tea. "I certainly wouldn't want Finley to grab me like that, so there's no reason he should be grabbing you."

"Finley is right about some things. I can be spoiled and selfish. To put a finer point on it, I can be absolutely awful to people." Eileen yanked on her mental reins, reminding herself not to wander too close to the whole truth. "I'm trying to be better. And I want us all to be friends, at least."

"I think we already are. Although I should probably come clean about something . . ."

Nicola scraped her thumbnail along the faded painted flowers on the side of her teacup.

"What could you possibly have to confess?" Eileen asked with a laugh. Nicola wasn't afraid to show her teeth, that was true, but Eileen had a hard time imagining that Nicola could have done anything under her roof worth being secretive about. She seemed too earnest, too sweet-natured.

"I made some accusations to Adam about you a few days ago."

"Accusations?" Eileen echoed, her smile already fading.

"I got upset the night you and Adam found that picture of his grandfather as a child. I think I just felt . . . on the outside of things. I got it into my head that you had some sinister grand plan for him you weren't telling us about."

Eileen couldn't scrape together two words so she just looked at Nicola, hoping her expression was neutral. Hoping that the deafening pounding of her heart didn't give her away.

"I know you have secrets," Nicola went on, voice a little softer. "And they're yours to keep. But I hope you'll share some of them with me, in time."

"That's very kind," Eileen said, voice thick. Somehow, Nicola's generous patience was worse than any.

"Do you want to play a game with me?" Nicola went on.

The Confession game flashed through Eileen's mind, and for a moment she thought Nicola might be propositioning her. It was enough to make her lightheaded.

"A game?" she repeated, throat dry.

"Not that kind of game," Nicola said with a titter. Was Eileen imagining it, or was there a faint blush in Nicola's cheeks? "I was thinking cards or Scrabble. I'm pretty decent at Scrabble, actually. You have all those board games in the parlor. You like games, right? It might be a soothing activity."

Eileen found, to her horror, that the walls of ice around her heart were beginning to thaw in the presence of Nicola Fairweather. It was as natural as an iced-over loch coming back to life in the presence of the spring sun, but it was still horrifying. Eileen wasn't in the business of caring about people. Historically, she was terrible at it.

But perhaps, for Nicola, it was worth it to try.

Perhaps, this time, it wouldn't all end in ruin.

"That's a lovely idea," Eileen said, and gave Nicola's hand a squeeze. "I can show you a game I like."

CHAPTER TWENTY-NINE

Finley

Finley walked ahead of Adam with his hands thrust deep into his pockets and his mouth set into a grim line. He kept walking, saying nothing at all, until he came to a small stone bridge Eileen's father had constructed over a babbling brook. Finley had come here with Eileen countless times as a child to look at the ducks and toss stones into the water, or by himself as a man to brood. He slumped against the railing, flicking a stray leaf down into the water below.

"Nice day," Adam ventured, sidling up to Finley.

Finley huffed through his nose. The day was dreary and ugly, just like his heart.

"You can go back to the house, you know," Finley said. "You don't need to play counselor; I'm not going to hurl myself into the river. Eileen would probably be grateful to see you."

"I don't want to see Eileen right now, I want to see you," Adam said, leaning over the railing so he could look into Finley's face.

Finley flickered a glance his way, taking in those earnest blue eyes, that curving, thin mouth.

I want to see you. Finley knew Adam hadn't meant it this way, but it was impossible not to ruminate on the fact that Eileen was the only one who had ever really *seen* him, not as the hired help or as someone's wayward son, but as a person. People looked past Finley all the time. It was his job as a staff member to be invisible, after all. But Eileen had always seen him, really seen him, as intelligent and strong, and when he had revealed his dark desires to her, she had responded in kind. She looked at all that wanting, all that ugliness and selfishness, and saw someone worthy of love.

Maybe that's why he was addicted to her.

Maybe that's why he never left.

"Hey," Adam said, jostling his shoulder against Finley's. "Are you with me? You seem miles away."

"I'm with you," Finley mumbled, picking up a stone and hurling it with all his might into the water. It broke the surface with a satisfying splash, shattering the pristine scene. Finley wanted to throw more rocks. He wanted to tear up the grass and knock the supports out of the bridge and fill the brook with debris, just to feel something. To spite Eileen's dead father, perhaps, or to spite Eileen herself.

Or perhaps Finley was just hard-wired for destruction, doomed to ruin everything he touched.

"I'm sorry for losing my temper," he said. "It was stupid of me. Eileen just gets under my skin sometimes."

"What did she say to you?"

"She was saying I ought to leave her. That I don't belong here."

"That doesn't sound very nice," Adam ventured in that broad Midwestern accent. Finley hadn't grown up around many foreigners, and his childhood impression of Americans had been shaped primarily by television. He sometimes saw Adam as a cowboy, roughshod and brazen, riding into Craigmar on his horse to kick up dirt and cause a ruckus. It was easy now to imagine Adam as some small-town sheriff, playing peacemaker in a shining star badge and leather chaps.

"Well, she didn't exactly say that," Finley admitted. "But I know what she meant."

"You two go at it like that often?"

"Sometimes."

Adam nodded sagely, pursing his lips.

"The way I see it, you might try to be kinder to each other. You're all the other has, all the way out here."

"That's exactly the problem," Finley said, pushing off the bridge to make his way back to the house alone. He didn't appreciate Adam's unsolicited advice, or the talent Adam had for rummaging around in his brain.

"Come on," Adam said, "don't run off. I've got something to say to you."

"Then you ought to say it," Finley said, rounding on

Adam fast, like a warning. Adam didn't look the least bit frightened. Instead, he clapped Finley on the shoulder.

"I wanted to thank you," Adam said. "I know Nicola and I crash-landed in your life, but you've been very good to us, better than we deserve. You've kept Nicola grounded the whole time. You've done the same for me too. You're a good person, Finley."

Finley doubted Adam was trying to make him want to throw up from guilt, but that was exactly the effect his words had. Sickly shame settled deep into his stomach, roiling and churning. He shrugged off Adam's shoulder.

"Listen, Adam, I do like you. Probably more than I ought. So that's why I'm going to tell you plainly that I'm not."

"Not what?"

"A good person."

Finley expected his response to shut the whole conversation down. He expected Adam to turn away and leave him to his own thoughts. But then, Adam did something entirely baffling, which Finley was coming to learn was incredibly characteristic.

He smiled. Not one of Eileen's taunting smirks, but a real smile, all teeth and goodwill.

"Well, I've always been a poor judge of character when it comes to my friends."

Friends. Finley considered Adam an acquaintance, perhaps a very intimate acquaintance, but he hadn't allowed himself to place Adam in the friend category in his brain. Sure, they took their meals together and talked together while walking the grounds and yes, sometimes even had almost-threesomes together, but he refused to let himself think of Adam as a real friend. That seemed dangerous, especially considering the very active role Finley had played in sealing his fate.

But then again, Adam was right. He really was alone out here, except for Eileen and Nicola. He had been alone out here his entire life.

It might be nice to get on better terms with Adam. It might be nice to have another man he could talk to, about some things at least.

Finley sniffed and stuck out his hand. Adam shook it, and then pulled Finley into a one-armed embrace, probably the one he used to greet his other friends back home. Finley's hand drifted up in shock to press between Adam's shoulder blades, seeking closeness despite his mental refusal to accept what was happening.

Then, just as quickly as it had begun, the hug was over.

Finley was left reeling by the unexpected display of affection. Heat crawled up the back of his neck.

"You're cold," Adam said simply. "You need a coat."

Maybe it was something about all Americans, or maybe it was something about Adam, but Finley found the way he offered up his goodwill without an ulterior motive uncomfortably sexy.

This was bad, Finley decided. Eileen might permit all sorts of indiscretions in her house, but only when she was the one pulling the strings.

Finley was doing it again, rushing to defend Eileen from her own bad behavior. The woman wasn't even here; who was he trying to please?

Fuck Eileen's plans. Hell, fuck Eileen. Finley was allowed to keep things for himself, never to be shared with her, and maybe this spark of interest was something he could nurse in private. It wasn't likely to go anywhere, anyway. What could it hurt?

"Walk me home?" Finley ventured, allowing himself the indulgence of a slight innuendo threaded through the words. It was so faint he doubted Adam could have picked up on it, but it still felt electric, thrilling, like Finley was a boy stealing a peek at his Christmas presents before his father caught him.

"Happy to," Adam said, and fell into step beside him.

They found Eileen and Nicola curled up in the parlor loveseat, peering down at the brightly lit phone screen in Eileen's hand. Nicola's brows were furrowed in concentration, her fingertips pressed to her lips.

"What if you move that little cherry cluster over to the left?" she asked. "Would that complete the pattern?"

"No," Eileen said, glued to her phone. She tapped it a few times, resulting in the sound of popping bubbles and chiming bells. She hadn't even heard Finley and Adam walk into the house. "We should remove the apples first, there are more of them. But I don't see how."

"You could use a power-up?"

"I could, but I consider that cheating."

"Since when do you have any moral scruples when it comes to winning?"

"It's not a matter of morality. Winning when there's more of a challenge is simply more satisfying."

Finley cleared his throat, standing awkwardly in the doorway with Adam at his side. It seemed rude to interrupt whatever strange feminine bonding ritual was going on as Eileen and Nicola tried to riddle out the right strategy to beat Eileen's fruit-matching game. Eileen tended to prefer analog games, but she always kept two or three games on her phone, dumping a small fortune in microtransactions into them in an effort to beat her own high scores.

"Oh," Eileen said, shaken from her reverie. She clicked off her phone screen. "You're back."

"We're back," Finley said.

Eileen glanced up at Finley through mascaraed lashes. Finley knew that look. It was her best approximation at an apology.

"Got all the nonsense out of your system?" Eileen asked.

Nicola elbowed her in the ribs.

"Because I've got it out of mine," Eileen added.

"Looks like we're both feeling better," Finley said, impressed by the show of personal responsibility, tiny though it was. What kind of spell had Nicola cast over Eileen to make her so agreeable?

"You know what I think we all need?" Adam asked, clasping Finley on the shoulder. Finley tried not to tense. Apparently, Adam was very physically effusive with his friends. "Brandy."

"And then," Finley added, "I think we're overdue for a level-set. Are we all in a place where we can talk things through like adults?"

"I'm game," Adam said.

"Me too," Nicola replied.

"You bring the brandy and I'll bring my best behavior," Eileen said.

Finley nodded. It was a start.

CHAPTER THIRTY

Eileen

Eileen poured herself a snifter of brandy to warm her bones and her disposition while the other three chatted. Finley was considerably more pleasant since his conversation with Adam; now he was lingering close to where Nicola was sitting in an armchair and saying something soft near her ear. Nicola smiled at him, a sunshiny smile without a hint of malice.

Eileen swallowed the last of her generous pour, shifting from foot to foot on the parlor rug. She wanted to integrate herself somehow into their private world of gentleness, but she didn't understand how to. She never had.

Eileen knew she wasn't easy to live with, and that she was harder to love. She couldn't blame Finley for taking his comfort where he could find it.

"So," Adam said, swirling the brandy around in his glass. He was sitting cross-legged on the parlor couch, looking boyish in his stockinged feet. "Faeries. The way I see it, continuing to deny the possibility is actually the least rational thing to do."

"Oh, thank God," Nicola said. "I was getting tired of watching you hem and haw about it."

"A near-death experience will put the fear of the fae in a man," Finley muttered.

"If these things are after me, I'd like to understand them better," Adam said. "And I'd like to better understand how I fit into Eileen's family's story."

"That sounds sensible," Finley offered. He sat down on the rug at Nicola's feet, and she raked her fingers idly through his curls. Eileen couldn't fathom Finley bending so easily for her, handing over control without a fight.

"Let's take it from the top," Adam said. "What do we know?"

"Faeries are real, and they aren't very nice," Nicola said, propping her dimpled chin in her free hand. "Nothing groundbreaking there. They're locked in some kind of blood feud with Eileen's family, which also includes Adam, since Adam's grandfather was Eileen's grandmother's adopted brother. Jury's out on the why and the when of that."

"I'm still trying to figure out why they went after me," Adam said. "Eileen and I aren't related by blood. Doesn't that matter?"

"What you've got to understand is that those creatures are ancient," Eileen replied, finally breaking her silence.

"They've been alive since the time when a man's name was one of the only things he had in the world. And trust me, they give those who are adopted into the family just as much hell as they give those who are born into it. DNA doesn't matter to them. You're a Kirkfoyle."

"That doesn't sound as romantic as it did a few days ago," Adam muttered. "So I'm walking around with a target on my back, is that it?"

"For the time being, yes. It's probably safest for you not to stray too far from the house, at least not unaccompanied."

Adam tensed, a muscle jumping in his jaw. "But I can't just stay here under house arrest for ever. What if I want to go into town? What if I want to leave? What if . . .?" He trailed off, gnawing his lower lip until it was cherry-red.

Eileen didn't know Adam as well as she ought to, but she knew that he had spent most of his adult life flitting from country to country, never staying in one place long enough to become bored or panicked by the feeling of being tied down. He was a wanderer by nature, which made the Kirkfoyle name branded on his skin no better than a death sentence. He would waste away if she kept him here, just like the Kirkfoyles before him who had gone mad from their confinement.

Eileen wished there was any other way. For one fleeting moment, she almost felt like she could be good enough to let him go, if she acted very quickly. But then the reality of her situation settled back in again, heavy and dark as a stormcloud, and she resigned herself to their shared fate.

"In the old stories, there's always a way out of a faery bargain," Nicola said. "It might not be very comfortable, and it might require cunning or even deceit, but it's possible. You've been living under this curse your whole life, Eileen. Surely there's some kind of loophole in the treaty we could exploit so Adam could leave safely?"

Eileen opened her mouth and closed it again. The truth was welling up inside her, gathering in the back of her throat like bile. Her stomach churned. She hadn't been very hungry for days now, and it was getting harder to deny that it was because she, on some level, felt convicted of her sins.

There was a loophole, she knew damn well. The only one she ever had been able to find in all her years of searching, the one she may never have found if she hadn't stumbled across it pressed between the pages of the journal stored in the floorboards beneath her bed. But if she told Adam now, everything would shatter. She had to wait.

Soon. She would tell him soon, and she would deal with the consequences then. But not yet.

"Adam, you're free to go wherever you please," Eileen lied. No need to use force to keep him here unless it was absolutely necessary. The illusion of freedom would work just as well. "As long as there's one Kirkfoyle living in this house, Craigmar is safe. They haven't been able to kill me yet. This is my cross to carry, cousin. Not yours."

"You can't just say that," Adam replied. "I've seen things here that I can never forget, we all have. I can't just go back to freelancing out of my studio in Michigan, not after I've finally found proof of all my grandfather's stories, and I found you, and . . ."

Adam's voice trailed off, betraying the tender sentiment that had taken root in his heart like an invasive plant, and Eileen stared at him in horror. No one could care for her that quickly. Not even when she was wearing her friendliest mask and offering herself up in every sexual scenario imaginable and pretending to be good, to be kind. No one who got close to her could *love* her that quickly, not even Finley, who had become inoculated to her poison over time just as she had learned to work around his thorns.

Adam gathered himself, soldiering forward.

"I've been waiting my whole life to make it out here and, to be perfectly honest, I care about everyone in this room, maybe more than I should. I can't just leave."

When this whole affair had started, she had done a very good job of constantly reminding herself that Adam was here for a purpose, and that he didn't have to like her, and that she didn't have to like him either. But something about his earnestness had worn away at the defenses she had built so carefully around her humanity, and now the guilt was starting to bleed in. She *did* like Adam Lancaster. She liked his easy smile and the way he talked with his hands and the way he somehow had enough room in his heart for her and Nicola both. She liked his ferocious curiosity, and how he approached the world with a mixture of hardline reason and awe.

She liked him, goddamnit, and that was never supposed to happen.

"Then you're just as doomed as I am," she said, swallowing down the softness that was threatening to burst from within her. Softness had never served her, and it wasn't about to start now.

"Have you considered a more aggressive approach?" he asked. "What about walling up the cave with rocks?"

"We tried that in the eighteenth century," Eileen said. "The boulders mysteriously came loose during the night and rolled down the hill towards the house, damaging the east wing."

"What about negotiating the contract?" Nicola asked. "Has anyone ever tried that?"

"Yes, a Kirkfoyle tried in the 1920s. He went out to the cave with every mind to make peace and was never heard from again."

"Nobody inside that cave has any interest in peace," Finley said.

"Why should they?" Eileen scoffed. "Legend has it they live for centuries. Why lift a finger to make amends when they can just wait my family out while we drop like flies?"

A somber atmosphere settled over the room, and Eileen glowered down at her hands. Suddenly, Adam slapped his thighs and shot to his feet, as though he couldn't bear to sit for a moment longer.

"I need air, and I need to think. I'm going into town."

"Not alone you aren't," Eileen said. "Finley, you're with him."

"I don't need a chaperone," Adam replied.

"Regardless, it's too dangerous for you to wander around alone. Do you really want to face whatever bit you out at the cave, or whatever grabbed you in the loch, again, alone? They can cause you plenty of distress without touching you, iron ring or no."

Adam fell silent at that.

"I need to stretch my legs anyway," Finley said, pulling himself to his feet. "And I won't say no to a porter from the pub. Adam, mind some company?"

"Not if you buy the first round," Adam said, arching a playful eyebrow. Finley smiled back, and Eileen once again noticed the way the air between them sometimes warmed, heated by barely hidden flirtation.

"Godspeed," she said, surrendering herself to whatever the night may hold. "And good luck."

CHAPTER THIRTY-ONE

Adam

Adam and Finley squeezed into a table in the darkest corner of the Hound and Grouse, knees jostling against each other. Adam hadn't been at Craigmar long but he already felt the place rooting down inside him, filling his chest with gorse flowers and creeping thistle. It wasn't home to him, but he felt strangely unsteady even a few miles away from the house, as though he had forgotten how to exist in a world beyond the boundaries of its sultry magic. He had convinced himself Craigmar was the fantasy world, but now he realized that it was only at Craigmar that he felt truly real. That the shadows of the pub swirled in the corners of his vision as though in a dream.

Finley started them off with two porters in sweating glasses, setting them down on the table with a decisive *thump* that roused Adam from his thoughts.

"Cheers," Finley said.

"*Sláinte*," Adam replied, clinking their glasses together.

"Nice accent. You're going native."

Adam took a long pull of his beer before replying.

"Just trying to keep up with you and Eileen."

They drank in awkward silence for a few more moments, disappearing half a beer each, and then Finley leaned across the table, crossing his hands on the wood. His iron earrings glinted in the firelight, a reminder of the debt they all had to pay to Craigmar, to its wild magic. Adam's iron ring chafed against his skin. He had asked Eileen once, over a late lunch of croissant sandwiches in the library, why Finley wore iron so faithfully if he wasn't a Kirkfoyle. Eileen's eyes had clouded over with emotion, and she had muttered something about faeries delighting in robbing Kirkfoyles of whatever it was they cared for most. Her response had confused him then. Now, Adam was starting to understand.

"I didn't thank you properly," Adam said eventually. "For pulling me out of the water."

"It was nothing," Finley said, shrugging one shoulder. "It was the decent thing to do."

"It was the thing for a decent *person* to do," Adam corrected.

Finley tugged on his lip with his teeth, looking away. He always broke eye contact when Adam got too serious with him, or looked at him too hard. "Thanks," he said eventually.

They drained their first beers quickly and Finley

disappeared to produce a second round. When he returned to the table, his face was lit up with delight.

"She says it's on the house," he said, nodding over his shoulder at the pretty red-headed bartender with well-worn smile lines who was running the show that night. She was probably ten years older than Adam, freckled and tall. "She says it's because you're easy on the eyes."

Adam glanced again at the bartender, who shot him a wink.

"That seems like trouble," he said, smiling despite himself.

"Good trouble," Finley corrected. "But only if you're up for it. Do you want me to get you her number?"

"Eh, probably not," Adam said, trying to play his disinterest as cool as possible. Finley didn't need to know how hard up he was for Eileen and Nicola *all the time*, how much of his waking thoughts were occupied with them. There was no room for anyone else. At least, not anyone who wasn't already under the heady spell of Craigmar. "You should get it for yourself, though. She's hot."

"Nah," Finley said, putting away more beer. "I've got my hands full with Nicola and Eileen. Or one for each hand, I suppose."

Adam's smile tightened, and it was only then that Finley seemed to realize he was irritating him. Adam had nothing against a little friendly kissing and telling, so long as no one was getting hurt or being outright degraded. But he still felt a hot jolt of jealousy inside him every time Finley talked about the girls, the kind that made his fingers itch, and

Adam was starting to fear that it had less to do with the girls than it had to do with Finley.

"Sorry," Finley said. "I didn't mean to be crass."

"Doesn't bother me," Adam lied, mostly because he didn't even know why he was bothered. Being bothered over anything Finley did was stupid.

"You seem bothered."

"Well, I'm not," Adam bit out, then covered his embarrassment by draining the rest of his second beer.

Finley tapped his fingers against his pint glass for a while, stewing in silence. Just about the time Adam was worried that he had somehow fucked up things between him and Finley even more, that they were going to have to muscle through this entire outing in silence, Finley made a confession.

"I wish I had any way to help you, or even any words of comfort to give you about this whole sordid affair, but I don't.

"Adam liked listening to him talk, liked the way he tossed antiquated turns of speech and five-dollar-words into otherwise normal sentences. It telegraphed so clearly that Finley had learned much of his vocabulary from reading, not necessarily by hearing those words spoken aloud in natural dialogue, and something about that endeared Adam to him greatly. Adam had always been lousy at reading: no focus, no ability to sit still. But he loved listening to people talk, especially when they used so many beautiful words.

"This story has been turning in on itself over and over

again since before any of us were born, and I won't pretend to have confidence that it's going to end any other way than the way it always has. So, sorry for that. Turns out I'm no good at cheering anyone up."

"Neither am I," Adam said.

"What I am good at, though," Finley said ponderously, rubbing the stubble on his chin, "is drinking."

An illicit thought, fueled no doubt by exhaustion and alcohol, flickered through Adam's mind: the ghostly sensation of that stubble scraping across his skin.

He should really call it a night. He and Finley were getting nowhere, and Nicola and Eileen would be waiting for them back at Craigmar. But there was a treacherous part of him that didn't want to walk away from this private moment with Finley. Adam had always craved novelty and adventure, and Finley had both in spades, but even more than that, Adam had come to respect Finley, no matter how grudgingly. He was an enigma Adam wanted to get to know better.

Intimately, if that was what was called for.

In the end, the devil of Adam's worse nature won out.

"You know what?" he said. "So am I. Round three?"

Finley grinned at him across the table, one perfect dimple appearing in his cheek, and Adam had enough presence of mind to know at that moment that he was well and truly fucked.

They went four rounds, all told, moving from porter to stout and then from stout to double pours of Highland whisky, pacing it out by sharing a basket of chips. By the end of the night they were acting like old friends, and Finley had been jostled by passers-by in the crowded bar so many times that he had circled around the table to sit pressed up next to Adam in the bench set into the wall. The entire side of Finley's body was pushed up against Adam, and the atmosphere was hot and close. Adam found himself short of breath, needing air.

"Do you want to get out of here?" Adam asked, and it was only after the words left his mouth that he heard the insinuation in them.

Finley swept his eyes all over Adam, and the American felt absolutely naked under his gaze.

"You're not driving in this state," Finley pronounced. "Want to get some night air to clear your head first?"

"I'd love that."

"Let me pay," Finley said, clapping Adam on the shoulders like they were brothers, like they were friends. Adam's stomach twisted needy and hot at the contact, but then Finley was gone, counting out money at the bar and chatting with the bartender. He made her laugh, a big bright laugh with her head thrown back. He grinned back at her, all dimples and shining eyes.

Was there anyone Finley couldn't charm?

Finley and Adam stumbled out into the cool Scottish night through the back entrance, finding themselves in a small red-brick alleyway. They were laughing at something, Adam didn't even know what, so hard they could barely speak. Finley leaned up against the wall of the alleyway, catching his breath with his hand pressed to his chest.

"You're not so bad, you know," Finley said with a lopsided smile. "In fact, I find you perfectly tolerable. I could even put up with you for a long while, if I was forced to."

The laughter dried up in Adam's throat. The world was spinning slower, the night quieter and velvety-soft around them.

"Tolerable?" Adam repeated, taking a step forward without really meaning to.

"Endurable," Finley said, like he *knew* the deft display of intelligence turned Adam on. "Bearable. Admissible, even, if you twist my arm about it."

That broke Adam. He took another step forward, right up to the brink of ruin, and braced his hands on either side of Finley's head. The other man's eyes darkened immediately, like he had gotten exactly what he wanted.

"What are you gonna do, Lancaster?" Finley challenged.

"You talk too much," Adam said, and crushed his mouth against Finley's.

Finley tasted like heather whisky and the sweet caramel notes of a porter, mixed with the unplaceable tang of something altogether unique to him. Adam felt like he was being resuscitated all over again, like he had felt when Finley had dragged him from the murderous green waters of the loch and brought him back to life. Heat and light bloomed inside his chest, delirious and perfect.

Finley kissed like he was trying to prove a point, chasing Adam's advance with his own nips and probing tongue. Somehow – it was hard to say in the haze of booze and lust – Adam ended up with his back against the brick and Finley's fists balled in his shirtfront. He had never been on the receiving end of Finley's commanding bedside manner, not like this, and he found that he liked the experience *very* much.

Finley kissed him again, punishingly, like they were at war. They were exposed in this alley, with grime underfoot and moonlight overhead, but Adam didn't care. Fuck decency, and fuck anyone who stumbled across them. He and Finley had been hurtling headlong towards this moment from the instant they met, and Adam wasn't about to back away from it now.

Finley pressed their bodies flush together, and Adam could feel his hard length digging into his thigh. Adam let out a low moan, pulling Finley in tighter. He could die like this, and die happy.

Eileen was going to kill him, and Nicola would tease him within an inch of his life about it. But his heart was thrumming and his skin was on fire and his jeans were painfully tight.

In for a penny, in for a pound, Adam thought.

His fingers dropped down to pluck open Finley's fly.

"Let me," he said, nearly pleading. God, what was he becoming?

Finley reared back, looking for all the world like a startled horse.

"Here? Now?"

"Let me suck you off," Adam said, dropping to his knees in the filthy alleyway. Normally he would care about things like cleanliness and not breaking public indecency laws, but right now, all he cared about was pushing Finley until he broke.

Finley didn't have another word to utter in protest. He simply let Adam unzip his jeans and free his cock from their confines, hissing in the dark as Adam gave an experimental stroke. Adam had seen plenty of men naked before, and he had taken plenty of them to bed, but nothing could compare to this experience. Having Finley in the palm of his hand, quite literally, feeling the muscles in the other man's thighs tense as Adam wrapped his lips around the head of Finley's cock. He tasted like soap and salt and skin-musk.

"Christ," Finley swore, threading his fingers through Adam's hair. "*Adam.*"

Adam made a pleased humming sound in his throat and took as much of Finley into his mouth as he could, applying himself with the vigor of a dedicated student. Finley kept swearing under his breath, his language getting progressively more colorful as Adam stroked him and licked the underside of his shaft. Adam could do this for an hour if Finley just kept *talking*.

Adam's back was braced against the wall of the alleyway, so when Finley started thrusting into his mouth, there was nowhere for Adam to go. He just lost himself in the sensation, stinging eyes slipping shut as Finley took his pleasure with rough abandon. His knees would be bruised in the morning, but he would count the markings as precious if it meant he got to enjoy this moment, just the two of them letting off steam under a velvety night sky.

Finley came quickly, spilling down Adam's throat with a grunt and a gasp. Adam sucked him clean, swallowing dutifully.

"Jesus, Joseph and Mary," Finley said, still trying to catch his breath. "You're good at that."

"I know," Adam said smugly.

Finley grasped his wrist and hauled him up, pulling him into another kiss. Adam nearly pulled away, convinced that no one would want to kiss him after he had just done that, but Finley didn't seem bothered in the slightest. He palmed Adam through his jeans as he slipped his tongue into his mouth, rubbing a delicious circle that made Adam squirm against the touch.

"My turn," Finley said, leaving no room for argument. He unzipped Adam's pants and slipped his hand down the front of his boxers, grasping his cock like it belonged to him. Adam sucked in a breath, the muscles in his stomach quivering.

"Fuck," he managed. "*Yes.*"

"You've been hard up for this for a while now, haven't you?" Finley said, a little bit careless and a little bit mean, like this didn't mean anything at all, but then he dropped his mouth to Adam's shoulder and pressed a kiss to the juncture of his neck with a gentleness that betrayed him. He kept kissing him like that, slow and exploratory, as he pumped Adam's cock with merciless expertise.

Once again trapped between the wall and Finley, Adam had no choice but to accept the waves of pleasure as they crested over him, building in the base of his stomach to an unbearable degree. Adam dug his fingers into the other man's shoulders, holding on for dear life.

"Finley," he rasped, "I'm going to—"

He never got a chance to complete his sentence, because he finished in a surge of sensation so strong it nearly blinded him. Finley sidestepped the mess, and kept stroking until Adam was entirely spent, so sensitive he considered begging Finley to stop. But Finley, who watched him with keen, studying eyes, stopped mere seconds before Adam had to ask, smoothing his hand up the plane of Adam's stomach to hold him against the wall with a firm palm on his chest. The touch steadied Adam, acting as a center of gravity to lean on while he caught his breath.

"I've wanted to do that since I met you," Finley confessed, still watching his face like Adam was *fascinating*, like he could observe him for a hundred years and not get bored.

Adam huffed out a laugh, his cheeks hot.

"Does that mean I win some kind of bet?"

Finley shoved him against the wall, playfully this time, and pressed one last firm kiss to the corner of his mouth.

"Don't let it go to your head."

A car drove by the alley, headlights skimming across their feet, and Adam remembered suddenly that they were in public.

"We should probably get out of here," Finley said, taking a few steps back. "We've been gone hours; the girls will be missing us."

Adam nodded, reality clearing through the haze of endorphins. The girls. Eileen. Nicola. Was this something Adam would have to apologize for? They had never nailed down the ever-shifting boundaries of their relationships to each other, and the rules seemed to change with the winds, or with the hurt feelings of those inside the house. Life tended to work out for Adam, in matters of career or money or love, but he was worried that perhaps there were things even he couldn't undo, trespasses he couldn't talk his way out of.

"Should we tell them?" Adam blurted. It wasn't a very suave thing to say, but he needed to know.

"Absolutely," Finley said, as though it wasn't a question. "I'd recommend gauging what kind of mood Eileen is in before you go unburdening your heart, however. She can be . . ."

"Temperamental," Adam supplied. Then, trying again for something that didn't sound so insulting. "Territorial."

"Sounds like we understand each other," Finley said, clasping Adam's arm as though they were sealing some kind of pact. Adam reeled slightly as they sought their balance on the knife's edge between lovers and friends. "Come on. I'm driving."

CHAPTER THIRTY-TWO

Nicola

Once it became apparent that the boys would not be back for some time, Nicola wandered up the narrow stairs to Eileen's room. She hadn't been up to this room yet, and she was nervous to knock. But Eileen called her inside, and Nicola walked in to find Eileen playing a very serious game of solitaire. Eileen's dark brows were creased in contemplation as she laid down cards just so on the white duvet of her bed. Nicola had imagined Eileen's room before out of curiosity, sometimes innocent, sometimes less so, and she had always imagined some kind of gothic chamber, perhaps adorned with taxidermized birds or elegantly displayed kink gear. But instead, the room was small and cozy, hung with landscapes and tapestries and decorated with girlish trinkets like carved hand bells and miniature porcelain figurines of shepherdesses. Eileen even had a caramel-colored teddy bear on her bed, an honest-to-God stuffed animal. It appeared so well-loved Nicola supposed it must be a family heirloom.

"It's getting dark," Nicola said, clutching the woven blanket she had swiped from her own room tighter around her shoulders. It was nearly summer, but the weather was still mild, and the house was perpetually drafty. "Should we call them?"

"I say if they're taking their time, let them," Eileen said, placing down one more card before looking up at Nicola. She was wearing a simple linen men's shirt and black trousers, her wild hair swirled up in an artful bird's nest on top of her head. "So long as they don't end up dead in a ditch or in the clink somewhere, I won't complain."

"Don't even say that," Nicola said, but she was chuckling. She had learned the contours of Eileen's dry sense of humor, and she had grown to appreciate it. "Are you hungry? I'm peckish."

"I suppose we ought to fend for ourselves if the boys won't be back in time for supper. Do you like charcuterie?"

"I love it," Nicola said. "Don't we have fresh grapes?"

"And honeycomb. Come on, let's fix a platter."

Nicola padded after Eileen down the stairs and into the kitchen, where she and Eileen arranged cheese, rosemary crackers, and the grapes and honeycomb onto a literal silver platter. This felt a little lavish to Nicola, and the silver itself was tarnished, so well-used the floral engraving had been almost entirely worn away. Eileen didn't seem to think there was anything odd about having a light meal on silver, but then again, she had been born into decaying finery.

Eileen produced a bottle of merlot from the cellar, and they carried their spoils into the library, where they sat close together on the couch. A little color returned to Eileen's cheeks in the glow of the fire, and Nicola warmed from the inside out as she sipped her wine.

"Do you like that?" Eileen asked, topping up Nicola's glass with another pour. "I'm more partial to chianti myself, but this is a nice vintage. Can you taste the clove? I like it when wine has that quality; the taste of earth."

"I'm not very good at the whole picking out tasting notes thing," Nicola said. "I'm more of a discount six-pack girl myself. Not very sophisticated."

"I think you're quite sophisticated," Eileen said, a playful sparkle in her eyes. "And cheap beer has its own rustic charms. Although you're an artist with an eye for color and texture; you can probably pick out more notes than you think. I'll show you. Go on. Take a sip."

Nicola hesitantly raised her glass to her lips, then swallowed with determination.

"A small sip," Eileen amended. "Don't swallow this time. Hold it against your soft palate. Let the wine caress your mouth."

Nicola blushed, feeling a bit silly for taking her time with something like drinking, which she usually did thoughtlessly as a means to an end, whether it was feeling included in a party or reaching that floaty headspace where she didn't feel so paranoid about everything she said making people leave her behind. But Eileen never broke eye contact, waiting patiently for Nicola to obey, and something about that focused attention made Nicola *want* to obey. It made her want to be good.

Nicola took a delicate sip of wine, letting it coat her tongue before she pressed the liquid up against the tender roof of her mouth.

"What do you taste?" Eileen asked.

"Wine," Nicola said, feeling even more foolish as she swallowed as slowly as she could. "Red wine? With . . . tannins?"

"Good. Again. Look for more."

Nicola brought her glass to her lips again, pausing this time to inhale deeply, the way she had seen people do in fancy restaurants.

"Maybe berries? A dark berry, not a strawberry. A blackberry?"

"Yes!" Eileen said, eyes alight with pleasure. "I get lots of blackberry. Good girl. Anything else?"

Nicola tried to ignore the way warmth pooled in her stomach at that phrase: *good girl*. Had anyone ever called her that? Certainly not with so much sincerity, like it wasn't a joke at all.

"Vanilla," Nicola pronounced with more confidence. It was easier to believe she was not only good but clever when Eileen encouraged her like that.

"Well done," Eileen said. "Appreciating wine isn't about skill, it's about speed. Slowing down enough to appreciate all the different forms pleasure may take."

"I still think you're better at that than I am," Nicola said, popping a grape into her mouth.

Eileen gave her a thin smile, like she was a cat who had caught the scent of a mouse in the walls.

"Hedonism can be learned. I'd say you've been a very diligent student."

A double entendre from Eileen wasn't uncommon, as she often spoke in riddles and suggestive metaphors. But it was hard not to feel, as they sat side by side alone in the great empty house, that there was something in that sentence that was meant especially for Nicola and Nicola alone.

With no audience to perform for, with no men around to titillate, Eileen's favor felt more real. More meaningful.

It felt like an invitation.

"Here's to lifelong learning," Nicola said, raising her glass. Eileen clinked their glasses together, eliciting a merry ting. Nicola understood Finley especially well in that moment. How he could fall so wholeheartedly for Eileen, despite her fickle whims and secrets and demands. How being looked at like this, like you were the center of Eileen's world, was more intoxicating than even the strongest wine.

Nicola knew, rationally, that Eileen was not the safest person to cozy up to, or at the very least, not the most honest. But she was so charismatic, black eyes reflecting Nicola's own troubled childhood and desire for a life lived to the fullest back to her, and she was so beautiful, and her hand was resting lightly on Nicola's knee.

"You're cold," Nicola said, brushing her fingers across Eileen's knuckles. "Do you want to go back to bed?"

"Not on your life," Eileen said, setting down her glass. "I'm having far too good a time with you. Here, let me stoke the fire."

Nicola sat patiently while Eileen expertly fed the fire, feeling for all the world like a princess being doted on by a noble suitor. When Eileen sat back down, the fireplace crackling merrily behind her, Nicola was so flustered by the display of chivalrous competency that it was all she could do to smile nervously.

"How is your book coming?" Eileen asked.

"Okay," Nicola said. "Although writing about made-up creatures seems silly when there are real supernatural creatures roaming around outside."

"It isn't silly," Eileen said, perfectly serious. "Children need tales of wonder to help them develop good brains. Besides, fairy tales teach us courtesy and safety. I'm sure there are a lot of lonely children out there who would do well to find a new friend in a book."

"Exactly," Nicola said, joy bubbling up inside her. "You understand. I didn't have . . . Well, I didn't have the most stable childhood, but books helped me to feel less alone."

"Same for me. I was sick all the time, stuck in this big old house with just my parents and the doctor for company. I never met many children my own age, outside of Finley. Books were my constant companions."

Nicola had wondered about all the children's books in Eileen's childhood bedroom, how she had seemingly neglected to get rid of any of them, but now she understood the sentimental attachment. It was so humanizing to imagine Eileen returning to *Peter Rabbit* and *The Adventures of Alice in Wonderland* over and over again, so . . . sweet.

"Do you think you and Finley would have gotten together if you weren't thrown together by circumstance like that?" she asked, and then immediately regretted it. Nicola was sometimes too earnest, too open with her curiosity. She often offended people accidentally. However, Eileen didn't seem upset, she only thought for a long moment.

"I think we would have found each other eventually," she said. "We're two sides of the same moon, him and I."

"But you also found Adam," Nicola ventured, emboldened to ask more questions after her first one wasn't shot down.

"Yes, I suppose I did. He was an unanticipated boon, I'd say."

"I'm going to tell him you said that," Nicola teased.

"You'd better not," Eileen replied with a smirk. "I'm trying to keep him on his toes."

"I'm impressed you can manage them both."

"You don't seem to have a problem managing them

yourself," Eileen said, nudging Nicola. They were seated even closer now, with their thighs and shoulders touching, ostensibly so they could both reach the charcuterie board. But they had finished dinner fifteen minutes ago. Was Eileen coming on to her? Nicola didn't know, and she felt like assuming wrong in this situation would be unilaterally disastrous.

"I've got a big heart," she said softly, her eyes dropping to Eileen's mouth. Eileen had forgone her slash of russet lipstick that day. Was it intentional, this flicker of vulnerability? This removal of her warpaint that, like a stoplight, forbade any but the most determined pilgrim from approaching the shrine of her lips?

"I've got a greedy heart," Eileen said, sliding her arm around Nicola's shoulder over the back of the couch. "I'm afraid I'm not a very nice person."

"Nice is different than good. And I think you're good, deep down."

"It would take a saint to see the good in me," Eileen said, one thumb brushing idly against Nicola's shoulder. The sensation sent a shudder down Nicola's spine. "Are you the maiden brave of spirit and pure of heart who's come to tame the dragon?"

Now Nicola felt drunk, not from wine, but from Eileen. Eileen was so close, and so warm, and she smelled like girlish pressed powder and the masculin-sap of the trees outside.

"Do you want to play a game with me, dove?" Eileen murmured, her sweet breath tickling Nicola's lips.

"Not a game," Nicola said quickly.

Eileen drew back immediately and opened her mouth in a panic, trying to course correct. Nicola caught her before she could fully retreat, cupping her face in her hand. Eileen's cheek was strangely cool, like she was clammy from the comedown of a fever.

"I don't want any games between us," Nicola said, swallowing hard and gathering her courage. "But I would like to kiss you."

Bewilderment flashed behind Eileen's eyes, as though she couldn't fathom that someone would want her without being tricked into the wanting. As though without the half-pretend fantasy world of a game, no one would ever put up with her.

Then, Eileen surged forward and kissed Nicola on the mouth.

Nicola made a soft sound of pleasure, opening her mouth further as Eileen cradled her jaw and stroked her hot tongue across Nicola's lower lip. Nicola let her hands roam, coming up to grasp Eileen's waist.

"Such a pretty girl," Eileen said breathlessly, leaning back down to kiss Nicola again and again. There was an awkward urgency to her kiss, heady though it was, a trembling in her hands as she gripped Nicola's hips. "Such a courageous maiden."

"You aren't the dragon," Nicola said between kisses. "You aren't a monster."

Eileen let out a strangled sound, like she had attempted

to speak and found herself incapable of it, and then she laid Nicola down on her back on the couch. Eileen leaned over her, bracing herself with one hand on the arm of the couch, and kissed Nicola until she was breathless.

Eileen's kiss was firm and exacting, like there was strategy behind it, like she was trying to kiss Nicola *exactly* right. Like all that mattered was figuring out how Nicola liked to be kissed. But Nicola liked a little bit of everything, most days, and she liked a lot of everything when it came to people she had been wistfully lusting after, so everything Eileen did felt good, even when her teeth bumped against Nicola's. As Nicola became more and more pliant, warming under Eileen's hands like clay in the fingers of a sculptor, Eileen kissed her with less self-consciousness. And when Eileen bit down on Nicola's earlobe and Nicola made a mewling sound, like a kitten crying for more attention, Eileen took a ragged breath and said,

"Can I touch you? Under that skirt I got you."

Nicola was nodding before her brain had even fully processed the request. She tugged her tweed skirt – tight enough to show off her ass, and now she *knew* Eileen had kept that in mind while picking it out – up over her hips, revealing her black cotton panties. Eileen brushed her fingers over their decorative pink satin bow reverently, then slipped her hand underneath the fabric.

Nicola gasped as Eileen slid her fingers through the

short blonde curls and down to where Nicola was wet and throbbing and needy. A wave of pleasure rolled through Nicola's belly as Eileen stroked her pussy, slow and experimental, like this was the first time she had touched another woman. Nicola remembered, with another wave of pulsing pleasure, that by Eileen's own admission, it was.

"Harder," Nicola whined. She tried to catch her breath, suppressing the urge to be bossy despite how badly she wanted more. "I like it harder. If you want to, you can—"

Eileen pressed the heel of her palm down against Nicola's clit, snatching the last of her words away. Not that Nicola could have managed to say anything anyway, because Eileen was kissing her again. Nicola tugged at the collar of Eileen's shirt, unfastening buttons and popping one off in the process, then slid her hand over Eileen's firm, high breasts. She wasn't wearing a bra underneath the silk, and Eileen shuddered as Nicola swiped her thumbs over Eileen's peaked nipples.

"I've got to get inside you, starling," Eileen said. "Please let me. Please, can I—"

Nicola pressed Eileen's hand down further with her own, canting her hips up to give Eileen's fingers even easier access. When Eileen slipped two cool fingers inside her, Nicola felt so full and so relieved that she could have cried.

"You're going to have to show me how you like it,"

Eileen said, dark hair tumbling over her collarbones as she shrugged her shirt off her shoulders. "Show me how you touch yourself when you're alone."

Nicola kept her hand on top of Eileen's as Eileen pumped her fingers in and out of Nicola, slowly at first and then faster as Nicola guided her touch. She was so swept up in the moment, in Eileen's fingers inside her and Eileen's perfectly bitable collarbones and petal-pink nipples right where Nicola could reach them with her mouth, that she didn't even hear the drums. Not right away.

At first, she thought it was simply her heartbeat hammering away in her ears, or some auditory trick brought on by distant thunder. But then that droning, unmistakable rhythm grew louder and louder, filtering into the house as though from far away.

"What is that?" Nicola asked, breaking the kiss. She couldn't say exactly why she was scared, but a deep ancestral memory stirred inside her, of fighting or freezing or fleeing.

Eileen withdrew her fingers and gripped Nicola's thigh, almost hard enough to bruise. She held her tight and she listened, more intent and more serious than Nicola even thought Eileen was capable of being.

There were definitely drums. And they were getting closer.

"Eileen?" Nicola whispered.

"Shut the windows and draw the curtains," she said

quickly, climbing off Nicola. There was an absolutely stricken expression on her face. In that moment, she looked like the most miserable girl in the world. "And stay as quiet as you can."

CHAPTER THIRTY-THREE

Eileen

Eileen could still taste Nicola's strawberry lip oil as she frantically locked the windows and drew the shades, her heart pounding in her chest. It was a jarring thing, the taste of summer and girlish sweetness on her mouth while fear-soaked bile rose up in her throat.

The drums were closer now, along with the sound of those discordant bells that she heard in her dreams. Only this time, there was no waking up from the nightmare.

This had only ever happened once to her parents, she had been told, on a midwinter's night when the moon was full. Eileen had been an infant, and she had blessedly slept through the racket. Her parents said the faeries had them surrounded for hours, rattling the roof with the sounds of merriment without ever becoming visible through the windows. The assault had only ceased with the rising of the sun, just as James was threatening to walk right into the yard with his rifle and end it for good, whatever that meant.

Eileen wanted to be brave. She wanted to scoop Nicola up like a dashing hero out of one of Finley's adventure books and lock her away in her room for safekeeping. But Eileen was rooted to the spot with fear, dread crawling down her spine as the sound of high-pitched laughter filtered in through the roof, through the windows. Even up through the floorboards.

Eileen didn't care if this was a trick of the fae, or a trick of this old house, or a trick of her mind. She knew in the deepest pit of her stomach that they were surrounded, entirely at the mercy of whatever creatures had come to call on them.

This is it, Eileen thought. *They've finally come to get me.*

She scurried out into the hall long enough to lock the front door, as though that would do anything to help, then retreated back into the library, feeling feverish and more ill than she had in a long time.

She had thought perhaps that she would be the one to break, in the end. That she would surrender to the whispers in her dreams and march out in her nightclothes into the woods, to be so disoriented by old magic that she walked in circles until she starved, or maybe make it all the way into the cave just to hurl herself inside, right into the hungry mouth of her family's oldest enemy. But she had held out, all this time, and now the faeries had grown impatient. Now, they had come to her.

She didn't know whether to be proud of herself or not.

The music was deafening now, discordant chiming joined by screeching strings that rang through the library. The roof creaked, and dust and plaster drifted down onto Nicola's shoulders and dusted her hair. There was nowhere to run and nowhere to hide, but Nicola didn't know that. Nicola just looked confused and frightened, so Eileen did the only thing she could think to do. She pulled Nicola down with her onto the floor, where they curled up between the couch and the bookshelves to wait it out, or wait for death.

"What's happening?" Nicola whispered, touching Eileen's face with searching hands.

"I don't know," Eileen muttered. "I think—"

There was a deafening bang on the front door. Eileen nearly jumped out of her skin, nauseous with terror. God, she wanted to throw up.

All her planning, all her lies and schemes and careful patience, were all going to come to nothing. She was going to die, and Nicola was going to die with her, and Finley would find their bodies clutched together just like this. Maybe Adam would take up the Kirkfoyle mantle and care for whatever was left of the house, or maybe, the story would finally end here, a legacy engulfed in decay.

There was another bang, louder this time. Nicola gasped, burying her face in Eileen's shoulder.

Eileen ignored the cold sweat of terror breaking out all over her body, and she fixed her eyes on the library door.

Bang!

Bang!

The knocking grew until it sounded like someone was assailing the door with a battering ram. The floorboards shook with every strike.

Eileen slowly rose to her feet, her fingertips shaking.

"No," she said, as though flat-out refusal could somehow save them both from the inevitable.

Bang!

"No!" she shouted, her voice drowned out by the clamor.

There was one more thundering crash, and the front doors gave way with a weary creak. At that moment, the raucous music from outside ceased, plunging the house into silence.

Footsteps echoed from the foyer, growing clearer as they approached.

Finley pushed his way into the library, and then Adam. They looked confused, but not at all concerned.

"What are you doing in here with all the windows shut?" Finley asked. "And why did you lock the front door? I didn't have my keys."

"We knocked," Adam said, pointing over his shoulder with his thumb towards the door. "A couple of times. Are you guys all right? Nikki, why are you on the ground?"

"Adam," Nicola gasped, clambering to her feet. She rushed into his arms. "Oh my God, it was horrible. You didn't hear that, not any of it? You didn't see anything outside?"

"I don't know what you're talking about," Adam said, hands coming up instinctively to pet her hair. God, but he was *good*. Good in a way Eileen could never be, good without having to try. "Just slow down. What happened?"

Something about watching Adam soothe Nicola made Eileen's mind up for her. She had reached the absolute limits of her patience with this situation, and dragging her feet about getting it over and done with wasn't going to help anyone. Adam may desire her, Adam may even harbor a fondness for her on some days, but he would never look at her like that. He would never trust her, not entirely, and he would be right not to. No matter what Eileen did, no matter how she measured her words or tried to be patient or tried to share herself and Finley nicely, Adam would never enter into this of his own free will.

It was time to apply pressure.

Eileen stalked out of the library, brushing past Finley and ignoring the way he said her name over and over again. Her Christian name, and her pet name, the one that had taken form when he was just a child and couldn't pronounce Eileen and so had called her Eye-la, which then became—

"Isla," Finley snapped as she hauled herself up the stairs. "Where are you going?"

The longer she waited, the more likely Adam was to wander off and get himself snatched away, or Eileen was to go utterly mad from all of her nightmares and drown herself in the bathtub.

The journal was right where she'd left it, stowed at the foot of her bed beneath the same floorboard Arabella had wedged lose all those years ago. Of course Eileen had found it. She was her grandmother's progeny, wasn't she? Just as curious, and just as hungry for everything forbidden. Of course she had found it, and of course she had read it. Every last word.

If Arabella's parents had known about this journal, they would have surely destroyed it. But Arabella, like Eileen, had been as clever as she was paranoid. She knew how to hide the darkest secrets of her heart from those who would hate her for them.

Eileen stomped down the stairs, feeling wrung out and on the verge of collapse with a headache spiking in her temple. She strode back into the library, and everyone fell silent as she slammed the journal down on her father's desk.

"No more games," she said, voice nearly breaking. "I'm tired of games. I just want to tally the points and have it over and done with, now."

"What are you talking about?" Adam asked, appraising her warily. Finley was already putting plenty of distance between himself and Adam, clearing the blast radius as he braced for explosion. Of all the ways they had talked about this going, they hadn't imagined this. Eileen had braced for seduction or coercion or force or some blend of all three, but she hadn't accounted for losing her composure She hadn't accounted for the fae finally breaking her mind.

"You asked me how my grandmother disappeared," Eileen said, flipping open the book to the right page. She had read through the journal so many times that she could find it based on feel alone, the weight of the paper between her fingers guiding her. "Here's the long and the short of it. One night, some time after she had been married to a man of her parents' choosing and two years after the birth of my father, she ran. Out into the night, into a rainstorm, right towards the cave. She went inside, and she never came out again."

"When Adam asked you about that, you said you didn't know. Why?" Nicola asked, face dark with fury. Moments ago, she had been clinging to Eileen. Now, Nicola looked like she might like to hit her. "I knew you were lying about something. I should have trusted myself. I should have—"

"Your grandfather left Craigmar before my grandmother ran," Eileen went on. As much as she liked Nicola, there was no time left for arguments. She kept her eyes trained on Adam. Looking at Nicola's wounded expression hurt too much. "Right before her wedding, in fact. And perhaps because he was adopted or just the strength of his own will, he managed to stay away. I'm happy to give more details with time. But for now, time is exactly what we're out of."

"Eileen," Finley said, warningly. What could he possibly be warning her about? That she was coming on too strong and would put Adam off his appetite for her? That she was having an unflattering response to nearly having the roof of her house ripped off by a band of roving faeries who delighted in nothing more than trying to scare her to death? Surely he couldn't be asking her to back out. It was too late for that now.

"Hush, Finley," Eileen snapped. She felt worn thin enough that she was sure if you held her up to a window, you could see light through her body. She couldn't handle a word of dissent from him right now. "Adam, I want to ask you—"

"I don't care what you want," Adam said. For the first time since he arrived, Eileen saw the coldness within him. The mean, imperious streak, the total disregard for human feeling that emerged only when he was pushed to his absolute limit. The expression on his face was breathtakingly cruel. It was like looking into a mirror. "I don't want to hear another word out of you unless it's explaining that whole story to me, slowly, in a straight line, so it makes goddamn sense. One minute you're talking about your grandmother; the next minute you're talking about my grandfather . . . Why did he leave this place?"

Eileen glanced to Finley, more out of instinct than anything else. He had always been her reprieve, her safe place to be as ugly or as selfish as she wanted without any real consequence. But now, despite the part he had played in all this, he couldn't even look at her. He just stared into the fire, like a holy man averting his eyes from a sin so terrible he couldn't bear to witness it.

He hadn't said a word, and yet she had never felt so abandoned by him in her entire life.

"Fine," she said, kicking the chair out from under her father's desk and gesturing for Adam to sit down in it. Adam didn't obey her, standing in defiance. She balled her hands into impotent fists at her sides and seethed. "*Fine.* Let's have it all out in the open and over and done with, shall we?"

Eileen flipped through her grandmother's journal, back to the page where the writing was jagged and the paper was stained with tears, and she began to read.

CHAPTER THIRTY-FOUR

Robert

Robert Kirkfoyle sulked on the stairs as his sister bid her suitor farewell in the foyer. It was an old-fashioned word, *suitor*, but there was no other word for the friend of a family friend who had started hanging around Arabella, always with their parents just a room away tittering over tea about what a perfect match they were. Robert hadn't bothered to learn his name: it was Daniel or Darren or something like that, and it didn't matter anyway, because Arabella would get tired of him soon and stop taking his calls.

Still, Robert couldn't help but feel a hot protective prick when Arabella let her suitor kiss her on her cheek, or on her mouth, or even on her neck in the few stolen moments after family goodbyes when they thought no one could see.

Robert saw. He always saw what everyone else in the house didn't want to.

Right now, the suitor was murmuring something to his sister while he hugged her long and lingering, smoothing his hand down the back of her dress to rest right above the curve of her ass. Arabella giggled in response, tossing her hair, which had been curled into gleaming show-pony ringlets.

Robert watched, and he seethed. His sister could do whatever she liked; she was twenty years old. She could carry on with whoever she wanted, even if it was some too-old square-jawed blockhead from Stirling who could barely carry an interesting conversation and didn't care about anything eighteen-year-old Robert might have to say.

Arabella could do whatever she pleased. But that didn't mean Robert had to like it.

Arabella gave her suitor one more kiss and then waved goodbye as he strode off into the rainy night. There had been unseasonable lightning in the distance all evening, along with the rumble of thunder.

A storm was about to break. Robert could feel it.

Arabella all but skipped up the stairs, her silky dress flowing around her long legs. It was flimsy, not suited for the weather, but Robert's sister somehow never got cold. Even when he shivered, she thrived. Like she was a serpent clad in nothing but gleaming scales.

"Spying again, Robbie?" she asked, pausing on the landing beside him.

"It's hardly spying if you're carrying on in plain sight," he said.

"Well, you've always liked to look," she replied, voice light and airy as she leaned against the banister.

Robert's chest tightened. They never talked about it, the way she sometimes stripped down to nothing but stockings and panties and changed dresses while he sat on her bed gossiping, the way he always tried to avert his eyes but could never succeed, not completely. They never talked about all the times they had broken loose from lessons to run out to the loch, peel off all their clothes, and dive into the bracing waters together, a pastime that had felt much more innocent when they were children. And they certainly hadn't talked about last week, when Robert had passed by one of the bathrooms to find the door ajar, revealing Arabella lounging in the tub with her hair piled on top of her head and one of their father's cigarettes smoldering between her fingers.

They hadn't talked about the way her eyes had flickered to the crack in the door before she had continued as though she were entirely alone, as though Robert wasn't riveted to the spot, watching. Watching Arabella run her hand idly over her breasts and over the soft curve of her stomach down into the water, between her legs.

They certainly hadn't talked about the way she had only arched her back more and rubbed herself more vigorously when he pressed his hand down against his hardening cock. They hadn't talked about the way Robert had slipped his hands beneath the waistband of his trousers and stroked himself beneath the thin fabric of his boxers, making her moan. And they hadn't talked about how they had stayed like that for a whole damning minute. Touching themselves with nothing between them but a doorway and a few feet of tiled floor, desperately trying to pretend they weren't aware of what the other was doing.

But Robert *knew* she knew. They had grown up together after all, and they both knew damn well how he hung on her every word, how every one of their arguments had an increasing undercurrent of desperation these days. Like they ached to get a rise out of each other in every conceivable way that didn't involve touching each other.

Robert knew it was wrong. Just because it wasn't something the courts could find him guilty of, that didn't mean it was right, and just because Arabella wasn't his blood, that didn't mean she wasn't his sister. It didn't mean wanting her wasn't a sin he could burn for.

But Arabella was all he had ever known, his tormentor and protector, and she had grown up just as lovely as he had grown up curious and strong. How was he not supposed to love her, when she was so cruel and so clever? How was he not supposed to long to touch her, with her skin like milk and her hair dark as night?

"Thank God he's finally gone," Robert said, steering the conversation into safer waters. "I would have been sick if I had to listen to Mother fawn over him for another minute."

"Oh, be nice," Arabella said. "He's not so bad, you know."

"He's stupid, Belle."

"He comes from a good family and he makes me laugh. Most importantly, he's taken with me. That counts for something."

"You're actually thinking of going steady with him," Robert said, with a little laugh to cover up his betrayal. Arabella might be flighty, but she was a romantic at heart just as surely as Robert was. This was a change in her tune he didn't like.

"More than steady," she said, tangling her fingers together in an anxious knot. She was putting on that city girl air she had picked up at the cinema, trying to speak with bored disaffection, but Robert didn't buy it. "He asked me to marry him, you know."

"When? Just now?"

"In the parlor, with Mother and Father. You would have seen it if you had been there and not up here sulking. He got down on one knee and everything. It was very romantic."

Robert stared at his sister, struggling to scrape together words. They had sworn to each other years ago they wouldn't marry unless it was for love. Arabella had said she would sooner become a wild abbess sworn to the land than consent to nuptials with a bore of their parents' choosing. Robert had said he would rather be a wandering vagabond without a home than settle down with someone with no taste for adventure. He hadn't been lying about any of it. Had she?

"But, Belle, you said—"

"Whatever I said, I was a child when I said it, and I'm an adult now. He's a sound match, Robbie. And he's got enough money to keep this place running for at least a few decades more. Mother and Father are happy for me. I hope you can be too."

Robert could have let it go. He could have given her a stiff hug, forced a smile, and congratulated her on her upcoming wedding. He could have sat through picking out flowers and the dress and the cake and then sat in the front row of the church and clapped like everyone else. If he had been younger, he might have. If he had more to lose, he *certainly* would have. But he was a grown man already suffocating under the weight of his parents' double-sided expectations, and the only thing he had ever had to lose was standing right in front of him in a silk dress, telling him she was going to marry another man.

"You can't marry him," Robert said. He wished he could be more articulate and come up with a convincing argument on the spot. But there was none. There was only his heart, and the way it beat and bled for her.

"Why can't I?" she dared.

"You *know* why."

"Do I?"

"Belle," he groaned. "Come on. You know that I . . . The way we are, I thought . . . Last week, when you were in the bath and you saw me standing there—"

"The things you do when you're bored and there's no one else around," she said, glancing down at her satin shoes so she wouldn't have to look him in the eye when she broke his heart, "Those aren't the things you want to do for the rest of your life."

Robert felt like she had punched the wind out of him. This wasn't right. This wasn't the way any of this was supposed to go, if either of them ever plucked up the courage to be honest about the way they adored each other, the way they trusted only each other, the way they slipped handwritten initiations under each other's doors to the games of chase-and-seek that had only grown more deliciously aggressive as they had gotten older. Last Boxing Day, Arabella had found him in the broom cupboard before dragging him into the hallway, straddling his chest, and pinning his hands above his head with a triumphant grin. Why would she have done that if she didn't feel the same way he did?

Robert pushed up from the wall he had been slouching against and drew himself up to his full height. He was tall for a boy his age, much taller than Arabella, and she glared up at him with watery eyes as he stood over her.

"Is that all I am to you?" he demanded. "A toy you can take up when you're bored and discard when someone else comes around?"

"God, don't be dramatic—"

"I'm not being dramatic; I'm being honest. If I have to be the first one to say it, I will. I love you, Belle. I love you as my family and I always will, but you must know by now that I love you more than that, too."

"You're just confused," Arabella said, trying to slip past

him in a whip of hair and a rustle of silk. Robert caught her wrist tightly. When she spun around to glare at him, he softened his grip, rubbing a circle into her palm with his thumb.

"Please don't do this," he said, and now he was begging, all intentions to stand up for himself as a man forgotten. "I know you don't want to marry him. You always told me you would rather go live with the birds in the trees and eat nothing but nuts and berries than be sold off to some minor aristocrat. That's exactly what's happening here! I don't know why you can't see that—"

"You aren't a girl, Robbie," she snapped so ferociously that he recoiled. "You don't know what it's like to be in my position. I *have* to marry and I *have* to have babies. Otherwise our family will be destroyed. How I feel about that doesn't matter."

"Then marry me," he said, panic making him rash. He scrubbed a hand over his face, over his stubbled jaw and overheated throat. "Have babies with me, if that's what you want."

"This is exactly what I was afraid of. You're too attached to me, Robbie. I had hoped if you saw me with someone else you would let me go and—"

"I can take care of you, Belle, as your brother or as your husband, or as both if that's what you want. Marry me, and I swear to God you'll never be bored. I promise I'll—"

"Oh, please don't," she said, tears gathering in earnest in her eyes now. "I've already said yes to him, Robbie. I have a real future with him. There is no future for you and I. Our parents would kill us both."

"I don't care about them," he declared, pulling her in closer. Robert latticed their fingers together even as he pressed his body against hers, just like they had when they were little and making a pact. "I only care about what you want. Tell me what you want, Arabella. That's all I'm asking."

"I want you to let me go," she said, her voice a self-betraying whisper.

She had always been a bad liar.

Robert wordlessly hooked his hands under his sister's thighs and scooped her up, sitting her in the reading nook built into the windowsill. The trio of stained-glass hares gazed down at them from above with dead marble eyes, their linked ears illuminated by distant lightning.

"Tell me to go then," Robert said, hands braced on either side of her hips, lips inches away from the kiss they had been denying themselves for years. "Make me believe you don't want me and I'll *go*. Come on, send me away. Say it like you mean it."

Arabella glared at him as though she hated him more than anyone else in the world, and Robert just stood there, letting her hate him. He refused to touch her, but he also refused to draw away. No matter how this played out, it would be Arabella's decision what happened next.

Then, all at once, she made a frustrated noise and surged forward to crush her mouth against his.

Robert cradled her face in his hands, her skin smooth as porcelain and twice as cool, and he kissed her back. They wrestled for dominance for a moment, like this was just another expression of sibling rivalry, but then at Robert's gentle urging, Arabella slowed down. Her breathing deepened as he kissed her deep and soft, reverent as a priest. She gripped his wrists in her trembling hands, letting him take his time with her and treat her as gently as he had wanted to since they were both teenagers.

Robert pulled her in tighter, ignoring the distant murmur of their parents' voices downstairs. She was warmer now, a hot flush spreading across her skin as he pushed the silk up over her thighs and around her hips. He dug his fingers into her flesh, just hard enough to leave a half-moon indent with his short nails.

"I can't," she gasped, breaking the kiss.

Robert released her as though he had been burned, tugging his sister's dress back down over her legs.

"I'm sorry," he began, the apology a deeply rooted childhood impulse. "I don't want to hurt you, I—"

"I can't be with you," she said, decisive as she scrubbed stray tears off her face. "Please don't kiss me again."

"Belle—" he said, voice broken into pieces. She shrank away from him and slipped down from the windowsill.

"I think it's best if you and I don't talk much for a while," she said, hurrying off into the dark. "At least until the wedding is over."

Robert was left alone on the landing, his sister's tears

drying on his cheeks and a hot yearning in his blood and sickening shame heavy as a stone in his stomach. He felt like he was being torn to pieces, like part of him was already sitting at that wedding and part of him was ten years old chasing after the sound of his big sister's laughter and part of him was eternally standing on this landing, reliving the kiss he would never be able to recover from. His parents' voices grew downstairs, punctuated by the ringing of champagne glasses and the sound of laughter.

They were already celebrating. They had pawned off their daughter and now Robert would be left alone with them. The disregarded son who had only been adopted as an entertaining diversion for their beloved offspring. No matter how much they said they loved him, Robert saw it clearly, the difference in the ways they looked at him and looked at Arabella.

He hated Craigmar, hated its dreary old paintings of people who looked nothing like him and its drafty corridors and its hallways that led nowhere. He hated his parents for bringing him out here and he hated his sister for being exactly what she was: a half-feral creature more in love with the land outside their window than she would ever be with him. He was too human for this place, too fallible and needy. He would never be good enough, either for his parents or for Arabella.

Making up his mind with the brutal finality of someone who had been considering the unthinkable for months, Robert strode into his room and yanked the black leather duffel out from under his bed. He had travelled with it only a few times, since he typically only travelled with Arabella and she was rarely permitted to leave Craigmar, but now he stuffed it full of clothes torn from his dresser.

There was no rhyme or reason to any of this, and he was crying through most of it, but within ten minutes he had most of his toiletries and his identifying documents and his best pen stuffed into the bag, along with stationery and stamps, a pair of trainers, and his dog-eared copy of *Gulliver's Travels*. He plucked up Tammany the teddy before deciding it was better to travel as light as possible, with no reminder of his family with him. He settled Tam into the pillows of his bed and then flipped the lights off and crept into the hallway. Maybe the bear would be better appreciated by another child, better suited to this place.

He might be Arabella's brother, but he wasn't a Kirkfoyle. Not in any of the ways that mattered.

Robert hustled quietly down the stairs and let himself out the kitchen door, far away from where his parents were chatting in the parlor. Arabella was somewhere in the house, probably crying her eyes out and waiting for him to come apologize, but he wouldn't be apologizing. There was nothing else to say. This place was rotting him from the inside out, making him a slave to unnatural desires, and the best thing he could do for any of them was to leave.

Robert strode out into the night just as a cold rain began to fall. He turned his coat up against the wind.

It was a rocky walk to Wyke, but from there he could warm up in the Hound and Grouse and hitch a ride into the nearest large city. From there, he could go anywhere in Scotland, or in Britain, or in the world.

He had always wanted to travel, unmoored from Craigmar's dark, demanding magic and the disapproving glances of his parents. Perhaps now, at the other end of the world, he would find a happiness previously thought impossible.

CHAPTER THIRTY-FIVE

Eileen

Eileen wiped the back of her hand across her mouth as she finished reading the shaky and fragmented diary entry from the night Robert ran away. Eileen was shaking too now, although she wasn't totally sure why. Maybe it was the bottomed-out drop in her adrenaline levels after the fear, or all her illnesses conspiring against her at once, or just the way Adam was looking at her, like he wanted to take her to pieces in the most precise, clinical way possible.

"You knew. You knew exactly why my grandfather was here, and why he left."

"Yes," Eileen said, glad to have the secret out of her at last. No matter the consequences, at least she felt lighter. "From what I can gather he travelled around Britain and the continent for some time before settling in the States. Taking up the name Lancaster in the process, of course.

He would play War of the Roses with Arabella when they were small, pretending to behead each other in the garden. She was always York. He was always Lancaster."

"Why would you keep this from me?" Adam asked. She had expected him to be angry, but right now he seemed more wounded. This, somehow, was worse.

"I needed time to convince you. It would have worked better if you had come to certain conclusions yourself, if you had believed they were your own idea. But time isn't something we're spoiled for at the moment, so—" Eileen dropped down on one knee, only swaying slightly, and held her hand out to Adam. "Adam Kirkfoyle, will you marry me? Please?"

Nicola let out a high, delirious laugh, like she had stumbled into a carnival sideshow.

"Finley, what's really going on here?" she demanded. "Say something."

Finley just glared at the ground, unable to meet anyone's eyes. Nicola took a step back from him, as though she had only just realized he might not be entirely trustworthy.

"Oh, be serious," Adam scoffed. "Marry you? Stop this, Eileen. It isn't funny."

"I'm not joking. I'm asking you to marry me. Now. Please."

"You're not thinking straight," Adam went on, leaving her there bruising her knees on the ground like an idiot. She knew she was twisting his arm, but she thought he might like the gesture of a formal proposal all the same.

She believed that important things should be done properly, after all.

"You don't love me. You don't even know me."

"Maybe I do love you," she snapped, with a ferocity that surprised her. Her head pounded, a blinding pain shooting through her ocular nerve. "Or I could come to love you, in time. Love doesn't matter right now, all that matters is that our family line survives. Generally, the only way to make a new Kirkfoyle is to birth one, or adopt one. Marriage bonds don't hold the same weight, not to the fae. But you're *already* a Kirkfoyle, you're already family, and I hope to God marrying you works just as well as having a child by you. But for now, this is what I can do to survive. This is the only way."

Adam stared at the journal, and he stared at Eileen, and then, he looked down at the ring of iron on his finger.

"Is this . . . a wedding ring?"

"It was my father's ring. And he used it to make a promise to my mother, yes."

"How long have you been planning this?" Adam demanded. "Since you and I first kissed, since the night we found that photograph, since—"

Now he was starting to *get* it. Eileen always got bored when people couldn't keep up with the speed of her chess moves. It was a relief, even an ugly one, to finally have her strategy understood.

"Since before," she said, ripping the truth up from herself like a weed. "Since I found that childhood picture of your grandfather in the attic months ago and hung it on the wall for you to find. It took you longer than I expected to put the pieces together, I'll admit."

"You . . ." Nicola took a shaky breath. Her hands were balled into fists at her side. "You planted that picture? You knew the whole time?"

"Who do you think called you both out here?" Eileen said, resisting the urge to roll her eyes. "Who do you think sent Adam's mother that old letter, knowing it would make its way to him? I've spent my entire life searching for a way out of this treaty, Adam. Did you really think I wouldn't have discovered you?"

The room fell silent as a morgue. Both Adam and Nicola were looking at her like she was some kind of a monster, and maybe she was a monster, maybe she was the villain in this story, but she still deserved some small semblance of happiness, goddamnit. If not happiness, then relief.

"We can do it quickly," Eileen said, rising to her feet. She slid open a drawer in her father's desk and pulled out the yet-to-be-signed marriage certificate in a manilla folder, the one she had her out of town solicitor draft up weeks ago. "We've got two witnesses, and I have the paperwork right here. We'll handle the courts later, and the Church, if you care about that sort of thing. But I'm hoping this will be enough to hold them at bay, for now. Then we can all decide what to do together."

"I'm not doing anything with you." Adam spoke each

word with vehemence. She could practically see the poison drip from his mouth.

"You don't have much of a choice," she said, feeling rotted from the inside out. "It was always going to be you and me. It's in our blood. And I do like you, Adam; I like you an awful lot. There can be a happy ending here if you just try and see it. I can give you everything you've ever wanted, I will forbid you nothing, I will indulge your every fantasy and wish. You can have Nicola if you want, and Finley, if he'll have you. You can have full run of the land and full rights to the house and unlimited access to me in any way you want me. I just need you to stay."

"That's not how this works, Eileen. You can't just barter people away, and you can't just force me to marry you, for *God's sake*. You let me believe we were friends! You let me think that I . . . that I belonged somewhere, that you wanted me for myself, not to use as leverage."

"I let you believe what you wanted to believe," Eileen said quietly. "I gave you a gift by letting you think that you were a chosen one. What man doesn't want to be a hero? You can still be a hero, Adam. Please. Save me from this. Save us both."

"Did you know about this?" Nicola demanded. Not to Eileen, but to Finley. Eileen's great forbidden love and the golden girl who Eileen had come to begrudgingly treasure stared at each other for a long, miserable moment, the truth settling around them like iron chains.

"Nicola—" Finley began, soft enough to betray himself.

"God, you knew!" Nicola said, barking out a mean laugh. He opened his mouth to explain, but she didn't let him. "This whole time! Since the pub, isn't that right? Since you invited us out here and into Eileen's sticky little spiderweb. You'll really do anything she asks you, won't you? She calls and you come. She snaps her fingers, and you crawl like a dog."

"Nicola," Finley said, more firmly, raising his voice over hers.

"You were happy to get close to me, to fuck me, and then turn around and s*acrifice* Adam and throw me away like trash!" Nicola shrieked, her composure shattered like glass. Her fists trembled at her sides like she wanted to hit him. "I let you chase me and hurt me, I let you inside me, I let you make me believe that you cared about me and it was all a trick!"

"It wasn't a trick," he said quickly, taking a step towards her. "Nicola, please, I truly admire you, I love being with you, I didn't mean—"

Nicola picked up the nearest item, which was one of the thick history books Finley carried around like security blankets and left scattered around the house, and hurled it at him with impressive force. Finley managed to catch it, but not before it clipped him hard in the chest.

"Don't come a step closer," Nicola said, holding out a menacing finger. "Don't you touch me."

"Will you please just let me explain myself?" Finley

snapped. "There are things going on here you could never understand, and I just—"

Nicola kept shouting at him, screaming really, and Finley matched her volume, doing a piss-poor job of trying to calm her down. Eileen didn't much care what they had to say to each other; that could all be sorted out later. She herself had an explosive temper that settled down quickly, transgressions forgotten with a sweet kiss and a smile, surely this would be the same. The ringing in her ears was so loud she could barely hear anyway, and she had a job to do.

Eileen picked up her father's fountain pen and signed her name with a flourish at the bottom of the marriage certificate. It felt a bit like signing her death warrant, but Eileen ignored the dread in her stomach. Any life was better than a slow death, than watching her family home and her own mind succumb to faery torments. "Vivere militare est" was her family motto after, all. To live was to fight.

"Your turn," she said, holding the pen out to Adam. A single drop of ink dripped from the razor-sharp nib, like blood from a wound.

"Fuck you," Adam said. He ripped the iron ring from his finger and threw it at her feet.

Then Adam Lancaster turned from her and stormed out of the room, and Eileen watched her final hope in the world run from her.

CHAPTER THIRTY-SIX

Adam

Adam didn't bother with a coat, or a scarf. He barely bothered with shoes. He was so angry he couldn't see straight, so violated that he thought he might throw up everything he had eaten at the pub, and he was still just drunk enough from his whiskies and porters that getting the fuck out of this house seemed not only like a good idea, but like the *only* idea.

Adam shoved past Finley through the library doors, walking so quickly down the hallway it bordered on a run. He headed for the kitchen, to the closest exit, where his muddy boots had been drying out by the door.

He would come back for Nicola soon, and they would figure something out. They could leave together, or they could tie Eileen to a chair and waterboard her until she released all her secrets. He would think of something, anything. But for now, the bone-deep urge to run was too strong to ignore. It had been building for a week inside him, kept at bay only by the strange companionship he had found with his loves and friends. But now, all the goodwill was gone and Adam felt *trapped*, trapped in a way so total and so crushing that he didn't even have the words to express it, and he needed to get *out*.

Fuck Eileen, and every kind word she had ever given him, every lingering kiss or tight hug or insistence that he was worthy of this legacy, that he deserved to be here, to enjoy the privileges of a life of leisure. And Finley, *fuck* Finley. Finley who had made him feel like perhaps they could be true friends, who had earned Adam's respect a dozen times over with his practicality and humor, who handled him with rough, calloused hands and smiled at him in a way that made Adam feel like he was on fire.

None of it was real. Nicola hadn't been kidding when she called this place a spiderweb. Eileen was the black widow at the heart of it all, wrapping them up in silks and sweetness as she prepared to devour them, and Finley was just her servant, a spider wearing the colors of a friendlier insect to trick passerby into getting stuck.

They had trapped him in a fantasy, one that was only growing darker and more sordid with every passing day.

Nicola had been right. He wasn't the prince in this story. He was the human sacrifice.

Adam yanked on his shoes and burst through the kitchen doors, ignoring Finley barking his name behind him. Eileen, hot on both their heels, yelled from the doorway as he stalked across the grass, pleading for him to come back inside. He even ignored Nicola stumbling out behind him into the yard and shouting something about his ring. He needed to be alone, and he couldn't face her right now, not when he was drowning in the guilt he felt about bringing her out here and involving her in this brutality. He should have left her in America, or put her right back in the car and driven them both to safety the moment he laid eyes on Eileen. He should have known better.

Adam strode out across the green, swallowing down the lump in his throat as the lashing wind brought tears to his eyes. The manor house loomed behind him, ever-present and unescapable, no matter how far he walked.

Craigmar had its roots in him now, and he could feel them burrowing deeper, wrapping tighter around his organs as they called him home. If there had ever been a point where he could return unscathed to his normal life, he had passed it. Maybe the moment he kissed Eileen, or the day he agreed to help her search for their shared family history. Or maybe it had been when he had first set foot on Craigmar soil. The play had been set in motion with his arrival, and now Adam was trapped on stage under the hot lights, doomed to either recite his assigned lines or fall into ruin.

Adam kept walking, with nothing but the rustling tree branches to break the silence, not even sure of where he was going. But then he heard a voice, high and urgent, cutting through the wind. He slowed and turned to see three specks moving from the house towards him. Eileen waving frantically, trying to call him back, and Finley and Nicola running at top speed out front. It was Nicola who was shouting, over and over again, as though trying to warn him of something.

Adam was never able to make out what she was saying, because the ground opened up beneath him, and a sinkhole stinking of bitter herbs and rot and ancient mineral water swallowed him whole.

Epilogue

The earth wrapped the boy in a loving embrace, cushioning his descent with lichen and loam. Craigmar's secret subterranean passages opened wide as they pulled him down into the dark and damp. It had been so long since there was a Kirkfoyle beneath the earth, so long since that hot, noble blood had enriched the soil. When the boy ripped his forearm open on a sharp stone as he tumbled into the deepest chambers of the earth, the mycelium and microscopic bugs and filaments of roots from the trees above lapped greedily at his offering, all the sweeter for his suffering.

The boy lay a long while in darkness, still as though in a slumber with his cheek pillowed on moss. Then he groaned, like his body was one big bruise, and cracked open an eye.

The packed earth beneath his feet held steady as he pressed his palms against the dirt, trying to get his bearings. It was dark down here, that unspoiled dark of caverns where no light had reached for centuries, and he was human yet. His eyes weren't strong enough for the dark, nor glamoured to pierce the shadows.

The bioluminescent mushrooms did their best to glow valiantly for him, pulsing blue light softly through the chamber at the intervals of their shared heartbeat. The boy moved his limbs tentatively, like he was checking for broken bones.

Then, just as the boy was beginning to hyperventilate, taking shallow panicked breaths in the dark, footsteps approached.

Craigmar would know that sound anywhere, the leisurely click of the gleaming boots of their beloved keeper.

The boy heaved in a breath, ready to pull himself to his feet and fight, but suddenly there was a boot on his shoulder, holding him down.

The boy craned his chin up as far as it would go.

The king underground stood over him, all sinuous grace with skin the color of burnished bronze and hair spilling over his shoulders in a cascade of jet. He wore an ankle-skimming black oilcloth cloak, battered from the weather and splattered with mud, and the hunting attire that had been the height of fashion the last time he had ventured aboveground. It could have been ten years ago, or a hundred. Craigmar was too old to keep track of such minuscule increments.

The king gave the boy a thin-lipped smile, his almond-shaped eyes glittering like shards of onyx. They were black all the way through, black as a night without stars.

"*Eileen's eyes*," the boy gasped, only loud enough for the earth to hear.

"Easy, little knight," the king said, in that voice like icy water, clear and crisp and entirely devoid of human warmth. "No need to draw your blade just yet."

"Who are you?" the boy demanded.

"I'm the oldest friend your family has," the king replied.

"I've never seen you before," the boy blustered. He was trying to buy time.

"You might not have seen me," the king went on, unhurried. This was his domain, after all. He had more time to fritter away than any mortal man could dream of. He could wait until the boy acquiesced, if that was what it took. The boy would get hungry eventually, after all. Thirsty. Starving for warmth and a gentle touch. "But I've certainly seen you."

"When?"

"At night, when you sleep. And during the day, when you were playing your little game of pain with the Kirkfoyle girl by my mushroom ring."

"Let me go," the boy demanded, panic rising in his voice.

"There's nowhere else to go. Not home, and not into

the past. There is only the now, and the gateway I offer you into the future. Will you step through it with me? I can make it quite pleasurable for you. And I will explain everything you long to understand, in time."

The king removed his boot from the boy's shoulder and then held out the hand of peace to him.

"Welcome home, Adam Kirkfoyle," he said, smiling with a mouthful of pointed teeth. "I've been so desperate to meet you."

The boy held his breath as he deliberated and Craigmar held its breath with him, every bit of flora under the earth trembling and tense. Craigmar ached for equilibrium, for the veil so long drawn between the aboveground and the belowground to fall away. It longed for bloody, euphoric catharsis, and for the old magic to rush back in and reign supreme.

In the end, there was no other option besides the one that had been put before him. It was the only path that had ever been laid before any Kirkfoyle who walked the road of this story.

With a shuddering sigh of surrender, the boy took the king's hand and let him pull him to his feet.

Acknowledgments

The Orbit team has worked tirelessly on both sides of the Atlantic to bring this book to you, and I cannot thank every editor, proofreader, designer, typesetter, marketing staffer, and publicist enough. I especially want to thank Nadia Saward, who had enough faith in me to buy an erotic gothic queer kinky polyamorous folkloric romance without batting an eye. Thanks for proving that those words do indeed go together in places that aren't just my head, and for supporting me in my endeavor to be bold with this one. To my agent, Tara Gilbert, thank you for holding me down professionally in every conceivable way as I build a career in this rollercoaster industry: I perpetually owe you a fruit basket.

Thank you to Elizabeth Unseth, for taking me along on the adventure to the Scottish coastline where we stumbled across the real-life Craigmar; your kindheartedness reminds me that there is good in this world worth preserving. Thank you to Elias Eells, for your level pragmatism and spry humor; I can't wait to vibrate air with you over and over again until we're old and gray and sipping 50/50s on a porch somewhere. Thank you to Elizabeth Kilkoyne, for being one of the finest damn writers I have ever met, and a ferociously loving friend who has rescued every single one of my books from muddy middle ruin; I wish you gentle ease and astronomical success. Thank you to Sydney Shields for vibing on the same wavelength with me so hard we could power a small city; may our mastermind hot girl antics never end.

Thank you to Laura Samotin, who saved this plot from falling to pieces almost as many times as she saved my faith in my own goodness. Thank you for sharing visions in the astral with me and for making me a braver writer in ways nobody else was ever capable of; you tenderize my heart like meat.

And as always, thank you to Kit Mayquist, for being the stalwart light that guides me through the labyrinth of my own mind, even when it's so dark I can hardly see. Thank you for loving me with a faithfulness and patience I didn't think existed in the real world, and for proving to me that romance reaches its zenith in honest trust and laughter free of fear. You're the plot doctor and astrological advisor and happy ending I never even dared to dream of.

Thank you to all the established romance authors, titans in my heart, who were kind to me as I fumbled along looking for my door into this genre. Thank you especially to those who never hesitated to share their advice and in some cases their research with me: Katee Robert and Sierra Simone and Elizabeth May. I wouldn't have been brave enough to break into this space without your encouragement.

I owe some of my greatest thanks to my inspirations, to those books that helped me find the right shape for this story. I especially owe a debt to the way Emily Brontë's *Wuthering Heights* made wild things take root in my soul, and to the pricking ache and tearstained catharsis of Sierra Simone's Thornchapel series. I wish I could thank every single fairy tale I read growing up for planting their mythic seeds in my heart as well, but instead I'll thank my mother, who always encouraged me to read, and shared her most precious books of folklore with me.

Finally, thank you to every reader, from the most casually curious pilgrim to the most dedicated devotee, for coming along on this wild ride with me. Your enthusiasm is the fuel for my creative furnace, and it keeps me going on days when melancholic ennui or artistic frustration or the state of the world makes it hard to write. I never get tired of delighting you all and doing my best to melt your brains. Sorry about the cliffhanger; it's going to get worse before it gets better but it will be worse in a hot way, I promise.

In the meantime, be good to each other, and keep yourself safe and well for me. Sláinte!

About the Author

S.T. Gibson is the *Sunday Times* bestselling author of *A Dowry of Blood*, *An Education in Malice* and *Evocation*.

Find out more about S.T. Gibson and other Orbit authors by registering for the free monthly newsletter at orbit-books.co.uk